Behind you, the voice came, urgent and loud now. *Coming up behind you. Loaded gun. You've become a threat. Pointed at your head*.

He was not speaking. He was thinking.

I betrayed no response. I continued staring at him questioningly, yet as casually as I could.

Now, now, now. Hope to God he can't hear the footsteps behind him.

He was testing me. I felt sure of it. Mustn't respond, mustn't show fear, that's what he wants, he wants some little sign, some glimmering of fear in my face, wants me to whip around suddenly, flinch, show him I can *hear* it.

'Then I really *should* be getting along,' I said calmly.

I heard: *Does he?*

'Well,' Rossi said. 'We can talk next time.'

I heard: *Either he's lying, or –*

I watched his face; saw that his mouth hadn't moved.

Once again I felt that creeping dread, a tingling on my skin, and my heart began to beat much too quickly.

Rossi looked at me, and I felt sure I saw resignation in his eyes. I had, for the time being at least, fooled him, I thought. But there was something about Charles Rossi that told me I would not fool him for long.

Joseph Finder was born in Chicago in 1958 and was educated at Yale College and the Harvard Russian Research Center. Fluent in Russian and a frequent visitor to Russia, he has written widely about Russian affairs, international politics, and Intelligence for *The New York Times*, *The Wall Street Journal*, *The New Republic* and *The Times*. His first novel, *The Moscow Club*, published to great acclaim in thirty countries, predicted the coup that ended the Soviet Union. He lives in Boston with his wife, Michele Souda, and their daughter.

EXTRAORDINARY
POWERS

....

Joseph Finder

ORION

An Orion paperback
First published in Great Britain by Orion in 1994
This paperback edition published in 1995 by Orion Books Ltd,
Orion House, 5 Upper St Martin's Lane, London WC2H 9EA

A CIP catalogue record for this book is available
from the British Library.

ISBN: 1 85797 361 5

Printed and bound in Great Britain by
Clays Ltd, St Ives plc

To Michele
and to our daughter on the way

ACKNOWLEDGMENTS

I am grateful for the kind assistance of Richard Davies and Samuel Etris of the Gold Institute; Gerald H. Kiel and Bill Sapone of McAulay Fisher Nissen Goldberg & Kiel; Ed Gates of Wolf Greenfield & Sacks; Dr Leonard Atkins and Dr Jonathan Finder; and, in Paris, Jean Rosenthal and my friends at the Paris Métro system.

Also, Peter Dowd and Jay Gemma of Peter G. Dowd Firearms, Elisabeth Sinnott, Paul Joyal, Jack Stein, Pat Cooper, Martha Shenton, and my great friends Bruce Donald and Joe Teig. The brilliant Jack McGeorge of the Public Safety Group was, as usual, both an invaluable source and enormously generous with his time.

My thanks, too, to Peter Gethers, Clare Ferraro, and Linda Grey at Ballantine, and the terrific Danny Baror of Henry Morrison, Inc. Thanks, as well, to my friends and sources in the intelligence community, who've come to learn the meaning of that ancient Chinese curse, 'May you live in interesting times.'

Henry Morrison was, as ever, not just a marvelous agent and reader but a valued editor and brainstormer as well. I continue to be awed by, and indebted to, my brother Henry Finder, brilliant editor and indispensable counsel. And to my wife, Michele Souda – editor, adviser, and literary critic, who was there from the start – my thanks and love always.

The weapons of secrecy have no place in an ideal world. But we live in a world of undeclared hostilities in which such weapons are constantly used against us and could, unless countered, leave us unprepared again, this time for an onslaught of magnitude that staggers the imagination. And while it may seem unnecessary to stress so obvious a point, the weapons of secrecy are rendered ineffective if we remove the secrecy.

–Sir William Stephenson, in
A Man Called Intrepid

Former KGB agent seeks employment in similar field. Tel: Paris 1–42.50.66.76.

–classified advertisement in the
International Herald Tribune.
January 1992

Extraordinary Powers

Espionage tradecraft jargon utilized in certain former Warsaw Pact intelligence services. Refers to the permission granted a highly trusted clandestine officer, in extremely rare circumstances, to violate his employer's standing orders if need be in order to accomplish a mission of vital importance.

A NOTE TO THE READER

The events of last September and October that so shook the world will, of course, never be forgotten. But few if any details of what happened during those extraordinary weeks have been revealed to the public.

Until now.

Several months ago, on November 8, I received at my home in Manhattan a package delivered via Federal Express. The package, weighing 9.3 pounds, contained a manuscript, part typewritten and part handwritten. Subsequent investigation failed to determine who had sent it. The Federal Express company was able to ascertain only that the sender's name on the bill was false (the point of origin was Boulder, Colorado) and that it had been paid in cash.

Three independent handwriting analysts, however, were able to confirm something I already knew – the handwriting was that of Benjamin Ellison, a former operative for the Central Intelligence Agency and later an attorney with a prominent law firm in Boston, Massachusetts. Ellison had presumably made arrangements for this manuscript to be sent in the event of his death.

Although I was hardly a close friend of Ben Ellison's, we were roommates for one semester as Harvard undergraduates. He was a good-looking fellow, of medium height and trim build, with thick dark brown hair and brown eyes. I remember him as being easygoing, quite likable, and possessed of an infectious laugh. I had met his wife, Molly, a few times and liked her quite a bit. When Molly's father, the late Harrison Sinclair, was Director of Central Intelligence, I interviewed him on several instances; but that is the extent of my acquaintance with Sinclair.

1

As a very good series of investigative articles in *The New York Times* documented recently, there is little doubt that Ben and Molly's disappearance in the waters off Cape Cod, Massachusetts, a week after the events recorded in this manuscript, was suspicious at best. A number of reliable intelligence sources have confirmed for me in off-the-record interviews what the *Times* articles speculate – that Ben and Molly were probably murdered, likely by agents connected with the Central Intelligence Agency, because of the knowledge they possessed. Until their bodies are located, however, we cannot know the truth.

But why me? Why would Ben Ellison have chosen to send his manuscript to me? Perhaps it was because of my reputation as a reasonably fair-minded (or at least I like to think so) writer about foreign affairs and intelligence. Perhaps it was the success of my most recent book, *The Demise of the CIA*, which originated as an exposé I did for *The New Yorker*.

But most likely, I think, it was because Ben knew me and trusted me: he knew I would never turn his manuscript over to the CIA or any other government agency. (I doubt Ben ever anticipated the numerous death threats I have received over the phone and in the mail in recent months, the subtle and not-so-subtle campaign of intimidation by my contacts in the intelligence community, and the massive legal effort by the CIA to squelch publication of this book.)

To say the least, Ben's account at first struck me as shocking, bizarre, even incredible. But when the publishers of this book asked me to verify the authenticity of Ellison's account, I undertook lengthy interviews with those who knew Ellison in the legal and intelligence communities as well as extensive investigation in several European capitals.

And so I am confident in stating that Ben's version of these alarming events, astonishing though it may be, is an accurate one. The manuscript I received was obviously written in haste, so I have taken the liberty of editing it for publication and correcting a few largely inconsequential errors. Where necessary, I have interposed newspaper accounts to augment his narrative.

Controversial though this document will no doubt be, it is the first complete story we have of what really happened during that fearsome time, and I am pleased to have had a part in bringing it to the light of day.

– James Jay Morris

The New York Times

CIA Director is Killed in Automobile Accident

Harrison Sinclair, 67, Helped Agency Cope with a Post-Cold-War World

Successor Not Yet Named

BY SHELDON ROSS

SPECIAL TO THE NEW YORK TIMES

WASHINGTON, March 2 – The Director of Central Intelligence, Harrison H. Sinclair, was killed yesterday when the automobile he was driving plunged into a ravine in rural Virginia, 26 miles from CIA headquarters in Langley, Virginia. He was killed instantly, agency spokesmen say. There were no other victims.

Mr Sinclair, who had been head of the CIA for less than a year, was one of the agency's founders in the years after World War II. He leaves a daughter, Martha Hale Sinclair . . .

PROLOGUE

The story begins, appropriately enough, at a funeral.

The coffin of an old man is being lowered into the ground. The mourners surrounding the grave site are as somber as any funeral-goers, but they are conspicuously well dressed, radiating power and wealth. It is an odd sight: on this gray, drizzling, cold March morning, in a small rural cemetery in Columbia County in upstate New York, you can see United States senators, Supreme Court justices, the various scions of the New York and Washington power establishments, picking up wet clods of soil and flinging them atop the coffin. They are surrounded by black limousines, BMWs, Mercedeses, Jaguars, and the assorted other vehicles of the rich, powerful, and elect. Most of them have come a long distance to pay their respects; the graveyard is miles from anywhere.

I was there, of course, but not because I am famous, great, powerful, or elect. I was at the time merely an attorney in Boston – for Putnam & Stearns, a very good firm, and earning a respectable salary – and I felt distinctly out of place among the luminaries.

I was, however, the deceased's son-in-law.

My wife, Molly – more formally, Martha Hale Sinclair – was the only child of Harrison Sinclair, a legend of the American Establishment, an enigma, a master spy. Hal Sinclair had been one of the founders of the Central Intelligence Agency, then a renowned Cold Warrior (a dirty job, but someone had to do it), later a Director of Central Intelligence, brought in to rescue the foundering Agency during its post–Cold War identity crisis.

Like his friend William Casey before him, Sinclair died

during his tenure as director. We are all fascinated by the specter of a CIA director dying while in office – what secrets, one wonders, did the old spymaster take with him to the grave? And indeed, Hal Sinclair took an extraordinary secret with him when he went. But on the cold, overcast morning of his funeral, neither Molly nor I nor any of the VIPs gathered so mournfully knew it.

Without question, the manner of my father-in-law's death seemed suspicious. He had perished a week earlier in a car accident in rural Virginia. It was late at night; he had been driving to an emergency meeting at CIA headquarters in Langley, and the car had been run off the road by an unidentified vehicle, then exploded in a ball of flames.

One day before the 'accident,' his executive assistant, Sheila McAdams, had been found murdered in an alley in Georgetown. The Washington police concluded that she'd been the victim of a mugging – her purse and jewelry were missing. Molly and I, to be honest, suspected from the start that both her father and Sheila had been murdered, that there was no mugging, and no 'accident,' and we were not alone in our suspicions. *The Washington Post, The New York Times,* all the television networks, hinted as much in their coverage. But who would have done such a thing? In the bad old days, of course, we would all be quick to blame the KGB or some other dark, mysterious arm of the Evil Empire, but the Soviet Union no longer existed. American intelligence no doubt still had its enemies – but who would want to assassinate, if that's the right word, the director of the CIA? Molly also believed that her father and Sheila had been having an affair, which isn't quite as scandalous as it seems, since Sheila was single, and Molly's mother had died some six years before, leaving Sinclair a widower.

Although Hal Sinclair was a remote, even cryptic figure, I had always felt a closeness to him, from the first time Molly introduced us. Molly and I had been friends in college, more like pals – she was a freshman when I was a senior – and there was unquestionably a spark of attraction between us, but each of us was involved with another. I was seeing Laura, whom I

6

married immediately after college. Molly was involved with some lunk she tired of after a year or so. But Hal Sinclair took to me, and recruited me to the Agency upon my graduation from Harvard, nudging me toward the clandestine service, apparently figuring me for a better spy than I turned out to be. As it happened, this line of work tapped into a dark and violent side that made me a superb if reckless operative – much feared, including by myself.

So for two very tense years before I entered Harvard Law, I worked for the Central Intelligence Agency as a clandestine operative. I did quite well at it too – until the tragedy in Paris. That was when I quit the Agency and went into the law, not regretting the decision for a moment.

It wasn't until I returned from Paris a widower, after the incident I still find hard to speak of, that Molly and I began to see each other seriously. Molly, the daughter of the man who was soon to become the Director of Central Intelligence, applauded my decision to leave the espionage business behind me. She had seen firsthand, after all, what it could do to a family, the strains it had put upon her own family, and she wanted no part of it.

Even after Hal Sinclair became my father-in-law, I saw little of him, and never got to know him well. We saw each other only at the occasional family gathering (he was the quintessential workaholic, a committed Company man), where he seemed to regard me with a certain warmth.

But as I said, the story begins at Harrison Sinclair's funeral. It was there, as the mourners began to disperse, shaking hands with one another under their black umbrellas, walking quickly back to their cars, that a tall, lanky man in his early sixties, with tousled silver hair, slipped up to me and introduced himself.

His suit was rumpled, his tie askew, but beneath all the sloppiness, his clothes were expensive: a double-breasted charcoal wool suit of impeccable tailoring and a striped shirt that looked like it had been custom-made for him in Savile Row. Although I'd never met him, I recognized him at once as Alexander Truslow, an old CIA man of considerable renown.

Like Hal Sinclair, he was a pillar of the Establishment, with a reputation for moral rectitude. For a few weeks during the Watergate scandal of 1973–4, he served as acting Director of Central Intelligence. Nixon disliked him – largely because, it was said, Truslow refused to play ball with the Nixon White House and involve the CIA in the cover-up – and moved swiftly to replace him with a political appointee more to his liking.

Soft-spoken and elegant in his slightly disheveled way, Alex Truslow was one of those well-mannered, well-bred WASP Yankee types, like Cyrus Vance or Elliot Richardson, who radiate fundamental decency. He had retired from the Agency after Nixon passed him over, but naturally he never aired any gripes about the president; that would be ungentlemanly. Hell, I would have called a press conference, but that was not Alex's way.

After casting around a bit, doing the lecture circuit, he had formed his own international consulting firm, based in Boston, which was known informally as the 'Corporation.' The Corporation advised corporations and law firms around the world on how to deal with an ever-changing, ever-baffling world market. Not surprisingly, given Truslow's upstanding reputation in the intelligence community, the Corporation also worked quite closely with CIA.

Alexander Truslow was one of the most respected, eminent men in the intelligence community. After Hal Sinclair's death, Truslow was known to be on the shortlist to replace him. For reasons of morale in CIA's ranks alone, Truslow should have been named, so popular was he among the younger officers and the old boys alike. True, there were grumblings about Truslow's work in the 'private sector.' And then there were those with good reason to fear a 'new broom.' Even so, as he introduced himself to Molly and me, I silently wagered that I was shaking hands with the next Director of the CIA.

'I'm terribly sorry,' he said to Molly. Truslow's eyes were moist. 'Your father was a wonderful man. He'll be sorely missed.'

Molly only nodded. Did she know him? I couldn't tell.

'Ben Ellison, is that right?' he said, shaking my hand.

'Good to meet you, Mr Truslow,' I said.

'Alex. I'm surprised we haven't run into each other around Boston,' he said. 'You may know I'm a friend of Bill Stearns's.' William Caslin Stearns III is the senior partner of Putnam & Stearns, and himself an old CIA man. Also, my boss. Such were the circles in which I moved.

'He's mentioned you,' I said.

A few minutes of awkward chat followed as we walked toward where the cars were parked, and then Truslow got to what was clearly his main point. 'You know, I've mentioned to Bill that I'd be very much interested in having you do some legal work for my firm.'

I smiled pleasantly. 'I'm sorry, but I haven't had anything to do with CIA or intelligence or anything of that sort since I left the Agency. I don't think I'm the one you want.'

'Oh, your background has nothing to do with it,' he persisted. 'It's purely business, and I'm told you're the best intellectual-property attorney in Boston.'

'You've been badly misled,' I said with a polite chuckle. 'There are lots better than me.'

'You're too modest,' he replied gently. 'Let's have lunch sometime soon.' He gave a lopsided smile. 'All right, Ben?'

'I'm sorry, Alex. I'm flattered – but I'm afraid I'm not interested. My loss.'

Truslow looked directly at me with his sad brown eyes. They reminded me of a basset hound's. He shrugged, and shook my hand again.

'Then it's *my* loss, Ben,' he said, smiled forlornly, and disappeared into the back of a black Lincoln limousine.

I suppose I shouldn't have been surprised that it wouldn't end there. But I could not help thinking it odd that he would want to hire me, and by the time I understood why, it was too late.

Part One

THE CORPORATION

The Independent
Is Germany on the Verge of Collapse?

FROM NIGEL CLEMONS

IN BONN

In the bleak months since the stock market crash that has plunged Germany into its worst economic and political crisis since the 1920s, many here have come to believe that this country, once Europe's powerhouse, is on the verge of collapse.

In a violent demonstration yesterday in Leipzig, over one hundred thousand people protested the economic privation, plummeting standard of living, and sudden loss of thousands of jobs throughout the nation. There were even widespread calls for a dictator to restore Germany to its former greatness.

In recent days there have been food riots in Berlin, outbreaks of neo-Nazi and right-wing extremist terrorism, as well as an enormous rise in street crimes especially in what was formerly West Germany. The nation is nearing the end of a fiercely contested election of the next chancellor, and ten days ago the head of the Christian Democratic Party was assassinated.

Government sources here continue to blame the recent German crash on the global recession as well as on the fragility of the recently integrated national stock market, the Deutsche Börse.

Some observers pointedly recall that the last economic crisis of this magnitude, during the Weimar era, gave rise to Adolf Hitler.

1

The law offices of Putnam & Stearns are located in the narrow streets of Boston's financial district, amid granite-fronted bank buildings: Boston's version of Wall Street, with fewer bars. Our offices occupy two floors of a handsome old building on Federal Street, on the ground floor of which is a respectable old Brahmin bank famous for laundering money for the Mafia.

Putnam & Stearns, I should probably explain at this point, is one of the CIA's 'outside' law firms. It's all perfectly legitimate; it doesn't violate the Agency's charter (which prohibits them from domestic shenanigans; *international* shenanigans are apparently okay). Fairly often, the CIA requires legal counsel in matters involving, say, immigration and naturalization (if they're trying to spirit an intelligence defector into the country) or real estate (if they need to acquire property, a safe house, or an office or anything else that can't be traced to Langley). Or, and this is Bill Stearns's particular expertise, moving funds around, in and out of numbered accounts in Luxembourg or Zurich or Grand Cayman.

Putnam & Stearns, though, does a lot more than the CIA's dirty work. It's a general practice, white-shoe firm comprising some thirty lawyers, twelve partners, who practice a range of law from corporate litigation to real estate to divorce to estates to tax to intellectual property.

That last item, intellectual property, is my specialty: patents and copyrights, who invented what, who stole whose invention. You remember a few years back when a famous sneaker manufacturer came up with a gimmick that allowed the wearer to pump the shoe up with air, for a cost of a mere hundred and fifty dollars a pair. That was my handiwork – the legal work, I mean; I devised an ironclad patent, or as ironclad as you can realistically get.

For the last several months I had been keeping twenty-four large dolls in my office, which no doubt disconcerted my stuffier clients. I was helping a toy manufacturer out in Western Massachusetts defend his Big Baby Doll line of products. You probably haven't heard of Big Baby Dolls. This is because the claim was settled against my client; I'm not proud of it. I did much better restraining a cookie company from using in its TV ads a little animated creature that suspiciously resembled the Pillsbury Doughboy.

I was one of two intellectual-property lawyers at Putnam & Stearns, which officially makes us a 'department,' if you count the paralegals and legal secretaries and all that. This means the firm gets to advertise that we're a full-service legal corporation, here to handle all your needs, even your copyrights and your patents. All your legal needs serviced under one roof. One-stop shopping.

I was considered a good attorney, but not because I loved it or took much interest in it. After all, as the old saw has it, lawyers are the only persons in whom ignorance of the law is not punished.

Instead, I am blessed with a rare neurological gift, present in less than 0.1 percent of the population: an eidetic (or photographic, as it's colloquially known) memory. It doesn't make me smarter than anyone else, but it certainly made my life easier in college and law school, when it came time to memorize a passage or a case. I can see the page, as if it were a picture, in my mind. This capability is not something I generally let people know about. It's not the sort of thing that wins you many friends. And yet it is so much a part of who I am, and always has been, that I must constantly be mindful not to let it set me apart from others.

To their credit, the founding partners, Bill Stearns and the late James Putnam, spent nearly their entire earnings their first few years on interior decoration. The office, all Persian rugs and fragile antiques from the Regency period, exudes a stifling, hushed elegance. Even the ring of the telephone is muted. The receptionist, who's (naturally) English, sits at an antique library table whose surface is polished to a high gloss. I have seen clients, real estate moguls who in their own lairs strut around barking orders to their minions, walk into our reception area as cowed and discomfited as chastened schoolboys.

It was a little over a month since Hal Sinclair's funeral, and I was rushing to a meeting in my own office. I passed Ken McElvoy, a junior partner who had been enmeshed in some unspeakably dull corporate litigation for almost six months. He was carrying a huge stack of depositions and looked miserable, like some wretch out of *Bleak House* or something. I gave poor Dickensian McElvoy a smile and headed for my office.

My secretary, Darlene, gave me a quick wave, and said: 'Everyone's there.'

Darlene is the funkiest person in this firm, which isn't hard to accomplish. She usually wears all black. Her hair is dyed a jet black; her eye shadow is midnight blue. But she's fiercely efficient, so I don't give her any grief.

I had called this meeting to resolve a dispute that had been carried out through the mail for more than six months. The matter concerned an exercise machine called the Alpine Ski, a magnificently designed device that simulates downhill skiing, giving the user not only the aerobic benefits you get from something like the NordicTrack, but at the same time, a serious muscular workout.

The Alpine Ski's inventor, Herb Schell, was my client. A former personal trainer in Hollywood, he had made a bundle with this invention. Then suddenly, about a year ago, cheaply produced ads began to run on late-night television for something called the Scandinavian Skier, unmistakably a knockoff of Herb's invention. It was a lot less expensive too: whereas the real Alpine Ski sells for upward of six hundred dollars (and Alpine Ski Gold for over a thousand), the Scandinavian Skier was going for $129.99.

Herb Schell was already seated in my office, along with the president and chief executive officer of E-Z Fit, the company that was manufacturing Scandinavian Skier, Arthur Sommer; and his attorney, a high-powered lawyer named Stephen Lyons, whom I'd heard of but never met.

On some level I found it ironic that both Herb Schell and Arthur Sommer were paunchy and visibly in lousy shape. Herb had confided to me over lunch shortly after we met that, now that he was no longer a personal trainer, he'd grown tired of working out all the time; he much preferred liposuction.

'Gentlemen,' I said. We shook hands all around. 'Let's resolve this thing.'

'Amen,' Steve Lyons said. His enemies (who are legion) have been known to refer to him as 'Lyin' Lyons' and his small, aggressive law firm as 'the Lyons den.'

'All right,' I said. 'Your client has blatantly infringed my client's design, down to the last claimed feature. We've been through all this dozens of times. It's a goddamned Chinese copy, and unless this is resolved today, we are prepared to go into federal court and seek an injunction. We'll also seek damages, which, as you know in cases of willful infringement, are *treble*.' Patent law tends to be a very mild, rather dull way to earn a living – the bland leading the bland, I like to call it – and so I cherished my few opportunities to be confrontational. Arthur Sommer flushed, presumably with anger, but said nothing. His thin lips curled up in a small, tight smile. His attorney leaned back in his chair: ominous body language if ever there was such a thing.

'Look, Ben,' Lyons said. 'Since there really isn't any cause of action here, my client is generously willing to make a courtesy settlement offer of five hundred thousand. I've advised him against it, but this charade is costing him and all of us –'

'Five hundred thousand? Try twenty times that.'

'Sorry, Ben,' Lyons said. 'This patent isn't worth the paper it's printed on.' He clasped his hands together. 'We got an on-sale bar here.'

'What the hell are you talking about?'

'I have evidence that Alpine Ski went on sale more than a year before the patent filing date,' Lyons replied smugly. 'Sixteen months before, to be exact. So the damned patent's not valid. On-sale statutory bar.'

This was a new approach on his part, and it was unsettling. Up to now, all we'd been hashing out, in letter after letter, was whether Scandinavian Skier materially resembled Alpine Ski: whether it infringed the claims of the patent, to put it in legalese. Now he was citing something called the 'on sale' doctrine, under which an invention can't be patented if it was 'in public use or on sale' more than a year before the date that the patent was applied for.

But I did not let on my surprise. A good attorney must be a skilled bullshit artist. 'Nice try,' I said. 'That's not really *use*, Steve, and you know it.' It sounded good, whatever it meant.

'Ben –' Herb interrupted.

Lyons handed me a legal file folder. 'Take a look,' he said. 'Here's a copy of a newsletter put out by the Big Apple Health Club in Manhattan that shows their latest piece of equipment – the Alpine Ski – almost a year and a half before Mr. Schell applied for his patent. And an invoice.'

I took the folder, glanced at it without interest, and handed it back.

'Ben –' Herb said again. 'Can we talk for a minute?'

I left Lyons and Sommer in my office while Herb and I talked in a nearby vacant conference room.

'What the hell is this all about?' I asked.

'It's true. They're right.'

'You sold this thing more than a year before you applied for a patent?'

'Two years before, actually. To twelve personal trainers at health clubs around the country.'

I stared at him evenly. 'Why?'

'Christ, Ben, I didn't know the law. How the hell are you supposed to test these things out unless you get it out there? You have no idea the kind of abuse machines like this take in gyms and health clubs.'

'So you were able to make improvements along the way?'

17

'Well, sure.'

'Ah. How fast can you get me a document from your corporate headquarters in Chicago?'

Steve Lyons was beaming with triumph as we came in. 'I assume,' he said with what he probably took to be sympathy, 'that Mr Schell has filled you in.'

'Yes, indeed,' I said.

'Preparation, Ben,' he said. 'You ought to look into it.'

The timing was exquisite. At that moment my personal fax machine rang and squealed and began to print out a document. I walked over to the fax, watched it print out, and as it did so, I said: 'Steve, I only wish you'd saved us all the time and expense by doing a little reading in your case law.'

He looked at me, puzzled, his smile dimming somewhat.

'Ah, let's see,' I said. 'It would be 917 Fed Second 544, Federal Circuit 1990.'

'What's he talking about?' Sommer audibly whispered to Lyons. Lyons, unwilling to shrug in my presence, merely stared at me, uncomprehending.

'Is that true?' Sommer insisted.

Lyons's facial expression did not change. 'I'd have to look it up.'

The fax machine cut the paper, a staccato punctuation mark. I handed it to Lyons. 'Here's a letter from the manager of the Big Apple Health Club to Herb Schell, containing his thoughts about the Alpine Ski, his notes on how it was holding up and what about it might be reconfigured. And suggestions for modifications.'

At that point Darlene walked in, silently gave me a book – *Federal Reporter 917, 2d Series* – and left. Without even looking at it, I handed it to Lyons.

'This some sort of game you're playing?' Lyons managed to stammer.

'Oh, not at all,' I replied. 'My client sold prototypes during a period of testing, and gathered performance data from the sold version. Therefore the "on-sale" doctrine doesn't apply, Steve.'

'I don't even know where you're getting this –'

'Manville Sales Corp. v. Paramount Systems, Inc. Fed Second 544.'

'Oh, come off it,' Lyons retorted. 'I never even heard of –'

'Page 1314,' I said as I returned to my chair, leaned back, and folded my legs. 'Let's see.' In a monotone, I recited: 'The policies that define the on sale and public use bars do not support invalidation of the patent even though, more than one year prior to filing a patent application, the patentee installed a fixture at a state highway rest station under construction. A period of outdoor testing of the invention was necessary to determine whether it would . . .'

Lyons, in the meantime, sat with the book open on his lap, following along, mouthing the words. He finished the sentence for me: 'it would serve its purpose.'

He looked up at me, slack-jawed.

'See you in court,' I said.

Herb Schell left that morning much happier and almost ten million dollars richer. And I had the pleasure of a parting colloquy with Steve Lyons.

'You knew that fucking case word for word,' he said. 'Word for word. How the hell did you do that?'

'Preparation,' I said, and shook his hand firmly. 'Look into it.'

2

Very early the next morning I had breakfast at the Harvard Club in Boston with my boss, Bill Stearns.

Which was when I learned I was suddenly in some serious trouble.

Stearns had breakfast there every morning: Mrs Stearns, a wan Wellesley housewife, apparently did little else beside serve as a volunteer for the Museum of Fine Arts. I imagined that she slept late, with an eyeshade on, and that since the time their two kids had left the nest for their foreordained lives as junior Boston Brahmins (Deerfield, Harvard, investment banking, alcoholism), he hadn't had a single breakfast at home.

His table at the Harvard Club was always the same, against the plate-glass window overlooking the city. Invariably he'd have the Harvard Club's special shirred eggs (Stearns considered the late twentieth-century aversion to cholesterol an evanescent fad, like the sixties). Sometimes he'd eat by himself, with *The Wall Street Journal* and *The Boston Globe*, sometimes with one or more of the senior partners, to discuss business and golf.

Every once in a long while I'd join him. In case you suspect we engaged in conspiratorial, old-boy-network chitchat about the Central Intelligence Agency, I should make it plain that Bill Stearns and I normally talked about sports (which I know just enough about to banter) or real estate. Occasionally – this morning, for instance – there was something of gravity Bill wanted to discuss.

Stearns is the sort of person who's considered avuncular by those who don't know him. He's in his late fifties, gray-haired,

20

ruddy-faced, bow-tied, somewhat pot-bellied. His two-thousand-dollar suits from Louis of Boston look, on him, as if they came off the wrong rack at Filene's Basement.

The truth is that after those two nightmarish, violent years of clandestine CIA work, I found the very safeness of my legal career at Putnam & Stearns deeply reassuring. But it was my service at CIA that got me recruited to Putnam & Stearns. Bill Stearns was formerly Inspector General of the Central Intelligence Agency under the legendary Allen Dulles, the Director of Central Intelligence from 1953 to 1961.

When I was hired at Putnam & Stearns nine years ago I made it very clear that my intelligence background notwith-standing, I would refuse to have anything to do with the CIA. My brief CIA career was the past, I told Bill Stearns, and that was that. Stearns, to his credit, had shrugged theatrically and said, 'Who said anything about CIA?' There was, I'm convinced, a twinkle in his eye. I think he figured that in time I'd relent, that it would be easy business for me. He knew that the Agency feels much more comfortable in dealing with its own, that there'd be all kinds of pressure on me to do whatever legal work the Agency wanted, and that I'd give in. Why else would an ex–field officer like me come to work for an old-boy firm like Putnam & Stearns? The answer, of course, was the money, which was substantially more than any other firm was offering me.

I didn't know why Bill Stearns had invited me to breakfast that morning, but I strongly suspected something was up. I busied myself with my blueberry muffin. I'd had way too much coffee already, and I figured a little solid matter in my stomach would anchor me. I've always hated business breakfasts; I believe Oscar Wilde had a point when he said that only dull people are brilliant at breakfast.

As our food arrived, Stearns pulled a copy of *The Boston Globe* from his briefcase.

'You read about First Commonwealth, I assume,' he said.

His tone immediately alarmed me. 'I didn't see the *Globe* this morning,' I said.

He slid it across the table.

I scanned the front page. There, just below the fold, was a headline that made me feel immediately queasy.

INVESTMENT FIRM CLOSED BY FEDERAL GOVERNMENT it read. And in smaller letters: FIRST COMMONWEALTH ASSETS FROZEN BY SEC.

First Commonwealth was a small money-management firm based in Boston which managed all my money. Despite the grandiose name, it is a tiny place, a boutique firm run by an acquaintance of mine, with fewer than half a dozen clients. It was the firm that paid my mortgage each month, the place where virtually all my money was stashed.

Until this morning.

Unlike Stearns, I am not rich. Molly's father left an insignificant amount of cash, some stock certificates and bearer bonds, and the title to his house in Alexandria, which was mortgaged to the hilt. He also left her, curiously, a document he'd signed and notarized, giving her full and absolute right of beneficiary to all accounts in his name foreign and domestic under the laws of blah blah blah . . . The details would numb your brain, as would most details pertaining to the law of estates and trusts. I say 'curiously' because, as Harrison Sinclair's only surviving heir, she was automatically entitled to beneficiary rights. No piece of paper was necessary. All right, so maybe Sinclair was the overly cautious type.

Me, he left exactly one item: an autographed copy of the memoirs of CIA director Allen Dulles, *The Craft of Intelligence*. It was a first edition, and it was inscribed 'For Hal, With deepest admiration, Allen.' A nice bequest on Sinclair's part, but hardly a fortune.

When my father died some years back, I inherited a little over a million dollars, which after estate taxes immediately became half a million. I transferred all of it to First Commonwealth because of its good reputation. The head of the firm, Frederick 'Doc' Osborne, I knew from various legal dealings, and he always struck me as shrewd. Was it Nelson Algren who said, Never eat at a place called Mom's and never play cards with a guy named Doc? And that was before the days of money managers.

22

You may wonder, of course, why someone as shrewd as I'm supposed to be would put all his money in one place. I have often wondered the same thing myself, to be frank, and still do. The answer, I suppose, is twofold. Doc Osborne was a friend, and he had a terrific reputation, and therefore it seemed unnecessary to diversify. And I had always treated my inheritance as a nest egg, a chunk of money I preferred not to touch, since I was making a decent salary. And I suppose, too, it's like that old saw about the shoemaker's children never having any shoes: the guys who work with money are often pretty mindless about their own.

I dropped my fork, felt sick to my stomach. Rapidly calculating, I realized at once that unless I could somehow wrest my money back from First Commonwealth, I would immediately go bankrupt – my salary, generous though it was, wouldn't even cover my mortgage. In the present soft real estate market in Boston, I'd be unable to sell my house except at a tremendous loss.

The veins at my temples throbbed. I looked up at Stearns.

'Help me out here,' I said weakly.

'Ben, I'm sorry –' Stearns said through a mouthful of shirred egg.

'What does this mean? This stuff isn't my expertise, you know that.'

He took a swallow of coffee and set down the cup noisily in the saucer. 'Here's what it means,' he said with a sigh. 'Your money's frozen, along with that of all other First Commonwealth clients.'

'By whom? Who has the authority to do that? And for what?' I ran my eyes wildly up and down the *Globe* article, trying to glean some sense from it.

'The Securities and Exchange Commission. Plus the U.S. attorney's office in Boston.'

'Frozen,' I said dully, disbelieving.

'The U.S. attorney's office isn't saying much – they said it's a pending investigation.'

'Investigating *what*?'

'All they said was something about securities law violations and RICO statutes. They said it might take at least a year to release the assets, pending the outcome of the SEC's investigation.'

'*Frozen*,' I said again. 'My God.' I ran a hand across my face. 'All right. What can I do about this?'

'Nothing,' Stearns said. 'Nothing except wait this out. I can have Todd Richlin talk to a friend of his at the SEC' – Richlin was Putnam & Stearns's resident financial genius – 'but I wouldn't hold my breath.'

I looked out the window at the miniature streets of Boston thirty-some floors below us – the green of the Public Garden and the Common resembling the green-sprayed lichen of a toy train set; the magnificent tree-lined Commonwealth Avenue; and running parallel to it, Marlborough Street, where I lived. If I were the suicidal type, it would have made a good spot from which to jump. 'Go ahead,' I said.

'Both the Securities and Exchange Commission and the Justice Department, acting through the U.S. attorney's office in Boston, have shut down First Commonwealth, apparently for alleged drug ties.'

'Drug – ?'

'Well, the word is that Doc Osborne's involved in some kind of money-laundering scheme for drug types.'

'But *I* have nothing whatsoever to do with whatever shit Doc Osborne is into!'

'It doesn't work that way,' he replied. 'Remember when the Fed shut down that big discount brokerage in New York, Drexel Burnham? They literally went in and put handcuffs on people and put a sticker on the door. I mean, you could take a tour of the place a year later and you'd see cigarettes still in ashtrays, half-full cups of coffee, all that.'

'But Drexel's clients didn't lose their cash!'

'Well, look at Marcos of the Philippines, or the Shah of Iran – sometimes they just seize all the money and let it earn interest – for good old Uncle Sam.'

'Seize all the money,' I echoed.

'First Commonwealth literally has a padlock on the door,' Stearns went on. 'Federal marshals have seized all the computer equipment, all the records and documentation, sequestered –'

'So when can I get my money?'

'Maybe in a year and a half you'll be able to pry the money loose. Probably longer.'

'What the hell am I going to do?'

Stearns exhaled noisily. 'I had a drink last night with Alex Truslow,' he said. Then, daubing his mouth with a linen napkin, he added casually: 'Ben, I want you to free up time for Truslow Associates.'

'My schedule's a little cramped, Bill,' I said. 'Sorry.'

'Alex could mean upward of two hundred thousand dollars in billable hours this year alone, Ben.'

'We've got half a dozen attorneys as qualified as I am. More qualified.'

Stearns cleared his throat. 'Not in all ways.'

His meaning was clear. 'As if that's a qualification,' I said.

'He seems to think it is.'

'What does he want done anyway?'

The waitress, a large-bosomed woman in her late fifties, refilled our coffee cups and gave Stearns a sisterly wink. 'Pretty routine stuff, I'm sure,' Stearns said, brushing crumbs off his lapel.

'So why me? What about Donovan, Leisure?' That was another white-shoe law firm, based in New York, founded by 'Wild Bill' Donovan, the head of the OSS and a major figure in the history of American intelligence. Donovan, Leisure was also known to have links to the CIA. For something as secretive as intelligence, it's amazing how much is 'known' or 'rumored.'

'No doubt Truslow does some work with Donovan, Leisure. But he wants local counsel, and of the Boston firms, there aren't many he feels as comfortable about as he does us.'

I was unable to suppress a smile. ' "Comfortable," ' I repeated, savoring Stearns's delicacy. 'Meaning he needs some sort of extracurricular espionage work, and he wants to keep it all in the family.'

'Ben, listen to me. This is a wonderful opportunity. I think this could be your salvation. Whatever Alex wants, I'm sure he's not going to ask you to get back into clandestine work.'

'What's in it for me?'

'I think something could be arranged. An emergency loan, say. An advance as a lien against your equity stake in the firm. Taken out of your end-of-the-year share of the firm.'

'A bribe.'

Stearns shrugged, took a deep breath. 'Do you believe your father-in-law died in a genuine accident?'

I was uncomfortable at hearing him articulate my private suspicions. 'I have no reason to disbelieve the version I was told. What does this have to do with –'

'Your language betrays you,' he said angrily. 'You sound like a fucking bureaucrat. Like some Agency public affairs officer. Alex Truslow believes Hal Sinclair was murdered. Whatever your feelings about CIA, Ben, you owe it to Hal, to Molly, and to yourself to help Alex out in any way you can.'

After an uncomfortable silence I said, 'What does my legal ability have to do with Truslow's theories about Hal Sinclair's death?'

'Just have lunch with the guy. You'll like him.'

'I've met him,' I said. 'I have no doubt he's a prince. I made a promise to Molly –'

'We could all use the business,' Stearns said, examining the tablecloth, a sign that he'd just about reached the end of his patience. If he were a dog, he'd emit a low growl at this point. 'And you could use the money.'

'I'm sorry, Bill,' I said. 'I'd rather not. You understand.'

'I understand,' Stearns said softly, and began waving for the check. He was not smiling.

'No, Ben,' Molly said when I returned that evening.

Normally she is effervescent, even playful, but since her father's death she was, understandably, a very different person. Not just subdued, angry, despondent, mournful – the range of emotions anyone goes through with the death of a parent – but uncertain, hesitant, introspective. It was a very different Molly these last few weeks, and it pained me to see her like this. 'How can this be?'

I didn't know how to respond, so I just shook my head.

'But *you're* innocent,' she said, on the edge of hysteria. '*You're* a lawyer. Can't you do something?'

'If I had been smart enough to spread my money around, this wouldn't have happened. Twenty-twenty hindsight.'

She was making dinner, something she does only when she needs the therapeutic benefits that cooking provides. She was wearing one of my rattier college sweatshirts and oversize jeans and stirring something in a saucepan that smelled like tomatoes and olives and lots of garlic.

I don't think you would call Molly Sinclair beautiful the first time you saw her. But her looks grow on you so that after you've known her for a while, you're amazed to hear anyone express the opinion that she's anything less than stunning.

She's a little taller than I, five foot ten or so, with an unruly mop of kinked black hair; blue-gray eyes and black lashes; and a healthy, ruddy complexion, which I think is her finest feature. I've always considered her somewhat mysterious, slightly distant, no less so now than when we met in college, and she's graced with a serene temperament.

Molly was a first-year resident in pediatrics at Massachusetts General Hospital, and at thirty-six she was older than anyone else in her year, since she started late. Which is very Molly: she's a serious procrastinator, especially when she has better things to do. In her case, this meant trekking through Nepal for more than a year after college. At Harvard, even though she knew she'd eventually end up in medicine, she majored in Italian, writing her thesis on Dante – which meant she was fluent in Italian but not so fluent in organic chemistry.

Molly was forever quoting that line from Chekhov, to the effect that doctors are the same as lawyers, but while lawyers merely rob you, doctors rob you and kill you too. She loved medicine, though, far more than she cared about material possessions. She and I had often talked – half seriously – about quitting our jobs, selling this albatross of a house, and moving somewhere rural, where we'd open a clinic to treat poor kids.

The Ellison-Sinclair Clinic we'd call it, which sounded like a psychiatric hospital.

She turned down the heat on the sauce, and together we walked to the sitting room off the kitchen, which, like every room in the house, was a mess of lumber, spackling compound buckets, copper pipes, and such, and everything covered with a fine layer of plaster dust. We sat down in the overstuffed armchairs that were protected temporarily with plastic drop cloths.

Molly and I had bought a beautiful old town house in Boston's Back Bay, on Marlborough Street, five years ago. Beautiful, that is, on the exterior. The interior was *potentially* beautiful. It was the height of the market, a few months before the bottom fell out – you'd think I'd have been smarter, but like everyone else I figured real estate prices had to keep skyrocketing – and the house was what real estate ads sometimes call a 'handyman's dream.' 'Roll up your sleeves,' the ads say, 'and use your imagination!' The realtor didn't call it a handyman's dream, but then, the realtor also didn't tell us about the arthritic plumbing, the carpenter ants, or the rotten plasterboard. People used to say in the 1980s that cocaine was God's way of telling you you have too much money. In the 1990s, it's a mortgage.

I got what I deserved. The renovation was an ongoing project not unlike the construction of the pyramids at Giza. One thing led to another. If you want to repair the crumbling staircase you must put in a new load-bearing wall, which necessitates . . . well, you get it.

At least there were no rats. I have always had a rat phobia, an irrational, uncontrollable terror of the little beasts beyond the revulsion everyone else experiences. I had ruled out several houses before this, houses Molly adored, because I was convinced I'd glimpsed the silhouette of a rat. Exterminators were out of the question; I believe that rats, like cockroaches, are fundamentally nonexterminable. They will survive us all. Every once in a while, while we were browsing in a video store, Molly would have a little fun at my expense by pulling out a cassette of the rat horror movie *Willard* and suggesting we rent it for the evening. Not funny.

28

And as if we needed more stress, we had been arguing for months about whether to have a child. Unlike the normal pattern – the woman wants one while the husband doesn't – I wanted a kid, or several kids, and Molly vehemently didn't. I thought it odd for a pediatrician such as she to insist that the secret of raising a kid right is not to be its parent. As she saw it, her career was just getting started, and the timing was all wrong. This always touched off the fiercest quarrels. I'd say I was willing to split the responsibilities with her equally; she'd counter that no male in the history of civilization has ever shared the child-raising duties equally. The plain fact was, I was ready to have a family – when my first wife, Laura, died, she was pregnant – and Molly wasn't. So the arguments continued.

'We could sell Dad's house in Alexandria,' she began.

'In this market we'd make next to nothing. And your father didn't leave you anything. He never cared much about money.'

'Can we take out a loan?'

'Using *what* as collateral?'

'I can moonlight.'

'That's not going to do it,' I said, 'and you'll just wear yourself out.'

'But what does Alexander Truslow want with you?'

What, indeed, when the world swarms with lawyers far more qualified? I didn't want to repeat Stearns's suspicion that Molly's father had been murdered: in any case, that didn't explain why Truslow wanted to sign me on. No reason to upset her further.

'I don't like to think about why he wants me,' I said lamely. Both of us knew it had to do with my CIA background, probably with my fearsome reputation, but that still didn't answer *why*, precisely.

'How was the NICU?' I asked, meaning the neonatal intensive-care unit at Massachusetts General Hospital, where, since her father's funeral, she had been doing her rotation.

She shook her head, refusing to let me off the hook. 'I want to talk about this Truslow thing,' she said. She fingered one of

29

her curls anxiously and said, 'My father and Truslow were friends. Trusted colleagues, I mean, not necessarily close personal friends. But he always liked Alex.'

'Fine,' I said. 'He's a good person. But once a spy, always a spy.'

'The same could be said for you.'

'I made a promise to you, Mol.'

'So you think Truslow wants you to do clandestine work for him?'

'I doubt it. Not at my billing rate.'

'But it involves CIA.'

'No question about that. CIA is the Corporation's single biggest client.'

'I don't want you doing it,' Molly said. 'We talked about it already – that's your past. You made a clean break – stay away.'

She knew how important it was to me to separate myself from the clandestine operative work that brought out the icy ruthlessness in me. 'That's my instinct too,' I said. 'But Stearns is going to make it as hard for me to say no as he possibly can.'

Now she got up and knelt on the floor facing me, her hands on my knees. 'I don't want you working for them again. You promised me that.' She was rubbing her hands back and forth on my thighs as she spoke, seducing me away, and fixed me with a beseeching stare, more inscrutable than usual. 'Is there anyone you can talk to about this?' she asked.

I thought for a moment, and at last said, 'Ed Moore.'

Edmund Moore, who was retired from the Agency after thirty-some years, knew more about the inner workings of the CIA than just about anyone else in the world. He had been my mentor in my brief intelligence career – my 'rabbi,' in intelligence argot – and he was and remained a man of rare instincts. He lived in Georgetown, in a wonderful old house, and he seemed to be busier now, since his retirement, than in his active days in the Agency: reading seemingly every biography ever published, attending meetings of CIA retirees, luncheons with old CIA cronies, testifying before Senate subcommittees, and doing a million other things I couldn't keep track of.

'Call him,' she said.

'I'll do better than that. If I can clear my calendar tomorrow afternoon, or the day after, I'll fly to Washington to see him.'

'If *he* can spare the time to see *you*,' Molly said. She had begun to arouse me, no doubt her very intention, and as I leaned forward to kiss her neck, she suddenly exclaimed, 'Oh, great. Now the damn putanesca sauce is burning.'

I followed her into the kitchen, and as soon as she had turned off the burner – the sauce was now a hopeless cause – I encircled her from behind. Things were so charged between us that with a little nudge in either direction, we could be embroiled in an endless argument, or . . .

I kissed her right ear and made my way slowly downward, and we began to make love on the floor of the sitting room, plaster dust or no plaster dust, pausing only long enough for Molly to go find her diaphragm and put it in.

That evening I called Edmund Moore, who delightedly invited me to join him and his wife for a simple dinner at their home the next evening.

The next afternoon, having postponed three eminently postponable meetings, I caught the Delta shuttle to Washington National Airport, and as dusk began to settle over Georgetown, my taxi crossed the Key Bridge, rattled over the cobblestones of N Street, and pulled up to the wrought-iron fence in front of Edmund Moore's town house.

3

Edmund Moore's library, in which we sat after dinner, was a magnificent two-story affair lined with shelves of oak inset with cherry. The second tier was ringed with a catwalk; several library ladders rested against the first-tier cases. In the dim lighting the room seemed to glow amber. Moore had one of the finest personal libraries I had ever seen, which included an impressive collection of books about espionage and intelligence. Some of them were accounts by Soviet and East Bloc defectors, which Ed Moore had placed with American and British publishers, in the years when the CIA did such things. (Openly, anyway.) Entire bookcases were devoted to the works of Carlyle, Dickens, Ruskin. They had the look of those books you could purchase by the yard from an interior decorator to simulate the look of an old baronial library, but I knew that Ed Moore had painstakingly collected them all at auctions and in bookshops in Paris and London, and in second-hand stores and barns throughout the U.S., and no doubt had read them all, at one time or another.

A fire crackled in the fireplace, illuminating the room with a cozy ocher light. We sat in worn leather armchairs before the flames. He sipped a 1963 vintage port of which he was especially proud; I had a single-malt.

I appreciated the atmosphere Moore had so carefully arranged for himself. In his town house we were no longer in Georgetown in the 1990s, crammed with video rental places, Tan-O-Ramas, and Benettons, but in Edwardian England. Edmund Moore was a midwesterner, really an Oklahoman, but over his years with CIA he'd become as tweedy and Ivy League as any Yalie or Princetonian in his generation. It wasn't an affectation; that was simply what happened after

32

enough time in an organization like the CIA. In fact, the Agency had changed around him. During the sixties, when Ivy League campuses were torn by strikes and drugs, the Agency began to recruit from safer, midwestern schools of more fundamental values. Thus, as one Company friend put it, the 'polyesterization' of the CIA. And here was this quaint Oklahoman who could have walked into a lecture room at Linsley-Chittenden Hall at Yale in the forties and no one would have batted an eye. 'Gentility,' Moore once told me, 'is what is left over from rich ancestors after the money is gone.' In fact, though, Moore had married into a lot of money – Elena's grandfather had invented something essential having to do with the telephone.

'You don't miss it, at all, do you?' he asked with a mischievous smile. He was a small, almost pixielike man in his late seventies, with a small dome-shaped bald head and heavy black-framed glasses that magnified his eyes enormously. His brown tweed suit hung on him, making him seem even more diminutive. 'The glamour, the travel, the first-class hotels . . . ?'

'. . . The beautiful women,' I added helpfully, 'and the Michelin three-star restaurants.'

'Ah, yes.'

Moore, who had been chief of the Europe Division of the Operations Directorate while I was stationed in Paris – my boss, to put it simply – knew full well that the life of a clandestine operative actually meant unending tedious 'fitness reports,' cables, lousy restaurants, and cold, rainy parking lots. After Laura's murder, Moore had all but shoved me out the door of Langley headquarters, arranging my interview with Bill Stearns in Boston. He felt strongly that it would be a serious mistake for me to remain in the Agency after what had happened. For a while I resented him for it, but I soon came to realize that he had my best interests at heart.

Moore was a shy, bookish man – an unlikely operations type, where the prevailing personality is boisterous, aggressive, canny. You would have pegged him for an analyst, an intelligence type, according to Agency nomenclature. Not at all a spymaster. He taught history at the University of Oklahoma at Norman before he was recruited to Army intelligence in the Second World War, and he was still an academic at heart.

Outside, the wind howled, driving torrents of rain against the tall French doors at one end of the library, rattling the glass. The doors gave onto a beautifully landscaped garden, at the center of which was a small duck pond.

The rainstorm had begun during dinner, which was a somewhat overdone pot roast served by Moore's diminutive wife, Elena. We chatted about innocuous subjects – presidential politics, the Middle East, the upcoming German general elections, gossip about mutual acquaintances – and the painful one, the death of Hal Sinclair. Both Ed and Elena expressed their sincere condolences. After dinner Elena excused herself to go upstairs, leaving us to talk.

Her entire married life, I imagined, had been spent excusing herself to go upstairs, or out of the room, or out for a walk, leaving her husband to talk shop with whatever spook happened to have dropped by. But she was far from colorless and retiring; she wielded her strong opinions, laughed often, and, at once playful and feisty, she reminded me of the actress Ruth Gordon.

'I take it, then, that the sedentary life suits you well?'

'I like the sedateness of my life with Molly. I look forward to having a family. But being an attorney in Boston isn't the most exciting way to earn a living.'

He smiled, took a sip of port, and said, 'You've had enough excitement for several lifetimes.' Moore knew about my past, about what the Agency disciplinary board termed my 'recklessness' in the field.

'That's one way to put it.'

'Yes,' he agreed, 'you were something of a hothead. But you were young. And you were a good agent, which is the main thing. God, you were fearless. We were afraid we'd have to rein you in. Is it true you put a Camp instructor out of commission?'

I shrugged. It was true: during my training at the CIA's

Camp Peary, a martial arts instructor had scissored me in a choke hold in front of my fellow students and proceeded to taunt me, goad me. And suddenly I was overcome by a slow, cold wave of anger. It was as if some corrosive fluid had seeped into my abdomen, then flooded the rest of my body, giving me a glacial composure. Some ancient portion of my hindbrain seemed to take over; I was a primitive, ferocious animal. I reached out with the heel of my right hand and slammed his face, breaking his jaw. The incident immediately passed into Camp lore, told and retold, embellished and embroidered over drinks late at night. From then on I was regarded warily, like a hand grenade with the pin out. It was a reputation that served me well in the field, and it caused me to be selected for assignments that were deemed too risky for the others. But it was at the same time a trait that sickened me; it warred with my sober, analytical side; it simply wasn't who I was.

Moore crossed his legs and sat back. 'So tell me why you're here. I assume it's nothing we could have discussed over the telephone.'

Not, certainly, without a secure phone, I thought; the Agency takes those privileges away from you upon retirement, even from such an institution as Edmund Moore.

'Tell me about Alexander Truslow,' I said.

'Ah,' he said, and arched his brows. 'You're doing some work for him, I take it.'

'Considering it. The truth is, Ed, I'm in a bit of financial trouble.'

'Ah.'

'You might have heard about a small firm in Boston called First Commonwealth.'

'I think so. Drug money or something?'

'It's been shut down. Along with all my liquid assets.'

'I'm terribly sorry.'

'So suddenly Truslow Associates is looking quite a bit more appealing to me. Molly and I could use the money.'

'But isn't your specialty intellectual property, or patents, or whatever it's called?'

'That's right.'

35

'I'd have thought Alex would require the services of someone –'

He paused for a moment to sip his port, and I put in, 'Someone more adept at hiding money in international bolt holes?'

Moore gave a faint smile, and nodded. 'Yet perhaps you're just what he needs. You did have a reputation as one of the finest, most highly skilled operatives in the field –'

'A loose cannon, Ed, and you know it.'

A 'loose cannon' was, I imagine, just one of many labels given me by my colleagues and superiors in the Agency. I was regarded with fear, wonder, and a good deal of puzzlement. It was the fieldwork, the exposure to danger and the threat of violence, that would bring out my dark side. Some considered me fearless, which wasn't true. Others considered me reckless, which was closer to the truth.

The fact was that at certain times, a ruthless and frightening Ben Ellison would take over. It was something that, once I was aware of it, deeply unsettled me, and eventually led to my leaving the Agency.

Before Paris I was detailed to Leipzig to get my feet wet. My cover was as a trade official. One of my first assignments was to debrief and protect a rather nervous informant, a Red Army soldier stationed nearby. They'd chosen me because I had studied Russian at Harvard, and was almost fluent. And I carried out the mission flawlessly, and so I was rewarded – promoted, in a sense – with a far more dangerous task.

I was ordered to escort an East German defector, a physicist, from Leipzig to a border crossing a good distance away, at Herleshausen. The Mercedes I was driving had been fitted with a specially constructed compartment behind the seat, in which the physicist was concealed. At the checkpoint we went through the routine, the wheeled mirror apparatus shoved under the car to check for Germans trying to escape that miserable country, all that. A BND man had been sent up from headquarters in Pullach to meet us on the other side. As I went through the passport and immigration block, congratulating myself on a job well done, the BND man made the mistake of showing himself. Someone on the East German side recognized him, and suspicion instantly fell upon me.

Suddenly three, then seven *Volkspolizei* emerged from the booth and surrounded the car. One stood before me and indicated with an outstretched hand that I should halt.

According to Agency procedures, I should have acted innocent and perplexed, and stopped. Under no circumstances was a human life to be taken. That wasn't how the game worked.

And as I sat there, I thought of the small, sweaty physicist curled up in the tiny airless compartment between the backseat and the trunk. My precious cargo. The man was brave. He was risking his life, when it would have been so much easier to do nothing.

I smiled, looked to my left and my right, and then straight ahead. The Vopo blocking my way – a Stasi *Kommandant*, I later learned – gave me a smug smile.

I was boxed in. It was a classic box technique; we had learned it at Camp Peary. The only thing to do was to surrender. You did not take a life; the consequences would be grave.

And then something came over me, that same glacial fury that had come over me when I broke the martial arts trainer's jaw. It was as if I were in another world. My heartbeat did not accelerate; my face did not flush. I was calm – but overtaken by a desire to kill.

Break the box, I told myself. *Break the box*.

I floored the gas pedal.

Never will I be able to expunge from my memory the sight of the *Kommandant*'s face as it rose up to meet the windshield. A rictus of terror; disbelief in the eyes.

Tranquil, floating in a reptilian calm, I stared straight ahead. Everything was in slow motion. The *Kommandant*'s eyes locked on mine, pools of abject fear. He saw in my eyes the supreme indifference. Not fury, not desperation – but that icy calm.

With an awful thud the *Kommandant*'s body was thrown

into the air. There was a shower of gunfire, and I was across the line, my cargo safe.

Later, of course, I was reprimanded by Langley for taking 'unnecessary' and 'reckless' measures. But off the record my superiors let me know in subtle ways that they were secretly pleased. After all, I had gotten the physicist out, hadn't I?

But what remained with me was not pleasure in an assignment accomplished, not pride in an act of bravery of heroism, but a queasiness. For a minute or so at the border crossing I had become almost an automaton. I could have driven right into a brick wall. Nothing scared me.

And that scared me.

'No, Ben,' Moore continued. 'You were hardly a loose cannon. You were possessed of a rare combination of prodigious intellect and . . . brass balls. What happened to Laura wasn't your fault. You were one of the best. Moreover, with your photographic memory, or whatever that's called, you're quite an asset.'

'My . . . *eidetic* memory, as the neurologists call it, may have been a big deal in college and law school, but these days, with electronic data bases all over the place, it's nothing special.'

'You've met with Truslow?'

'I met him at Hal's funeral. We talked for about five minutes. That's it. I don't even know what he wants me to do yet.'

Moore got to his feet and walked across the room to the French doors. One of them was rattling more than the others; he adjusted and locked it, quieting the noise. As he returned, he said: 'Do you remember that famous civil rights case that was filed against CIA in the early 1970s? A black man applied for an analyst position there and was turned down for no good reason?'

'Sure.'

'Well, it was Alex Truslow who, in the end, resolved the case. And saw to it that the Agency's personnel office never again discriminated on the basis of race or sex. It was extraordinary – he had a vision of a CIA that was a true meritocracy, that wouldn't permit its old guard to trample the rights of minorities to enter its ranks. A lot of old-timers still bear a grudge against him for that – he let all those minorities into the lily-white old-boys club. And, as you might have heard, he's probably going to be named to replace your father-in-law.'

I nodded.

'How much do you know of what he's doing?' Moore asked.

'Virtually nothing. "Security work" for the Agency, I understand. Procedures Langley can't or won't do.'

'Let me show you something,' Moore said, once again rising, this time beckoning me to follow. With a grunt he mounted the wooden spiral staircase to the library's second level. 'Someday soon I won't be able to climb these stairs,' Moore said, short of breath. 'At which point I'll move all my Ruskin up here, where I need never see it again. Vile stuff – never liked the nasty old son of a bitch. That's what happens when cousins marry. Here we go. My booty.'

We had advanced about ten feet along the catwalk, past drablooking morocco-bound volumes, until Moore came to a stop at a wainscoted stretch of wall between shelves. He nudged a panel until it popped open, revealing a metal file drawer painted institutional gray.

'Nice,' I said. 'Did you have the boys from Technical Services build that for you?' In truth, it was rather a poor hiding place to anyone who knew the first thing about breaking and entering, but I wasn't about to tell him that.

He pulled the drawer open. It gave a low, rusty moan. 'No, actually it was here when I bought the house in 1952. The rich old manufacturer who built this place – some coot out of an Edith Wharton novel, I'll bet – liked secret compartments. There's a sliding panel in the fireplace mantel I never use. Little did he know his town house would eventually end up in the hands of a bona fide spook.'

The drawer seemed to contain intelligence files, at least from what I could tell by scanning the index tabs. 'I didn't know they let you take files with you when you retired,' I said.

He turned to me and adjusted his eyeglass frames. 'Oh, they don't.' He smiled. 'I'm trusting your discretion.'

'Always.'

'Good. I haven't violated any national security acts, *really*.'

'Did someone give these to you?'

'You remember Kent Atkins, from Paris station?'

'Certainly. He was a friend.'

'Well, he's in Munich now. Deputy station chief. He stuck his neck out to get these for me. The very least I could do is take the precaution of hiding them at home from prying burglars or what have you.'

'So I take it the Company doesn't know.'

'I doubt they've even noticed,' he said, and pulled out a manila folder. 'This is what Alex Truslow is up to. Do you know much about what your father-in-law was doing before his death?'

The rain was beginning to let up. Moore had spread out an array of files on a well-burnished oak library table near the French doors. They concerned the abolition of the KGB and the East Bloc intelligence services: the steady flow of secrets, and personnel, from Moscow and Berlin and everywhere else behind what was once called the Iron Curtain. There were extracts from debriefings of KGB officials who were attempting to sell their secrets for protection in the West, or who were offering bundles of files for sale to the CIA or to Western corporations. There were decoded cables reporting morsels of information seeping out of KGB stations around the world, which (I could tell at the briefest glance) had the potential for being explosive.

'You see,' Moore said gently, 'there's quite a bit of information that we'd all just as soon had remained buried in the Lubyanka.'

'What do you mean?'

He sighed. 'You know about the Wednesday Club, I'm sure.'

I nodded. The Wednesday Club was a regular social gathering of former CIA muckamucks – former directors and deputy directors and so on who enjoyed each other's company enough to eat lunch together at a French restaurant in Washington every Wednesday. The younger folks in the Agency called it the Fossils Club.

'Well, there's been quite a bit of talk in the last few months about just what we're seeing coming out of what used to be the Soviet Union.'

'Anything useful?'

'Useful?' He looked at me intently, owlishly, over his glasses. 'Would you consider it useful to receive irrefutable documentary proof that the Soviet Union engineered the assassination of John F. Kennedy?'

I started for a second, then shook my head. 'I don't think it would make Oliver Stone very happy,' I said.

He burst out laughing. 'But for a second you believed me, didn't you?'

'I know your sense of humor quite well.'

He laughed a few moments longer, then pushed his glasses up his nose. 'We've had KGB and Stasi generals coming over and trying to sell us information on KGB assets around the world. Names of people who worked for them.'

'I'd think that would be a great boon.'

'Maybe, in some historical sense,' Moore said, and removed his glasses. He massaged the bridge of his nose. 'But who really cares much now about some washed-up old Red who cooperated thirty years ago with a government that no longer exists?'

'I'm sure some people do.'

'No doubt. But that's not what interests me. A few months ago at one of our Wednesday lunches I heard a story about Vladimir Orlov.'

'The former chairman of the KGB?'

'More precisely, the *last* chairman of the KGB, before Yeltsin's people did away with it. Where do you imagine a fellow like that goes when his job is pulled out from under him?'

'Paraguay or Brazil?'

Moore chuckled. 'Mr. Orlov knew better than to hang

41

around in his dacha outside Moscow, waiting for the Russian government to decide to prosecute him for doing his job to the best of his ability. He went into exile.'

'Where?'

'That's the problem.' He selected a stapled set of papers from the table and handed it to me. It was a photocopy of a cable from a CIA officer in Zurich station reporting the appearance of one Vladimir I. Orlov, former chairman of the Soviet KGB, in a café on Sihlstrasse.

He was accompanied by Sheila McAdams, executive assistant to Director of Central Intelligence Harrison Sinclair. The cable was dated less than one month earlier.

'I'm not sure I understand,' I said.

'Three days before Hal Sinclair died, his executive assistant and – I trust I'm not revealing anything you don't already know – *mistress*, Sheila McAdams, met in Zurich with the ex-chief of the KGB.'

'So?'

'The rendezvous was apparently cleared by Sinclair himself.'

'Presumably they were transacting some sort of business.'

'Of course,' Moore said impatiently. 'The following day, the name of Vladimir Orlov disappeared from most CIA data banks, at least those accessible to all but the top five or six officials. Then Orlov himself disappeared from Zurich. We don't know where he went. It was as if Orlov had given Hal's assistant some quid pro quo in exchange for removing him from our sonars, our sights. But we'll never know. Two days later Sheila was killed in that alley in Georgetown. Next day Hal perished in that awful "accident." '

'So who would have murdered them?'

'That, my dear Ben, is exactly what Alexander Truslow would like to know.' The fire was dying, and Moore poked at it idly. 'There's turmoil in the Agency. Terrible turmoil. A dreadful power struggle.'

'Between – ?'

'Listen to me. Europe is in a frightful mess. Britain and France are in bad shape, and Germany's virtually in a depression. The specter of feuding nationalist elements –'

'Yes, but what does that have to do –'

'The talk – it is only talk, I grant you, but it is from supremely well-connected Agency retirees – is that certain elements within the Agency have found a way to insinuate themselves into the chaos in Europe.'

'Ed, that's awfully vague –'

'Yes,' he said, so sharply that it startled me. '*Certain elements* . . . and *insinuate* . . . and all the other muzzy little phrases we employ when all we know are wisps. But the point is, old men who should be playing golf and enjoying bone-dry martinis are frightened. Friends of mine who used to run the organization speak of enormous sums of money changing hands in Zurich –'

'Meaning that we paid off Vladimir Orlov?' I interrupted. 'Or that he paid *us* off for protection?'

'Money isn't the point!' His too-even teeth were an unnatural yellow.

'Then what is?' I asked gently.

'Let me just say that the skeletons haven't yet begun to emerge from the closet. And when they do, the CIA may well join the KGB on the ash heap of history.'

We sat for a long time in silence. I was about to remark *And would that be so bad?* when I glimpsed Moore's expression. His face was now chalk-white.

'What does Kent Atkins think?'

He was silent for half a minute. 'I don't really know, Ben. Kent is scared to death. He was asking *me* what *I* thought was going on.'

'What did you tell him?'

'That whatever these Agency renegades are trying to accomplish in Europe will not simply involve the Europeans. It will directly involve us as well. It will involve the world. And I shudder to think what sort of conflagration is in store for us all.'

'Meaning what, specifically?'

He ignored my question, gave a small, rueful smile, and shook his head. 'My father died at the age of ninety-one, my mother at eighty-nine. Longevity runs in my family. But none of them fought in the Cold War.'

'I don't understand. What sort of conflagration, Ed?'

'You know, in his last few months in office, your father-in-law was quite obsessed with saving Russia. He was convinced that unless CIA took serious action, forces of reaction would take over in Moscow. And then the Cold War would be a sweet memory. Maybe Hal was onto something.'

He clenched his small liver-spotted fist, and pressed it against his pursed lips. 'We take risks, all of us who work for Central Intelligence. The rate of suicide is quite high, you know.'

I nodded.

'And although it's actually quite rare for any of us to be killed in the line of duty, it happens.' His voice softened somewhat. 'You know that.'

'You're afraid you're going to be killed?'

Another smile, a shake of the head. 'I'm approaching eighty. I don't plan to live my remaining years with an armed guard beside my bed. Assuming they'd provide one. I see no reason to live in a cage.'

'But have you received any threats?'

'None at all. It's just the patterns that have me worried.'

'Patterns – ?'

'Tell me this. Who knew you were coming to see me?'

'Just Molly.'

'No one else?'

'No.'

'There's always the telephone.'

I peered at him closely, wondering whether the paranoia had closed in on him, as it had done on James Angleton in his last years. And as if he could read my thoughts, Moore said, 'Don't worry about me, Ben. I have all my marbles. And certainly my suspicions could be wrong. If and when anything happens to me, it will happen. It's just that I'm allowed to be scared, aren't I?'

I had never known him to be hysterical, so his quiet fear unnerved me. All I could say was 'I think you're probably overreacting.'

He smiled, a slow, sad smile. 'Maybe so. Maybe not.' He

reached for a large manila envelope and slid it across the table toward me. 'A friend . . . or, rather, a friend of a friend . . . sent this to me.'

I opened the envelope and removed an eight-by-ten glossy color photograph.

It took me a few seconds to recognize the face, but the instant I did, I felt sick to my stomach.

'Jesus Christ,' I said. I was transfixed with horror.

'I'm sorry, Ben. But you had to know. It rather settles any doubts as to whether Hal Sinclair was murdered.'

I stared, my head reeling.

'Alex Truslow,' he went on, 'may be the last, best chance the Company has. He's been valiantly trying to rid CIA of this – for want of a better word, *cancer* – that afflicts it.'

'Are things really that bad?'

Moore gazed at the reflection of the room in the dark panes of the French doors. His eyes got a far-off look. 'You know, years ago, when Alex and I were junior analysts at Langley, we had a supervisor who we knew was fudging an assessment – grossly exaggerating the threat posed by an Italian extreme-left splinter group, just so that he could double the size of his operating budget. And Alex faced him down. Called him on it. Even then the guy had brass balls. He had a kind of integrity that seemed out of place, almost bizarre, in such a cynical outfit like the Agency. As I recall, his grandfather was a Presbyterian minister in Connecticut, from whom Alex probably inherited that kind of ethical stubbornness. And you know something? People came to respect him for it.'

Moore took off his glasses, closed his eyes, and massaged them. 'Only problem is, I'm not sure there are any others left like him. And if they get to him the way they got to Hal Sinclair . . . well, who knows what might happen?'

4

I didn't get to bed until well after midnight. It was too late to catch the last shuttle back to Logan, and Moore wouldn't hear of my staying in a hotel, what with the various empty rooms in his house now that his children had all left. So I spent the night in his comfortable guest bedroom on the third floor and set the digital alarm clock for six A.M. so I could get to the office at a decent hour.

About an hour later I suddenly sat up in bed, my heart pounding, and switched on the bedside lamp. The photograph was still there. Molly must never see this, I told myself. I got up from the bed, and, in the bright yellow lamplight slipped the photograph into the manila envelope and zipped it into a side compartment in my briefcase.

I switched off the light, tossed and turned for a few moments, until I surrendered and put the light back on. I could not sleep. As a rule I avoid sedatives, in part because of my Agency training (one must always be ready to bound out of bed on an instant's notice), and in part because, as an intellectual-property attorney, the last thing I need during the day is the hangover from anything sleep-inducing.

So I put on the television and looked for something suitably soporific. C-SPAN usually does it for me. On CNN, as it turned out, was a news-talk program, *Germany in Crisis*. Three journalists were discussing the German situation, the German stock market crash, and the resulting neo-Nazi demonstrations. They appeared to be in rather heated agreement that Germany was in imminent peril of succumbing to another dictatorship, which would present the world with a terrifying prospect. And, being journalists, they seemed quite certain about it.

One of them I recognized immediately.

He was Miles Preston, a British newspaper correspondent. Ruddy-cheeked, a sparkling wit, and (unlike most Brits I know) a fitness fanatic, I had known him since my early Agency days. He was a bright, extremely well-informed, impressively well-connected fellow, and I listened closely to what he had to say.

'Let's call a spade a spade, shall we,' he was saying from CNN's Washington studio. 'The so-called neo-Nazis who are behind all this violence are just plain old Nazis. I think they've been waiting for this historical moment. Look, the Germans finally, after all these years, establish one unified stock market, the Deutsche Börse, and look what happens – it teeters and then collapses, right?'

I had met him during my assignment in Leipzig, having just graduated my training at the Farm. I was lonely: Laura was back home in Reston, Virginia, trying to sell our house so she could join me. I was sitting alone in the Thüringer Hof on Burgstrasse, a pleasant, bustling little beer cellar in the Altstadt, and I was probably looking bent out of shape, nursing a large mug of beer.

I noticed someone standing over me, clearly a Westerner. 'You look bored,' the man said in a British accent.

'Not at all,' I said. 'Drink enough of this stuff, and everybody seems interesting.'

'In that case,' Miles Preston said, 'may I join you?'

I shrugged. He sat at my table and asked, 'American? A diplomat, or something?'

'State Department,' I answered. My cover was as a commercial attaché.

'I'm with the *Economist*. Been here long?'

'About a month,' I said.

'And you can't wait to leave.'

'I'm getting a little tired of Germans.'

'No matter how much beer you drink,' he added. 'How much longer here?'

'A couple of weeks. Then Paris. Which I much look forward to. I've always liked the French.'

'Oh,' he said, 'the French are just Germans with good food.'

We hit it off, and saw each other, for drinks or dinner, a number of times before I was transferred to Paris. He seemed to believe my State Department cover, or at least didn't question it. He may have suspected I was with the Agency, I don't know. On one or two occasions when I was dining with Agency friends at the Auerbachs Keller, one of the city's few decent restaurants and popular with foreigners, he walked in, saw me, but didn't approach, perhaps sensing that I didn't want to introduce him. This was something I liked about him: journalist or not, he never tried to pry for information or ask intrusive questions about what I was *really* doing in Leipzig. He could be blunt-spoken to the point of crassness – a source of much humor between the two of us – but at the same time he was capable of extraordinary tact. We were both in the same line of work, which may have been what drew me toward him. Each of us was hunting and gathering information; the only difference was that I was doing it on the shady side of the street.

Now I picked up the bedside phone. It was after one-thirty in the morning, but someone answered at CNN's Washington office, no doubt a young intern, who gave me the information I needed.

We met for a very early breakfast at the Mayflower. Miles Preston was as hearty and charming as I remembered him.

'Did you ever remarry?' he asked over his second cup of coffee. 'What happened to Laura in Paris, my God, I don't know how you ever survived it –'

'Yes,' I interrupted. 'I'm married to a woman named Martha Sinclair. A pediatrician.'

'A doctor, eh? Could be trouble, Ben. A wife must be just clever enough to understand her husband's cleverness, and just stupid enough to admire it.'

'She may be a little too bright for my own good. How about you, Miles? As I recall, you had a rather steady stream of women.'

'Never did the dirty deed. Ah, well, if only you could fall into the arms of a woman without falling into her clutches, hmm?' He chortled quietly and signaled the waiter for a third cup of coffee. 'Sinclair,' he murmured. 'Sinclair . . . You didn't marry the scion of the proprietor of the Company Store, did you? Not Harrison Sinclair's daughter?'

'That's the one.'

'Then please accept my condolences. Was he . . . murdered, Ben?'

'Subtle as always, Miles. Why do you ask?'

'I'm sorry. Forgive me. But in my business, I can't ignore rumors.'

'Well, I was hoping you might be able to enlighten *me* on that,' I said. 'Whether he was or not, I have no idea. But you're not the first to suggest as much to me. And it doesn't make any sense to me – my father-in-law just didn't have personal enemies, so far as I know.'

'But you mustn't think in terms of personalities. Think instead in terms of politics.'

'How so?'

'Harrison Sinclair was known to be a vociferous supporter of helping out Russia.'

'So?'

'A lot of people don't want that.'

'Sure,' I said. 'Plenty of Americans oppose throwing money at the Russians – good money after bad, and all that. Especially in a time of global financial difficulty.'

'That's not what I mean. There are people – no, let's call them *forces*, Ben – who want Russia to collapse altogether.'

'What sort of forces?'

'Consider this: Eastern Europe is a total disaster. It's full of valuable natural resources, and it's roiling with dissent. Many Eastern Europeans have forgotten Stalinism already, and they long for dictatorship again. So it's ripe for the picking. Wasn't it Voltaire who said, "The world is a vast temple dedicated to Discord"?'

'I don't entirely follow your logic.'

'*Germany*, man. Germany. The wave of the future. We're about to see a new German dictatorship. And it won't happen accidentally, Ben. It's been in the planning for a good long time. And those planners don't want to see a revived, strengthened Russia. Bear in mind how the German-Russian national rivalry so dominated this century's two world wars. A weak Russia ensures a strong Germany. Maybe – just maybe – your father-in-law, a strong advocate of a strong, democratic Russia, got in the way. By the way, who's slated to take his place?'

'Truslow.'

'Hmm. Bit of a stickler, isn't he, our Alex? Not exactly a favorite of the old boys. Shouldn't be surprised if he took a little spill himself. Well, I've got a squash game. Being a bachelor, you understand, I have to keep in shape. Your American ladies have become *so* demanding these days.'

An hour later at National Airport, just before I boarded the shuttle to Boston, I left a message with Alexander Truslow's office, agreeing to meet with him.

5

The taxicab, a battered Town Taxi missing a door handle on the right rear side and driven by a borderline psychotic, pulled up to my house at quarter after nine. I quickly changed clothes – Molly was still at work – and drove the Acura to work. And only fifteen minutes late.

Darlene fixed me with a level stare and said, 'You had a nine o'clock conference call, or did you forget?'

'I was detained in Washington,' I said. 'On business. Could you call with my apologies, and reschedule?'

'What about Sachs? He waited about half an hour.'

'Shit. Could you get me his number? I'll call him myself.'

'Also' – she handed me a pink message slip – 'Molly called. Said it's urgent.'

I wondered what could possibly be so urgent that Molly would call at this time of the day, when she's normally on rounds at the hospital. 'Thanks,' I said, and entered my office, brushed past the row of twenty-four three-foot Big Baby Dolls, and sank into my leather desk chair. I sat there thinking for a moment, considered asking Darlene to put through the conference call, and instead dialed Molly's page number. No response; I left a message with the page operator.

I had work to do, a good bit of it, made all the worse by my lateness, but I was in no condition to concentrate on patent law. I picked up the phone to buzz Bill Stearns's office, then changed my mind and replaced the handset. My meeting with Truslow was set for tomorrow morning, but then, Stearns probably already knew that.

I have one of those pin sculptures that are impossible to describe unless you've seen them. It's called an 'executive toy.'

I made an impression of my fist out of hundreds of round-headed pins, then admired the 3-D sculpture for a while. My other executive toy is an electronic basketball hoop on a slick-looking acrylic backboard, mounted on the wall across from my desk. I tossed the black and white leatherette ball, swished it in, and it shouted in a fevered electronic voice, 'Great shot!' then emitted a great prerecorded frenzied crowd-cheer. Very out of place in this stuffy firm.

'*De nada*,' I said.

Ten minutes later, and still no call from Molly.

There was a soft knock on the doorjamb, and Bill Stearns entered, wearing his Ben Franklin reading glasses.

'I'll meet with Truslow,' I said.

I paused, looked at him sharply, felt my breath catch.

'Alex will be very pleased.'

I exhaled slowly. 'That's nice. But I haven't decided, yet. I'm agreeing only to talk with him.'

He arched his eyebrows slightly, quizzically.

'How much would his business mean to the firm?' I asked.

Stearns told me.

'I wouldn't see my share of that until the end of the year,' I said, 'after the profits are calculated, right?'

Now his brows furrowed slightly. 'What are you getting at, Ben?'

'Simply this. Truslow wants me to represent him, and so do you. I happen to have a rather sudden need for a little cash.'

'And?'

'I want him to pay *me*. Directly. Up front.'

Stearns removed his glasses, folded them with a flick of the wrist, and put them in his breast pocket. 'Ben, that's highly –'

'It can be done. I'll see Truslow, sign on with him, and he transfers a six-figure retainer directly to my account. Then we've got a deal.'

Stearns hesitated a moment before shaking my hand. 'Tough son of a bitch. Sometimes I forget that. All right, Ben. We've got a deal.' He turned as if to leave, then turned back. 'What changed your mind?' He came into my office, eased himself into one of the leather 'client chairs,' and crossed his legs.

'I could get brownie points and say it was your powers of persuasion,' I said.

He smiled. 'Or?'

'I'll go for the brownie points,' I replied, giving a half-smile. I pressed my open palm against the pin sculpture, creating a 3-D cyborg replica of my hand. 'Listen,' I said after a moment's silence, just as Stearns was turning once again to go. 'I had a talk with an old Agency friend last night.'

Stearns nodded, staring blankly into the middle distance.

'He's been looking into Harrison Sinclair's death.'

He blinked a few times and said, 'So?'

'He believes it had something to do with the KGB.'

He rubbed his eyes with both hands and moaned. 'Old Cold Warriors don't let go of their illusions very easily, do they? The KGB, and the Evil Empire, were truly great villains in their time. Really first-rate. But the KGB hasn't existed for a few *years* now. And even when it did, they didn't do things like assassinate directors of Central Intelligence.'

I considered showing him the photograph Ed Moore had given me, but just then the telephone buzzed.

'It's Molly,' came Darlene's voice, metallic and flat.

I punched the button, picked up immediately.

'Molly –' I began.

She was crying, her words slurred, almost indecipherable. 'Ben . . . something awful . . .'

I rushed into the corridor, toward the elevator, easing my coat on as I ran. Past Bill Stearns, hunched in conversation with Jacobsen, a bright new associate. Stearns looked up, gave me a quick, piercing, *knowing* glance as I ran.

As if . . . almost as if he knew.

6

A thousand years ago, it seems, I went through six months of CIA basic training at the 'Farm' – Camp Peary, Virginia – where I learned everything from how to make a brush pass to how to pilot a small plane to how to aim a pistol from a moving car. One of my tradecraft instructors casually remarked that we would be learning the spy's black arts so thoroughly that they would in time be automatic, almost instinctual. No matter what might take us by surprise, even years later, our bodies would know how to react a split second *before* our brains. I didn't believe it; after my years as an attorney, I felt sure, my instincts must surely have faded.

I parked the Acura, not in our space behind the building, but a block and a half away, on Commonwealth Avenue.

Why? Instinct, I suppose; the ingrained habits of my time in the field.

Molly had discovered something terribly upsetting, something she couldn't talk about over the phone. That was all, but still . . .

I raced down the alley that ran behind our block of attached town houses, approaching our building's back entrance, pausing at the door before taking out my key. Then, momentarily reassured, I entered and stole quietly up the dark, wooden back stairs.

Just the normal house noises. The ticking of heat coursing through pipes; the refrigerator cycling on; the whirring of countless mechanical objects that run our home.

Anxiously, my entire body tensed, I entered the long, narrow room that would someday be our library, but for the time being was barren. The floor-to-ceiling bookcases lay empty, the oil paint still not quite dry a day after it had been applied by Frank, the painter we'd hired.

I was about to cross over to the staircase and up to the bedroom when, in my peripheral vision, I noticed something.

Molly and I had stacked our books in this room, by subject, ready to put up on the shelves the moment they were dry. They stood in neat piles against one wall, covered with a clear plastic drop cloth. Next to them, also covered with a drop cloth, were the oak file drawers I had refinished a few years ago, filled with our personal files.

Someone had been through them.

They had been searched, expertly but noticeably. The drop cloths had been lifted and replaced incorrectly, so that now they were draped with the paint-bespattered surface *inside*, not outside.

I drew closer.

The books, still in orderly piles, were arranged differently. But nothing seemed to have been taken; the signed copy of Allen Dulles's *The Craft of Intelligence* was still there. Upon yet closer inspection, I could see that our files were in an entirely different order, some index tabs facing the wrong way, Molly's medical school files where my law school files had been, everything slightly askew.

Nothing seemed, at first glance at least, to be missing. Merely rifled.

I had been meant to see this.

Someone had been in the house, had looked through our belongings. Had deliberately replaced them wrongly. So that I would notice. As . . . what? a warning?

My heartbeat accelerating, I hastened up the stairs and found Molly in the bedroom, curled up fetuslike in the very center of our king-size bed. She was still wearing her work clothes, the sort of outfit she always wore to the hospital – a pleated gray skirt, a salmon cashmere sweater – but her hair, normally pulled back, was in disarray. I noticed she was wearing the gold cameo locket her father had given her. It had belonged to his mother, and had been passed down through generations of Sinclairs and Evanses. I think she believed it was lucky.

'Honey?'

I came closer. Her eye makeup was badly smudged; she had been crying for a long time.

I touched my hand to the back of her neck, which was damp and hot.

'What happened?' I asked. 'What is it?'

Clutched to her breast was the manila envelope.

'Where did you get that?'

Shaking, her voice trembling, she could barely speak. 'Your briefcase,' she said. 'Where you keep the bills. I was looking for the phone bill this morning . . .'

With an awful sense of dread I remembered that I had switched briefcases at home earlier that morning. She opened her eyes, red-rimmed. 'I got out of work a couple of hours early, thanks to Burton, and decided to just crash,' she said slowly, thickly. 'I couldn't sleep. Too wired. I . . . decided to pay some bills, and I couldn't find the phone bill. I looked in your briefcase . . .'

The photograph that I was now holding was of Molly's father, after his death.

I had tried to protect her as much as possible from the horrible details of her father's death. So badly burned was Harrison Sinclair's body that an open coffin was out of the question. In addition to the terrible mutilation caused by the explosion of the gas tank, his neck had been nearly severed (during the crash, the forensic pathologist explained to me). I saw no reason for Molly to see her father this way; both she and I preferred that she remember him the way he was when they were last together, hale and ebullient and strong. I remember weeping in the morgue in Washington, seeing what was left of my father-in-law. Molly certainly didn't need to go through it.

But she insisted. She was a physician, she insisted; she had seen mutilation. Still, it's different if it's your own father; the sight had been, naturally, deeply traumatic. Mangled though her father's body was, she had been able to identify it, pointing out the faded blue tattoo of a heart on his upper shoulder (which he'd gotten one drunken night in Honolulu during his service in World War II), his college class ring, the mole on his chin. And then she entirely fell apart.

The photograph Ed Moore had given me had been taken after Hal's death but *before* the car crash. It was proof of his murder.

It was a neck-and-shoulders shot of Hal Sinclair, eyes wide and staring, as if fiery with indignation. His lips, abnormally pale, were slightly parted, as if he were about to speak.

But he was unquestionably dead.

Immediately beneath his jawline, reaching from ear to ear, was a large horrid gaping grin, from which protruded tissue of red and yellow.

Sinclair's neck had been deftly sliced from left carotid to right carotid. I knew the procedure well; we had been taught to recognize it at a glance. The flesh wound was accomplished with one quick stroke, prompting a sudden loss of arterial blood pressure in the brain.

To the victim it was as if someone had suddenly shut off the water. You collapsed almost instantly.

They had done this; they had murdered Hal Sinclair, they had for some unfathomable reason snapped a photo, and then they had put him in a car, and . . .

They.

I knew right away, of course, who *they* were.

In the trade, this was what is known as a 'signature,' or 'fingerprint,' killing, a type of murder preferred by a particular group or organization.

The carotid-to-carotid slice was a specialty of the former East German intelligence service, the *Ministerium für Staatssicherheit*, also known as the *Staatssicherheitsdienst*.

The Stasi.

That manner of execution was their signature, and this photograph was their calling card.

But it was the calling card of an intelligence service that no longer existed.

7

She wept silently, her shoulders shaking, and I held her. I kissed the nape of her neck, speaking softly.

'Molly, I'm sorry you had to see this.'

She grabbed a pillow with both fists, scrunched it up into her face, muffling her words. 'It's a nightmare. What they did to him.'

'Whoever did it, Mol, they'll catch them. They almost always do. I know that's no consolation.' I didn't believe it either, but Molly needed to hear the words. I didn't tell her my suspicions about how the house had been searched.

Now she turned over, her eyes searching my face. My heart squeezed. 'Who would do this, Ben? Who?'

'Everyone in public office is vulnerable to crazy people. Especially in a position as sensitive as Director of CIA.'

'But . . . it means Dad was killed first, doesn't it?'

'Molly, you talked to him the morning he was killed.'

She sniffled, reached for a tissue, squeezed her nose with it. 'That morning,' she said.

'You said there was nothing unusual in your conversation.'

She shook her head. 'I remember,' she said remotely, 'he was complaining about some intra-Agency power struggle he couldn't explain much about. But that's normal for him. He always felt CIA was an impossible agency to get under control. I think he just wanted to vent, but as usual, he couldn't say anything specific.'

'Go on.'

'Well, that's pretty much it. He sighed, said – no, that's right, he *sang*, "Fools rush in where wise men never go." In his lousy voice.'

'That's a Sinatra song, right?'

She nodded once, compressed her lips. 'His favorite. Hated the man, loved the music. Not exactly a profound sentiment. Anyway, he always sang that to me at bedtime when I was little.'

I got up from the bed, went to the mirror, and straightened my tie.

'Back to the office, Ben?'

'Yeah. I'm sorry.'

'I'm scared.'

'I know. So am I, a little bit. Call me again. Whenever you want.'

'You're going to sign on with Alex Truslow, aren't you?'

I tugged at my lapels, ran a comb through my hair, didn't answer. 'I'll talk to you later,' I said.

She looked at me oddly, as if trying to decide something, and at last said: 'How come you never talk about Laura?'

'I'm not –' I began.

'No. Listen to me. I know it's so painful to you it's unbearable. I know that. I don't want to dredge up anything like that, believe me. But given what happened to Dad . . . Well, Ben, I just want to know if your decision to work with Truslow has something to do with how Laura was killed, with some kind of attempt to *rectify* things or something –'

'Molly,' I said very quietly, warningly. 'Don't.'

'All right,' she said. 'I'm sorry.'

She was on to something, of course, although I wasn't aware of it at the time.

I found myself thinking quite a bit about Harrison Sinclair that day. One of my earliest memories of him was of his telling a dirty joke.

He was a tall, spare, elegant man with a full head of white hair, obviously a former athlete. (He had rowed crew at Amherst.) Hal Sinclair was an easy, charming man, at once dignified and playful.

At the time I was in college, one of only three Harvard students (and the only undergraduate) in an MIT seminar on

59

nuclear weapons. One Monday morning I entered the seminar room and saw that we had a visitor, a tall, well-dressed older man. He sat there at the coffin-shaped conference table, listening and saying nothing. I figured (accurately) that he was a friend of the professor's. Only much later did I learn that Hal, who was then the number-three man in CIA, the Director of Operations, was in Boston coordinating an espionage operation behind what used to be called the Iron Curtain involving MIT faculty members.

I happened that afternoon to be presenting a research paper I'd done on the fallacy of America's nuclear weapons policy of mutual assured destruction, or MAD. It was a pretty sophomoric effort, I recall. The last line of the paper said something dumb about MAD being 'MADness indeed.' Actually, I'm being unfair to myself; the paper was a pretty decent job of culling public sources on Soviet and American nuclear strategy.

Afterward, the distinguished-looking visitor introduced himself, shook my hand, told me how impressed he was. We stood around talking, and the man told an off-color but very funny joke about nuclear weapons, of all things. Then I noticed my friend Molly Sinclair come in the classroom door. We said hello, surprised to see each other outside of Harvard Yard.

Hal took the two of us out to lunch at Maison Robert, on School Street, in Old City Hall. (Molly and I have dined there exactly once since then, when I proposed to her; her reply was that she'd 'think about it.') There was a lot of booze, a lot of laughing. Hal told another off-color joke, and Molly blushed.

'You two should get together,' he said sotto voce to Molly, but not sotto enough that I didn't overhear. 'He's great.'

She blushed redder still, almost scarlet.

We were both obviously attracted to each other, but it wasn't to be for several years.

'It's good to see you again,' Alexander Truslow said. He, Bill Stearns, and I sat at a banquette at the Ritz-Carlton the next day. 'But I must confess: I'm a bit surprised. When we met at Hal's funeral, I distinctly sensed a lack of interest on your part.'

Truslow was wearing another elegant bespoke suit, rumpled as usual. The only rakish element was his bow tie, which was small, neat, navy blue, and awkwardly tied. I was wearing my best suit, a muted olive-gray glen check from the Andover Shop in Harvard Square; I suppose I wanted to impress the old fellow.

He fixed me with a mournful look as he buttered his fresh-baked roll.

'I assume you know about my brief intelligence career,' I said.

He nodded. 'Bill has briefed me. I understand there was a tragedy. And that you were completely exonerated.'

'So I'm told, yes,' I murmured.

'But it was a scarring, terrible time.'

'It was a time I don't much talk about,' I said.

'I'm sorry. It's the reason you quit the Company, isn't that right?'

'It's the reason,' I corrected him, 'I quit that entire line of work. For good. I made a solemn vow to my wife.'

He put down his buttered roll without taking a bite. 'And to yourself.'

'That's right.'

'Then we must speak frankly. Are you at all familiar with what my firm does?'

'Vaguely,' I said.

'Well, we're an international consulting firm. I guess that's the best way to put it. One of our clients, as I'm sure you know, is – your former employer.'

'Which badly needs consulting,' I said.

Truslow shrugged, smiled. 'No doubt. You understand I'm speaking now within the bounds of attorney-client privilege.'

I nodded, and he continued. 'For various reasons, they at times desire the help of an outside firm located well outside the Beltway. For whatever reason – maybe because I was with the Agency so long, I was almost part of the furniture – the powers that be at Langley trust me to do the odd job for them.'

I took a roll, which was by now cold, and bit into it. I noticed he was carefully avoiding saying 'CIA.'

'Oh, really,' Stearns said, putting a hand on Truslow's shoulder. 'Such ridiculous modesty.' To me, he added: 'You know Alex is on the shortlist to be named director.'

'I do,' I said.

'There must be a serious scarcity of qualified candidates,' Truslow said. 'We'll see what happens. As I was saying, Truslow Associates is engaged in a number of projects that Langley prefers, for one reason or another, not to be directly involved in,' he said.

Stearns put in: 'You know how congressional oversight and such can gum up the work of intelligence. Especially nowadays, with the Russian thing out of the picture.'

I smiled politely. This was a particularly common strain of conversation within the Agency, usually among those who wanted CIA to be liberated to do whatever the hell it wanted, like use exploding cigars on Fidel and assassinate third-world dictators.

'All right,' Truslow said, lowering his voice. 'The 'Russian thing,' as Bill puts it – the collapse of the Soviet Union – created a number of unique problems for us.'

'Sure,' I said. 'Without an enemy, what's CIA for? And then, who needs the Corporation?'

'Not quite,' he said. 'There are plenty of enemies, and unfortunately we'll always need a CIA. A reformed CIA, a *better* CIA. Congress may not realize that now, but in time it will. And as you know, CIA is retooling, concentrating far more on economic and corporate espionage. Defending American companies from those foreign countries that seek to steal their industrial secrets. Which is where the real battles of the future lie. Are you aware that shortly before his death, Harrison Sinclair established contact with the last chairman of the former KGB?'

'Through Sheila McAdams,' I said.

He paused, his chin up, surprised. 'That's right. But apparently Hal was in Switzerland too. *Both* he and Sheila met with Orlov. Think back to the death throes of the Soviet empire – the failed coup d'état attempt of August 1991. At that point the old guard knew the game was up. The Communist

Party bureaucracy was already in a shambles, the Red Army had turned tail and was now supporting Yeltsin – then seen as the only hope for preserving Russia, at least. And the KGB –'

'Which,' I interrupted, 'engineered the coup.'

'Yes. Engineered, masterminded the coup – though it's nothing to be proud of, the way it was bungled. The KGB knew that in weeks, perhaps months, it was going to be shut down.

'It was at that point that the Agency began to watch the Lubyanka especially closely. Watching to see whether it would accept its inevitable death sentence –'

'Or rage against the dying of the light,' I said.

'Well put,' Truslow said. 'In any case, it was at that point that the Agency began to detect an unusually heavy shipment of diplomatic "bags" – truckloads of mail sacks and cartons, to be exact – moving from Moscow to the Soviet embassy in Geneva. The recipient, and requisitioner, was the KGB's station chief.'

'If you'll excuse me,' Stearns said, and arose. 'I've got to get back to the office.' He shook Truslow's hand and departed. We were now, I realized, getting down to it.

'Do we know what was in the shipments?'

'Actually, no,' Truslow said. 'Something quite valuable, I imagine.'

'Which is why you want my help.'

Truslow nodded. He finally took a bite of his roll.

'How, exactly?'

'Investigation.'

I paused, considered. 'Why me?'

'Because –' He lowered his voice, and continued: 'Because I can't trust the boys at Langley. I need an outsider – someone who knows the ways of the Agency but is no longer connected.' He paused for a long time, as if wondering how frankly he could speak. Finally he shrugged. 'I'm in a bind: I don't know who in the Agency I can trust anymore.'

'Meaning what?'

He hesitated. 'Corruption is rampant at Langley, Ben. You've heard stories, I'm sure –'

'Some, yes.'

'Well, it's much worse than you can imagine. It's at the point of criminality – of outright rogue action.'

I recalled Ed Moore's warning: 'There's turmoil in the Agency. . . . A dreadful power struggle . . . Enormous sums of money changing hands . . .' At the time, it seemed the overheated, irrational doomsayings of an old man who'd been in the business too long.

'I need specifics,' I said.

'And you'll have specifics,' Truslow said. 'More than you'll care to know about. There's an organization – a sub rosa group, a council of elders . . . But we mustn't talk of these things here.'

Truslow's face had flushed. He shook his head.

'And what,' I asked, 'did Hal Sinclair have to do with these shipments?'

'Well, that's the mystery. No one knows why he met with Orlov, why he was so secretive about it. Or what was transacted, exactly. And then came word – rumors – that Hal embezzled a good deal of money –'

'Embezzled? Hal? You *believe* these rumors?'

'I'm not saying I believe them, Ben. I certainly don't want to believe them. Knowing Hal, I'm sure that – whatever the reason was that he met secretly with Orlov in Switzerland – it wasn't out of criminal intent. But whatever he was up to, there's good reason to believe that he was killed because of it.'

Had he seen the photograph Moore had given me? I wondered. But before I could ask, he resumed: 'The point is this: In a matter of days the United States Senate is about to commence hearings into the widespread corruption within CIA.'

'Public?'

'Yes. Some sessions will no doubt be closed to the press. But the Senate Select Subcommittee on Intelligence has heard enough of these rumors to look into it.'

'And Hal is implicated, is that what you're telling me?'

'Not publicly. Not yet. I don't even think the Senate has heard these tales. They have heard only that a good deal of money is missing. And so Langley internal affairs has hired me to look into this. To see what Hal Sinclair was up to in the last days of his life. To find out why he was killed. To find the missing money, to find out where it went, who was involved. The investigation must not be done in-house – the corruption is too rampant. Thus, Truslow Associates.'

'How much missing money are we talking about?'

He shrugged. 'A fortune. Let me leave it at that for now.'

'And you need me . . .'

'I need you to find out what Hal was doing, meeting with Orlov.' He looked up at me, his brown eyes bloodshot, moist. 'Ben, you still have the perfect right to say no. I'll understand. Given, especially, what you've been through. But from everything I'm told, you were one of the best in the field.'

I shrugged, flattered and appreciative, but not sure how to reply. Surely he'd heard tales of my 'recklessness.'

'You and I have a lot in common,' he said. 'I could tell that about you from the start. You're a straight shooter. You gave the Agency your all, but you always felt it could be better than it was. I'll tell you something: in all the years I've been with the Agency, I've seen its fundamental purpose jeopardized by ideologues and zealots on the left and the right. Angleton once said something to me: he said, Alex, you're one of the best we have – but the paradoxical thing is, what makes you so good at the work is the fact that on some level you disapprove of it.' Truslow laughed ruefully. 'At the time I denied it till I was red in the face. But in the end I realized he was right. My gut tells me you're a similar creature, Ben. We do what we think has to be done, but there's a part of us that stands aloof in disapproval.' He took a deep sip from his water glass and smiled to himself, seemingly embarrassed that he'd gone on so.

He slid the wine list across the tablecloth toward me, as if inviting me to make a selection. 'Could you glance at this, Ben? Pick out something nice.'

I opened the leather booklet and looked through it quickly. 'I like the Grand-Puy-Ducasse Pauillac quite a bit,' I said.

Truslow smiled and took the wine list back. 'What was on the top of page three?'

I thought for a second, brought the picture to memory. 'A Stag's Leap Merlot, '82.'

Truslow nodded.

'But I'm not much into performing like a circus animal,' I said.

'I know,' he said. 'I apologize. That's a very rare gift. How I envy you.'

'It allowed me to coast through any class at Harvard in which memorization was crucial – which included English, history, the history of art . . .'

'Well, you see, Ben, your . . . eidetic memory is a real advantage in work like this, an assignment that might well involve sequences of codes and the like. *If*, that is, you're still willing to accept. Incidentally, I'm completely amenable to the terms you and Bill worked out.'

The terms I extorted, he meant, but was too polite to say. 'Uh, Alex, when Bill and I discussed those terms, I had no idea what you wanted me for.'

'That's quite all right –'

'No, let me finish. If I understand you correctly – that what this comes down to is clearing Hal Sinclair's name – then I certainly have no intention to be mercenary.'

Truslow frowned, his expression stern. '*Mercenary?* For God's sake, Ben, I know about your financial plight. At the very least, this assignment will give me the excuse to help you out. If you'd like, I can even put you on our payroll as well.'

'Thanks, but not necessary.'

'Well, then,' he said. 'I'm glad you're on board.'

We shook hands, as if ritually consummating the deal. 'Listen, Ben, my wife, Margaret, and I are going to our place in New Hampshire tonight. Opening it up for the spring. We'd love it if you and Molly could have supper with us – nothing fancy, barbecue or whatever. Meet the grandkids.'

'Sounds nice,' I said.

'Tomorrow possible?'

Tomorrow was hectic, but I could clear some time. 'Yeah, sure,' I said. 'Tomorrow.'

*

For the rest of the afternoon I could barely concentrate. Could Molly's father seriously have been involved in some sort of conspiracy with the former head of the KGB? Was it possible that he had actually embezzled money – 'a fortune,' as Truslow put it? It made no sense.

Yet as an explanation for his murder . . . it did make a certain sense, did it not?

A knot of tension had formed in my stomach and evidently had no plans to untie itself.

The phone buzzed; Darlene announced that Molly was on the phone.

'What time are we meeting Ike and Linda?' She was calling from some noisy corridor in the hospital.

'Eight, but I'll cancel if you like. Under the circumstances.'

'No. I – I want to.'

'They'll understand, Mol.'

'Don't cancel. It'd be good to go out.'

There was, thankfully, no time to brood that afternoon. My four o'clock arrived punctually: Mel Kornstein was a rotund man in his early fifties, who wore too-stylish, expensive Italian clothes and his tinted aviator-style glasses always slightly askew. He had the distracted, unfocused look of a genius, which I believe he was. Kornstein had made a tidy fortune from inventing a computer game called SpaceTron, which you've no doubt heard of. If you haven't, basically it's a chase game, in which you, the pilot of a small spacecraft, are supposed to elude the evil spacecraft intent on destroying you and then planet Earth. This may sound silly, but the game is a marvel of computer technology. It's all done in 3-D so lifelike you're really convinced you're there – you really feel as if the comets and meteors and enemy spaceships and all that are coming right at you. This is accomplished by means of an ingenious software driver device Kornstein patented, a real breakthrough. Add that to his patented voice simulator that barks commands at you – 'Too far to the left!' or 'You're getting too close!' – and you have an explosion of color and sound, all on your home computer. And Kornstein's company had revenues of something like a hundred million dollars a year.

But now another software company had released a product so similar to SpaceTron that Mel Kornstein's revenues had plummeted. Needless to say, he wanted to do something about it.

He sank into the leather chair at the side of my desk, radiating darkest despair. We chatted for a few moments, but he was not in an expansive mood. He handed over to me a box containing the rival game, which was called SpaceTime. I popped it into my desktop computer, booted it up, and was astonished to see how close a copy it was.

'These guys didn't even *try* to be original, did they?' I said.

Kornstein removed his eyeglasses and polished them on a shirttail. 'I want to shut the fucking bastards down,' he said.

'Let's slow down a minute here,' I said. 'I'm going to have to make an independent determination as to how close the patent infringement is.'

'I want to screw the bastards,' he said.

'All in good time. Let's go through each of the claims in the patent, one at a time.'

'It's identical,' Kornstein said, putting his eyeglasses back on, still askew. 'Am I going to have a case here, or what?'

'Well, computer games are patentable on the same principles that govern, let's say, board games. You're really patenting the relationship between the physical elements and the concepts behind them, the way they interact.'

'I just want to screw 'em.'

I nodded. 'We'll do our best,' I said.

Focaccia was one of those fabulously hip, vaguely offensive, yuppie northern Italian restaurants in the Back Bay that serve a lot of arugula and radicchio, where all the patrons are young and beautiful and wear black and work in advertising. Between the clamor of voices and the thundering white man's rap music, the place is deafeningly loud too, which seems to be another requirement of pretentious northern Italian restaurants located in urban American settings.

Molly was late, but my closest friend, Ike, and his wife, Linda, were already shouting at each other across the table in what looked like a vicious marital argument but was just an attempt to communicate. Isaac Cowan and I had gone to law school together, where he specialized in defeating me at tennis. He's now got some corporate law job that's so unspeakably dull, even he can't bring himself to talk about it, but I know it has something to do with reinsurance. Linda, who was seven months pregnant at the time, is a shrink who mostly treats children. Both of them are tall, freckled, and redheaded – unnervingly similar in physical type – and I find them both easy to be with.

They were saying something about his mother coming for a visit. Then Ike turned to me and mentioned a Celtics game we had gone to last week. We talked a bit about work, about Linda's pregnancy (she wanted to ask Molly something about a test her ob-gyn was forcing upon her), about my backhand (virtually nonexistent), and eventually about Molly's father.

Ike and Linda had always seemed a little uncomfortable talking about Molly's famous father, never sure when they were prying, not wanting to seem *too* curious about him. Ike knew a little about my work for CIA, though I had made it clear I preferred not to say much. He knew, too, that I had been married before, that my first wife had been killed in an accident, and not much else. Naturally, that limited our conversation at times. They expressed their condolences, asked how Molly was doing. I knew I couldn't say anything about what had preoccupied me of late, certainly nothing about Hal Sinclair's murder.

While we were finishing our appetizers (as a matter of principle, no one ordered focaccia), Molly arrived, profusely apologetic.

'How was your day?' she asked as she kissed me. She gave me a look that was a second or two too long, which meant she was asking about Truslow.

'Fine,' I said.

She kissed Ike and Linda, sat down, and said, 'I don't think I can take this much longer.'

'Medicine?' Linda asked.

'The preemies,' Molly replied, medical jargon for

premature babies. 'Today I admitted twins and another baby, and the three patients together weighed less than ten pounds. I spend all my time taking care of these critically ill little things, trying to put in umbilical artery catheters, dealing with stressed-out families.'

Ike and Linda shook their heads sympathetically.

'Kids with AIDS,' she continued, 'or bacterial infections around the brain, and being on call every third night –'

I interrupted her. 'Let's leave all that behind for now, huh?'

She turned to me, her eyes widening. 'Leave it *behind*?'

'All right, Mol,' I said quietly. Ike and Linda, looking uncomfortable, concentrated on their Caesar salads.

'I'm sorry,' she said. I took her hand under the table. Work sometimes strung her out in this way, but I knew she still hadn't recovered from the shock of seeing that photograph.

Throughout dinner she was distant; she nodded and smiled politely, but her thoughts were obviously elsewhere. Ike and Linda no doubt attributed her behavior to her father's recent death, which was largely accurate.

In the cab on the way home we had a quarrel, in fiercely whispered tones, about Truslow and the Corporation and the CIA, everything she had once made me promise I would give up forever. 'Dammit,' she whispered, 'once you start dealing with Truslow, you're back in that awful game.'

'Molly –' I began, but she was not interruptable.

'Lie down with dogs and you get fleas. Dammit, you made a promise to me you'd never go back to that stuff.'

'I'm not going back to that stuff, Mol,' I said.

She was silent for a moment. 'You talked to him about Father's murder, didn't you?' she asked.

'No, I didn't.' A minor falsehood; but I didn't want to tell her about the alleged embezzlement or the Senate hearings.

'But whatever he wants you for, it has something to do with that, doesn't it?'

'In a sense, yes.'

The cabbie swerved to avoid a pothole, slammed on the horn, and cut into the left lane.

We were both silent for a moment. After a minute or so – as

if she'd been deliberately trying for some kind of dramatic effect – she said, too casually, even airily: 'You know, I called the Fairfax County medical examiner's office.'

Momentarily I was confused. 'Fairfax – ?'

'Where Dad was killed. To get a copy of his autopsy report. The law states that immediate family members can get copies if they want.'

'And?'

'It's sealed.'

'Meaning what?'

'It's not a public record any longer. The only parties allowed to see his autopsy report are the district attorney and the attorney general of the Commonwealth of Virginia.'

'Why? Because he's – was – CIA?'

'No. Because someone involved in the case decided something we already know. It was a homicide.'

We rode the rest of the way home in silence, and for some lunatic reason had another fight after we got back, and ended up going to bed furious at each other.

It's funny, but now I look back on that evening with fondness, because it was one of the last normal nights we'd ever spend together, just two nights before it happened.

8

That night, the last normal night in my life, I had the dream.

· I dreamed about Paris, a dream as lifelike as any waking nightmare, a dream I have suffered through perhaps thousands of times.

The dream always goes like this:

I am in a clothing store on the rue du Faubourg-St. Honoré, a men's clothing store that is a rabbit's warren of small, bright rooms, and I have lost my way, moving from room to room, looking for the rendezvous point I have laboriously arranged with the field agent, and at last I find a dressing room. It is the rendezvous spot, and there, hanging on a peg, is a sweater, a navy blue cardigan, which I take, as we have arranged, and in the pocket I find, as we have also arranged, a scrap of paper containing the coded message.

I spend too long poring over the message, and now I am late for the phone call I am supposed to make, and frantically, I go from room to room in this wretched store, looking for a telephone, asking for one, unable to locate one, until at last, in the basement of the building, I find a phone. It is a bulky, old-fashioned French phone, two-tone, tan and brown, and for some reason it will not work, try after try after try, and then – thank God! – it rings.

Someone answers the phone; it is Laura, my wife.

She is crying, pleading with me to come home, to our apartment on the rue Jacob, something horrible has happened. I am gripped with fear, and I begin to run, and in a few seconds (this is a dream, after all) I have arrived at the rue Jacob, at the entrance to my apartment building, knowing what I am about to see. This is the worst part of the dream:

thinking that if I don't go home, it won't have happened; but some horrified fascination impels me onward. I swim through the air, feeling nauseated.

A man is coming out of my building, wearing a thick woolen plaid hunter's shirt, Nike running shoes. An American, I am convinced, in his thirties. Although I can see him only from behind, I can see that he has a thick, unruly shock of black hair and – it is always the same detail – a long red ugly scar running along his jawline, from his ear to his chin. It is a terrible scar, and I can see it quite clearly. He is limping as if in great pain.

I don't stop the man – why should I? – but instead, as he limps away, I enter the building, smelling the odor of blood, which grows stronger as I climb the stairs to our apartment, and now the stench is unbearable, and I find myself retching, and then I am at the landing, and I can see the three bodies, splayed grotesquely in pools of blood, and one of them – it *can't be*, I tell myself – is Laura.

And at this point I usually awake.

But that is not quite the way it happened, of course. My dream, and it is always the same, has created a grotesque semiparable out of it.

As a case officer in Paris, I was charged with running several valuable deep-cover field agents, and a host of minor ones. I'd had one major success in Paris: I'd succeeded in rolling up a ring of Soviet military-intelligence spies operating out of a turbine plant outside the city. My cover was as an architect at an American firm. The apartment I had been given on the rue Jacob was small but sun-drenched, located in the sixth arrondissement, the best neighborhood in Paris, to my mind. I was fortunate; most of my fellow spooks were housed in the drab eighth. Laura and I had recently married, and she had no objection whatsoever to being moved to Paris: she was a painter, and there were few places she preferred to paint than Paris. She was small, irresistibly cute, with long blond hair that she wore up. We were pretty much intoxicated with love.

We had talked about having kids, and we both wanted

them. But what I didn't know was that she was pregnant, a fact that would have thrilled me. She never had a chance to tell me. I've always believed she wanted to tell me in her own way, at her own pace, after she'd had a chance to digest the news. All I knew was that she'd been feeling sick for several days – some sort of minor virus, I thought.

Around this time I was contacted by a low-level KGB officer, a filing clerk in the KGB's Paris station, who wanted to strike a deal. He had some information to sell, he said, which he'd run across in the archives in Moscow. In exchange, he wanted to defect, wanted financial security, protection, the works.

I followed all the standard procedures, cleared the first meeting with the CIA station chief, James Tobias Thompson. Case officers are always wary of what's called a 'blind date,' which means a meeting with an unknown agent at a place of his designation. There is always the risk that the whole thing is a trap.

But this agent, who called himself Victor, agreed to meet on *our* terms, which was heartening. I arranged a rendezvous, risky but vital. Three quick rings of a telephone at a flat somewhere in the sixth arrondissement signaled the location and time. Then, a 'chance' encounter in an expensive men's clothing store on the rue du Faubourg-St. Honoré, but unlike in the dream, it went swimmingly. A navy blue sweater was hanging on a peg in the dressing room, as it was supposed to be, left behind by a careless customer who decided against making a purchase, and in the pocket I left the scrap of an envelope, the encoded message, designating time and place.

The next day we met at one of the Agency's safe houses, really a grubby little apartment in the fourteenth. I knew that walk-ins generally didn't pan out, but you could never ignore them either: many of the greatest defectors in the history of intelligence have been walk-ins.

'Victor' was wearing a blond wig, obviously a wig; his olive complexion was that of a dark-haired man. Below his jawline was a long, thin, beet-red scar.

He seemed to be the real article, at least as far as I could ascertain. He promised me, the next time we met – if a deal could be arranged – a major, earth-shaking revelation. A document, he said, which he'd come across in the KGB archives. He mentioned a cryptonym: MAGPIE.

When my boss and close friend Toby Thompson debriefed me later, this little detail intrigued him. Apparently there was some substance to the case.

So I arranged a second meeting.

I have been over this a thousand times since then. Victor had contacted *me*, which meant he already knew my cover. And all the safe houses conveniently located were in use for debriefings and such. So, with Toby Thompson's approval and even encouragement, I arranged a second meeting, between Victor, Toby, and me, at my rue Jacob apartment.

Laura, despite her sporadic bouts of nausea, was out of town, or so I believed. The night before she had gone out to visit friends near Giverny, to explore Monet's gardens. She wasn't to return for two days, so the apartment was available.

I shouldn't have risked it, but that's easy to say now.

The meeting was to have been at noon, but I was detained at work on a transatlantic conference call to Langley on a secure trunk line, to the deputy director of Operations, Emory St. Clair. As a result, I arrived twenty minutes late, expecting Toby and Victor to be in the apartment already.

I remember seeing a dark-haired man striding purposively out of my building, wearing a plaid hunter's shirt, and dismissing him as a neighbor or visitor. I climbed the stairs, and something in the stairwell smelled somehow off. The odor got stronger as I neared the third floor: blood. My heart began to race.

When I arrived at the third-floor landing, I beheld a scene of unforgettable gruesomeness. Tangled on the floor, in pools of fresh blood, were two bodies: Toby . . . and Laura.

I think I must have cried out, but I can't be sure. Everything slowed down, became stroboscopic. Suddenly I was kneeling beside Laura, cradling her head, unbelieving. She wasn't supposed to be home; it wasn't her; this was some mistake.

Laura had been shot in the chest, in the heart, the

bloodstain spread over a large area of her white silk nightgown. She was dead. I turned, saw that Toby had been shot in the stomach, saw him shift in the lake of blood, heard him groan.

I don't remember anything after that. Someone showed up, I think. Probably I called someone. I can't have made any sense. I had lost my mind. They had to separate me from my poor dead Laura, who I was convinced I could revive if I tried hard enough.

Toby Thompson had survived, if barely; his spinal cord had been severed, and he would be paralyzed for life.

Laura was dead.

Later, some things were explained.

Laura had returned home early that morning, feeling sick. She had called me at work to say so, although for some reason I never got her message. Later, the autopsy revealed that she was pregnant. Toby had shown up at my apartment at a few minutes before noon, armed, in case anything untoward happened. He found the door ajar, the KGB man inside, holding Laura hostage at gunpoint. 'Victor' had then pointed his gun at Toby and fired, then turned and shot Laura. Toby had returned the fire, tried but failed to kill him before the pain overtook him.

What had happened, it seemed, was a Soviet retaliation targeted directly at me. But for what? For rolling up the turbine factory spy ring? Or for any of the several incidents in East Germany in which I wounded, and in a few cases killed, East German and Soviet agents? I had been set up by 'Victor,' and was to be taken in a shootout. But instead, Laura was killed – Laura, who wasn't supposed to be there – and I, detained by some freak twist of fate, was spared. I had fucked up, and I was alive, while Toby Thompson was condemned to a wheelchair for the rest of his life, and Laura was dead.

As to the dark-haired man in plaid whom I'd seen leaving my building: who else could it have been but 'Victor,' having shed his blond wig?

Much later it was decided that though I hadn't been at fault, I had nevertheless performed badly – sloppiness of procedure, largely, which I could not contest, even though Toby had given me an okay – and in a sense I was ultimately culpable for my own wife's murder and for Toby's paralysis.

My career was not necessarily over; I could have appealed to yet another administrative board. In time, I could have surmounted this.

But I couldn't bear it. I knew that I had as good as pulled the trigger myself.

The inquest went on for some time. Everyone who'd been even marginally involved, from secretaries to code clerks to Ed Moore, the chief of the Operations Directorate Europe Division, was questioned endlessly, administered polygraph tests. The inquest took over my life at a time when I had no inner resources left to draw from.

My wife and future child had been killed. My life seemed pointless.

Weeks went by. I was in purgatory. They'd put me up in a hotel a few miles from Langley. I would drive to 'work' every morning: a windowless white conference room on the second floor, where the interrogator (every few days there was a new one) would smile cordially, give me a firm, bureaucratic handshake, offer me a cup of coffee and a brown jar of Coffee-mate nondairy creamer, and a flat wooden coffee stirrer.

Then he'd pull out the transcript of yesterday's session. On the surface we were just two guys trying to figure out what went wrong over there in Paris.

In reality the interrogator was trying with all his might to trip me up on the slightest inconsistency, to find the tiniest hairline fracture in my composure, the most minuscule contradiction, wear me down, break me down.

After seven weeks of this – the manpower costs involved must have been extraordinary – the investigation was closed. No conclusion reached.

I was summoned to Harrison Sinclair's office. He was still the number-three man in the Agency, the Deputy Director for Operations. Although we had spoken only a few times, he acted as if we were old friends. I'm not saying he was insincere; more likely, he was doing his damnedest to put me at ease. Hal was a genuinely affectionate man. He put an arm around me, guided me over to a leather seat, and sat in the small leather couch next to me. He hunched toward me confidentially, as if he were about to brief me on some top secret operation, and then told me a joke about an old man and an old lady in an elevator in a retirement community in Miami. I remember only that the punch line was 'So, are you single?'

Although I felt as if my insides had turned to scar tissue in the last two hellish months, I found myself laughing, felt the tension ebbing, if only for the moment. We talked a bit about Molly. She was living in Boston after two years with the Peace Corps in Nigeria. She'd broken up with her college boyfriend – the lunk, as she referred to him.

She wanted me to give her a call when I felt I was ready to see people, Sinclair added. I said I would.

He told me that Ed Moore, the chief of the Europe Division, had decided I had to leave the CIA, that my career would always be clouded by questions. That although I was no doubt innocent, there would always be suspicions. The best thing for me to do was to leave. Moore, he said, was quite adamant.

I was hardly going to argue. I wanted nothing more than to curl up in a ball somewhere and sleep for days and then awake to find it was all a bad dream.

'Ed thinks you should go to law school,' Hal said.

I listened passively. What interest in law did I have? The answer, I later discovered, was not much, but what difference did that make? You can do something well that you don't care much for.

I wanted to talk to Hal about what happened, but he wasn't interested. He had a full schedule; he thought it best to maintain neutrality; he didn't want to rake over the past.

You'll be a great lawyer, he said.

He told a very funny, very dirty joke about lawyers.

We both laughed. That day I left CIA headquarters – for what I thought was the last time.

But I was to be haunted by the nightmare of Paris for the rest of my life.

9

Alex Truslow's weekend house in southern New Hampshire was less than an hour's drive from Boston. Molly, miraculously enough, was able to free up enough time to join me. I think she wanted to reassure herself that Truslow was all right, that I was not making a colossal error by agreeing to work for the Corporation.

The house, a rambling old beauty perched on a bluff above its own lake, was much larger than we had expected. White clapboard with black shutters, it was at once cozy and elegant. It looked as if it had begun as a humble two-room farmhouse a hundred years ago, and had gradually and steadily been added to until it sprawled, ungainly and serpentine, along the undulating crest. Here and there the paint was peeling.

Truslow was outside, tending the fire as we drove up. He was in casual attire: a plaid woolen shirt, bulky moss-green wide-wale corduroy pants, white socks, and boat shoes. He kissed Molly on the cheek, clapped me on the back, and pushed vodka martinis at us. I realized for the first time, consciously, what it was about Alexander Truslow that intrigued me. In certain striking ways – the mournful cast of the brow, the dogged honesty – he reminded me of my own father, who died of a stroke when I was seventeen, the summer before I went off to college.

His wife, Margaret, a slender, dark-haired woman of around sixty, came out of the house, wiping her hands on a bright red apron, the screen door clattering behind her.

'I'm sorry about your father,' she said to Molly. 'We miss him so much. So many people miss him.'

Molly smiled and thanked her. 'This is a wonderful place,' she said.

'Oh,' Margaret Truslow said, approaching her husband and touching his cheek fondly with the back of her hand, 'I hate it out here. Ever since Alex retired from CIA he's made me spend practically every weekend and every summer out here. I put up with it because I have no choice.' Her expression, doting and wearily amused, was the sort you might use on an errant but beloved child.

'Margaret much prefers Louisburg Square,' Truslow said. Louisburg Square was a small, exclusive enclave atop Beacon Hill, where Alexander Truslow owned a town house. 'You two live in the city, don't you?'

'Back Bay,' Molly said. 'You might have seen the Men at Work signs and the trash heaps. That's us.'

Truslow chuckled. 'Renovation, I take it?'

Before we could reply, two small children came tearing out of the house, a little girl of about three, bawling, being chased by a somewhat older boy.

'Elias!' Mrs. Truslow called out.

'Now, cut it out,' Alex said, scooping the girl up into his arms. 'Elias, don't torment your sister. Zoë, I want you to meet Ben and Molly.'

The little girl looked at us warily with a tear-stained face. She then buried her head against Truslow's chest.

'She's shy,' Truslow explained. 'Elias, shake hands with Ben Ellison and Molly Sinclair.' The boy, towheaded and pudgy, thrust a small fat hand at each of us in turn, before he ran off.

'My daughter . . .' Margaret Truslow began to say.

'My deadbeat daughter,' Truslow put in dryly, 'and her workaholic husband are at the symphony. Which means their poor kids have to have supper with their boring old grandparents. Right, Zoë?' He tickled the girl with one hand, holding her up with the other. She giggled, almost reluctantly, and then resumed crying.

'Our little Zoë seems to have an earache,' Margaret said. 'She's been crying since she got here.'

'Let me take a look,' Molly said. 'You probably don't have any amoxicillin around, do you?'

'Amoxi-what?' Margaret said.

'That's all right. I think I've got a 150cc bottle in the car.'

'An honest-to-goodness house call!' Margaret Truslow exclaimed.

'And no charge either,' Molly said.

Dinner was prime Americana – barbecued chicken, baked potatoes, and a salad. The chicken was delicious; Truslow proudly gave us his recipe.

'You know what they say,' he said as we tucked into our dishes of ice cream. 'By the time the youngest children have learned to keep the house tidy, the oldest grandchildren are on hand to tear it to pieces. Right, Elias?'

'Wrong,' Elias replied.

'Do you have children?' Margaret Truslow asked.

'Not yet,' I said.

'I believe that children should neither be seen nor heard from,' Molly said. 'Ever again.'

Margaret looked momentarily scandalized, until she realized that Molly was kidding. 'And that from a pediatrician!' she mock-scolded.

'Having kids was the greatest thing I ever did,' Truslow said.

'Isn't there some book,' Margaret said, 'called *Grandchildren Are So Much Fun, I Should Have Had Them First*?'

Both Truslows chuckled. 'There's some truth to that,' Alex said.

'You'll have to give all this up if you go back to Washington,' Molly said.

'I know. Don't think it hasn't been weighing on me.'

'You haven't even been asked yet, Alex,' his wife said.

'Quite right,' Truslow said. 'And to be honest, replacing your father is a rather daunting prospect.'

Molly nodded.

'Few things are harder to put up with than the annoyance of a good example,' I put in.

'And now,' Truslow announced, 'I hope you lovely women don't mind if Ben and I wander off somewhere and talk shop.'

'Fine with us,' his wife said with asperity. 'Molly can help me get the kids down. If she can bear to be around kids, I mean.'

'A few weeks ago,' Truslow said, 'the Agency apprehended a would-be assassin. A Romanian. Securitate.' We sat in a stone-floored room that he seemed to use as his study, both of us at a large ashwood table. The furniture in the room was old and worn; the only discordant note was the modern black telephone-and-scrambler unit on the desk.

'He was interrogated. He was tough.'

I didn't know what he was getting at, so I waited in silence, tensely.

'After several difficult interrogation sessions, he finally broke. But even then, he knew very little. A very professional job of compartmentalization. He said he had something to offer us. Something about Harrison Sinclair's murder . . .' His voice trailed off.

'And?'

'And before he was able to spill, he died.'

'One of the Agency's overzealous interrogators, I take it.'

'No. They were able to infiltrate the system, get to him, take him out. Their reach is impressive.'

'And who are *they*?'

'A person or persons,' he said slowly, ominously, '*within* CIA.'

'Do you have names?'

'That's the thing. They're very well insulated. Faceless. Ben, this group inside Langley – it's a group long rumored about. Have you heard of the Wise Men?'

'Yesterday you mentioned some sort of council of elders,' I said. 'But who are they? What are they after?'

'We don't know. Too well cloaked, behind a series of fronts.'

'And you're saying that these . . . "Wise Men" . . . were behind Hal's murder?'

82

'Speculation,' he replied. 'It's possible that Hal was *one* of them.'

I felt a little vertiginous. Hal, it appeared, had been killed by someone trained by the East German secret service, Stasi. Now Truslow was talking about a Romanian. How did the pieces fit? What was he implying?

'But you must know something about their identities,' I prompted.

'We know only that they've managed to syphon off tens of millions of dollars from various Agency accounts. All done in a highly sophisticated manner. And it appears that Harrison Sinclair pocketed some 12.5 million of it.'

'But you don't seriously believe that. You know how modestly Hal lived.'

'Listen, Ben. I don't want to believe that Hal Sinclair embezzled a cent either.'

'You don't *want* to believe it? What the hell are you saying?'

Instead of replying, Truslow handed me a manila file folder. Its label bore an Agency filing designation: Gamma One, which was a higher level of classification than I'd ever before been privy to.

Inside was an assortment of photocopies of checks, computer printouts, blurry photographs. In one photo, a man wearing a Panama hat was standing in some kind of lobby.

It was unquestionably Hal Sinclair.

'What's all this?' I asked, although I already knew.

'Hal at a bank in Grand Cayman, evidently waiting for an appointment with the bank's manager. The other shots are of Hal at a variety of banks in Liechtenstein, Belize, and Anguilla.'

'Proving nothing –'

'Ben, listen to me. I was one of Hal's closest friends. This knocked me out too. There were several days during which Hal was missing – sick, allegedly, or taking a brief vacation. And was unreachable, or he'd arrange it so that he called in to the office. Evidently that's when he'd make the deposits. They've got records of trips he made using several false passports.'

'This is *bullshit*, Alex!'

He sighed; this obviously distressed him. 'That's his signature on the registration papers for an *Anstalt*, a nonshare, limited-liability "letter box" corporation based in Liechtenstein. The true owner's identity, as you'll see there, is Harrison Sinclair. And we've got copies there of intercepted wire transfers of funds to Bermuda trust accounts. Liberian-owned, of course. Telephone records, telexes, wire transfer authorizations. A real maze, Ben. Layers upon layers, shells inside shells. It's proof, pure and simple, and it breaks my heart. But there it is.'

I didn't know what to make of it all; from everything I could tell, they had the goods. But it made no sense. My late father-in-law a con artist, an embezzler? You had to know him as I did to realize how hard that was to accept. Yet there's always that tiny seed of doubt. We never really know another person.

'The key lies in Sinclair's meeting in Zurich with Orlov,' he continued. 'Think: What does *Zurich* say to you?'

'Gnomes.'

'Hmm?'

'The gnomes of Zurich.' The phrase, I believe, was coined by a British journalist in the early sixties, referring to Swiss bankers, who are so helpful and discreet with mafiosi and drug 'kingpins,' as they're called.

'Ah, yes. Precisely. It's a safe guess that when he and Orlov met in Zurich, they were transacting something. It was no social call.' He added musingly: 'The head of the CIA and the last-ever head of the KGB.'

'Circumstantial,' I said.

'Perhaps. I hope to God there's an explanation for all this. I believe there may well be. So you understand, I hope, why I want you to clear his name. The Agency has hired me to locate an enormous sum of missing money – a fortune that will make the 12.5 million that Hal allegedly embezzled seem paltry. I need your help. We can kill two birds with one stone: we can at once find the money and establish Hal's innocence. Can I count on you?'

'Yes,' I said. 'Yes, you can.'

'It's maximum-clearance stuff, Ben, you understand that. You'll have to go through the usual rigmarole, the polygraph, the vetting, and so on. Before you leave tonight, I'm going to give you a scrambler for your office phone which is compatible with the scrambler on my personal phone at work. But I must be honest: there are many people who will seek to hinder your work.'

'I understand,' I said. The truth was, I didn't understand, or didn't understand fully, and certainly I had no idea what precisely he had in mind until the next morning.

10

I remember the events of the next morning with an eerie clarity.

The offices of Truslow Associates, Inc., occupied all four floors of a narrow old brick town house on Beacon Street (a short walk, I realized, from where Truslow lived on Louisburg Square). A brass plaque on the ornate front door announced: TRUSLOW ASSOCIATES, INC., with no explanation; if you had to ask, you weren't supposed to know.

The office was pleasantly upscale. You had to buzz to enter a small antechamber, where a well-coiffed receptionist checked you over, and then you were buzzed through to a sedate waiting room, quietly elegant and very expensively furnished. I waited for ten minutes or so, sunken in a comfortable black leather chair and browsing through *Vanity Fair*. The choice of magazines was that or *Art and Antiques* or *Country Life*: anything but *business* magazines, for heaven's sake. No unsightly copies of *Barron's* lying around here.

At exactly ten minutes past the scheduled appointment time, Truslow's secretary emerged from whatever more important business was detaining her (coffee and danish, I guessed) and escorted me up a set of creaky, carpeted stairs to Truslow's office. She was a classic executive administrative assistant, mid-thirties, pretty, and efficient, in a Chanel suit and belt and a power Chanel gold necklace. She introduced herself as Donna and asked if I wanted some Evian water, coffee, or freshly squeezed orange juice. I asked for a cup of coffee.

Alexander Truslow rose from behind his desk as I entered. The light in his office was so bright that I wished I'd brought sunglasses. It flooded in through the tall windows and bounced off the antique white walls.

Seated in a leather chair beside Truslow's desk was a roundshouldered, dark-haired, bulky man in his early fifties.

'Ben,' Truslow said, 'I'd like you to meet Charles Rossi.'

Rossi rose, gave me a bone-crushing handshake, and said, 'Good to know you, Mr Ellison.'

'Same here,' I said, though I doubted that would prove to be true. We both sat down, and I added, 'Ben.'

Rossi nodded and smiled.

The secretary set a cup of freshly brewed coffee in an Italian ceramic mug before me. It was very good. I extracted a yellow legal pad from my briefcase and my Mont Blanc rollerball.

After she had left, he typed something into the Amtel keyboard in front of him, the device that allowed him and his secretary noiselessly to communicate during meetings or phone calls.

'What we're about to discuss with you has to remain a matter of utmost secrecy.'

I nodded, took a sip of coffee. Some rich French-roast-plus-something-else blend; remarkably good.

'Charles, if you'll excuse us,' Truslow said. Rossi got up and left the office, closing the door behind him.

'Rossi is our liaison with CIA,' Truslow explained. 'He came down from Langley especially to work with you on this.'

'I'm not sure I understand,' I said.

'I got a call from Rossi last night. Given the sensitivity of the project we've been hired to do, the Agency, understandably, is concerned about security. They've insisted upon implementing their own clearance procedures.'

I nodded.

'It seems a bit excessive to me too,' Truslow went on. 'You've been vetted and cleared and all that nonsense. But before you can be cleared fully, Rossi would like to run you through some preliminary stuff. We're required, by contract with the Central Intelligence Agency, to flutter all outside employees.'

'I see,' I said.

He was referring to the polygraph, the lie detector, to which all Agency employees are subjected a few times in their careers – at the beginning of their service, periodically thereafter, and sometimes after vital operations or in extra-ordinary cases.

'Ben,' Truslow went on, 'you see, as the centerpiece of our investigation, we'd like you to track down Vladimir Orlov, and learn whatever you can about what happened in his meeting with your father-in-law. Orlov may have been playing a double game on Hal Sinclair, and I want to know whether he did or not.'

'Track Orlov down?' I said.

'This is about all I can tell you until you've been cleared. Once you've been fluttered, we can talk more.' He pressed a button on his desk, and Rossi returned.

Truslow came around the side of his massive desk and clapped Rossi's shoulder. 'I'll turn you over to Charlie at this point,' he said, and then gripped my hand. 'Welcome, friend.'

I could see Truslow turn once again to his Amtel and punch a button on his phone. As I left his office, I caught a last glimpse of him, a brooding, dark figure of intense energy silhouetted against the brilliant morning sunlight.

Charles Rossi drove me, in a dark blue government-issue sedan, across the river to an ultramodern building in the Kendall Square section of Cambridge, near the Massachusetts Institute of Technology and Raytheon and Genzyme and all the other high-powered, high-tech corporations.

Leaving the elevator on the fifth floor, we entered a very functional-looking reception area, all chrome and steel and industrial-gray carpeting and blond woods. On the wall that faced us was a drab nameplate that said DEVELOPMENTAL RESEARCH LABORATORIES: AUTHORIZED VISITORS ONLY.

I knew at once this was a CIA-owned operation. Everything about it – the unrevealing name, the anonymity, the for-bidding stillness – screamed Agency. I knew CIA ran labs and test facilities in the suburbs outside Washington, and in a building on Water Street in New York City; I hadn't realized they also had a facility in Cambridge, in the land of MIT, but it made perfect sense.

Saying very little, Rossi led me through a set of large metal doors, which he opened by inserting a magnetic card in a vertical slot. The doors opened, yielding a view of an enormous room containing row upon row of computer terminals. In front of most of them people sat typing.

'Not much to look at, huh?' Rossi observed as we stood at the room's entrance. 'Pretty dull stuff.'

'You should see our firm,' I replied.

He laughed politely. 'There's actually a range of projects going on here. Microdevices, automated cryptography, machine vision, things like that. Are you familiar . . . ?'

'Not terribly,' I admitted.

'Well, take automated cryptography. This is funded by DARPA, the Defense Advanced Research Projects Administration, a part of the Defense Department.'

I nodded as he escorted me toward one terminal, a SPARC-2 workstation, at which a wiry young bearded man seemed to be working furiously. 'Now, this terminal is made by Sun Microsystems, and it's "talking" to a supercomputer, a Thinking Machines Corporation CM-3.'

'I see.'

'Anyway, Keith here is developing plain-text encryption algorithms. That means codes that are, theoretically at least, unbreakable. In simple English, that will allow us to translate, encode top secret information into a form that'll resemble some innocuous-looking document in English – not non-sense, but real prose. Then, by means of speech recognition, our computers will be able to decrypt it – trapdoor codes, I mean, knapsack codes, that sort of thing.'

I didn't see, but I nodded anyway. Rossi, however, turned out to be quite observant. 'I'm yakking,' he apologized. 'Let me put it another way. An agent in the field will be able to encode a classified document into a script for an ordinary news program broadcast over the Voice of America. To anyone listening it won't sound like anything unusual, but the right computer will be able to decrypt it.'

'Nice.'

'Oh, anyway, there are a number of things we're working on. Microdevices, for instance, are being designed here – we have them made elsewhere, by a nanofabrication laboratory.'

'And what are they used for?'

He wagged his head back and forth, as if indecisively, and then said, 'These are tiny devices made of silicon and xenon, a few angstroms wide, which can, let's say, be placed undetectably into a computer, serve as a transmitting device. There are far more interesting uses, but I'm not really free to go into it. So, if I may . . .'

We returned to the white corridor, then entered another secured area, which Rossi accessed by inserting a different magnetic card in the vertical slot. He turned to me and observed simply, 'Security.'

Now we were in an entirely white, windowless corridor. A plaque directly in front of us said AUTHORIZED PERSONNEL ONLY.

Rossi led me down this corridor, through another set of doors, and into a peculiar-looking concrete chamber. At the center of the chamber was a smaller chamber, glass-enclosed, which contained a large white machine, maybe fifteen feet high by ten feet wide. It resembled a large square doughnut. Outside the glass walls was a bank of computer monitors.

'A magnetic resonance imager,' I said. 'I've seen them in hospitals. But this one looks quite a bit larger.'

'Very good. The MRI you usually see in hospitals might range anywhere from a .5 tesla to a 1.5 tesla – a tesla is a measure of the strength of the magnet inside. Once in a great while you might see a two tesla in highly specialized use. This is a four.'

'Awfully powerful.'

'But quite safe. And modified somewhat. I directed the modification.' Rossi's eyes roamed the bare concrete room as if distracted.

'Safe for what?'

'You're looking at a replacement for the old polygraph. A modified MRI will soon be used by the Agency in debriefing intelligence officers, defectors, agents, and so on, to provide a reliable mental "fingerprint." '

'Would you like to explain that?'

'I'm sure you're aware of the many drawbacks of the old polygraph system.'

I did, but I listened as he explained.

'The old polygraph technique relies on blood pressure cuffs and electrodes that measure galvanic skin responses, sweat, changes in skin temperature, and so on. It's crude, and it's only – what? – sixty percent reliable. If that.'

'All right,' I said impatiently.

Rossi continued patiently: 'The Soviets didn't even use the thing, as you may know. They gave seminars on how to beat it. For God's sake, do you remember the time when twenty-seven Cuban DGI double-agents working against us were cleared by CIA flutter?'

'Sure,' I said. It was part of Agency lore.

'The damn thing registers only emotional responses, as you know. Which vary widely depending upon temperament. And yet the flutter is the cornerstone of so much of our intelligence operations. Not only for the CIA, but for the DIA and NSA and a number of intelligence agencies and divisions. Their operational security all hangs on this, establishing bona fides and reliability of product, even screening applicants and recruits.'

'And it's easy to defeat,' I added.

'Embarrassingly easy,' Rossi agreed. 'Not just sociopaths or people who don't register the normal range of human emotions, guilt and anxiety, pangs of conscience, and what not. But any trained professional can beat the machine using any of a number of drugs. Even doing something simple like causing oneself physical pain during the test can skew the results. Stepping on a thumbtack, for Christ's sake.'

'Okay,' I prompted him.

'So, with your permission, I'd like to get started, and have you on your way back to Mr Truslow.'

11

'Half an hour,' Rossi told me, 'and you should be out of here. And on your way.'

We stood in the outer MRI chamber, inspecting 3-D computer reconstructions of the human brain, rendered on a computer's color monitor. On the screen in front of me, a lifelike image of a brain rotated and then flew apart, section by section, like a pink grapefruit.

One of Rossi's lab assistants, a small, dark-haired former MIT graduate student named Ann, sat at the monitor and called up the various images. The cerebral cortex, she explained to me in a soft, little-girl voice, was made up of six layers. 'We've discovered that there is a discernible difference between the appearance of the cortex in someone who's telling the truth and someone who's lying,' she said. She added confidentially, 'Of course, I still have no idea whether this originates in the neurons or in the glial cells, but we're working on that.'

She produced a computer image of a liar's brain, which seemed to be shaded somewhat differently from the nonliar's brain.

'If you want to take off your jacket,' Rossi said, 'you'll be more comfortable.' I did so, and removed my tie, placed them both on the back of a chair. Meanwhile, Ann went into the inner chamber and began adjusting the machine.

'Now, anything metal,' he went on. 'Keys, belt buckles, suspenders, coins. Your watch too. Since it's really just one big magnet, anything made of steel or iron is going to fly out of your pockets. The magnet can stop your watch, or at least screw it up pretty badly.' He chortled good-humoredly. 'Also, your wallet.'

'My wallet?'

'The thing can demagnetize things like bank cards, magnetic strips, stuff like that. You don't have a steel plate in your head or anything like that, right?'

'No.' I finished emptying my pockets and placing the contents on a lab table.

'All right,' he said, leading me into the inner chamber. 'This might feel a bit claustrophobic. Does that bother you?'

'Not especially.'

'Excellent. There's a mirror in there too, so you can see yourself, but a lot of people don't like looking at themselves lying flat in the machine. I guess it suggests to some people what they're going to look like in their coffins.' He chortled again.

I lay down on the white platform, and Ann strapped me in. The straps around my head fit snugly and were cushioned with sponges. The whole setup was vaguely uncomfortable.

Slowly she moved the platform into the center of the machine. Inside the doughnut hole was, as they said, a mirror, enabling me to see my head and torso.

From somewhere in the room I heard Ann's voice:

' – to start the magnet.'

Then, from a speaker inside the machine, I heard Rossi's voice: 'All right in there?'

'I'm fine,' I said. 'How long does this take?'

'Six hours,' the voice came back. 'I'm kidding. Ten, fifteen minutes.'

'Very funny.'

'All set?'

'Let's get on with it,' I said.

'You'll hear a pounding noise,' Rossi came back, 'but you'll still be able to hear my voice over that. Okay?'

'Okay,' I said impatiently.

The head guard made it impossible to move my head, which was an unpleasant feeling. 'Let's get on with it.' Suddenly a loud jackhammerlike sound started, a rhythmic thudding, spaced less than a second apart.

'Ben, I'm going to ask you a series of questions,' came Rossi's voice, metallic. 'Answer yes or no.'

'This isn't my first flutter,' I said.

'I understand,' came the metallic reply. 'Is your name Benjamin Ellison?'

'Yes,' I said.

'Is your name John Doe?'

'No.'

'Are you a physician?'

'No.'

'Have you ever had an extramarital affair?'

'What is this?' I said angrily.

'Please, just bear with me. Yes or no.'

I hesitated. Like Jimmy Carter, I have felt lust in my heart. 'No.'

'Were you employed by the Central Intelligence Agency?'

'Yes.'

'Do you live in Boston?'

'Yes.'

I heard a female voice from the room, Ann's voice, and then a male voice coming from somewhere nearby. Then Rossi's amplified question: 'Were you an agent for Soviet intelligence?'

I gave a sputter of disbelief.

'Yes or no, Ben. You understand these questions are designed to test the parameters of your anxiety levels. Were you an agent for Soviet intelligence?'

'No,' I said.

'Are you married to Martha Sinclair?'

'Yes.'

'Holding up okay in there, Ben?'

'I'm fine,' I said. 'Continue.'

'Were you born in New York City?'

'No.'

'Were you born in Philadelphia?'

'Yes.'

'Are you thirty-eight years old?'

'No.'

'Are you thirty-nine years old?'

'Yes.'

'Is your name Benjamin Ellison?'

'Yes.'

'Now, Ben, I want you to lie for the next two questions. Is your legal specialty real estate law?'

'Yes,' I said.

'Have you ever masturbated?'

'No.'

'Now the truth. When you worked for American intelligence, did you at the same time work for the intelligence service of any other nation?'

'No.'

'Since the termination of your employment with the Central Intelligence Agency, have you been in touch at any time with any intelligence officer formerly associated with what was once the Soviet Union or the Soviet Bloc nations?'

'No.'

There was a long pause, and then Rossi's voice came again. 'Thanks, Ben. That'll do.'

'So get me out of here already.'

'Ann will have you out in a minute.' The jackhammering stopped as suddenly as it had begun, and the silence was an enormous relief. My ears felt thick. I heard voices again, distantly: the lab techs, surely.

'All set, Mr Ellison,' came Ann's voice as she pulled the platform back. '*I hope to God he's all right.*'

'Excuse me?' I said.

'I said, we're all set.' She reached down and unstrapped the head guard, then undid the Velcro restraints at my ankles and thighs.

'I'm all right,' I said. 'Except for my hearing, which I imagine will recover in a couple of days.'

Ann gave me a penetrating look, furrowed her brow, and then said, 'You'll be fine.' She helped me off the platform.

'That wasn't so bad,' she said as I got to my feet, adding angrily, '*Didn't work didn't work.*'

'What didn't work?'

She looked at me, puzzled again. She hesitated a moment, then said, 'Everything went fine.' I followed her to the outside room, where Rossi stood, his hands in the pockets of his suitcoat, in a relaxed stance.

'Thanks, Ben,' he said. 'Well, you're all clear. No surprise. The computer-enhanced images – the snapshots of your brain-wave activity, in effect – indicate you were being entirely truthful, except when I asked you to lie.'

Rossi then turned around to pick up a sheaf of files. I approached to retrieve my belongings, and heard him mutter something about Truslow.

'What about Truslow?' I asked.

He turned around, smiling pleasantly. 'What do you mean?'

'Were you talking to me?' I asked.

He stared at me for a full five seconds. Shook his head. His eyes stared coldly.

'Forget it,' I said, but of course I'd heard him. We'd been standing no more than three feet apart; there was no way I could have misheard him. Something about Truslow. Baffling. Perhaps he didn't realize he'd spoken aloud.

I turned my attention to the array of belongings on the table next to us, the watch and belt and coins and so on, and Rossi said again, as clearly as the last time, '*Is it possible?*'

I looked at him and said nothing.

'Did it *work?*' came Rossi's voice again, somewhat indistinct, a little distant, but –

– and this time I was quite certain –

– his mouth had not moved.

He had not spoken a word. The realization sank in, and I felt my insides turn to ice.

Part Two

THE TALENT

The Pentagon has spent millions of dollars, according to three new reports, on secret projects to investigate extrasensory phenomena and to see if the sheer power of the human mind can be harnessed to perform various acts of espionage. . . .

– The New York Times, *January 10, 1984*

Financial Times
Europe Fears Nazi Rule in Ravaged Germany

BY ELIZABETH WILSON

IN BONN

In the three-man race for Chancellor of Germany, Mr Jurgen Krauss, leader of the reborn National Socialist Party, appears to be overtaking both the moderate candidate, Christian Democratic Party leader Wilhelm Vogel, and the incumbent. . . .

In the wake of the German stock market crash and the subsequent depression, there are widespread fears here and around Europe of a resurgence of a new form of Nazism. . . .

12

We stared at each other for a moment, Rossi and I.

In the long months since that instant, I've never been able to explain this aspect to anyone's satisfaction, least of all mine.

I heard Charles Rossi's voice almost as clearly, almost as distinctly, as if he'd spoken to me.

Not quite as if he'd spoken aloud. The timbre was different from the spoken voice, the way a long distance telephone connection sounds at once different from a clear, local one. A little less distinct; a little distant, a trace muffled, like a voice heard through a cheap motel room plasterboard wall.

There was an unmistakable difference between Rossi's spoken voice and his – what else can I call it? – his 'mental' voice, his *thought* voice. The spoken voice was somehow crisper; the mental voice was softer, smoother, more rounded.

I was able to hear Rossi's thoughts.

My head began to pound, a throbbing, vicious pain that localized at my right temple. Around everything in the room – Rossi, his gaping assistant, the machinery, the rubberized lab coats that hung on hooks by the door – was a shimmering rainbow of an aura. My skin began to prickle unpleasantly, flushing hot and then cold, and I could feel a wave of nausea overtake my stomach.

There have been volumes upon volumes written on the subject of extrasensory perception and psychic phenomena and 'psi,' the vast majority of which is packed with nonsense – I know, I've probably read every bit of it – but not one theorist ever speculated that it would be like this.

I could *hear* his thoughts.

Not all of his thoughts, thank God, or I would surely have

gone crazy long ago. Certain ones, things that entered his mind with sufficient urgency, sufficient intensity.

Or at least so I came to realize much later.

But at that moment, at that moment of realization, I had not put all of this together the way I have by now. I only knew – *knew* – that I was hearing something that Rossi *had not spoken aloud*, and it filled me with a bottomless dread.

I was on the edge of a precipice; it was a struggle now to keep from losing my mind entirely.

At that moment I was convinced that something in me had snapped, some thread of my sanity had broken; that the magnetic forces of the MRI machine had done something terrible to me, had somehow precipitated a nervous breakdown, that I was losing my grip on reality.

And so I responded in the only way I could: absolute denial. I wish I could claim credit for being shrewd, or clever, say I *knew* even then I must keep this strange and awful development to myself, but that wasn't the first thing that came to me. My instinct was to preserve some semblance of sanity – not to let on to Rossi that I was hearing things.

He spoke first, quietly. 'I didn't say anything about Mr Truslow.' He was probing me, watching my eyes from this uncomfortably close distance.

I said slowly, 'I thought you did, Charlie. Must have misheard.'

Turning to the lab table, I gathered my wallet, keys, coins, and pens, and began putting them in my pocket. As I did so, I backed slowly, casually, away from him. The headache intensified, the cold flush. It was a full-blown migraine.

'I didn't say anything at all,' Rossi said levelly.

I smiled dismissively, nodded. Wanted to sit down somewhere, tie something around my forehead, squeeze the pain from it.

He gave me another long, penetrating stare, and –

– and I *heard*, a murmur: *'Does he have it?'*

With forced joviality, I said, 'So if we're all through for the day –'

Rossi eyed me suspiciously. Blinked once, twice, and said, 'Soon. We need to sit down and talk for a couple of minutes.'

'Look,' I said. 'I have a terrific headache. A migraine, I'm pretty sure.'

I was at least six feet away from him now, putting my suit jacket back on. Rossi was still watching me as if I were a boa constrictor coiling and uncoiling in the middle of his bedroom. In the silence I strained to hear another of these murmurs, these faint voices.

Nothing.

Had I imagined these last few moments? Had they been hallucinations, like the shimmering aura that surrounded all the objects in the room? Would I come to my senses now, after this momentary departure from sanity?

'Are you prone to migraines?' Rossi asked.

'Never had one before. The test must have caused it.'

'That's impossible. It's never happened before, not in any test of the magnetic resonance imager, ever.'

'Well,' I said, 'in any case, I should be heading back to the office.'

'We're not quite done here,' Rossi said, turning back toward me.

'I'm afraid –'

'We'll be done shortly. I'll be right back.'

He went off in the direction of the adjacent room in which the computer banks were being monitored. I watched him approach one of the computer techs and say something quick and furtive. The tech handed him a small sheaf of printouts.

Then Rossi returned, bearing the computer images from the lie-detector test. He sat at a long, black-topped laboratory table and gestured for me to sit opposite him. I paused a moment, considered, and then sat obligingly.

He spread out the images on the lab table. Looked them over, his head bowed, seeming to consult them. We sat perhaps three feet apart.

I heard Rossi's voice, muffled but astonishingly clear: *I believe you have the ability*.

He said: 'Here, you'll notice, is your brain at the outset of the test.'

He pointed to the first image, which I drew closer to inspect. 'Unchanged, for the most part, throughout the test, because you're telling the truth.'

I heard: *You must trust me. You must trust me.*

Then he indicated a final set of images, which even I could tell were colored somewhat differently – yellow and magenta along the cerebral cortex rather than the normal rust and beige. He described with a finger the areas that manifested change.

'Here, you're lying.' He smiled quickly and added with unnecessary politeness, 'As I asked you to do.'

'I see.'

'I'm concerned about your headache.'

'I'll be fine,' I said.

'I'm concerned that this machine might have caused it.'

'The noise,' I said. 'The noise is probably what did it. I'll be fine.'

Rossi, head still bent, nodded.

I heard: *It will be so much easier if we trust each other.* The voice seemed to fade out for a moment, and then came back: – *to tell me.*

He did not reply, and so I said, 'If there's nothing further . . .'

Behind you, the voice came, urgent and loud now. *Coming up behind you. Loaded gun. You've become a threat. Pointed at your head.*

He was not speaking. He was thinking.

I betrayed no response. I continued staring at him questioningly, yet as casually as I could.

Now, now, now. Hope to God he can't hear the footsteps behind him.

He was testing me. I felt sure of it. Mustn't respond, mustn't show fear, that's what he wants, he wants some little sign, some glimmering of fear in my face, wants me to whip around suddenly, flinch, show him I can *hear* it.

'Then I really *should* be getting along,' I said calmly.

I heard: *Does he?*

'Well,' Rossi said. 'We can talk next time.'

I heard: *Either he's lying or –*

I watched his face; saw that his mouth hadn't moved. Once again I felt that creeping dread, a tingling on my skin, and my heart began to beat much too quickly.

Rossi looked at me, and I felt sure I saw resignation in his eyes. I had, for the time being at least, fooled him, I thought. But there was something about Charles Rossi that told me I would not fool him for long.

13

I sat, stunned, in the back of a taxicab making its way through the broad, clogged streets near Government Center toward my office. My head throbbed worse than ever, and I felt constantly on the edge of being sick to my stomach.

It is an understatement of the highest order to tell you that I was in the early stages of some sort of deep, wild panic. My world had been turned upside down. Nothing made sense anymore. I was deeply afraid that I was on the verge of losing touch with sanity altogether.

I was hearing voices now, voices unspoken. I was hearing, to put it plainly, the *thoughts* of others almost as clearly as if they had spoken them aloud.

And I was convinced I was losing my mind.

Even now I'm unable to put straight what I knew then and what I concluded much later. Had I really 'heard' what I thought I'd heard? How was this possible? And, more directly to the point, what precisely did Rossi and his lab assistant mean by asking themselves, 'Did it work?' It seemed to me there was only one possible explanation: *they knew*. Somehow, they – Rossi and his lab assistant – were not stunned that the MRI had done to me what it did. For there was no doubt in my mind that it was the MRI that had somehow altered my brain's hard-wiring.

But did Truslow know what had happened?

And yet a minute after thinking this whole thing through lucidly, I found myself wondering, in a panic, whether I had taken a left turn into lunacy.

As the taxi crawled through traffic, my thoughts grew increasingly suspicious. Was that 'lie detector test' business merely a pretext, a way to compel me to undergo this procedure?

Had they, in short, *known* what would happen to me?

Again: had Truslow known?

And had I fooled Rossi? Or did he know that I had this strange and terrible new ability?

Rossi, I feared, knew. Normally, when someone says something that echoes in some way what we've been thinking – we've all had moments like that – we respond with surprise, often delight. It is no doubt pleasurable on some level to find another human being connecting with us in such a way.

But Rossi didn't seem surprised. He seemed – how would I describe it? – alert, alarmed, suspicious. As if he'd been waiting for such a development.

I wondered, as I reflected on that scene with Rossi, whether I had really convinced him that there was nothing out of the ordinary in my response – that I merely *seemed* to be tuned in to his thoughts, that it was nothing more than coincidence.

As the cab pulled into the financial district, I leaned forward to give the driver directions. The driver, a middle-aged black man with a sparse beard, sat back in his seat distractedly as he drove, as if in a reverie. Separating us was a scuffed Plexiglas partition. I spoke into the speaker holes, and suddenly realized something startling: I wasn't 'hearing' the driver. Now I was totally confused. Had this talent subsided, or disappeared altogether? Was it the Plexiglas, or the distance, or something else? Again: had I imagined the occurrence altogether?

'Take a right here,' I said, 'and it'll be the large gray building on the left.'

Nothing. The sound of the radio, an all-talk station chattering along at low volume, and the occasional burst of static from his CB, but nothing else.

Had the MRI done something to my brain that had disappeared as quickly as it had appeared?

Totally confused now, I paid him and entered the building lobby, which was crowded with people returning from their early lunches, noisy with their babble. Along with a sizable crowd of lunchtime returnees, I pressed my way into the elevator, pushed the button for my floor, and – I will admit it – tried to 'listen' or 'read' or whatever you call it, but the various loud conversations made that impossible in any case.

My head throbbed. I felt claustrophobic, nauseated. Perspiration dripped down the back of my neck.

Then the elevator doors shut, and the crowd fell silent, as it so often does in elevators, and it happened.

I could hear, kaleidoscopically, snatches of words – or, as it seemed to me at that moment, *smears* of words and phrases, the way a record or tape sounds when you play it backward (or *did* in the days before digitally recorded sound, when the technology actually allowed you to do such tricks). The woman next to me – pressed up against me by the crush of people – was a serene-looking woman of around forty, plump and red-haired. Her expression was pleasant, a slight smile. But I could hear at the same time a voice – it had to be coming from her – that came in surges, distant and then distinct, fading in and out, like voices on a party line. *Stand it can't stand it*, the voice went. *Do it to me he can't do it to me he can't.* Startled by the contrast between this woman's pleasant demeanor and the thoughts that bordered on the hysterical, I turned my head toward the man on my left, who looked like a lawyer, in a lawyerly pinstripe suit and horn-rimmed glasses, early fifties, his expression one of vague boredom. And then it came, a distant shout in a male voice: *minutes late they've started without me the bastard* . . .

I was 'tuning in,' without consciously doing it, the way you can listen for a familiar voice in a crowd, selecting for a certain timbre, a certain sound. In the silence of the elevator, it was simple.

The bell sounded and the doors opened onto the reception area of Putnam & Stearns. I brushed past several of my colleagues, barely acknowledging them, and found my way to my office.

Darlene looked up as I approached. As usual, she was wearing black, but today it was some sort of frilly high-necked thing that she probably imagined was feminine. It looked as though she'd picked it up at a Salvation Army.

As I neared her, I heard: *'something seriously wrong with Ben.'*

She started to say something, but I waved her away. I entered my office, silently greeted the Big Baby Dolls who kept their silent vigil against one wall, and sat down at the desk. 'Hold my calls,' I said, closed my office door, and sank into my chair, safe at last in the solitude. For a very long time I sat in absolute silence, staring into the middle distance, squeezing my throbbing temples, cradling my head in my hands, and listening only to the hammering of my heart.

A little while later I emerged to ask Darlene for my messages. She looked at me curiously, obviously wondering whether I was all right. Handing me a pile of pink message slips, she said, 'Mr Truslow called.'

'Thanks.'

'You feeling any better?'

'What do you mean?'

'You got a headache, right?'

'Yeah. A nasty migraine. "A headache so bad it *shows*." '

'You know, I've always got some Advil here,' she said, pulling open a desk drawer that revealed her stash of medications. 'Take a couple. I get migraines too, every month, and they're like the worst.'

'The worst,' I agreed, accepting some of the pills.

'Oh, and Allen Hyde from Textronics wants to talk to you as soon as possible.' Mr. Hyde was the beleaguered inventor of Big Baby Dolls who was on the verge of making a settlement offer.

I said, 'Thanks,' and scanned the messages. Darlene had turned to her IBM Selectric – yes, we still use typewriters at Putnam & Stearns; in certain instances the law requires typewriters, not laser printers – and returned to her frenetic typing.

I could not stop myself from moving close to her desk, then leaning forward and trying.

And it came, with that same damned clarity. *Looks like he's losing it*, I heard in Darlene's voice, and then silence.

'I'm okay,' I said quietly.

Darlene spun around, her eyes wide. 'Huh?'

'Don't worry about me. I had a tough meeting this morning.'

She gave me a long, frantic look, then composed herself. 'Who's worried?' she said, turning back to the typewriter, and I heard, as if in the same conversational tone, *Did I say anything?* 'Want me to get Truslow on the line?'

'Not yet,' I said. 'I've got forty-five minutes before Kornstein, which goes right into Lewin, and I need to get some fresh air or my head's going to explode.' What I really wanted was to sit in a dark room with the blankets over my head, but I figured that a walk, painful as it might be, would do as much to alleviate the headache.

As I turned back to my office to get my overcoat, Darlene's phone trilled.

'Mr Ellison's office,' she said. Then: 'One moment, please, Mr. Truslow,' and she punched the hold button. 'Are you here?'

'I'll take it.'

'Ben,' Truslow said when I picked it up in my office. 'I thought you'd be returning to chat.'

'Sorry,' I said. 'The test ran on longer than I anticipated. I've got a crazy day here. If you don't mind, let's reschedule.'

A long pause.

'Fine,' he said. 'What did you make of this Rossi? He seems a bit thuggish to me, but maybe I worry too much.'

'Didn't have much of a chance to size him up.'

'In any case, Ben, I understand you passed the lie detector with flying colors.'

'I trust you're not surprised.'

'Of course not. But we need to talk. I need to brief you fully. The thing is, a little wrinkle has turned up.'

There was a smile in his voice, and I knew.

'The President has asked me to go to Camp David,' he said.

'Congratulations.'

'Congratulations are premature. He wants to talk things over with me, his chief-of-staff says.'

'Sounds like you got it.'

'Well . . .' Truslow said. He seemed to hesitate for a moment, but then he said, 'I'll be in touch very soon,' and he hung up the phone.

I walked up Milk Street to Washington Street, the pedestrian mall sometimes called Downtown Crossing. There, along Summer Street, the gulf between the two great, rival downtown department stores, Filene's and Jordan Marsh, I wandered aimlessly among pushcart vendors selling popcorn and pretzels, Bedouin scarves, Boston tourist T-shirts, and rough-knit South American sweaters. The headache seemed to be subsiding. The street was, as usual, teeming with shoppers, street musicians, office workers. Now, though, the air was filled with sounds, a bedlam of shouts and mutterings, sighs and exclamations, whispers and screams. Thoughts.

On Devonshire Street I entered an electronics shop, blankly examined a display of twenty-inch color television sets, fended off the salesman. Several of the sets were tuned to soap operas, one to CNN, one to a Nickelodeon rerun of a black and white TV show from the fifties that may have been *The Donna Reed Show*. On CNN the blond anchorwoman was saying something about a United States senator who had died. I recognized the face flashed on the screen: Senator Mark Sutton of Colorado, who had been found shot to death at his home in Washington. The police in Washington believed the slaying was probably not politically motivated, but instead committed during an armed robbery.

The salesman approached again, saying, 'All the Mitsubishis are on sale this week, you know.'

I smiled pleasantly, said no thanks, and went out to the street. My head throbbed. I found myself standing close to passersby at stoplights and crossings, *listening*. One attractive young woman with short blond hair, in a pale pink suit and running shoes, stood next to me while the Don't Walk sign flashed at Tremont Street. In normal circumstances we all keep a certain social distance from strangers; she was standing a few feet away, immersed in her own thoughts. I bent my head toward her in an attempt to share some of those thoughts, but she scowled at me as if I were a pervert, and moved quite a distance away.

People were bustling past too quickly for my feeble, novice efforts. I would stand, craning my neck this way and that as unobtrusively as I could, but nothing.

Had the talent disappeared? Had I simply imagined the whole thing?

Nothing.

Had the power merely faded?

Back on Washington Street, I spotted a newsstand, where a clot of people were buying their *Globes* and *Wall Street Journals* and *New York Timeses*, and when the Walk sign flashed, I crossed over to it. A young guy was looking at the front page of the *Boston Herald* – MOB HIT MAN NABBED it said, with a picture of some minor Mafia figure who'd been arrrested in Providence. I moved in close, as if contemplating the pile of *Heralds* in front of him. Nothing. A woman, thirtyish and lawyerly, was scanning the piles of papers, looking for something. I moved in as close as I could without alarming her. Nothing there either.

Was it gone?

Or, I wondered, was it that none of these people was upset enough, angry enough, scared enough, to be emitting brain waves – is that how it worked? – of a frequency I could detect?

Finally, I saw a man in his early forties, dressed in the natty apparel of an investment banker, standing near the piles of *Women's Wear Daily*, blankly staring at the rows of glossy magazines. Something in his eyes told me he was deeply upset about something.

I moved in closer, pretending to be inspecting the cover of the latest issue of *The Atlantic*, and tried.

– to fire her she's going to bring up that whole fucking business about the affair God knows how she'll react she's a fucking loose cannon would she call Gloria and tell her ah Jesus what am I going to do I don't have any choice so goddamned stupid to fuck your secretary –

I stole a furtive glance at the banker, and his dour face had not moved.

By this time I had formulated a number of what I guess you could call understandings, or perhaps theories, about what had happened, and what I should do.

One: The powerful magnetic resonance imager had affected my brain in such a way that I was now able to 'hear' the thoughts of others. Not all people; perhaps not most, but at least some.

Two: I was able to 'hear' not all thoughts but only those that were 'expressed' with a fair degree of emphasis. In other words, I only 'heard' things that were thought with great vehemence, fear, anger. Also, I could 'hear' things only at close physical proximity – two or three feet away from a person, maximum.

Three: Charles Rossi and his lab assistant were not only not surprised at this manifestation, but were actually expecting it. That meant they had been using the MRI for this express purpose, even before I came on the scene.

Four: The uncertainty they felt indicated that either it had not worked in the proper way before, or it had rarely done so.

Five: Rossi did not know for certain that this experiment had succeeded on me. Therefore, I was safe only as long as I did not let on that I had this ability.

Six: Therefore, it was only a matter of time before they caught up with me, for whatever purposes they intended.

Seven: In all probability, my life would never be the same. I was no longer safe.

I glanced at my watch, realized I had strolled far too long, and turned back toward the office.

Ten minutes later I was back at the offices of Putnam & Stearns, with a few minutes to spare before my next appointment. For some reason I suddenly found myself recalling the face of the senator I had seen on the CNN newscast. Senator Mark Sutton (D.-Col), shot to death. I remembered now: Senator Sutton was the chairman of the Senate Select Subcommittee on Intelligence. And – was it fifteen years ago? – he had been Deputy Director of Central Intelligence, before he'd been appointed to fill a Senate vacancy, and then was elected in his own right two years later.

And . . .

And he was one of Hal Sinclair's oldest friends. His roommate at Princeton. They had joined the CIA together.

That made three CIA types now dead. Hal Sinclair and two trusted confidants.

Coincidences, I believe, occur everywhere except in the intelligence business.

I buzzed Darlene and asked her to send in my four o'clock.

14

Mel Kornstein entered, in an Armani suit that looked untailored and did little to conceal his girth. His silver tie was stained with a bright yellow half-moon of what appeared to be egg.

'Where's the asshole?' he asked, giving me a soft, damp handshake and looking around my office.

'Frank O'Leary will be here in about fifteen minutes. I wanted to give us a little time to go over some things.'

Frank O'Leary was the 'inventor' of SpaceTime, the computer game that is an exact rip-off of Mel Kornstein's amazing SpaceTron. He and his attorney, Bruce Kantor, had agreed to a conference to initiate the exploratory stages of some sort of agreement. Ordinarily that would mean they realized they'd better settle, that they'd lose big if it ever went to trial. A lawsuit, as lawyers like to say, is a machine you enter as a pig and come out a sausage. Then again, they could be showing up simply as a courtesy, but lawyers aren't much into courtesy. It was also entirely possible that the two just wanted to display their gladiatorial confidence, try to rattle us a bit.

I was not at my best that afternoon. In fact – though my headache had by this time mostly disappeared – I could barely think straight, and Mel Kornstein picked up on this. 'You with me here, Counselor?' he asked querulously at one point when I lost the thread of argument.

'I'm with you, Mel,' I said, and tried to concentrate. I'd found that if I didn't *want* to pick up a person's thoughts, I generally didn't. What I mean is that I discovered, sitting there with Kornstein, that I wasn't bombarded with thoughts on top of conversation, which might have been unbearable. I could listen to him normally, but if I wanted to 'read' him, I could do so simply by focusing in a way, homing in.

Obviously I can't describe this adequately, but it's like the way a mother can single out the voice of her child playing on the beach from the voices of dozens of other children. It's a bit like listening to the jumble of voices on a party line, some of them more audible than others. Or maybe it's more like the way, when you're speaking on a cordless phone, you can hear the ghosts of other people's conversations overlapping your own. If you listen with some effort, you can hear everything clearly.

So I found myself listening to Kornstein's voice, rising in aggrievement and falling in despair, and realizing that I could hear only his spoken voice if I so desired.

Fortunately, I regained some footing by the time O'Leary and Kantor showed up, effusing cordiality. O'Leary – tall, red-haired, bespectacled, thirtyish – and Kantor – small, compact, balding, late forties – made themselves right at home in my office and sank into their chairs as if we were all old chums.

'Ben,' Kantor said by way of greeting.

'Good to see you, Bruce.' Good old casual chummy banter.

Only the attorneys are supposed to talk at these conferences. The clients, if they appear at all, are there only for their attorney's ready reference; they're supposed to keep silent. But Mel Kornstein sat there, fuming, refusing to shake hands with anyone, and couldn't restrain himself from blurting out, 'Six months from now you're going to be washing dishes at McDonald's, O'Leary. Hope you like the smell of french-fry grease.'

O'Leary smiled calmly and gave Kantor a look that said, *Will you handle this lunatic?* Kantor bounced the look over to me, and I said, 'Mel, let Bruce and me handle this right now.'

Mel folded his arms and smoldered.

The real point of this meeting was to determine one simple thing: had Frank O'Leary seen a prototype of SpaceTron while he was 'developing' SpaceTime? The similarity of the games wasn't even in question. But if we could prove beyond any

114

doubt that O'Leary had *seen* SpaceTron at any point before it went on the market, we won. It was as simple as that.

O'Leary maintained, naturally, that the first time he saw SpaceTron was in a software store. Kornstein was convinced that O'Leary had somehow gotten an early prototype of the game from one of his software engineers, but of course he couldn't prove his suspicion. And here I was, trying to fence with Bruce Kantor, Esq., the feisty little bantam.

After half an hour Kantor was still making noises about restraint of trade and unfair practices. I was finding it hard to concentrate on his line of argument, in that half-dazed state I'd been in since the morning, but I knew enough to realize he was just blustering. Neither he nor his client was going to give an inch.

I asked, for the third time, 'Can you say for absolutely certain that neither your client nor any of his employees had any access to any of the research or development work that was going on at Mr Kornstein's firm?'

Frank O'Leary continued to sit impassively with folded arms, looking bored, and let his attorney do the heavy lifting. Kantor leaned forward, gave his saucy little smile, and said, 'I think you're scraping the bottom of the barrel, Ben. If you've got nothing else –'

And then I heard, in that gauzy, soft-focus tone that I'd begun to recognize, Frank O'Leary's voice mutter something. I could barely make it out, but I tilted my head forward, pretending to be consulting my legal pad, and concentrated to separate it from Kantor's chatter.

Ira Hovanian, O'Leary was saying.

Jesus, if Hovanian spills –

'Ah, Bruce,' I said. 'Perhaps your client can tell us a little about Ira Hovanian.'

Kantor frowned, looked annoyed, and said, 'I don't know what you're –'

But O'Leary grabbed his arm and whispered something into Kantor's left ear. Kantor looked at me quizzically for a moment, then swiveled around, and whispered something back.

I consulted my yellow pad and tilted my head and began to listen, but at that instant Kornstein tapped me lightly on the shoulder. 'What does Ira Hovanian have to do with anything?' he whispered. 'How did you know about Ira Hovanian?'

'Who is he?' I asked.

'You don't –'

'Just tell me.'

'He's a guy who quit the company a couple of months before SpaceTron came out. A shlemazzel.'

'A what?'

'I felt sorry for the schmuck. He lost a shitload in stock options. I guess he found a better job somewhere else, but if he had stayed, he'd be a rich man by now.'

'Did he sell trade secrets?'

'Ira? Ira was a nothing.'

'Listen to me,' I said. 'For some reason, O'Leary knows that name. It means something to him.'

'You didn't mention –'

'It's something I picked up recently,' I replied. 'All right, let me think for a minute.' I turned away from Kornstein, and feigned deep concentration on the scribblings on my yellow pad. Several feet away, O'Leary and Kantor were deep in whispered colloquy.

– stole a working prototype from the safe. He had a combination. Sold it to me for twenty-five thousand bucks and the promise of another hundred grand when we started turning a profit.

I took notes as quickly as I could, and continued to listen, but the voice faded out. O'Leary was smiling, visibly relaxed now, and his thoughts were placid, therefore unreadable.

I was about to turn back to Kornstein to ask him about this, when suddenly I picked up another flow.

. . . burned him. What the hell was he going to do? He's the guy who committed the illegal act, right? So who's he going to turn to?

Now Kantor swiveled back toward me and said, 'Let's meet again in a day or two. We've gone on long enough today.'

I reflected for a few seconds and said, 'If that's what you and your client would like, that's fine. If anything, that will give us time for an additional deposition of Mr Hovanian, who has already given us some interesting information concerning a prototype of SpaceTron and a company safe.'

Kantor looked supremely uncomfortable. He unfolded his legs, then folded them again, and pulled nervously at his chin with a thumb and forefinger.

'Look,' he said, his voice a few notes higher than before, 'bluff all you like. But let's not waste each other's time. If a minimum settlement is what you want, I think it would be in my client's interest just to get all this stuff behind him, so we'd be prepared to make a –'

'Four point five million,' I said.

'*What?*' he gasped.

I stood up and extended my hand. 'Well, gentlemen, I've got some depositions to take. With your knowing cooperation in the concealment of a felony, as the attorney of record I think we should have an interesting trial. Thank you for coming.'

'Hold on a second here,' Kantor blurted out. 'We can come to an agreement of –'

'Four point five,' I repeated.

'You're out of your mind!'

'Gentlemen,' I said.

The two clients, O'Leary and Kornstein, were staring at me, dumbstruck, as if I'd suddenly pulled down my trousers and danced a jig on my desk. 'Jesus,' Kornstein said to me.

'Let's – let's talk,' Kantor said.

'All right,' I said, and sat down. 'Let's talk.'

The meeting broke up forty-five minutes later. Frank O'Leary had agreed to pay an outright settlement of $4.25 million in one lump sum, payable within ninety days, with a further stipulation that SpaceTime would remove its flagship computer game from the market forthwith.

Shortly before lunch, O'Leary and Kantor, considerably more subdued, filed out of my office. Mel Kornstein gave me a humid, bearlike embrace, thanked me profusely, and left, beaming for the first time in months.

And I sat alone in my office, ignoring the ringing phone,

and tossed a perfect hook-shot into my electronic hoop. It emitted a wild packed-Boston-Garden cheer and shouted tinnily, '*Score!*' I grinned to myself like an idiot, wondering how long this peculiar good fortune could last. As it happened, it lasted for precisely one day.

15

My mistake, as it turned out, was that classic error of the novice intelligence operative: neglecting to assume that you're being watched.

The problem was that I had lost my bearings. My world had turned upside down. The normal logic of my staid, ordered, lawyerly life no longer applied.

We go through our lives by rote, I think, doing our jobs and performing our duties as if with blinders on. Now, suddenly, the blinders were off. How could I possibly be as circumspect, as cautious, as I once might have been?

I was able to leave the office early enough to make a stop before home. When the elevator arrived, it was empty – too late, as usual, for the evening rush – and I got in.

I needed desperately to talk to someone, but who, in truth, could I talk to? Molly? She would immediately think I had gone off the deep end. Like all physicians, her world was a very rational one. Of course I would have to tell her at some point – but when? And what about my friend Ike? Possible, I suppose; but at this point I couldn't risk telling anyone.

Two floors below, the elevator stopped, and a young woman got in. She was tall, auburn-haired, with a little too much eye makeup, but with a nice full figure, and her silk blouse accented her large breasts. We stood there in the normal silence shared by elevator passengers who do not know each other but happen to be standing in a metal box a few feet apart. She seemed distracted. Both of us were busily looking up, watching the numbers change. My headache, that terrible welling-up of pain, was all but gone, thank God.

I happened to be thinking about Molly, in fact, when I
'heard' it –

what he's like in bed.

I glanced over at her, instinctually, assuring myself once
again that she hadn't said anything aloud. Her eyes seemed to
catch mine for a split second, but turned back toward the
flashing red numerals in the panel above the door.

I concentrated now, and I picked up more.

*nice ass. Probably a pretty strong guy. Looks like a lawyer,
which means he's probably the real conservative boring type but
one night who cares.*

I turned again, and this time her eyes met mine for an
instant, a second too long.

If ever a woman were available, she was. I at once felt a
strange spasm of guilt. I was privy to her most intimate
fantasies, her private calculations, her daydreams. It was a
terrible violation. It violated all the rules we human beings
have developed for flirtation, the dance of cues and hints and
suggestions, which works so well because nothing is ever said,
nothing is ever certain.

I knew this woman would go to bed with me. Ordinarily,
you can never be certain no matter what the body language.
Some women like to flirt, to take things to the brink just to see
if they're sufficiently desirable to lead a man that far. Then
they'll pull back, playing along with social conventions,
feigning unwillingness, a need to be wooed. The whole game,
which has baffled both men and women since we all began
standing upright (and likely before then), relies upon our
inability to know what is in the minds of others. It is premised
upon uncertainty.

But I *knew*. I knew with absolute certainty what this woman
was thinking. And for some reason I found this deeply
upsetting, as if I'd just become an outsider to the normal rules
of human behavior.

I'm also quite aware that another man might have taken
immediate advantage of the situation. And why not? I knew
she was willing; I found her attractive enough. Even if she
affected a lack of interest, I could see – or 'hear' – through it,

knowing just what to say and when to say it. The power was enormous.

Well, I'm no more virtuous than any man. It's just that I was in love with Molly.

And it was at that point that I realized that my relationship with Molly could never be quite the same.

The Boston Public Library was not too busy at this time of the early evening, and I was able to get the pile of books I'd ordered within twenty minutes.

The literature on extrasensory perception is actually quite extensive. A number of books had (reasonably) sober-sounding titles like *Psychic Discoveries Behind the Iron Curtain* and *The Scientific Basis of Telepathy*. Some, on the other hand, had such unpromising titles as *Develop Your Mind Potential!* or *Anyone Can Have ESP*; those I discarded after the briefest scan. Some of the serious-seeming ones turned out, after a few minutes of reading, to be not so serious after all – they'd dressed up a lot of speculation and the slimmest evidence in pages full of statistics and learned references. Finally I was down to three volumes that seemed to hold out hope: *Psi* (which turned out to be a jargon abbreviation of 'psychic'), *Recent Findings in Parapsychological Phenomena*, and *The Frontier of the Mind*.

I felt a little strange looking through these books, speculative as they were. It was a bit like a migraine sufferer poring over volumes that hypothesized that there just might *possibly* be such a thing as a migraine headache. I wanted to shout out to the library's hushed, cavernous interior: 'It's not goddamn theoretical! I *have* it!'

Instead, I plowed through the studies. Apparently, amid all the quacks and the loonies there were a number of credentialed, credible scholars who believed that certain human beings possessed the ability to read minds in one way or another. Among them were a few Nobel laureates and some prominent researchers at Duke, UCLA, Princeton, Stanford, Oxford, the University of Freiburg in Germany. They studied such subspecialties as 'psychometry' and 'psychokinesis.'

121

Mostly these scientists had attained recognition in more traditional fields of research and drew little or no serious attention for their work in parapsychology, despite the occasional article in respected science journals like Britain's *Nature*.

What it seemed to come down to was this: perhaps a quarter of all human beings, at one time or another, experience some form of telepathy. Most of us, however, refuse to allow ourselves to accept it. I read a number of accounts that seemed plausible. A woman is dining with friends in New York City and suddenly feels *certain* that her father has died. She rushes to the phone – and the father, indeed, died of heart failure in a hospital at the moment she felt it. A college student feels a sudden, unexplained urge to call home, and learns that his younger brother has been in a terrible car accident. Most often, I learned, people receive 'signals' or 'feelings' while asleep and/or dreaming, because it is at those times that we are least hindered by our skepticism.

But none of this really applied to what had happened to me. I wasn't experiencing 'feelings' or 'signals' or 'urges.' I was 'hearing' – there's no other word for it – the thoughts of others. Yet not at a distance. In fact, more than a few feet away, I could not 'hear' a thing. Which meant that I was receiving some sort of transmissible signal from the human brain. Nothing in these books dealt with that.

Until I came across an intriguing chapter in *The Frontier of the Mind*. The author was discussing the use of psychics by various police forces throughout the United States, and by the Pentagon during a search for MIAs in Vietnam. There was a reference to the Pentagon's use of a psychic in January 1982, in a hunt for General Dozier, who had been kidnapped by the Red Brigades in Italy.

And then I spotted a reference to a 1980 article in the U.S. Army's house journal, *Military Review*, on 'the new mental battlefield.' It discussed the 'great potential' of 'the use of telepathic hypnosis' in warfare – psychic warfare, the article called it! There was a mention of Soviet 'psychotronic' weapons – the use of parapsychology to sink U.S. nuclear submarines – and of the National Security Agency's use of a psychic to crack codes.

The book continued on to discuss a rumored 'psychic task force' in the basement of the Pentagon, maintained under the highest of security and headed by an assistant chief of staff for intelligence.

And then, on the next page, I came across a reference to a top secret CIA project involving the intelligence possibilities of extrasensory perception.

The project, according to this account, was terminated in 1977 by the new Director of Central Intelligence, Admiral Stansfield Turner. At least, the author speculated, it was terminated *officially*. Very little was known about the project, the author said, except one name associated with it, obtained from a renegade CIA officer. It was the name of the project's director.

The name was Charles Rossi.

Deeply anxious now and disoriented, I needed to get some exercise, to clear my head and think rationally.

For a couple of years now I have belonged to an athletic club on Boylston Street that I like mostly for its proximity both to work and to home. Its clientele is a real mix, lawyers and businessmen, salesmen and midlevel executives, real jocks, and so on; the gym facilities are top-notch. I could never prevail upon Molly to work out with me. She was of the opinion that we all have a finite number of heartbeats, and she didn't want to waste hers on some Nautilus machine. And she called herself a physician.

I changed out of my work clothes and into a pair of shorts and a T-shirt, and worked out on the rowing machine for twenty minutes, thinking all the while about what I had read at the library.

In the strictest sense I was not reading the thoughts of others, I'd concluded. I was able to receive the low-frequency brain waves generated by one single part of the brain, the speech center in the cortex. In other words, I was hearing words and phrases as they were converted from abstract thoughts and ideas into words, as they were given form in speech, preparatory to their being uttered aloud. Apparently, if my theory was right, when certain thoughts occur to us with the right force or passion or emotion, we *pre*articulate them – ready them for speaking, even if we will never speak the words. And it is at those moments that the brain gives off signals perceptible to – well, to me.

If only I knew more about how the brain functioned! But I could scarcely risk consulting a neurologist at this point: no one could be trusted, really, to keep my condition a secret.

All of this was going through my mind as I got off the rowing machine, my gray T-shirt already stained dark with sweat, and got on the Stairmaster. This particular torture device requires you to pump up and down on a set of pedals while grasping on to a handlebar, all the while standing vertical, while a bright red computer display keeps track of your pain.

On the next Stairmaster was a portly gentleman of about fifty in a light blue T-shirt and white shorts, spewing droplets of sweat onto the machine's metal base, rivulets of perspiration running down his ears, nose, jaw, and brow. He was wearing wire-rim glasses that were fogged over. I had once talked to him at the club – I don't remember what about – and I seemed to remember his name was Alan or Alvin or something, and that he was a vice president at a troubled Boston bank, the Beacon Guaranty Trust. Because of a history of lousy management added to the nation's economic woes, Beacon was slowly going down the tubes. Alan or Alvin, as I recall, was a perennially depressed man, and who could blame him?

Pumping away at the Stairmaster as he was, Al didn't notice me. His eyes were hooded, his mouth half open, his breathing labored.

It was not my intention, because I wanted to be alone with my thoughts and mine alone, but I could not help hearing what I did.

Catherine's uncle, maybe?

No. The SEC will get right on to that. Those bastards don't miss a trick.

That's just as illegal as my selling my own stock.

Gotta be a way.

I couldn't pick up everything he was saying. His thoughts came in and out, loud and then faint, clear and then indistinct, like a shortwave radio picking up some distant foreign station.

But all that stuff about the SEC and illegality drew my attention right away. I tilted my head ever so slightly toward Al's heaving, dripping body.

The stock's going to just goddamn rocket. How come I'm not allowed to buy stock in my own company? Doesn't seem right. Wonder whether anyone else on the board of directors is thinking what I'm thinking. Of course they are. They're all trying to figure out a way to get rich off this.

This monologue was getting more and more interesting, and I strained to tune in without seeming too obvious about it. Al, lost in his greedy little thoughts, seemed oblivious of me.

So let's see. The announcement is made tomorrow, two o'clock p.m. Every financial analyst in the country, and hundreds of thousands of shareholders, see that poor beleaguered old Beacon Trust is now being acquired by the rock-solid Saxon Bancorp and everyone and their grandmother will be buying badly undervalued shares of Beacon. We're going to go from eleven and a half to fifty or sixty in two days. Jesus. And I gotta sit on my hands? There's gotta be a way. Maybe one of Catherine's rich lady friends. Maybe her uncle can work something out that's insulated from me enough – buy up Beacon tomorrow morning in someone else's name –

I found my heart beginning to thud rapidly. I had just learned what could be described only as the ultimate insider information. Beacon Trust was going to be acquired by Saxon. The deal was going to be announced tomorrow. Alan or Alvin was one of probably only a handful of insiders, executives and attorneys, who knew about the deal. The stock of Beacon would certainly shoot up, and anyone who had advance knowledge could become a rich man. Al was scheming out a way to get rich off it himself, if he could find a way that wouldn't attract the hound dogs of the SEC. I doubted he'd be able to pull it off.

125

But I could.

Tomorrow I could, in a matter of hours, make a killing in shares of Beacon Trust that would make the disappearance of my half-million-dollar nest egg seem inconsequential.

There was no way in the world anyone could connect me to Beacon Trust. My firm did no business with Beacon (we wouldn't deign to). I would have to make a point of not even saying hello to Al: better we didn't even exchange a word.

What could the Securities and Exchange Commission possibly do? Bring me into a courtroom, facing a jury of my peers, and charge me with mind reading with intent to profit illegally? The chairman of the SEC would be locked up in a rubber room before they could even file the paperwork.

I got off the Stairmaster, sweating profusely. I'd done a good three-quarters of an hour on the torture equipment without even realizing it.

16

Twenty minutes later or so, I heard a key turn in both front door locks, then heard Molly's voice calling out, 'Ben?'

'You're late,' I said, feigning irritation. 'Tell me what's more important – the life of an infant, or my supper?'

I looked up, gave her a smile, and saw that she looked exhausted.

'Hey,' I said, getting up to embrace her. 'What's wrong?'

She shook her head slowly, wearily. 'Tough day.'

'Ah,' I said, 'but now you're home.' I wrapped my arms around her and kissed her, a good, long, extended kiss. I gave her bottom a squeeze and pressed myself hard against her.

She slid her hands, cold and dry, down my back, under the elastic band of my shorts. 'Mmm,' she said. Her breath was hot on the back of my neck.

Now I slipped my hands under her blouse, up under the white cotton fabric of her bra, felt her warm, erect nipples, stroked.

'Mmmph,' she said.

'Upstairs?' I asked.

She moaned quietly, then gave a brief shiver.

– *the kitchen* – I heard.

I leaned toward her, still running my fingertips over her right breast, squeezing the thickened nipple.

– *do it in the kitchen. Standing up. Ah, right here* –

I got up, took her by the shoulders, and gently maneuvered her from the sitting room into the kitchen, then pushed her back against the burnished, scarred oak table top.

Her thoughts. It was wrong, it was evil, it was shameful, but, carried away in my lust, I couldn't stop myself –

127

Oh, yes –

She moaned softly as I pulled off her blouse.

– my other breast. Don't stop. Both breasts –

Obediently, I caressed both her breasts with my palms, then bent my head down and sucked first one nipple, then the other.

Don't move –

I continued to suck and lick, all the while pushing against her until she was lying flat on the table, safely clear of the bowls. I had never seen *The Postman Always Rings Twice*, but I remembered the iconography of it; hadn't Lana Turner and John Garfield done it on the kitchen table too?

Now, still nuzzling her breasts, I pressed my erect member against her thigh, grinding slowly, and as I began to undo the drawstring of her sweatpants, I heard

– No. Not yet.

And, obeying her unspoken wishes, I turned my full attention to her breasts, dallying there longer than I otherwise might have.

We did in fact make love on the kitchen table, losing one cheap china bowl to the commotion, but neither one of us much noticed the crash. It was, I have to say, the most erotic, intense sex I had ever had. Molly had been so carried away, she had forgotten to insert her diaphragm. She came time after time, the tears flowing down her cheeks. Afterward we lay tangled in each other's arms, wet with sweat and musky with the fluids and odors of lovemaking, on the couch in the sitting room next to the kitchen.

Yet when it was over, I felt enormously guilty.

They say that all human beings are sad after sex. I believe that it is only men who experience the postcoital blues. Molly looked at once blissful and disoriented, stroking my now-flaccid, reddened, drained penis.

'You weren't protected,' I said. 'Does that mean you've changed your mind about kids?'

'No,' she said dreamily. 'I'm not at the fertile part of my cycle right now. Not much of a risk. But that was great.'

128

I felt increasingly guilty and predatory and generally evil. I had violated her in a fundamental way, I felt. By responding to her every unspoken desire, I had in a terrible sense manipulated her, engaged in a reprehensible dishonesty.

I felt shitty.

'Yeah,' I said. 'That was great.'

Our wedding was held on the grounds of a lovely old estate outside Boston. The day is still a blur. I remember bustling around, looking for my cummerbund and studs and a pair of half-decent black socks to wear.

Shortly before the ceremony began, Hal Sinclair caught hold of my elbow. In his tuxedo he was even more distinguished-looking than when I first met him: his white hair glowed against his tanned, long, narrow, handsome face. He had a cleft chin, thin lips, laugh lines around the eyes and mouth.

He seemed angry, but I quickly realized he was being stern, and I'd never seen him stern before.

'You take care of my daughter,' he said.

I looked at him, expecting him to crack a joke, but his mien was unrelievedly somber.

'You hear me?'

I said I did. Of course I will.

'You take care of her.'

And it suddenly hit me, like a punch to the solar plexus. Of course! My last wife had been killed. Hal would never, ever say it, but were it not for my failure to follow correct procedures, Laura would be alive. Were it not for my bungling.

You killed your first wife, Ben, he seemed to be saying. *Don't kill your second one.*

My face flushed hotly. I wanted to tell him to go fuck himself. But not my future father-in-law, not on the day of my wedding.

I replied, as warmly as I could, 'Don't you worry about it, Hal. I will.'

*

129

'I've got a client, Mol,' I said later as we drank vodka and tonics at the kitchen table. 'A normal, totally sane guy –'

'What was he doing at Putnam & Stearns?' She took a sip from the icy glass. 'Excellent. Lot of lime, the way I like it.'

I chuckled. 'So this client, who seems totally on the level, asked me if I believe in the *possibility* of extrasensory perception.'

'ESP.'

'So this client insisted he can, in a way, pick up on the thoughts of others. Sort of "read" them.'

'Okay, Ben. What's your point?'

'So, he tried it on me, and I'm convinced. I guess, what I want to know is, do you accept the possibility?'

'No. Yes. How the hell do I know? What are you getting at?'

'You ever hear of such a thing?'

'Sure. On *The Twilight Zone*, I think there might have been some episode like that. A kid in a Stephen King book, too. But listen, Ben – I – we need to talk.'

'All right,' I said warily.

'A guy accosted me at the hospital today.'

'What guy?'

' "What guy?" ' she echoed sardonically. 'You know damned well what guy.'

'Molly, what are you talking about?'

'This afternoon. At the hospital. He said you told him where to find me.'

I put down my drink. 'What?'

'You didn't talk to him?'

'I promise you, I have no idea what this is all about. Someone "accosted" you?'

'Not "accosted," I don't mean that. There was this guy, you know, a guy sitting outside the NICU, in the waiting area, and I guess he'd sent in word for someone to get me. I didn't recognize him. He had that sort of official look – the gray suit and the blue tie and all that.'

'Who was he?'

'Well, that's the thing. I don't know.'

'You don't –'

'Listen,' she said sharply. '*Listen* to me. He asked if I was Martha Sinclair, the daughter of Harrison Sinclair. I said yes, who was he? but he asked if he could talk to me for a couple of minutes, and I said all right.'

She looked at me, her eyes red-rimmed and bloodshot, and continued. 'He said he'd just talked to you, that he was a friend of my father's. I assumed that meant he was an Agency employee, since he sort of had that look, and he wanted to talk to me for a couple of minutes, and I said okay.'

'What'd he want?'

'He asked if I knew anything about an account my father had opened before his death. Something about an access code or something. I didn't know what the hell he was talking about.'

'*What?*'

'He didn't talk to you, did he?' she said, failing to suppress a sob. 'Ben, it's a lie, it has to be.'

'You didn't get his *name*?'

'I was in a state of shock! I could barely talk.'

'What did he look like?'

'Tall. Very light skin, almost an albino. Light blond hair. Strong-looking, but somehow, I don't know, feminine. Epicene. He said he was doing security work for the Central Intelligence Agency,' she said in a small, thin voice. 'He said they were investigating – what he called Dad's "alleged embezzlement," and he wanted to know whether my father had left me any papers, gave me any information. Left any *access codes*. Anything.'

'You told him they have their heads up their collective asses, didn't you?'

'I told him there was some horrible mistake, you know, what kind of proof did they have, all that. And the guy just said something like, I'll be in touch again, but in the meantime, think very hard about anything your father might have told you. And then he said –'

Her voice cracked, and she covered her eyes with one cupped hand.

'Go on, Molly.'

'He said the embezzlement was, in all likelihood, connected to my father's murder. He knew about the photo of –'
She closed her eyes.

'Go ahead.'

'He said there was a lot of pressure from the Agency to make these allegations public, release them to the news media, and I said, but they couldn't do that, it was a lie, you'd ruin his reputation. And he said, We'd hate to do that, Ms Sinclair. All we want, he said, is your cooperation.'

'Oh, my God,' I moaned.

'Does this have anything to do with the Corporation, Ben? With whatever you're doing for Alex Truslow?'

'Yes,' I said. 'Yes, I think it does.'

17

Early the next morning – and it had to have been early, because Molly had not yet gotten up to go to work – I opened my eyes, looked around the room as I habitually do, and saw from the digital clock-radio that it was not even six o'clock.

Molly was asleep next to me, curled into the fetal position, her hands clasped to her chest. I like looking at her asleep: I like the little-girl vulnerability and seeing her hair mussed up and her makeup off. She has the ability to sleep far more deeply than I. Sometimes I think she enjoys sleep more than sex. And indeed, she inevitably awakes in a buoyant mood, happy and refreshed, as if she'd just returned from a wonderful though brief vacation.

Whereas I awake dyspeptic, dazed, grumpy. I got out of the bed, walked across the cold wooden floor, and went to the john, hoping the noise would wake her up. But she couldn't be lured away from whatever she was dreaming. Then I approached her side of the bed, sat down on the edge of it, and leaned my head down toward hers.

I was startled to 'hear' something.

It was nothing coherent, none of the brief snatches of ordered thought that I'd been able to pick up the day before.

I heard bits and pieces of sounds almost musical, tonal, that didn't sound like any language I'd ever heard. It was as if I were dialing a radio's tuning knob in some foreign country. And then – a cluster of words that made perfect sense. *Computer*, I heard, and then something that sounded like *fox* and then, clearly a hospital dream now, *monitor*, and then, suddenly, *Ben*, and then more of the musical nonsense phrases.

And then Molly was awake. Had she felt my breath on her

face? Her eyes opened slowly, focusing on me. She jolted upright. 'What is it, Ben?' she asked urgently.

'Nothing,' I said.

'What time is it? Is it seven?'

'It's six.' I hesitated, then said: 'I want to talk.'

'I want to sleep,' she grumbled, and closed her eyes. 'Talk later.' She rolled over on her side and clutched the pillow.

I touched her shoulder. 'Mol, honey. We have to talk now.'

Eyes closed, she mumbled, 'Okay.'

I touched her shoulder again, and her eyes opened again. 'What?' She sat up slowly.

I moved over on the bed, and she made room for me.

'Molly,' I began, and then paused.

How do you say this? How do you explain something that doesn't even make sense to oneself?

'Hmm?'

'Mol, this is going to be really hard to explain. I think you're just going to have to listen. You're not going to believe me, I expect – certainly *I* wouldn't believe it – but for now, just listen. Okay?'

She regarded me suspiciously a moment. 'This has something to do with the guy at the hospital, doesn't it?'

'Please, just listen. You know this CIA man came over and asked me to submit to an MRI polygraph exam.'

'So what are you saying?'

'I think the MRI did something to me – to my brain.'

Her eyes widened, then her eyebrows went up, worried. 'What happened, Ben?'

'No, listen. This is tough. Do you believe in at least the *possibility* that some human beings possess an extrasensory perception?'

'This client you talked about last night,' she said. 'There isn't any client, is there?' She groaned. 'Oh, Ben.'

'Listen, Molly –'

'Ben, I've got some friends you can consult with. At the hospital –'

'Molly –'

'Very good, very smart people. The chief of the adult psychiatric division is an especially –'

'For Christ's sake, I haven't flipped out.'

'Then –'

'Look, you know there have been a number of studies in the last few decades that demonstrate – not conclusively, but at least persuasively if you're of an open mind – the *possibility* that some of us are able to perceive the thoughts of others.

'Look,' I went on. 'In February of 1993, a psychologist from Cornell gave a paper at the annual meeting of the American Association for the Advancement of Science. This is a matter of public record. He presented hard statistical evidence that ESP exists – that human beings actually can read the thoughts of others. His paper was accepted for publication by the most prestigious journal in psychology. And the chairman of Harvard's psychology department said he was "quite persuaded." '

She seemed to be pouting, not even looking at me any longer, but I continued, undeterred. 'Until recently I never paid any attention to that kind of stuff. The world is full of hucksters and charlatans, and I'd always dismissed *those* kind of people as naive, if not worse.'

I was rambling now, desperately trying to sound as rational and grounded and lawyerly as possible. 'Let me get to the point. The CIA, the old KGB, and a number of other intelligence agencies around the world – I think Israel's Mossad too – have historically been interested in the espionage possibilities of people who possess even a modicum of – for want of a better word – "psychic" abilities. There are well-funded programs to search out such people – this is a fact – and try to employ them for intelligence purposes. When I was with the Agency, I remember hearing rumors about a special program. And I've done a fair bit of reading about it by now.'

Molly was shaking her head slowly, though I couldn't tell whether this was in disbelief or sorrow. She touched my knee with her hand and said, 'Ben, do you think Alex Truslow is involved in this?'

'Hear me out,' I said. 'When I . . .' My voice trailed off as I thought of something.

'Hmm?'

I held a hand up to silence her. I tried to make my mind a blank, then concentrated. Surely, if she was as upset as she seemed –

Rosenberg, I heard as clearly as anything. I bit my lower lip and continued to concentrate.

have let him do this fucking Truslow work. It's got to be so hard on him to come back into contact with these spook types after giving all that up, after what happened to him, it's got to take a toll. Stan Rosenberg will make time for him today if I ask him to as a special favor . . .

I said: 'Molly, you're going to call Stan Rosenberg, right? That's the name, isn't it?'

She looked at me sadly. 'He's the new chief of psychiatry. I've mentioned him to you before, haven't I?'

'No, Molly. Never. You were thinking it.'

She nodded, and looked away.

'Molly. Humor me for a second. I want you to think of something. Think of something I can't possibly *know*.'

'Ben,' she said, a wan smile on her face.

'Think of – think of the name of your first-grade teacher. *Do it*, Molly.'

'Okay,' she said patiently. She closed her eyes, as if thinking very hard, and I cleared my mind and heard it –'

Mrs Nocito.

'It's Mrs Nocito, isn't it?'

She nodded. Then she looked up at me, exasperated, and said, 'What's the point of all this, Ben? Are you having fun?'

'Listen to me, dammit. Something happened to me in Rossi's MRI lab. It altered my brain in some way, did something. I came out of it with an ability to – how can I explain this? – to hear, or read, or *something* – listen in on the thoughts of others. Not all the time, and not all thoughts. Only things that others think in anger or fear or arousal – but I can do it. Obviously someone discovered that a very powerful magnetic resonance imaging machine can alter the brain, or at least *some* brains –'

136

Five five five oh seven two oh. When he goes in the bathroom, or when he goes downstairs, I'll call Maureen. She'll know what to do –

'Molly. Listen to me. You're going to call someone named Maureen. The phone number is 555–0720.'

She looked at me dully.

'There's no way I could know that, Molly. No way. Believe me.'

She continued looking at me, her eyes shining with tears, her mouth slightly agape. 'How did you do that?' she whispered.

Oh, thank God. Thank God. 'Molly, I want you to think of something – something I couldn't *possibly* know you're thinking. Please.'

She brought her knees up to her chest, hugged them against her, and compressed her mouth.

Trollope. I've never read Barchester Towers. I want to read that next. Next vacation . . .

'You're thinking you've never read Trollope's *Barchester Towers*,' I said very deliberately.

Molly breathed in slowly, audibly. 'Oh, no. Oh, no.'

I nodded.

'Oh, no,' she said, and I was taken aback to see her face overtaken with an expression, not of excitement, but of enormous fear. 'Oh, Ben,' she said. 'Please. No.'

She pulled at her chin in an unconscious gesture of deep reflection. She got out of bed and began pacing. 'Would you agree to see someone at the hospital?' she asked. 'Like a neurologist, someone whom we can talk this over with?'

I thought for a moment. 'No, I don't think so.'

'Why not?'

'Who's going to believe me?'

'If you do to them what you did to me – if you just *demonstrate* it – how could they *not* believe you?'

'True. But what's the point? What would we learn?'

She flailed her hands about, then brought them down to her sides. 'How this happened,' she said, her voice taking on that shrill edge of tension. 'How it could possibly have happened.'

'Molly,' I said, turning to face her as she toyed with a conch shell on the dresser. 'It happened. No one's going to tell me anything I don't know.'

She looked at me. 'How much does Alex Truslow know, do you think?'

'About me? Probably nothing. And I didn't let Rossi know – at least, I don't *think* I did –'

'Did you talk to Alex about this?'

'Not yet.'

'Why not?'

'I . . . don't know.'

'Call him now.'

'He's at Camp David.'

She looked at me quizzically.

'Meeting with the President,' I explained.

'The directorship. I see. Did you tell Bill Stearns?'

'No, of course not.'

She paused. 'Why not?'

'What do you mean, why –'

'I mean, what are you afraid of?'

'Molly, come on –'

'No, Ben, think this through for a second.' She returned to the side of the bed and sat next to me, still toying with the conch shell's pink labia. 'Truslow Associates is hired to locate a missing fortune. It's top secret work, so some guy from CIA flies down and, in the guise of fluttering you, puts you through this protocol. A superior lie detector. As they told you. So maybe it does work that way. Okay. So what makes you think they're *aware* that this same superpowerful MRI also has some sort of – well, let's call it a subsidiary effect – of rearranging the human brain, or a tiny *part* of the human brain? In such a way that people thus exposed develop the ability to listen to the brain waves of others? I mean, how do you know they *know* what it did to you, what it *could* do to a person?'

'After what you went through yesterday – the guy at the hospital – how can you think otherwise?'

'Ben,' she said in a small voice after a moment's silence.

'Hmm?'

She turned to me, close enough to kiss, her face worried. 'When we – when we made love last night. In the kitchen.'

I drew myself up straight involuntarily, guiltily. 'Uh-huh?'

'You were doing it, weren't you?'

'Doing –'

'You were reading my mind, weren't you?' The sharpness had returned to her voice.

I smiled tensely. 'What makes you –'

'Ben.'

'You and I don't need extrasensory perception,' I began with false joviality.

She pulled herself away from my embrace. 'You did, didn't you?' Now she was angry. 'You were listening in on my thoughts, on my fantasies, right?'

Before I could say yes, she spat out, 'You bastard!'

She stood up, hands on her hips, facing me squarely. 'You son of a bitch,' she said quietly. 'Don't ever do that to me again.'

18

Molly's reaction, I suppose, was understandable. There is something creepy and awful about knowing that your inner-most thoughts, which we all take for granted are inaccessible to anyone but ourselves, can be eavesdropped upon.

We'd just enjoyed the best sex we'd ever had, Molly and I, and now it must have seemed to her cheap, fraudulent. But why? Logically, this power enabled me to know something we normally can never know, what another person secretly wants, and to give it to her.

Right?

Yet one of the things that makes us intelligent, thinking beings is the ability *not* to share our thoughts with others – to decide what to disclose and what to keep a secret. And here I was, trespassing across that line. Molly seemed especially distant when we kissed good-bye an hour after that. But after what she'd just learned about me, who could blame her?

I suppose that on some level I had hoped to awake that morning and realize I had dreamed the whole thing, that I would now go back to my safe and reassuring work as a patent lawyer, go through my rounds of conferences and meetings as usual.

This may strike you as a bit odd. After all, the ability to read the thoughts of others is one of those stock fantasies or daydreams that many of us keep to ourselves. There are those on the lunatic fringe who buy books or tapes that promise to teach them extrasensory perception. At one time or another we have all wished for such a power.

But you do not want it, not really. Take my word for it.

*

As soon as I arrived at the office and chatted a bit with Darlene, I shut my office door and called my broker, John Matera, at Shearson. I'd moved a few thousand dollars from my savings account to my Shearson brokerage account. That, plus the small equity I still had in some blue chips – mostly Nynex and other utilities – would give me enough money to play with. In effect, I was gambling with the money that Bill Stearns had advanced me to stave off bankruptcy, poverty, and ruin.

But it was a sure thing, after all.

'John,' I said after a few pleasantries, 'what's Beacon Trust selling at?'

John, who is a gruff, plainspoken type, replied without pause, 'Nothing. It's free. They're giving it away to anyone who's foolish enough to express an interest. What the hell do you want that dogshit for, Ben?'

'What's the asking price?'

He gave a long, soulful sigh. There was a clicking of computer keys, and then he said, 'Eleven and a half asked, eleven bid.'

'Let's see,' I said. 'For thirty thousand dollars, that means I can get – what? –'

'An ulcer. Don't be a lunatic.'

'John, just do it.'

'I'm not allowed to give you advice,' John said. 'But why don't you think this over and call me when you've come to your senses.'

Over his vehement protestations, I put in an order for 2800 shares of Beacon Trust at up to eleven and a quarter. Ten minutes later he called to say that I was the 'proud owner' of 2800 shares of Beacon Trust at eleven, and couldn't resist adding, 'Chump.'

I smiled to myself for a few seconds, and then screwed up the courage to call Truslow. Suddenly remembering that he said he was going to Camp David, I momentarily panicked. It was imperative that I reach him, find out whether what had happened to me was *intended*, whether he knew . . .

But how to reach him?

I first called Truslow Associates, where his secretary

informed me that he was out of town and couldn't be reached. Yes, she said; she knew who I was, knew I was a friend, but even she didn't know how to get in touch with him.

Next, I called his Louisburg Square home. The phone was answered by a woman (a housekeeper, presumably) who said that Mr Truslow was out of town – 'in Washington, I believe' – and that Mrs Truslow was in New Hampshire. She gave me the New Hampshire phone number, and at last I reached Margaret Truslow. I congratulated her on Alex's selection, then told her I needed to reach him immediately.

She hesitated. 'Can't this wait, Ben?'

'It's urgent,' I said.

'What about his secretary? Is it something she can handle for you?'

'I need to talk to Alex,' I said. 'At once.'

'Ben, you know he's in Maryland, at Camp David,' she said delicately. 'I don't know how to reach him, and I have a feeling this isn't a good time to disturb him.'

'There *has* to be a way to reach him,' I insisted. 'And I think he'll want to be disturbed. If he's with the President or something, fine. But if he's not . . .'

Sounding somewhat annoyed, she agreed to call the person at the White House who had first contacted Alex, to see if her husband could be reached. She also agreed that she'd relay my request that when and if Truslow called me, he do so only over a portable scrambler.

Partners' meetings at Putnam & Stearns are as dull as partners' meetings anywhere, except perhaps on television, on *L.A. Law*. We meet once a week, on Friday mornings at ten, to discuss whatever Bill Stearns wants us to discuss, decide whatever must be decided.

In the course of this particular meeting, over coffee and very good sweet rolls from the firm's caterer, we went over a number of matters ranging from the dull (how many new associates should we hire for the upcoming year?) to the mildly sensational (should the firm agree to take on the representation of a well-known Boston underworld crime lord – no, make that *alleged* crime lord – who happened to be the brother of one of the state's most powerful politicians, and who was being charged with fraud by the state Lottery Commission?).

The answers: No on the crime lord and six on the associates. If it weren't for the sole item of business that involved me – could I make a good case to a giant food conglomerate that would impress them into hiring me in their suit against *another* food conglomerate over who stole whose formula for a fake fat – I would have been unable to keep my attention on the business at hand at all.

I was feeling unsettled and decidedly unlawyerly, as if I could burst out of my skin at a moment's notice. Bill Stearns, at the head of the coffin-shaped conference table, seemed to be giving me too many glances. Was I being paranoid? Did he *know*?

No, the real question was: How *much* did he know?

I was tempted to try to tune in on the thoughts of my fellow partners as they doodled or spoke up, but, truth to tell, it was difficult. So many of the partners were on edge, nervous, irritated, angry, that the din, the hubbub, arose as one great wall of sound, or one wall-to-wall pile rug of chatter, out of which I could barely sort one person's thoughts out from another's spoken words. Yes, I've described the qualitative difference – the difference in timbre – in the thoughts I was able to receive as compared with the normal spoken voice. But the difference is a subtle one, and when too much was going on, I simply got confused and frustrated.

Yet I couldn't *stop* receiving the random thought. So one moment I would hear Todd Richlin, the firm's financial whiz, discussing billables and receivables and deliverables and at the same time I could hear, overlaid, his frenetic, edgy thoughts – *Stearns just raised his eyebrows, what does that mean?* and *Kinney's trying to jump in and embarrass me, that asshole*. And over that would come interjections by Thorne or Quigley, something about hiring an outside consultant to train our basically illiterate associates in writing and speaking, and then *their* thoughts over that. So what I ended up with was a nightmarish babble of voices, which gradually drove me to distraction.

143

And all the while, whenever I looked toward the head of the conference table, Bill Stearns seemed to be looking at me.

Soon the meeting began to take on that accelerated rhythm that always indicates we've got less than a half hour left. Richlin and Kinney were locked in some sort of gladiatorial struggle over the course of Kinney's corporate litigation involving Viacorp, a huge entertainment concern in Boston, and I was still trying to clear my head of all the babble, when I heard Stearns adjourn the meeting, rise quickly from his seat, and stride out of the room.

I ran to catch him, but he continued a brisk pace down the hallway.

'Bill,' I called out.

He turned around to look at me, his eyes steely, and did not break his stride. He deliberately, it seemed, was keeping a good physical distance between us. The jovial Bill Stearns was gone, replaced by a man of severe, frighteningly intent demeanor. *Did he, too, know?* 'I can't talk to you now, Ben,' he said in a strange, peremptory voice I'd never heard him use before.

A few minutes after I returned to my office, a call was put through from Alexander Truslow.

'Jesus Christ, Ben, is this something important?' His voice had that odd, flat tone that a scrambler imparts.

'Yes, Alex, it is,' I said. 'Is this a sterile line?'

'It is. Glad I thought to bring the device with me.'

'I hope I didn't call you out of a meeting with the President or something.'

'Actually no. He's meeting with a couple of his Cabinet members on something to do with the German crisis, so I'm cooling my heels. What's up?'

I gave him an abbreviated account of what had happened in 'Development Research Laboratories,' and, as sparely as I could, I told him about what I was now able to do.

A long, long pause ensued. The silence felt infinite. Would he think I'd lost my mind? Would he hang up?

When he finally spoke, it was almost in a whisper. 'The Oracle Project,' he breathed.

'What?'

'My *God*. I've heard tales – but to think –'

'You *know* about this?'

'God in heaven, Ben. I knew this fellow Rossi was once involved in such an undertaking. I thought . . . Jesus, I'd heard they'd had some success, that it worked on one person, but the last I heard, Stan Turner had shot the whole project down, quite some time ago. So that's what he was really up to. I should have known there was something fishy about Rossi's story.'

'You weren't informed?'

'Informed? They told me this was a regulation flutter. You see what I meant when I told you that something's afoot. The Company's out of control. Dammit all, I don't know who the hell I can trust anymore –'

'Alex,' I said. 'I'm going to have to sever my links with your firm entirely.'

'Are you sure, Ben?' Truslow protested.

'I'm sorry. For my safety, and Molly's – and yours – I'm going to have to lay low for a while. Stay out of sight. Cut off all contacts with you or anyone else associated with CIA.'

'Ben, listen to me. I feel responsible – I'm the one who got you involved in all this in the first place. Whatever you decide to do, I'll respect your decision. Part of me wants you to press on, to see what these Agency cowboys want from you. Part of me wants to tell you to just head up to our weekend place and hide out for a while. I don't know what to tell you.'

'I don't know what the hell has happened to me. I still haven't fathomed it. I don't know if I ever will. But –'

'I have no right to tell you what to do. It's up to you. You may want to talk to Rossi, suss out what he wants from us. Perhaps he's dangerous. Perhaps he's merely overzealous. Use your judgment, Ben. That's all I can tell you.'

'All right,' I said. 'I'll think it over.'

'In the meantime, if there's anything I can do –'

'No, Alex. Nothing. Right now there's nothing anyone can do.'

As I hung up, another call came in.

'A man named Charles Rossi,' Darlene announced over the intercom.

I picked it up. 'Rossi,' I said.

'Mr Ellison, I'm going to need you to come in as soon as possible and –'

'No,' I said. 'I have no arrangement with CIA. My arrangement was with Alexander Truslow. And as of this minute, the arrangement is over.'

'Now, hold on a second –'

But I had hung up.

19

John Matera, my Shearson broker, was so excited he could barely get his words out. 'Jesus,' he said. 'Did you hear?'

We were speaking on Shearson's recorded line, so I said innocently, 'Hear what?'

'Beacon – what happened to Beacon – they're being bought out by Saxon –'

'That's terrific,' I said, feigning excitement. 'What does that mean for the stock?'

'Mean? *Mean?* It's already up *thirty* fucking points, Ben. You've – you've like *tripled* your money, and the day's not even over yet. You've already raked in over sixty thousand dollars, which ain't half bad for a couple hours' work. Christ, if you could've bought call options –'

'Sell it, John.'

'What the *fuck* – ?'

'Just sell, John. Now.'

For some reason I didn't feel elated. Instead, I felt a dull, acid wave of fear wash over my insides. Everything else I'd been through in the last few hours I could on some level dismiss as my imagination, as some sort of terrible delusion. But I had read a human being's mind, had thereby learned inside information, and here was the concrete evidence of it.

Not just for me, but for anyone else who might be watching me. I knew there was a serious risk that the SEC would be suspicious of such a quick turnover; but I needed the cash, and I let it get the better of my good sense.

I gave him quick instructions on what to do with the proceeds, which account to place it in, and then I hung up. And called Edmund Moore in Washington.

*

The phone rang, and rang, and rang – there was no answering machine; Ed Moore had always considered such contraptions gauche – and when I was about to hang up, it was answered by a male voice.

'Yes?'

The voice of a young man, not Ed's. The voice of someone in a position of authority.

'Ed Moore, please,' I said.

A pause. 'Who's calling?'

'A friend.'

'Name, please.'

'None of your business. Let me speak to Elena.'

In the background I could hear a woman's voice, high and keening, her cries rising and falling rhythmically. 'Who is it?' the woman's voice called out.

'She's unable to come to the phone, sir. I'm sorry.'

In the background the cries became louder, then became words: 'Oh, my Lord!' and 'My baby. My baby' and a loud, anguished gasping.

'What the hell is going on?' I demanded.

The man covered the phone, consulted with someone, and then came back on the line. 'Mr Moore has passed away. His wife discovered him just a few minutes ago. It was a suicide. I'm sorry. That's all I can say.'

I was stunned, almost speechless.

Ed Moore . . . a *suicide*? My dear friend and mentor, that diminutive, feisty, and, above all, enormous-hearted old man. I was too dazed, too shocked, even to shed the tears for him I knew I would.

It couldn't be.

A suicide? He had talked about vague threats against him; he had feared for his life. Surely it was no suicide. Yet he *had* seemed so disoriented, even unbalanced, when we spoke.

Edmund Moore was dead.

It was no suicide.

I called Mass. General and had Molly paged. I trusted her

148

good sense, her sound advice, and I needed it now more than ever.

I was deeply scared. There's a macho tendency among new clandestine-officer recruits to belittle and mock fear, as if it somehow demeans your competence, your virility. But the experienced field men know that fear can be your greatest ally. You must always listen to, and trust, your instincts.

And my instincts now told me that this sudden talent had put both Molly and me in great danger.

After a long wait the page operator got on and said, in a cigarette-husky voice, 'I'm sorry, sir, there's no answer. Would you like me to connect you to the neonatal intensive-care unit?'

'Yes, please.'

The woman who answered at the NICU had a slight Hispanic accent. 'No, Mr Ellison, I'm sorry, she's already left.'

'Left?'

'Gone home. About ten minutes ago.'

'*What?*'

'She had to leave suddenly. She said it was an emergency, something about you. I assumed you knew.'

I hung up and hurried toward the elevator, my heart racing.

Rain was coming down in sheets, gusted by winds of almost gale force. The sky was gunmetal gray, streaked with yellow. People walked by in yellow slickers and khaki raincoats, their black umbrellas turned inside out by the howling wind.

By the time I mounted the steps to my town house, drenched during the short walk from the taxi to the front door, it was twilight, and all of the lights in the house seemed to be off. Strange.

I hurried into the outside foyer. Why would she have gone home? She was scheduled to spend the night in the hospital.

The first peculiar thing I noticed was that the alarm was off. Did that mean she was in the house? Molly had left after I did that morning, and she was always scrupulous – even a little

149

obsessive – about turning the alarm on, though there was little if anything for anyone to steal.

When I unlocked the front door, I noticed the second peculiar thing: Molly's briefcase was there, in the foyer, the briefcase she took with her wherever she went.

She must be home.

I switched on a few lights and quietly climbed the stairs to our bedroom. It was dark, and there was no Molly. I climbed another flight of stairs to the room she uses as her study, though at that point it was in a dismaying state of renovation.

Nothing.

I called out: 'Mol?'

No reply.

The adrenaline began to course through my bloodstream, and I made a series of mental calculations.

If she wasn't here, could she be on the way? And if so, who or what had caused her to come home? And why hadn't she tried to call me?

'Molly?' I called out a little louder.

Silence.

I descended the staircase rapidly, my heart thudding, switching on lights as I moved.

No. Not in the sitting room. Not in the kitchen.

'Molly?' I said loudly.

Complete, utter silence in the house.

And then I jumped as the telephone rang.

I leapt to pick it up, and said, 'Molly.'

It wasn't Molly. The voice was male, unfamiliar.

'Mr Ellison?' An accent, but from where?

'Yes?'

'We must talk. It is urgent.'

'*What the fuck have you done with her?*' I exploded. '*What the –*'

'Please, Mr Ellison. Not over the telephone. Not in your house.'

I breathed in slowly, trying to slow my heartbeat. 'Who is this?'

'Outside. We must meet right now. It is a matter of safety for both of you. For all of us.'

'Where the hell –' I tried to say.

'Everything will be explained,' came the voice again. 'We will talk –'

'No,' I said. 'Right now I want to know –'

'*Listen*,' the accented voice hissed through the receiver. 'There is a taxi at the end of your block. Your wife is in it right now, waiting for you. You must go left, down the block –'

But I did not wait for him to finish. Throwing the handset to the floor, I whirled around and ran toward the front door.

20

The street was dark, quiet, slick with rain. A slight drizzle fell, almost a mist.

There it was, at the end of the block, a yellow cab, a few hundred yards off. Why at the *end* of the block? Why *there*? I wondered.

And as I set off, running, accelerating, I could make out, in the taxi's backseat, the silhouette of a woman's head, the long tangle of dark hair, unmoving.

Was it in fact Molly?

I couldn't be sure at this distance, but it might – it *had* to – be. Why, I thought wildly, my legs pumping, was she there? What had happened?

But something felt wrong. Instinctually, I slowed to a fast walk, my head whipping to either side.

What was it?

Something. One too many strollers on the street at this time of night, in the rain. Walking too casually. People normally stride through rain to get *out* of it . . .

But was I being paranoid?

These were normal passersby, certainly.

For just an instant, a split second really, I caught a glimpse of one of the pedestrians. Tall, gaunt, wearing a black or navy blue raincoat, a dark knit watchcap.

He appeared to glance at me. Our eyes locked for a millisecond.

His face was extraordinarily pale, as if it had been bleached entirely of color. His lips were thin and as pale as the rest of his face. Under his eyes were deep yellowish circles that extended to his cheekbones. His hair, or what I could see of it beneath his cap, was a pale strawlike blond, swept back.

And just as quickly, he glanced away, casually.

Almost an albino, Molly had said. The man who had 'accosted' her at the hospital, who had wanted to know about any accounts, any money Harrison Sinclair might have bequeathed to her.

The whole thing seemed wrong. The call, Molly sitting in the cab: it *smelled* wrong, and my years of Agency training had taught me to smell things a certain way, to see patterns, and –

– and something caught my eye, a tiny flash of something, a glint of something – metal? – in the light of the lamp across the narrow street.

I heard it then, a faint *shoosh* of cloth against cloth, or cloth against leather, a familiar sound distinct against all the ambient street noises, a *holster*, could it be?

I flung myself to the pavement, just as a deep male voice shouted: '*Get down!*'

Suddenly the silence was shattered by a frightful cacophony.

The next moment was a terror, a hellish confusion of explosions and screams – the *phut-phut* of silencer-equipped semi-automatic pistols, the metallic shrieks of bullets creasing the hoods of the cars in front of me. From somewhere came a squeal of brakes, and then an explosion of glass. A window had been blown out somewhere – a stray shot?

I got up into a crouch, trying to determine where the gunfire was coming from. I moved with lightning speed, my brain whizzing through a million calculations.

Where was it coming from?

Couldn't tell. Across the street? Off to the left? Yes, to the left, from the direction – the direction of the cab!

A dark figure was running toward me, another shout, which I couldn't understand, and then, as I flung myself to the pavement again, another explosion of gunfire. This time the shots were perilously close. I felt a piece of something sting my cheek, my forehead, felt the pain of the sidewalk scraping against my jaw. Something pricked my thigh. And then the windshield of the car I was crouching behind exploded into a milky webbing.

I was trapped; my unknown assailants had moved in closer, and I was unarmed. Frantically, I dove under the car, and then came another round of silenced shots, an agonized yelp, and the squeal of tires . . .

and silence.

Absolute silence.

The shooting had momentarily ceased. From under the car's chassis I could just make out a circle of light directly across the street. In it sprawled a man's body, dark-clad, his face turned away, the back of his head a horrifying mess of blood and tissue.

Was it the pale man I had glimpsed a few seconds earlier?

No, I saw at once. The dead man's build was stockier, shorter.

In the silence my ears still rang from the shots and the explosions. For a moment I lay there, afraid to move, terrified that the slightest motion would indicate my position.

And then I heard my name.

'Ben!' A voice, somehow familiar.

The voice was closer now. It came from the window of an approaching vehicle.

'Ben, are you all right?'

Momentarily I was unable to reply.

'Oh, Christ,' I heard the voice say. 'Oh, God, I hope he wasn't hit.'

'Here,' I managed to say. 'I'm right here.'

21

A few minutes later I was sitting in the back of a bulletproof white van, dazed.

Seated in the front compartment, behind the uniformed driver and separated from me by a panel of thick glass, was Charles Rossi. The interior of the van was elegantly appointed: a small inset television screen, a coffeemaker, even a fax machine.

'I'm glad you're all right,' came Rossi's amplified voice, metallically emanating from a two-way intercom. The glass that divided us appeared to be soundproof. 'We need to talk.'

'What the hell was that all about?'

'Mr Ellison,' he said wearily. 'Your life is in danger. This isn't some sort of game.'

Oddly, I felt no anger. Was I numb from what I'd just gone through? From the shock of Molly's disappearance? What I felt, instead, was a distant, remote sense of indignation, an awareness that all was not right . . . Yet, strangely, no anger.

'Where's Molly?' I said dully.

Over the intercom Rossi sighed. 'She's quite safe. We want you to know that.'

'You have her,' I said.

'Yes,' Rossi replied as if from afar. 'We have her.'

'What have you done with her?'

'You'll see her soon,' Rossi said. 'I promise you that. You'll understand we did what we did for her safety. I promise you.'

His voice was soothing, reasonable, and plausible. 'She's safe,' Rossi continued. 'You'll see her soon enough. We're protecting her. You'll be able to speak with her in a few hours, and you'll see.'

'Then who tried to kill me?'

'We don't know.'

'You don't know too much, do you?'

'Whether it was one of our own, or others, we can't say yet.'

One of our own. Meaning CIA? Or others within the government? So how much did they know about me?

I reached over to the door handle and pulled up to open it, but it was locked from the inside.

'Don't try,' Rossi said. 'Please. You're far too valuable to us. I don't want you to get hurt.'

The van was moving now. I didn't know where, didn't quite understand. But I knew one thing now.

I said, 'I was hit.'

'Hmm? You appear to be fine, Ben.'

'No. I was hit.'

I reached down, felt the soreness on my upper thigh. I unbuckled my belt, slid down my pants. Found the needle mark, a tiny black dot surrounded by a red circular inflammation. I hadn't seen a dart; it wasn't a hypodermic needle. 'How'd you do it?' I asked.

'Do what?'

We were moving down Storrow Drive, into a traffic lane that pointed toward the expressways.

Ketamine, I thought.

Rossi's voice came, metallically: 'Hmm?'

I must have spoken aloud, but made an effort to keep my thoughts to myself.

Had they given me a benzodiazepine compound? No. It felt like ketamine hydrochloride. 'Special K,' as it was called on the streets, an animal tranquilizer.

The Agency occasionally had the need to administer ketamine to unwilling subjects. It produces something called 'dissociative anesthesia,' which basically means it makes you feel dissociated from your environment – you can *experience* pain, for instance, but not *feel* it; it separates the meaning from the sensation.

Or, at precisely the right dosage, you can remain alert but become amazingly agreeable, acquiescent, even though the self-preservation part of your brain warns you not to acquiesce.

If you want to make someone do something he otherwise wouldn't, it is the perfect drug.

I looked at the road, watched as we moved closer to the airport. Wondered idly what they were about to do to me.

Thought it couldn't be so bad, after all.

Nothing too bad.

Part of me, a distant, weak, small-voiced part, wanted to get the van door open, leap out, run.

But everything is basically all right, the stronger, closer, louder-voiced part reassured.

I am being tested in some way. Tested by Charles Rossi. That is all.

There is nothing they could learn from me, nothing of any value. If they were going to kill me, they would have done it long ago.

But such thoughts of danger are foolish. Paranoid. Unnecessary.

Everything is basically all right.

I could hear Rossi speaking to me calmly from hundreds of miles away.

'If I were in your position, given what's happened to you, I'd no doubt feel the same way. You think nobody knows – you don't quite believe it yourself. Sometimes you're elated at what you're suddenly able to do; sometimes you're scared out of your mind.'

'I don't have the vaguest idea what you're referring to,' I said, but my words came out flat and unconvincing, as if by rote.

'It would be much simpler, much better for all of us, if we cooperated instead of being antagonistic.'

I said nothing.

A moment of silence, and then he spoke. 'We're in a position to protect you. Somehow there are others who are aware of your participation in the experiment.'

'Experiment?' I said. 'You're referring to your MRI "polygraph" device?'

'We knew there was a one in a thousand – at best, one in one hundred – chance that the MRI would have the desired effect on you. Certainly we had good reason to believe, given the full medical evaluation in your Agency file, that you had all the necessary attributes – the IQ, the psychological profile, and particularly the eidetic memory. Precisely the right profile. Obviously we couldn't be certain, but there was significant cause for optimism.'

I absently traced a pattern on the burgundy-leather-upholstered seat.

'You weren't careful enough, you know,' he said. 'Even someone with your training, your skills, can be sloppy.'

All my alarms were ringing now. I could feel the skin on the back of my neck prickle unpleasantly. Yet my lazy, serene mind seemed utterly separate from my bodily instincts, and I felt myself nodding slowly.

He said, '. . . won't be at all surprised that your office and home telephones were tapped – all quite legally, by the way, given your possible involvement in the First Commonwealth debacle. Electronic devices were placed in several rooms of your house as well – we left very little to chance.'

I just shook my head slowly.

'Needless to say, we were able to monitor everything you said aloud – and you were somewhat indiscreet, both in your meeting the other day with Mel Kornstein and certainly in your conversations with your wife. I don't mean to be at all critical, because you had no reason whatever to suspect that anything was amiss. There was no reason to resort to your Agency tradecraft training, after all.'

I lowered my head to increase the blood supply to the brain, but that only made me dizzier. My head was swimming, and the headlights of the passing cars seemed far too bright, and my limbs felt heavy.

He said, his voice tinged with concern, 'It's a good thing too. If we hadn't had you under such close surveillance, we might not have picked you up in time.'

I stifled a yawn, tensing the tendons in my neck. 'Alex,' I started to say.

He said, 'I'm sorry we had to do this. You'll understand. It was a matter of protecting you from yourself. You'll understand when the ketamine wears off that we had to do this. We're on your side. We certainly don't want to see anything happen to you. We simply need you to cooperate with us. Once you listen to us, I think you'll cooperate. We can't make you do anything you don't want to do.'

'I guess good legal help . . . scarce,' I mumbled.

'You represent a great hope to some very good people.'

'Rossi . . .' I said. My speech was slurred; my mouth and tongue seemed lazy. 'You were . . . the project director . . . the CIA psychic project . . . Oracle Project . . . your name . . .'

'You're very, very valuable to us,' Rossi said. 'I don't want anything to happen to you.'

I said, 'Why . . . you sitting up there . . . what do you have to hide?'

'Compartmentalization,' he said. 'You know the golden rule in the intelligence business. With your ability, it would be dangerous for you to know too much. You'd be a threat to all of us. Better to keep you as ignorant as possible.'

We had pulled up now before some unmarked terminal at Logan Airport.

'In just a few minutes there's a military aircraft departing for Andrews Air Force Base. Soon, you'll want to sleep, and you should.'

'Why . . .' I began, but somehow I couldn't finish my sentence.

Rossi replied, a beat later, 'Everything will be explained soon. Everything.'

22

The last thing I remembered was talking with Charles Rossi in the van, and then I found myself groggily awake in some sort of barren airplane cabin that looked very much like a military plane. I became aware that I was strapped down horizontally, to a seat or a stretcher or something.

If Rossi was on the flight, I couldn't see him anywhere, certainly not from this angle. Seated nearby were men in some sort of military uniform. Guarding me? Did they think I planned to escape at ten thousand feet? Didn't they realize I was unarmed?

The ketamine that had been injected into me on the street must have been extremely potent, because even now I was unable to think clearly. Nevertheless, I tried.

Destination was Andrews Air Force Base. Likely, I was headed for CIA headquarters. No. That would make no sense. Rossi knew I had the ability to read thoughts, and so the *last* place he'd want to bring me was Langley. He seemed to know what I *couldn't* do – couldn't perceive brain waves through glass, or at a distance of more than a few feet – which told me that he had been through this extraordinary thing before.

But was the ability still in effect? I had no idea now. How short-lived was it? Perhaps it had faded as quickly as it had come.

I shifted in my seat, pulled against the restraints, and noticed my guards turn their heads, tense.

Had that been Molly in the cab or not? Rossi had said they had her, safe and sound. But a *cab*? And parked down the street? It had to have been a decoy, someone who looked very much like Molly placed in the cab in order to lure me down the block. But had Rossi's people done it? Or the unnamed, unspecified 'others'?

And who were these others?

I managed to croak out, 'Hey!'

One of the guards rose, came near me (but not, I noticed, *too* near). 'What can I do for you?' he asked pleasantly. He was in his early twenties, crew cut, tall, and massively built.

I turned my head toward him, looked him directly in the face. 'I'm sick,' I said.

He furrowed his brow. 'My instructions –'

'I'm going to vomit,' I said. 'The drugs. I just want to let you know that. Do whatever the fuck you're instructed to do.'

He looked around. One of the other guards frowned and shook his head.

'Sorry,' he said. 'Can I get you a glass of water or something?'

I moaned. 'Water? Jesus. What's that going to do? There has to be a john around here.'

The guard turned back to the other one, whispered something to him. The other was gesticulating with what seemed to be indecision. Then the first one turned toward me and said, 'Sorry, buddy. The best I can do is offer you a pan.'

I shrugged, or tried to, bound as I was by the restraints. 'Have it your way,' I said.

He went to the front of the cabin and returned shortly with what looked like an aluminum bedpan, which he placed alongside my head.

I did my best to simulate the sounds of nausea, coughed and retched as he held the pan next to my mouth, his head no more than a foot and a half away, a look of deepest distaste curling his mouth.

'Hope they're paying you well for this,' I said.

He didn't reply.

I did my best to focus my muddled, ketamine-befogged brain.

. . . *not hit him* . . . I heard.

I smiled, knowing what that was all about.

I coughed again.

Then: *what for . . .*

And, a few seconds later: . . . *what he did it's Company business never tell us probably some espionage conviction doesn't look like the type looks like a goddamned lawyer.*

'Guess you're not so sick after all,' the guard said, pulling the pan away after a few seconds.

'What a relief,' I said. 'But don't move that thing too far away.'

I knew, number one, that it was still working; and, number two, that there was nothing I could learn from this guy, who had been kept deliberately ignorant of who I was and where I was going.

In a short while I drifted back to a dreamless sleep.

The next time I awoke I was seated in the back of still another vehicle, this one a standard-issue government Chrysler. My limbs ached.

The driver was a tall, late-thirtyish man with a salt-and-pepper crew cut, wearing a dark blue parka.

We were entering a particularly rural section of Virginia now, somewhere outside of Reston, leaving behind the International Houses of Pancakes and the Osco Drugstores and the hundreds of little shopping malls for wooded, twisty two-lane roads. At first I wondered whether we were headed for Langley by some circuitous route, then I saw we were headed in another direction entirely.

This was safe-house country – the part of Virginia where the CIA maintains a number of private homes used for Agency business: meeting with agents, debriefing defectors, and such. Sometimes they're apartments in large anonymous suburban buildings, but far more often they're unremarkable split-level ranches with cheap furniture rented by the month, one-way mirrors in garish frames, vodka in the freezer, and vermouth in the refrigerator.

Ten minutes later we pulled up to a set of ornamental wrought-iron gates set into a wrought-iron fence over fifteen feet high. The gate and fence were spiked and looked high-security. Probably electrified. Then the gates swung open electrically, permitting us to enter a long, dark wooded expanse that suddenly ended after a few hundred yards, giving way to a long, circular drive in front of a large brick Georgian house that in the evening darkness seemed almost foreboding. One room on the third floor was lit up, a few on the second floor, and a large room on the first floor whose curtains were drawn. The outside entrance was lit up as well. I wondered what it cost the Agency to rent this impressive residence, and for how long.

'Well, sir,' the driver said. 'Here we are.' He spoke with the soft twang you hear in so many government employees who have emigrated to Washington from the Virginia environs.

'Right,' I said. 'Thanks for the lift.'

He nodded quite seriously. 'Best of luck, sir.'

I got out of the car and walked slowly across the gravel drive and the flagstone entranceway, and as I approached the front door, it swung open.

Part Three

THE SAFE HOUSE

The Wall Street Journal

The CIA in Crisis

President Reportedly Close to Naming New CIA Head

Some Wonder Whether a New Broom Can Really Sweep Clean

Is Spy Agency Out of Control?

BY MICHAEL HALPERN

STAFF REPORTER OF THE WALL STREET JOURNAL

Amid ugly rumors swirling in Washington of vast illegal activity within the Central Intelligence Agency, the President is said to be close to naming a new director.

The latest speculation centers on a career Agency officer, Alexander Truslow, who is generally well regarded by Congress and the intelligence community.

But many observers are concerned that Mr Truslow faces the difficult, even insurmountable, challenge of attempting to rein in a CIA that is widely believed to be out of control.

23

I should not have been at all surprised to see the man in the wheelchair, regarding me calmly as I entered the vast, ornate sitting room. James Tobias Thompson III had aged terribly since I'd last seen him, the incident that had ended my Agency career, but, far more tragically, had ended a wonderful woman's life and paralyzed a man from the waist down.

'Good evening, Ben,' Toby said.

His voice, a low rasp, was just barely audible. He was a trim man in his late sixties, wearing a conservatively cut blue serge suit. His shoes – which rarely if ever touched the ground – were black brogues, polished to a high shine. His full head of hair, worn a little long for a man of his age, especially an Agency veteran, was pure white. In Paris, when I had last seen him, it was jet black with dabs of gray at the temples. His eyes were hazel; he looked both dignified and dispirited.

Toby's wheelchair rested against an immense stone fireplace, in which, oddly, a great artificial fire blazed. Oddly, I say, because the room in which I stood, which must have been some fifty feet across and a hundred feet long, with a ceiling almost twenty feet high, was airconditioned to an uncomfortably cold temperature. For some reason I remembered that Richard Nixon liked crackling fires in the air-conditioned Oval Office in the middle of the summer.

'Toby,' I said, approaching him slowly to shake his hand. But instead, he gestured to a chair that was a good thirty feet away from him.

Seated in a wing chair to one side of the fireplace was Charles Rossi. Not far away, on a small damask-upholstered sofa, were two young men in the cheap navy suits I always associated with the Agency's security types. Almost certainly they were carrying weapons.

'Thanks for coming,' Toby said.

'Oh, don't thank me,' I said, masking my bitterness. 'Thank Mr Rossi's people. Or the Agency chemists.'

'I'm sorry,' Toby said. 'Knowing you and your temperament, I didn't think we could bring you in any other way.'

'You were quite clear,' Rossi interposed, 'that you were unwilling to cooperate.'

'Well done,' I said. 'That drug really saps the will. Do you plan to keep me on a drip to ensure compliance?'

'I think once you've heard us out fully, you'll be more cooperative. If you decide not to cooperate, there's nothing we can do about it. A caged animal makes a poor field agent.'

'Then go ahead,' I said.

The straight-back chair in which I sat seemed to have been placed especially for me in such a way that I could see and speak to Rossi and Thompson. Yet it was, I noticed, at a great distance from all of them.

'The Agency found you folks a nice safe house this time,' I said.

'It's actually owned by an Agency retiree,' Toby said, smiling. 'How've you been?'

'I'm fine, Toby. You look well.'

'As well as can be expected.'

'I'm sorry we've never had a chance to talk,' I said.

He shrugged and smiled again as if I'd made a flippant, foolish suggestion. 'Agency rules,' he said. 'Not mine. I wish we had too.'

Rossi was watching me silently. I continued: 'I can't tell you how sorry –'

'Ben,' Toby interrupted. 'Please don't. I've never blamed you. These things happen. What happened to me was lousy, but what happened to *you*, to Laura . . .'

We fell silent for a moment. I listened to the hiss of the deep orange gas flames as they licked the ceramic pine cones.

'Molly,' I began.

Toby put up a hand to silence me. 'She's fine,' he said. 'Fortunately – thanks to Charles – you are too.'

'I think I'm owed a little explanation,' I said mildly.

'You are, Ben,' Toby agreed. 'I'm sure you understand that this conversation isn't taking place. There is no record of your flight to Washington, and the Boston police have already buried a report of random gunfire on Marlborough Street.'

I nodded.

'I apologize for placing you at such a distance from us,' he resumed. 'You understand the need for the precautions.'

'Not if you have nothing to hide,' I said.

Across the room, Rossi smiled to himself and said, 'This is a highly unusual situation, one we didn't entirely plan on. As I've explained, keeping you out of physical proximity is the only way I know of to ensure the sort of need-to-know compartmentalization this operation requires.'

'What operation is that?' I asked quietly.

I heard a low mechanical whir as Toby adjusted his chair to face me squarely. Then he spoke, slowly, as if with great difficulty.

'Alex Truslow brought you in to do a job. I wish Charles hadn't engaged in the trickery he did. He'll be the first to admit, he's no den mother.'

Rossi smiled.

'It's an ends-and-means game, Ben,' Toby said. 'We're after the same end as Alex; we're simply employing a different means. But let's not lose sight of the fact that this is one of the most exciting and important developments in the history of the world. I think that once you hear us out, you'll choose to go along with us. If you choose not to, that's fine.'

'Go ahead,' I said.

'We selected you some time ago as our most likely subject. Everything about your profile seemed right, the photographic memory, the intelligence, and so on.'

'So you *knew* what would happen,' I said.

'No,' Rossi said. 'We'd failed time and time again.'

'Hold on a second,' I said. 'Hold on. How much exactly do you know?'

'Quite a bit,' Toby said calmly. 'You now have the ability to receive what's called ELF – the extremely low frequency radio waves that the human brain generates. Do you mind if I smoke?' He took out a pack of Rothmans – I remembered now that Rothmans were the only brand he smoked when we knew each other in Paris – and tapped it against the arm of the wheelchair until one slid out.

'If I did mind,' I replied, 'I doubt the smoke would bother me at this distance.'

He shrugged, and lighted the cigarette. Exhaling luxuriantly through his nostrils, he continued. 'We know this . . . talent, for want of a better word, has not abated since it emerged. We know you're sensitive only to thoughts that are occasioned at moments of strong feeling. Not yours, but those of whomever you're trying to "hear." This gibes rather neatly with Dr Rossi's long-standing theory that the intensity of thought waves, or ELF, would be proportional to the intensity of one's emotional reaction. That emotion varies the strength of the electrical impulses discharged.' He paused to inhale again and then said huskily, through the exhaled smoke, 'Am I in the ballpark?'

I only smiled in reply.

'Of course, Ben, we'd be much more interested to hear your experiences than to listen to ourselves gas on like this.'

'What led you to think of using the magnetic resonance imager?'

'Ah,' Toby said. 'For that I turn to my colleague Charles. As you may or may not know, Ben, for the last few years I've been on the DDO staff at home.' He meant that he was serving in the Deputy Directorate of Operations – the covert-action boys, to oversimplify – at the CIA's Langley headquarters. 'My area of responsibility is what they call special projects.'

'Well, then,' I said, feeling an odd sense of vertigo. 'Perhaps one of you gentlemen can explain what this . . . project, as you seem to be calling it, is all about.'

Toby Thompson exhaled with a finality, and stubbed his cigarette out in a crystal ashtray on the carved oak end table next to him. He watched the plume of blue smoke rise and curl in the air, then turned back toward me.

170

'What we're talking about,' he said, 'is a matter of the highest security classification.' He paused. 'And it is, as you can imagine, a long and rather complex story.'

24

'The Central Intelligence Agency,' Toby said, his eyes fixed on some middle distance, 'has long had an interest in . . . shall we say . . . the more *exotic* techniques of espionage and counterespionage. And I don't just mean that wonderful invention, the Bulgarian umbrella, whose tip injects deadly ricin.

'I don't know how much of this you know from your Agency days –'

'Not much,' I said.

Toby looked at me sharply, as if surprised to be interrupted. 'And our team, of course, observed you at the Boston Public Library doing research, so you must know at least something of what's in the public record. But the real story is far more interesting.

'You have to keep one major thing in mind: the reason most government undertakings are cloaked in deepest secrecy is *fear of ridicule*. It's as simple as that. And in a society like ours, a country like the United States, which prides itself on hard-headed pragmatism . . . well, I think the founders of the CIA recognized that the greatest risk to their existence came not from public outrage but public derision.'

I smiled appreciatively and nodded. Toby and I had been good friends, before the incident, and I had always enjoyed his dry sense of humor.

'So,' he continued, 'only a handful of the most senior officers, historically, have ever known of the Agency's work in this area. I wanted to make sure we were very clear on that.' He looked directly at me, then tilted back his head slightly. 'Experiments in parapsychology, as you no doubt already know, go back to at least the 1920s at Harvard and Duke – serious experiments undertaken by serious scholars, but of course never taken seriously by the scientific community at large.' He gave a wry smile and added, 'Such is the structure of scientific revolutions. Of course the world is flat; how could it be otherwise?

'The first groundbreaking work was done by a man named Joseph Banks Rhine at Duke in the late twenties and early thirties. I'm sure you've seen the Zener cards.'

'Hmm?' I murmured.

'You know, those famous ESP cards of five symbols, the square, triangles, circles, wavy lines, and straight lines. In any case, Rhine and his successors learned that some people have the talent – very few people, as it turns out – and in varying degrees. The vast majority, of course, do not. Or, as some scholars postulated, more have the *potential* to develop the talent than they realize, but our conscious mind blocks it out.

'Anyway, a number of laboratories in the decades since the 1930s engaged in research into parapsychology in its many forms, not just extrasensory perception. There was Dr Rhine's Foundation for Research on the Nature of Man, of course, but there was also the William C. Menninger Dream Laboratory at Maimonides Medical Center in Brooklyn, which did some interesting work in dream telepathy. Certain of these labs were funded by the National Institute of Mental Health – fronting for the Central Intelligence Agency.'

'But the CIA wasn't founded until – what? – 1949,' I said.

'Well, we came to this belatedly. As early as 1952, according to Agency archives, there was serious interest expressed in the *possibilities* of this research. Mostly this meant locating individuals with psychic abilities. But the early Agency officials seemed far more concerned with cloaking the work –'

'For fear of ridicule,' I interrupted. 'But how the hell did the CIA deal with these psychics? I mean, either the psychics were for real or they weren't. And if they were for real, they'd *know* they were meeting with people from an intelligence agency.'

Toby smiled, slowly and lopsidedly. 'True enough. It was a

real problem, from what I've read. They employed a double-blind security system, using two middlemen. But as I said, we came to this belatedly. Spurred on, naturally, by the Soviets.'

Rossi cleared his throat and remarked, 'The Cold War had its uses.'

'Indeed,' Toby resumed. 'Going back to at least the 1960s, the Agency began hearing credible reports of Soviet military efforts in parapsychology. I think it was around that time that a small cell of senior Agency people decided to fund an in-house study of the espionage possibilities of ESP. But what a treacherous undertaking! For every person who may have some glimmering of the ability, there are hundreds of hucksters and nutty old ladies with crystals. In any case, you may remember hearing about the Apollo 14 flight to the moon, in 1971, when the astronaut Edgar Mitchell performed the first ESP experiment in space. Didn't work, by the way. In those years – the early years, I think of them as – we and the Armed Forces Medical Laboratories and NASA were spending almost a million dollars a year on parapsychology research. Peanuts, yes, but then we were whistling in the dark anyway.

'Then came a series of classified reports, in the early 1970s, from the Defense Intelligence Agency, predicting that we would soon be endangered by Soviet psychic research, which was enabling the KGB and the GRU and the Soviet Army to do such neat tricks as ascertain the deployment of troops, ships, even military installations. Someone at the top of the Agency got serious about it. I don't suppose I'm spilling any secrets to tell you that Richard Nixon took a very strong interest in the program.

'Our intelligence confirmed by the mid-seventies that the Soviets had several secret parapsychological laboratories for military purposes, the main one in Novosibirsk. Then, in 1977, a reporter for the *Los Angeles Times* was arrested by the KGB in Moscow while attempting to obtain top secret documents from an institute of parapsychology. This really spurred the CIA, since now both sides knew that the other knew . . .

'Anyway, within the Agency, the program was so top secret

174

that the term ESP never appeared anywhere, in any documents. It was called "novel biological information transfer systems"! A few years later, after my . . . accident . . . I was brought in to head the project, to accelerate it – or scrap it. "Shit or get off the pot," I was instructed.'

I nodded. 'And you decided to shit.'

'In a manner of speaking. Certainly I was as much of a skeptic as anyone has ever been. I was quite hostile to all this foolishness, and I thought I was being given some make-work, time-wasting rehabilitation crap, the sort of thing they give a washed-up operations expert whose legs don't work anymore.

'But then' – here he waved his hands in Rossi's direction – 'then one day I met Dr Charles Rossi, and I learned about something that I knew at once would change the world.'

'Can we get you anything?' Toby asked just as my curiosity was piqued. 'You like Scotch, don't you?'

'Why not?' I said. 'It's been a long day.'

'Certainly has. And the ketamine appears to have worn off, so booze should be okay. Wally, Scotches all around – no, Charles, you like vodka, isn't that right?'

'On the rocks,' Rossi said. 'A touch of pepper ground over it, if you please.'

One of the security people got to his feet – he was, I now saw, definitely wearing a shoulder holster – and ambled out of the room. A few minutes later, during which we all sat in silence for some reason, he returned with a tray of drinks. Obviously he was not trained in the art of butlery, but he managed to serve each of us without spilling a drop.

'So tell me this,' I said. 'Why am I not able to scan you?'

'At this distance –' Rossi said.

'No. I wasn't even able to scan your security guy here, just now, when he gave me my drink. Nothing comes across. What's going on?'

Toby watched me for a moment, thinking. The strong light made hollows of his eyes. 'Jamming,' he finally said.

'I don't understand.'

'ELF. Extremely low frequency radio waves.' He swept a

175

hand around the room. 'The RF equivalent of inaudible white noise is being emitted from speakers set up throughout the room, broadcast on the same frequencies that the human brain in effect "broadcasts" on. This makes it impossible for you to pick anything up.'

'So you won't mind if we sit a little closer.'

Toby smiled. 'We don't like taking chances.'

I nodded, decided to drop it. 'All this CIA work on ESP – I thought it was terminated by Stan Turner in 1977.'

'Officially, yes,' Rossi said. 'In fact, it was simply buried in the bureaucracy under deep cover, so that hardly any personnel within the Agency knew of its existence.'

Then Toby continued his narrative. 'Until then, our efforts had concentrated on how to locate those few talented individuals. They're few and far between. The question soon became, how can you actually *instill* the power? Is it possible? It seemed far-fetched, seemed in fact absolutely impossible. Charles . . . well, Charles can tell you himself.'

Rossi shifted in his chair, took a deep breath, and exhaled slowly. 'In the early 1980s,' he said, 'I was working with a small California firm, developing something the Pentagon found most interesting. It was, in simple terms, an electronic paranoia inducer – a "psychic neuron disrupter," they called it, which would "jam" the synaptic connections between the brain's nerve cells. In effect, this would do electronically what the drug LSD often does. Nasty stuff, really, but then, the Pentagon are the folks who brought us napalm, courtesy of Dow Chemical. Anyway, this project thankfully went nowhere, but then one day I got a call from Toby, who offered me double my salary and lured me from the sunny climes of Southern California to this lovely metropolis. I continued my work on the effects of electromagnetic stimuli on the human brain. Initially, we were intrigued by the notion of mind control. I was concentrating on ELF, extremely low frequency radio waves, as Toby said. You see, the brain generates electrical signals. So I was attempting to learn whether we could transmit strong signals *in the same frequencies* that the brain transmits in, to induce confusion, even death.'

'Charming,' I said.

But Rossi ignored me. 'Nothing there either. But we had discovered the possibilities of ELF. I came upon research done by Dr Milan Ryzl of the University of Prague involving hypnosis. Dr Ryzl had discovered that certain people can, under hypnosis, relax themselves, relax their inhibitions, to such an extent that they can receive images by telepathy. That set me thinking.

'And it turned out, quite by coincidence, that in 1983, in a hospital in the Netherlands, a middle-aged Dutchman underwent a routine examination in a magnetic resonance imager and emerged with a measurable, documented extrasensory perception. His doctors were aghast. The man and his doctors were immediately visited by agents of Dutch, French, and American intelligence, who all confirmed the report. *The man had the ability actually to hear the thoughts of others in close proximity*. Neurologists attributed this to the intense magnetizing effect of the MRI on the man's cortex.'

'Did the power last?' I asked.

'Not exactly,' Rossi replied. 'The man went mad, actually. He began to complain of terrible headaches, of awful noises, and one day he literally ran his head into a brick wall and killed himself.' He took a long sip of vodka.

'Then why didn't the MRI work like this on everyone?' I asked.

'Exactly what I wondered about,' Rossi said. 'The MRI has been in use around the world since 1982, and this was the first report of such an astonishing occurrence. Upon scrutiny of this Dutch gentleman, the Dutch-French-American joint team concluded that this man possessed certain characteristics that must have been prerequisites. For one thing, he was extremely bright, with an IQ, according to the Stanford-Binet test, of over 170. For another, he had an eidetic memory.'

I nodded once.

'There were other markers. The man had a highly developed verbal skill, but an equally developed mathematical and quantitative ability. I flew over to Amsterdam, and managed to meet with this Dutchman before he went off the deep end. When I returned to Langley, I attempted to reproduce this bizarre effect.

'We recruited males and females who seemed to have all the right markers, the intelligence, the memory, the verbal and quantitative abilities, et cetera. And, without revealing the exact nature of the experiment, we subjected them to the most powerful MRI we could locate. This particular model was manufactured by Siemens A.G., of Germany. We had it modified. But no success – until you.'

'Why?' I asked, draining my Scotch and placing the empty glass on the adjacent table.

'We don't know,' Rossi said matter-of-factly. 'If only we did, but we don't. Certainly you had the right markers. The intelligence, obviously, but also the verbal skills, the eidetic memory, which is found in fewer than 0.1 percent of the population at large. You play chess, don't you, Ben?'

'Not too badly.'

'Quite well, in fact. And you're a whiz at such things as crossword puzzles. I believe you even indulged in Zen meditation at one time.'

'I "indulged" in it, yes,' I said.

'We studied the records of your training at Camp Peary very closely,' Toby Thompson put in. 'You were eminently suitable – but of course, we had no idea that you'd be a success.'

'You seem strangely uninterested in a demonstration of my abilities,' I said, addressing them both.

'Quite the contrary,' Rossi said. 'We're quite interested. *Extremely* interested, in fact. With your permission, we'd like to put you through a number of tests tomorrow morning. Nothing too arduous.'

'That hardly seems necessary,' I replied. 'I'd be glad to give you a demonstration right now.'

There was a moment of uncomfortable silence, then Toby chuckled. 'We can wait.'

'You seem to know a good deal about this condition. Perhaps you can tell me how long it's going to last.'

Rossi paused again. 'That we don't know either. Long enough, I hope.'

'Long *enough*?' I said. 'Long enough for what?'

'Ben,' Toby said softly, 'we've brought you here for a reason, as you've guessed. We need to run you through a series of tests. And then we need your help.'

'My help,' I said, not bothering to conceal my hostility. 'What sort of "help" are you talking about?'

A long beat of silence in the cavernous room, and at last Toby spoke. 'Spy stuff, I guess you'd call it.'

I sat there, unmoving, for what seemed like five minutes, as the men watched me. 'I'm sorry, gentlemen,' I said, standing. I turned slowly toward the door and began walking.

The two security guards rose, and one of them strode to the doorway, blocking my path, while the other took up a position behind me.

'Ben!' Toby called out.

'Really, Ben,' Rossi said almost simultaneously.

'Please sit down,' I heard Toby say calmly. 'Now, I'm afraid, you don't have much of a choice.'

25

One of the things I learned in my Agency days was when to persist and when to quit. I was outnumbered – not just by the two guards, but by whoever else they had in the house, and I knew there had to be others. I'd calculated the odds of an escape, and they were against me ten thousand to one, a hundred thousand to one.

'You're putting us in a difficult position,' Toby said to my back.

I turned around slowly. 'So much for caged animals.'

He was looking at me with just the slightest trace of anxiety. 'We – I – do *not* want to resort to compulsion. We'd much rather appeal to reason, to duty, to the basic decency I know you have.'

'And to my desire to see my wife again,' I said.

'There's that, yes,' he admitted. Nervously, he closed his fingers into a loose fist and then opened them, closed and opened.

'And, of course, you've already told me quite a bit,' I said. 'I "know too much," right? Isn't that the expression? So I have the absolute right to walk out of here, but I probably wouldn't make it to the gate.'

Exasperated, Toby said: 'You're being ridiculous. After what we've told you, why in the world would we want to do anything to harm you? If for no other reason than scientific –'

'Did the Agency arrange the freezing of my money too?' I asked bitterly. I felt the muscles in my legs tense, begin to cramp. My stomach was queasy; beads of perspiration sprang to my brow. 'That fucking First Commonwealth thing?'

'Ben,' Toby said after a long silence. 'We'd much rather

180

keep things positive, appeal to reason. I think once you hear us out, we can come to some agreement.'

'All right,' I said at last. 'That much I'm willing to do. Let's hear it.'

'It's late, Ben,' Toby said. 'You're tired. More to the point, I'm tired, but then, I tire easily. In the morning, before you're brought to Langley for tests, we'll all talk again. Charles?'

Rossi murmured his assent, gave me a quick, penetrating glance, and left the room.

'Well, Ben,' Toby said when we were alone. 'I believe the housekeeping staff has put out everything you'll need tonight, a change of clothes, toiletries, and whatnot.' He smiled gently. 'A toothbrush.'

'No, Toby. You've forgotten one detail. I want to see Molly.'

'I can't let you see her yet, Ben,' Toby said. 'It's just not physically possible.'

'Then I'm afraid we're not going to come to any sort of agreement.'

'She's not in the area.'

'Then I want to speak to her on the phone. *Now.*'

Toby assessed me for a moment, and then gave another hand signal to the security men. One of them left the room and returned with a black touch-tone telephone, which he plugged into a jack near me, placing the phone on the adjacent end table.

Then the guard lifted the handset and punched a long series of numbers. I counted: eleven digits, which may have meant long distance, and then another set of three. An access code, probably. Then two more digits. The guard listened impassively for a moment and then said, 'Ninety-three.' He listened again, and handed the phone to me.

Before I could say anything, I heard Molly's voice, high-pitched, anguished.

'Ben? Oh, God, is it you?'

'I'm here, Molly,' I said as reassuringly as I could.

'Oh, God, are you all right?'

'I'm – I'm fine, Molly. Are you – ?'

'Okay. I'm okay. Where did they take you?'

'A safe house somewhere in Virginia,' I said, watching Toby. He nodded, as if in confirmation. 'Where the hell are you?'

'I don't know, Ben. Something – a hotel or an apartment, I think. Outside Boston, not too far.'

I felt my anger rise once again. Addressing Toby, I said, 'Where is she?'

Toby paused. 'Protective custody in the Boston suburbs.'

'*Ben!*' Molly's voice came out of the receiver urgently. 'Just tell me these people are –'

'It's okay, Mol. As far as I know. I'll know more tomorrow.'

'It's all connected,' she whispered, 'connected with that – with that –'

'They know,' I said.

'Please, Ben. Whatever the hell is going on, why am *I* involved? They can't *do* this! Is this legal? Can they –'

'Ben,' Toby said. 'I'm afraid we're going to have to disconnect the call now.'

'I love you, Mol,' I said. 'Don't worry about it.'

'Don't *worry* about it?' she said incredulously.

'Everything will be under control soon,' I said without believing it.

'I love you, Ben.'

'I know,' I said, and then I heard a dial tone.

I put down the handset. 'You had no business scaring Molly this way,' I said to Toby.

'It was for her protection, Ben.'

'I see. The way I'm being protected.'

'That's right,' he said, ignoring my sarcasm.

'Maximum security,' I persisted. 'We're as safe as any two prisoners can be.'

'Come on, Ben. Tomorrow, after we've talked, you'll be free to walk out.'

'And now? What about now?'

'Tomorrow,' he replied. 'Tomorrow, hear us out. If you want to leave then, I promise you, I won't stand in your way.'

With an electric hum he guided his wheelchair across the

long expanse of Persian carpet toward the door. 'Good night, Ben. They'll show you to your room.'

It was at that point that an idea occurred to me and, thus preoccupied, I followed the two guards out to the main staircase.

26

The room they had provided for me was large and comfortable, furnished in the style of a Vermont country inn, spare and elegant. Against one wall was a plump, king-size bed draped in a white chenille spread. After this long, exhausting day, it looked supremely inviting, but I couldn't sleep yet. There was a dark walnut armoire and matching end tables; I noticed after brief inspection that they were immobile, somehow bolted down. The adjoining bathroom was spacious and elegant as well: green Italian marble floor, the walls tiled in white and black porcelain, the fixtures of 1930s vintage.

The floor, which creaked reassuringly as I walked, was covered in pale wall-to-wall carpeting. A few paintings had been placed, tastefully, here and there: oil paintings of nautical aspects, done in a nondescript style. Those, too, were fastened to the wall. It was as if they were expecting a violent animal who might at any moment decide to fling objects around the room.

A set of heavy floor-length drapes, striped in broad bands of maroon and gold, concealed a set of windows, finely leaded. I saw at once that the windows were reinforced with a fine, almost invisible, metallic webbing, which no doubt made them at once shatterproof and electronically alarmed.

I was a prisoner.

This particular room in this 'safe house,' I decided, was probably used to keep intelligence defectors or other agents with whom they couldn't be too careful. That category obviously included me.

For all intents and purposes, I was a hostage, despite Toby's gilded rhetoric. They had caught me here, like an exotic laboratory specimen, to be run through a set of extensive tests and then pressed into service.

But everything about this setup smacked of improvisation. Usually, when an operation is preplanned, every angle is covered, every detail thought through, sometimes ridiculously so. Often, of course, things still go wrong – SHIT HAPPENS, as the bumper sticker says – but not for want of planning. But I sensed that arrangements here had been hasty, ad hoc, jury-rigged, and that gave me hope.

They held Molly captive, but I would be able to negotiate her release much more readily if I were free. I had to move at once.

Even then, as I changed out of my ripped, soiled suit (a casualty of the shootout on Marlborough Street) I knew that Molly was going to be all right. It was quite possible that they were indeed protecting her – in addition to which, of course, they wanted to keep her separated from me as a means of suasion. You know, tie the girl up to the railroad tracks so that you'll change your mind, right? Well, there wouldn't be any express train coming, and the worst that would happen from this was that Molly would have subjected her captors to a severe tongue-lashing. I knew how the Agency liked to apply pressure.

As for *me*, however – well, that was another story. Ever since I had acquired this extraordinary talent, my life was in danger of one sort or another. And now I had the simple choice of cooperating, or . . .

Or what?

Hadn't Toby spoken the truth – why would they want to take out the only living, successful subject of their top secret project? Wouldn't it be like killing the goose that laid the golden eggs?

Or would the need for secrecy take precedence over everything else?

Perhaps, though . . . perhaps I could take matters into my own hands.

For I had an unquestionable advantage over other human beings, at least as long as it lasted, and it showed no signs of diminishing. And – this was what told me that my incarceration was hastily, even sloppily, arranged – I had been able to acquire some useful information from one of my guards.

Toby, or whoever was running this operation, had taken the precaution of requisitioning guards who were absolutely uninformed about me, or about the project itself. But naturally, they had to be fully briefed about the details of their *own* security operations.

As one of the guards – Chet, his name was – took me upstairs to the third-floor bedroom in which I was to be kept, I walked beside him, as close as I could. He had evidently been ordered not to engage me in discussion, and to keep a good distance from me.

But he had *not* been instructed not to *think*, and thinking is one of the few human activities over which we have no control.

'I'm concerned,' I said to him as we mounted the first staircase. 'How many of there are you?'

'I'm sorry, sir,' Chet said with a brusque dip of his head. 'I'm really not permitted to speak with you, sir.'

I raised my voice in mock anger. 'But how the hell do I know I'm *safe*? How many of you are going to protect me? Can't you at least tell me that?'

'I'm sorry, sir. Please step back.'

By the time he had ushered me into my bedroom, I had learned that there would be two stationed in front of my room throughout the night, that Chet was on the first shift, that he was glad of it, and that he was insatiably curious to know who I was and what I had done.

I spent the first hour or so carefully inspecting the room, looking for the transmitting devices (they had to be there, but I couldn't locate them) and such. Beside the bed was a clock-radio, which was a likely candidate for a bug.

But the radio was a mistake.

At about half past one in the morning I knocked on my bedroom door to summon the guard. The door opened after a few moments to reveal Chet. 'Yes?'

'Sorry to bother you,' I said. 'It's just that my throat is

parched, and I wonder whether you can get me a glass of seltzer.'

'There should be a little refrigerator in there,' he said tentatively, but he was tense, his body as tightly coiled as a clock spring, his hands at his sides, as he'd been taught.

I smiled sheepishly. 'All gone.'

He looked annoyed. 'It'll be a few minutes,' he said, then closed the door. I expected that he would call downstairs on the walkie-talkie, since he had been given instructions under no circumstances to leave his post.

About five minutes or so later there was a soft knock on the door.

By now I had the clock-radio on full blast, an AM rap station, raucous and rhythmic. And the shower was running, filling the bathroom with steam. The bathroom door was open, and steam billowed into the bedroom.

'I'm in the shower,' I yelled. 'Just put it anywhere, thanks.'

A different uniformed guard entered, bearing a tray, on it a bottle of French mineral water – nice touch, I thought – and looked around the room appraisingly for a few seconds, trying to decide where to put it down, and that was when I lunged.

He was a professional, well trained, but so was I, and that two or three seconds that I had on him was just enough to take him by surprise. I tackled him to the floor, the tray and water tumbling noiselessly onto the carpet. He recovered with impressive speed and reared up, knocking me aside momentarily, his left arm smashing into my jaw, a painful, wounding blow.

That old glacial calm came over me.

The radio blasted on and on, stridently: 'DOWN she gotta go DOWN now I really gotta . . .' and the white noise of the shower drummed and above this racket very little could be heard, of course, and –

The tray was a terrific weapon, and with my right hand I swept it off the floor and chopped it *back* toward him, toward his throat, toward the vulnerable cartilaginous area that shielded his jugular, and with great force *smashed* the wooden tray's narrow edge into his adam's apple, winding him, and he

187

groaned as his legs scissored upward to pin me, and I heard, suddenly – . . . *can't . . . shoot . . . mustn't shoot . . . fucker . . .*

And I knew I had him, I knew what he *wouldn't* do. This was his real vulnerability, the reason he wasn't reaching for his gun, and just as his fists formed themselves into cudgels, I managed to get my arms into a locked wedge, crashing into his abdomen, toppling him backward against the massive oak arm of the stolid overstuffed armchair, the back of his head cracking audibly against the wood, and with a *whoof* the air came out of his lungs, and he suddenly slackened, his mouth open, and slid to the floor.

Unconscious. He was hurt, but not badly. He would be out for ten, maybe twenty minutes.

And over it all the radio voice was ranting, ranting.

I had, I knew, maybe a few seconds before the back-up guard entered, suspicious about the delay.

The unconscious guard had a gun in his shoulder holster, an excellent Ruger P90 .9mm semiautomatic, which I had trained on though rarely had occasion to fire in action. I pulled it out, inserted the spare cartridge, released the gun's safety, and –

Looming over me was another guard, not Chet, but another one, on the early morning shift, and his gun was pointed at me.

'Drop it,' he commanded.

We faced each other, both frozen.

'Easy,' he said. 'No one's going to get hurt if you drop it. Lower it slowly to the floor, let go, then –'

I had no choice.

I stared at him blankly and pulled the trigger.

Aimed to hurt him only, not to do any serious harm.

A sudden sharp explosion, a flash of light, that acrid smell. He'd been hit, I saw at once, in the thigh, and he did what came naturally: he dove down. He wasn't a trained killer; that much I had read earlier, and the information was priceless.

Now I stood over him, the Ruger pointed at his head.

The look in his eyes was a combination of great pain, from

the gunshot, and enormous fear. I heard a great anguished rush of words –

no God no God no he'll do it please God

– and said very quietly, 'If you move, I'm going to have to kill you. I'm sorry.'

His eyes widened still farther, and his lower lip trembled involuntarily. I disarmed him and pocketed his weapon.

I said, 'You stay there quietly. Count to one hundred. If you move before then – if you make one fucking noise – I'll come after you.' And, stepping out of the room, I shut the door, heard it lock automatically, and I was out in the darkened corridor.

27

Crouching down now, I crept along the oak-wainscoted walls of the hallway and quickly surveyed the situation.

At one end of the hall glowed a light that seemed to be coming from an open door. Perhaps there was someone there. Just as likely there was no one. The room was, I surmised, used by the guards while awaiting the change in shift, where they had their coffee.

I thought: would there be anything in the room I might need?

No. Unlikely, and not worth the risk.

I continued along the edge of the hall, away from the light.

Suddenly I heard a static crackle, loud and metallic. It was coming from a walkie-talkie that the second guard had left in the hallway when he entered my bedroom. A signal, requesting confirmation. I didn't know the codes, couldn't fake it. Not worth trying.

That meant I had maybe a minute or so before someone would come from elsewhere in the house to investigate why nobody was answering his query.

Darkness everywhere, a long series of closed doors. I knew only as much of the layout of the palatial house as I'd managed to garner while they brought me up.

I was walking *away* from the main staircase now. The main staircase had to be dangerous territory, far too central; but I was convinced there would be a back stairway, for servants.

And there was.

Unlit and narrow, the treads wooden and worn, the servants' stairs were located at the end of this wing of the house. I descended, walking as lightly as I could, but still the creaks echoed in the stairwell.

By the time I reached the second floor, there were footsteps above. Running footsteps, then shouted voices. They had discovered my escape much more quickly than I'd hoped they would.

They knew I was in the house still, somewhere, and I had no doubt that all entrances were guarded; all had now been put on alert, and I was trapped.

Looking first up, then down, I knew I couldn't make it all the way to the first floor.

But what was on the second?

No choice; I had to take a chance. I sprinted out of the dark stairwell and into the second-floor corridor, but this one was not carpeted as the hallway upstairs had been, and my footsteps rang out with an alarming clatter. The voices were growing louder, nearer.

The only light came from the moon outside, shining meekly into a window at the end of the corridor, and I spun around, dashed toward the window, poised to pull it open and *jump*, dammit all, before I realized that the window overlooked not soft, spongy lawn but asphalt.

An asphalt, or macadam, car-park area depressed into the ground, a good twenty-five feet below me, a suicidal plunge. Nothing to break my fall. I couldn't do it.

Then came the alarm, the shrilling of hundreds of bells, deafening, throughout the house, coming from all over, and now all the lights were *on*, a brilliant halogen blaze illuminating the hall, illuminating everything, flashing on and off and on, and the ringing kept on.

For God's sake, *move*! I shouted inwardly.

Move, yes, but where?

Running desperately along the hall, away from the window, toward the main central staircase, I tried door after door, and then, four, five, six doors later, one *opened*.

A bathroom, small and dark, its window opened a crack, and through the crack came a cool draft. The vinyl shower curtain rustled and fluttered in the breeze, and that was it, of course.

I tore the shower curtain off its hooks, and it fell to the floor.

The alarm's ringing seemed even louder now, insistent. There was a crash somewhere, the slam of a door, shouts.

Now what?

Break the box!

Only a goddamned shower curtain. If only I'd thought to take a bedsheet!

Tie it to something, I thought wildly. Tie it. Hook it somewhere. Something stable.

But there was nothing! Nothing to hold the length of vinyl, to anchor me as I climbed out of the window, and there was certainly no time to mess around, because the footsteps were thundering closer, closer. They *had* to have followed me to the second floor, and as I looked around desperately, my heart thudding crazily, I heard, not twenty feet away in the hall, 'On the right! Move it!'

Raising the window all the way, I found a screen, cursed aloud, and clawed at it, at the goddamned release pins at the base, but it was frozen in place, wouldn't move, and I backed up and *dove* –

And hurled through the window, through the screen, and into the night air, my body contorted awkwardly, trying to break my fall.

And crashed to the ground – dirt, not sod, but cold, hard earth, which rose up to meet me and crack against my shoulders and the back of my neck, and I sprung immediately to my feet, somehow twisting my ankle a bit, bellowing out in pain.

Trees ahead of me, a small copse of trees, just barely visible in the darkness, but now illuminated by the flashing alarm lights mounted into the third-floor eaves, now dark, now light.

An explosion of gunfire.

Behind me, to my left, then a whiz of something awfully close, the sting of something against my ear, and I dove down. The gunshots kept up, erratic, close, and I scuttled along the grass and into the trees, thank God. A natural cover, protection. Just feet away a tree trunk splintered, then another one, and I put on one last agonizing burst of speed, running through the dizzying pain in my ankle and my shoulders, and I was at the fence.

Electrified, yes?

A fifteen-foot fence, solid black wrought iron, burglar-proof, high security . . . high tension? Was it possible?

I could scarcely turn around now, couldn't turn back, couldn't stop, I had a few seconds' lead time on them, that was all, but now I heard them coming into the yard, in my direction, many of them, it seemed, and the gunshots were back now, they had located me, but their aim was off; the trees blocked their line of sight.

I inhaled a deep breath and took the measure of the situation. The house is surrounded by nature, set in the rolling Virginia woods, which means trees and animals, squirrels and chipmunks that skitter here and there, up and down fences, and –

I threw myself toward the fence, grasping a horizontal section as a handhold, and climbed up, toward the spiked top, up, and, hesitating a mere split second, which seemed an eternity, grabbed the ominous black spears atop the fence –

And felt the cool, hard iron.

No. Not electrified. Squirrels and chipmunks would wreak havoc on an electrified fence, wouldn't they? You wouldn't do it. I spun my legs around carefully, just grazing the sharpened spikes, and *over*, and dropped to the moist spongy grass below, and I was out.

Behind me the mansion was flashing, the lights pulsing, the clamor shattering the night's stillness.

I ran, hearing shouts and running footsteps behind me, but they were on the other side of the fence, and I knew I had them.

I ran, and ran, wincing, probably moaning aloud, but keeping my stride, until the road bent, and I was at a junction that I had noticed as we arrived, and as I dashed up the dark, narrow road, I saw a pair of headlights coming toward me.

The car was moving along at a good clip, not too fast, not too slow, a Honda Accord. I saw it as it approached, and I considered waving it down, but I couldn't be sure.

It had come from the main highway, but I had to be careful, and as I slowed down, its headlights suddenly went bright, blindingly so, and then another set of headlights came up behind me, high beams, and suddenly I was *caught* between the two vehicles, the Honda facing me, and behind me, another car, larger, American-make.

I spun, but the cars had hemmed me in, and then two others came out of the darkness, brakes squealing, pulling up alongside the other.

I was blinded by four sets of headlights, and I spun around again, tried to figure a way of escape, but knew there wasn't one, and then I heard a voice coming from one of the cars.

Echoing in the night. 'Nice try, Ben,' came Toby's voice. 'You're as good as ever. Please, get in.'

I was surrounded by men and guns pointed at me, and slowly I lowered the Ruger.

Toby was seated in the back of a van, one of the last vehicles to arrive. He was speaking through the window. 'Terribly sorry,' he said calmly. 'But nice try all the same.'

28

They drove me in a plain government car, a dark blue Chrysler sedan, to Crystal City, Virginia. We entered an anonymous looking office building with an underground parking garage. I knew the CIA owned several buildings in Crystal City and its environs; this was certainly one of them.

I was escorted by the driver into an elevator and up to the seventh floor, through a plain governmental-looking corridor painted bureaucrat tan. ROOM 706 was painted in a black curve on frosted glass. Inside, a receptionist greeted me and showed me to an inside office, where I was introduced to a bearded, fortyish, Indian neurologist named Dr Sanjay Mehta.

You will no doubt wonder whether I attempted to read the thoughts of my driver, the people I passed in the corridor, the neurologist, and so on; and the answer, of course, is yes. My driver was another Agency employee, as uninformed as my last driver. I learned nothing there. The most I learned, walking down the hallway, was that I was indeed in a CIA building where work was being done on scientific and technical matters.

With Dr Mehta, things were different. As I shook his hand I heard, *Can you hear my thoughts?*

I hesitated for a moment, but I had decided not to play coy, and I responded aloud, 'Yes, I can.'

He gestured to a chair, and thought: *Can you hear everyone's thoughts?*

'No,' I told him. 'Only those who . . .'

Only those of a particular salience – such as those accompanied by powerful emotions, is that right? I heard.

195

I smiled, and nodded.

I heard a phrase of something, in a language I didn't know, which I assumed was Hindi.

For the first time, he spoke. 'You don't speak Hindi, Mr Ellison, do you?' His English was British-accented.

'No, I don't.'

'I am fully bilingual, which means that I can think in Hindi or in English. What you're telling me, then, is that you don't *understand* my thoughts when they're in Hindi. You *hear* them. Is that right?'

'Right.'

'But not *all* of my thoughts, of course,' he continued. 'I have thought a number of things in the last two minutes, in Hindi and in English. Perhaps hundreds of "thoughts," if one can so categorize the flow of the processing of ideas. But you were able to hear only those that I thought with great force.'

'I suppose that's right.'

'Can you sit there for a moment, please?'

I nodded again.

He got up from his desk and left the room, closing the door behind him.

I sat for a few moments, inspecting his collection of plastic souvenir paperweights, the kind that produce a snowfall if shaken, and soon I was picking up another thought. This time it was the timbre of a woman's voice, high and anguished.

They killed my husband, it went. *Killed Jack. Oh, God. They killed Jack.*

A minute later, Dr Mehta returned.

'Well?' he said.

'I heard it,' I said.

'Heard what?'

'A woman, thinking that her husband had been killed,' I replied helpfully. 'The husband's name is Jack.'

Dr Mehta exhaled audibly, nodding slowly. After a long silence he said, 'Well?'

'Well what?'

'You didn't "hear" anything just then, did you?' He gave the word "hear" the same spin I'd been mentally giving it myself.

'Just silence,' I said.

'Ah. But previously, it was a woman; you're right. That's quite interesting. I would have thought you'd pick up only that someone was in distress. But you don't perceive feelings; you actually seem to *hear* things, correct?'

'That's right.'

'Can you tell me exactly what you heard?'

I repeated it for him.

'Just so,' he said. 'Excellent. Can you distinguish between what you hear and what you "hear"?'

'The – I guess the timbre is different, the feel of the voice,' I attempted to explain. 'It's like the difference between a whispered and a spoken phrase. Or . . . or the way you can remember a conversation sometimes, inflections and intonations and all. I perceive a spoken voice, but it's much different from the audible voice.'

'Interesting,' he said. He rose, picked up a snowball paperweight of Niagara Falls from his desk, and toyed with it as he paced in a small area behind his desk. 'But you didn't hear the first voice.'

'I wasn't aware there was another one.'

'There was another one, a man, on the other side of this wall, but he was instructed to think placidly, if you will. The second one was a woman, in the same room, who was instructed to conjure up a horrifying thought and think it with a certain intensity. The room is soundproof, incidentally. The third attempt, which you say you also didn't hear, came from the woman, but this time she was a hundred yards or so down the hall, in another room.'

'You said she was "conjuring it up," ' I said. 'Meaning that her husband wasn't really killed.'

'That's right.'

'Which means that I was unable to distinguish between her genuine thoughts and her simulated ones?'

'You might say that,' Mehta agreed. 'Interesting, isn't it?'

'That's an understatement,' I replied.

For the next hour or so he ran me through a battery of tests, designed to ascertain how sensitive my 'gift' was, how strong

197

the emotions accompanying the thoughts had to be, how close the person had to be, and so on.

At the end he ventured an explanation.

'As you have already speculated,' Dr Mehta said, 'the magnetizing effect of the MRI on your brain produced this peculiar result.' He lighted a Camel straight. His ashtray was a tacky souvenir from a place called Wall Drug in South Dakota.

He exhaled a cloud of smoke, which seemed to enable him to think deeply. 'I don't know much about you, just that you're some kind of lawyer, and that you used to be with the Agency. I'd rather not know more than that anyway. As for me, I'm the chief of CIA's psychiatric division.'

'Psych tests, debriefings, and all that?'

'Basically. I'm sure my staff ran tests on you before they sent you to the Farm, before sending you wherever they sent you, and at the end of your term of duty. Your file's been pulled, so I couldn't know anything more about you than I do even if I wanted. Which I don't.' Another cloud of smoke, and then he continued: 'But if you expect me to enlighten you about your ability to read minds, I'm sorry to disappoint you. When Toby Thompson came to me a few years back, I thought he'd taken leave of his senses.'

I smiled.

'I frankly am not one of those who believed in human extrasensory perception. Not that there's anything inherently ludicrous about it. There's quite a body of evidence to suggest that certain animal species possess the ability to communicate that way, whether you're talking about dolphins or dogs. But I've never seen any evidence beyond highly unreliable anecdotal reports that suggest that we humans can do it.'

'I assume you've changed your mind now,' I said.

He laughed. 'Thoughts take place throughout the human brain, in the hippocampus and the frontal-lobe cortex and the neocortex. A colleague of mine, Robert Galambos, has theorized that thinking is "done" by the glial cells, not the neurons. You've heard about Broca's brain?'

I told him I'd only heard the term, but didn't know what it meant.

'The French surgeon Pierre-Paul Broca discovered an area of the human brain where language is produced, an area in the left frontal lobe. Broca's area is the seat of the speech mechanism. Another place, known as Wernicke's area, is where we recognize and process speech. That's in the left temporal and parietal lobes. I'm postulating that when one of these two areas, probably Wernicke's, is subtly altered somewhat by the powerful magnetism of the magnetic resonance imager, the neurons realigned. And that enables you to "hear" output, low frequency radio waves, from others' Broca areas. We've long known that the human brain puts out these electrical signals. What you're doing, I suspect, is simply *receiving* those signals. You know how sometimes we can "hear" ourselves think, as if in our own spoken voice?'

'Yes, sometimes.'

'Well, I'd theorize that at some point in the formation of such thoughts there's concurrent activity in the speech centers. And it's at that point that the electrical signals are generated. All right. So. Then two recent scientific findings set us to thinking, as it were.

'One was a study published in *Science* magazine two years or so ago, done by a team at Johns Hopkins that discovered they could actually produce a computer image of the *thinking* process of the brain. They hooked up electrodes to a monkey's brain, and used computer graphics to track the electrical activity in the motor cortex – that area of the brain that controls motor activity. So that in the instant before a rhesus monkey performed an action, they could see on the computer screen, a thousandth of a second in advance, the electrical activity in the monkey's brain. Amazing! We could actually see the brain thinking!

'And then, a couple of geobiologists at the California Institute of Technology discovered that the human brain contains something like seven billion microscopic magnetic crystals. In effect, bar magnets made of magnetite crystals, an iron mineral. They were wondering whether there was a link between cancer and electromagnetic fields, though there's no evidence yet that the magnetic crystals have anything to do with cancer. But my colleagues and I thought: what if we could use the magnetic resonance imager to somehow alter those little magnets in the human brain – to align them? Now, you're a patent attorney, so I assume you keep up with technological developments.'

'As a rule, yes.'

'Early in 1993, a stunning breakthrough was announced, almost simultaneously, by the Japanese computer giant Fujitsu, the Nippon Telegraph and Telephone Corporation, and Graz University of Technology in Austria. Using various techniques of biocybernetics, the collection of the electrical impulses put out by the brain by means of electroencephalography, human beings could actually control specially configured computers simply by *thinking* a command! By using their minds they could move a cursor around on a computer screen, even type letters. Well, that was it. At that point we knew it was possible.'

'So why can't you induce this in everyone?'

'That's the sixty-four-dollar question,' he said. 'It may have to do with the way your Wernicke's area is situated. Perhaps with the number, or density, of the neuronal cells there. Whatever it is about you that gives you an eidetic memory. To be honest, I have no idea. This is only sheerest speculation. But for whatever reason, for whatever confluence of reasons, it happened to you. Which makes you quite valuable indeed.'

'Valuable,' I said, 'to whom?' But he had already turned and left the room.

29

'I'm really quite satisfied,' Toby Thompson said, and indeed, he was visibly pleased with himself.

I sat in an antiseptic, brightly lit white interrogation room, watching Toby in an adjoining room through a large, thick pane of glass. The glass was smudged with fingerprints, and the room was so bright that it was easy to forget it was eight in the morning and I'd been up all night. The room was situated in an underground level of the same unlovely 1960s-vintage office building.

'Tell me something,' I said. 'Why the glass barrier? Why aren't you jamming the room with ELF like you did at the safe house?'

Toby smiled almost wistfully. 'Oh, we are. Better not to take chances. I don't much trust technology. Do you?'

But I was in no mood for banter, having been through more than an hour of Dr Mehta's testing. 'If I'd managed to escape . . .' I began.

'We'd have stopped at nothing to find you, Ben. You're much too valuable. Actually, our psychological profile of you indicated, unequivocally, that you would attempt an escape. So I'm not altogether surprised. You have to remember, Ben, that with your retirement from the Agency, you no longer have the colony odor.'

'The colony odor?'

'Entomology. Ants. You remember my interest in ants.'

Toby had in fact studied to become an entomologist before World War II moved him very far afield, to military intelligence, the OSS, and later the CIA. But he'd kept up his interest in ants, reading voraciously in the professional journals, staying in contact with an old friend of his from Harvard, E. O. Wilson, who was one of the world's great scholars of ants. Just about the only use for ants Toby had managed to find in his life, however, was in metaphors.

'I certainly do, Toby. The colony odor?'

'When one ant greets another, she runs her antennae over the other's body. If the other is an intruder from another species, she will be attacked. But if she's from the same species, and just, say, a different colony, she will be accepted. Yet she'll be offered less food until she acquires the same odor – the same pheromone – that the others in the colony have. Then she's one of them.'

'So, am I from a different colony?' I asked impatiently.

'Have you ever seen an ant offer its food? It's very intimate, very touching. The attack is of course very unpleasant. One, or both, dies.'

I ran my fingers over the brown fake-wood-grain-Formica-topped conference table at which I had been placed. 'All right,' I said. 'Now, tell me this: Who came after me the other night?'

'In Boston?'

'Correct. And "we don't know" isn't satisfactory.'

'But accurate. We really don't know. We *do* know that there's been a leak –'

'God*dammi*t, Toby,' I exploded. 'We have to level with each other.'

He raised his voice to a shout, which surprised me. 'I *am* leveling with you, Ben! As I told you, since my accident in Paris, I have been in charge of this project. They call it the Oracle Project – you know how the Covert-Op boys are so damned attached to their melodramatic code names – from the original Latin *oraculum*, from *orare*, to speak. The mind speaks, doesn't it?'

I shrugged.

'The Oracle Project is the Manhattan Project of telepathy – expensive, intensive, ultrasecret, and considered a hopeless cause by just about everyone who knows of its existence. Since the Dutch gentleman's several months of ESP – to be precise,

133 days, before he committed suicide – we have gone through more than eight thousand experimental subjects.'

'Eight *thousand*?' I exclaimed.

'The vast majority of these individuals, of course, knew only that they were undergoing medical experiments, for which they were reimbursed handsomely. Of all of them, two subjects emerged with some small manifestation of ESP, but the ability faded after a day or two. With you –'

'It's two days, and nothing has changed.'

'Excellent. Excellent.'

'But what the hell is this *for*? The Cold War is over, Toby, the damned –'

'Ah,' he said. 'Precisely wrong. Yes, the world has changed, but it's just as dangerous a place. The Russian threat is still there, waiting for another coup d'état or a total crash of the system, the way Weimar Germany was lying in wait for a Hitler to restore its ruined empire. The Middle East remains a caldron. Terrorism is rampant – we're entering the age of terrorism like we've never seen before. We need to cultivate this ability you now have – desperately. We need agents who can divine *intentions*. There will always be Saddam Husseins or Muammar Qadhafis or whoever the hell else.'

'So tell me this: Why the gunfire in Boston? The Oracle Project has been under way for – what? – five years?'

'Approximately.'

'And suddenly people are shooting at me. There's an urgency, obviously. Some people want something very badly, and very quickly. It makes no sense.'

Toby sighed, touched his fingers to the glass separating us. 'There's no more Soviet threat,' he said slowly. 'Thank God. But now we're facing a much more difficult, more diffuse threat: hundreds of thousands of unemployed East Bloc spies – watchers, wet workers – a real nasty bunch, many of them.'

'That's not an explanation,' I replied. 'Those are *assets*. Who the hell do they work for? And *why*?'

'*Damn* it,' Toby thundered. '*Who do you think took out Edmund Moore?*'

I stared at him. Toby's eyes were wide, frightened, teary. 'You tell me,' I said very quietly. 'Who killed him?'

'Oh, for Christ's sake, the public version is that he swallowed the barrel of his gun, a 1957 Agency-issue Smith & Wesson Model 39.'

'And?'

'The Model 39 is chambered for the 9mm Parabellum, right? It's the first 9mm made by an American manufacturer.'

'What the hell are you getting at?'

'The bullet that penetrated Ed Moore's brain came from the special 9mm x 18 cartridge. The cartridge used in the 9mm Makarov pistol. Follow me?'

'Soviet,' I said. 'Vintage late 1950s. Or –'

'Or East German. The cartridge was manufactured for the Pistole M. East German. I don't think Ed Moore would have used ammunition issued by the East German secret police in his old Agency pistol. Do you?'

'But the goddamned Stasi doesn't *exist* anymore, Toby!'

'East Germany doesn't exist. The Stasi doesn't exist. But Stasi *assets* exist. And someone is hiring them. Someone is *using* them. We *need* you, Ben.'

'Yes,' I said, raising my voice. 'Obviously. But to do *what*, dammit?'

He went through his ritual of extracting a pack of Rothmans, tapping it against the side of his wheelchair until one protruded, lighting it, then speaking fuzzily through the smoke.

'We want you to locate the last head of the KGB.'

'Vladimir Orlov.'

He nodded.

'But surely you know his location? With all the Agency's resources . . . ?'

'We know only that he's somewhere in northern Italy. Tuscany. That's it.'

'How the hell do you know that?'

'I never divulge sources and methods,' he said with a crooked smile. 'Actually, Orlov is a sick man. He's been seeing a cardiologist in Rome. That much we know. He's seen this fellow for years, since he first visited Rome in the late 1970s. This doctor treats a number of world leaders, with great discretion. Orlov trusts him.

'Also, we know that after his consultations with this cardiologist, he is driven back to some undisclosed location in Tuscany. His drivers so far have been admirably skilled at shaking the tail.'

'So do a black-bag job.'

'On the Italian cardiologist? We tried his office in Rome. No success; he must keep the files on Orlov well hidden.'

'And if I find Orlov?'

'You're Harrison Sinclair's son-in-law. Married to Hal's daughter. It's not entirely implausible for you to have business with him. He will be suspicious, but you can work it. Once you're in his presence, we want you to find out everything about whatever it was that he and Hal Sinclair discussed. Everything. Did Hal really steal a fortune? What did Orlov have to do with it? You speak Russian, and with your "talent" –'

'He doesn't have to say a word.'

'In one fell swoop you may be able to locate the missing fortune and clear Hal Sinclair's name. Now, it's entirely possible that what you learn about Hal will not please you.'

'Unlikely.'

'No, Ben. You do not want to believe that Harrison Sinclair was a crook, nor does Alex Truslow, nor do I. But prepare yourself for the possibility that this is what you'll discover, repugnant though it may be. This assignment will not be without risks.'

'From whom?'

He leaned back in his wheelchair. 'The most treacherous people in the intelligence business are one's own. You know, there was a great nineteenth-century entomologist named Auguste Forel who once observed that the greatest enemies of ants are – other ants. The greatest enemies of spies are other spies.'

He laced his fingers into a church steeple. 'Whatever deal Vladimir Orlov struck with Hal Sinclair, I'm sure he does not want it revealed.'

'Don't bullshit me, Toby,' I said. 'You don't believe Hal was innocent.'

He exhaled almost soulfully. 'No,' he admitted, 'I don't. I wish I could believe otherwise. But at the very least you might be able to find out what Hal was up to before he died. And why.'

'What *Hal* was up to?' I thundered. 'Hal is *dead*!'

Startled, Toby looked up. He seemed frightened, though by my outburst or by something else I couldn't tell.

'Who killed him?' I demanded. 'Who killed Hal?'

'Former Stasi employees, I would guess.'

'I don't mean the wet work. Who *ordered* his death?'

'We don't know.'

'These CIA renegades – the "Wise Men" Alex told me about?'

'Possible. Although perhaps – I know you hate to hear this, but consider it anyway – perhaps Sinclair was one of them. One of the so-called Wise Men. And perhaps there was a falling out.'

'That's one theory,' I said coldly. 'There must be others.'

'Yes. Perhaps Sinclair made some sort of deal with Orlov, something involving a great deal of money. And Orlov – out of greed or out of fear – had Sinclair killed. After all, wouldn't it be logical that some of these former East German and Romanian thugs would do some free-lance work for the man who used to be their boss?'

'I need to talk to Alex Truslow.'

'He's unreachable.'

'No,' I said. 'He's at Camp David. He's reachable.'

'He's in transit, Ben. If you must speak to him, try tomorrow. But there is no time to lose. This is a matter of the gravest urgency.'

'You plan to keep Molly, is that it? Until I deliver the goods?'

'Ben, we're desperate. Things are too vital.' He inhaled deeply. 'It wasn't my idea, by the way. I argued against it with Charles Rossi until I was blue in the face.'

'But you went along with it.'

'She's being treated exceptionally well, I promise you. She'll confirm that. The hospital has been told she's been called away on an urgent family matter. She'll have a peaceful rest for a few days, which she badly needs.'

I felt the adrenaline surge, and struggled mightily to keep my composure. 'Toby, I believe it was you who once told me that when an ant nest is under attack, the ants don't send out the young-men ants as guards, as soldiers. They send out the old-lady ants, you told me. Because it's okay if the old ladies get killed off. That's called altruism – it's better for the colony. Right?'

'We will do everything we can to protect you.'

'Two conditions,' I said.

'Yes?'

'First, this is the only assignment I will undertake for anyone. I will not be made a guinea pig, or an errand boy, or anything else for that matter. Is that understood?'

'Understood,' Toby said equably. 'Although I should hope at some point we could induce you to change your mind.'

I ignored him and went on. 'And second, you receive the information only after Molly is released. I'll work out the exact terms and arrangements. But it's going to be my game, with my rules.'

'You're being unreasonable,' Toby said more loudly.

'Perhaps. But it's a deal-breaker.'

'I can't allow it. It's against all accepted procedure.'

'Accept it, Toby.'

Another long, long pause. 'Dammit, Ben. All right.'

'All right, then,' I said. 'We have a deal.'

He put both palms flat on the table before him. 'We'll fly you to Rome in a few hours,' he said. 'There's not a minute to lose.'

Part Four

TUSCANY

International Herald-Tribune

Leader of Germany's National Socialist Party Assassinated

BY ISAAC WOOD

NEW YORK TIMES SERVICE

BONN – Jurgen Krauss, the fiery chairman of the reborn Nazi Party, who was the leading contender in the race for Chancellor, was shot and killed this morning in a rally here.

No one has yet claimed responsibility.

That leaves only two men in the contest to lead Germany, both of them considered centrists. While voicing sorrow at the violent end of Mr Krauss, diplomats expressed relief. . . .

30

I had been to Rome several times before, and never much liked it. Italy is without a doubt one of my favorite countries in the world, perhaps my single favorite, but I've always found Rome grimy, congested, and despondent. Beautiful, yes – Michelangelo's Campidoglio, St. Peter's, the Villa Borghese, the Via Veneto, are all striking in different ways, ancient, luxuriant, opulent – but overwhelming, threatening. And virtually everywhere you go in the city you somehow always end up at the monument to Victor Emmanuel II, a horrific typewriter-shaped structure of white Brescian marble, on the Piazza Venezia, shrouded in malign traffic fumes. Mussolini delivered his harangues here; I preferred to avoid it whenever possible.

The day I arrived was rain-swept and unpleasantly chilly. In the driving rain, the taxi stand in front of the international terminal at Fiumicino seemed a bit too forlorn to brave right away.

So I found a bar and ordered a *cafe lungo*, savored it for a long while, feeling the caffeine do battle with my jet lag. I had entered the country on a false passport, provided for me by those wizards of forgery in CIA's Technical Services section (in cooperation, let it be said, with the U.S. State Department).

My cover was Bernard Mason, an American businessman here to make some arcane arrangements with my corporation's Italian subsidiary. The passport they'd supplied me was admirably dog-eared; if I didn't know better, I'd have thought it had indeed been used on many international trips before, and by a slob. But of course it had been dummied up just for the occasion.

I polished off a second *cafe lungo* and a *cornetto* and made my way toward the rest room. The facility was simple, black and white, and clean. Against one wall, below a large mirror, was a row of sinks; facing them on the other side of the small room were four toilet stalls, the doors to which were painted a glossy black and went from floor to ceiling without a gap. The leftmost stall was occupied, and although the center one was vacant, I stood at the sink for a while, washed my hands, my face, and combed my hair, until the door to the left stall opened. A pudgy middle-aged Arab emerged, tightening his belt against his ample gut. He left without washing his hands, and I immediately entered the stall he had just vacated and locked it.

I lowered the toilet seat, climbed up on it, and reached up to the molded-plastic compartment near the ceiling. It lifted open easily, as promised, and there it was, a fat bundle. A padded manila envelope that contained, swaddled in clean cotton rags, a box of fifty .45 ACP shells and a sleek, matte black .45 semiautomatic pistol, a Sig-Sauer 220, brand-new and still oily from the manufacturer. The Sig is, I believe, the best pistol made. It has tritium night-sights, a four-inch barrel, six rifling grooves, and weighs around twenty-six ounces. I hoped I'd have no use for it.

I was in a foul mood. I had sworn I'd never return to this terrible game, and now I was back. And once again I would have to draw upon my dark, violent side, which I thought I had buried once and for all.

I wrapped it back up, slipped it into my carry-on bag, and left the envelope in the compartment, which I pressed closed.

As soon as I left the rest room and headed for the taxi stand, however, I felt something wrong. A presence, a person, a stirring. Airports are chaotic, hectic, bustling places, and so they are perfect for surveillance. I was being observed. I felt it. I can't say I *heard* or *read* anything – far too many people in too many little throngs, a Babel of foreign languages, and my Italian was only serviceable. But I sensed it. My instincts, once so finely tuned, then so long out of use, were slowly returning.

There *was* someone.

A compact, swarthy man, perhaps in his late thirties or early forties, wearing a green-gray sports jacket, lounging near the *farmacia*, his face mostly hidden behind a copy of the *Corriere della sera*.

I hastened my pace somewhat until I was outside. He followed me out: very unsubtle. Which concerned me. He didn't seem to worry about being noticed, which probably meant there were others. Probably also meant that they *wanted* me to notice.

I got into the next available cab, a white Mercedes, and said, 'Grand Hotel, *per favore*.'

The watcher was in a cab immediately behind mine, I saw at once. Probably by now there was another vehicle involved, perhaps two or three. After about forty minutes of crawling through the morning rush-hour traffic, the cab pulled up the narrow Via Vittorio Emanuele Orlando and in front of the Grand Hotel. At once, four liveried bellmen descended upon the cab to remove my luggage, load it onto a cart, help me out of the car, and escort me into the hotel's subdued, elegant lobby.

I tipped each one of them more than generously and gave my cover name at the reception desk.

The clerk smiled, said, '*Buon giorno, signore*,' and quickly inspected his reservation sheets. A troubled expression crossed his face. '*Signore* . . . ah, Mr Mason?' he said, looking up apologetically.

'Is there a problem?'

'There appears to be, sir. We have no record –'

'Perhaps under my company's name, then,' I offered. 'TransAtlantic.'

After a moment he shook his head again. 'Do you know when these were made?'

I slammed my open palm down on the marble surface of the reception desk. 'I don't *care*, dammit!' I said. 'This damned hotel screwed up –'

'If you need a room, sir, I'm sure –'

I signaled to the bell captain. 'No. Not here. I'm sure the Excelsior doesn't make these kinds of mistakes.' To the bell

213

captain I commanded: 'Bring my bags around to the service entrance. Not the front, the back. And I want a taxi to the Excelsior, on the Via Veneto. At once.'

The bell captain bowed slightly and gestured to one of the bellboys, who turned the cart with my luggage around and began to push it toward the back of the lobby.

'Sir, if there is some kind of mistake, I'm sure we can straighten it out very quickly,' the reception clerk said. 'We have a single room available. In fact, we have several small suites available.'

'I don't want to trouble you,' I said haughtily as I followed the luggage cart to the rear of the lobby, toward the service entrance.

Within minutes a cab pulled up to the rear of the hotel. The bellboy loaded the suitcase and carry-on bag into the Opel's trunk, I tipped him handsomely, and got in.

'The Excelsior, *signore?*' the driver said.

'No,' I said. 'The Hassler. Piazza Trinità dei Monti.'

The Hassler overlooks the Spanish Steps, one of the most pleasant locations in Rome. I had stayed here before, and the Agency had booked a room for me here, at my request. The Grand Hotel episode, of course, had been a ruse, and it seemed to have worked – I had lost the followers. I didn't know how long I could stay here unobserved, but for the time being, things seemed to be okay.

Exhausted now, I showered and collapsed onto the king-size bed, slipped between the luxurious, crisply ironed linen sheets, momentarily at peace, and drifted into a deep, much-needed sleep, which was troubled by apprehensive dreams about Molly.

A few hours later I was awakened by the distant honking of a horn somewhere near the Spanish Steps. It was midafternoon, and the suite was flooded with light. I rolled over, picked up the phone, and ordered a cappuccino and a bite to eat. My stomach was growling.

I looked at my watch and calculated that the business day

was just beginning in Boston. I placed a call to a bank in Washington where I still maintained an old but active account I'd opened years ago. My broker, John Matera, had indeed wired my Beacon Trust 'earnings.' (Earnings, of course, was the one thing they weren't.) No sense, I figured, in making it easy for the CIA to monkey around with my money. I knew their tricks and was determined not to trust them fully.

The coffee came fifteen minutes later, served in a large, deep gold-rimmed cup, with beautifully presented sandwiches: thick slices of moist white bread topped with paper-thin slices of prosciutto, arugula, a few slices of *pecorino fresco*, and ringed with beautiful deep red slices of tomato, glistening with fragrant olive oil.

I felt as alone as I'd ever felt. Molly, I was sure, was fine – was, in fact, being protected as much as she was being kept hostage. Still, I worried about her, about what they were telling her about me, how scared she was, how she was holding up. But I was convinced that she would not buckle; she would instead make her captors' lives hell.

I smiled to myself, and just then the phone rang.

'Mr Ellison?' came the American-accented voice.

'Yes.'

'Welcome to Rome. You've picked a nice time to come.'

'Thank you,' I said. 'It's much more comfortable here than it is in the States this time of year.'

'And a lot more to see,' my CIA contact said, completing the coded exchange.

I hung up.

Fifteen minutes later, in the soft light of a late Rome afternoon, I came out of the Hassler. The Spanish Steps swarmed with people, standing, sitting, smoking, taking pictures, shouting at each other, laughing at one another's jokes. I surveyed the bustling scene, felt terribly out of place amid the vivacity, and, my stomach already knotted with tension, got into a cab.

31

At the Piazza della Repubblica, not far from Rome's main train station, I rented a car at Maggiore, using my phony Bernard Mason driver's license and gold Citibank Visa card. (Actually, the credit card itself was real; but the bills run up by the fictitious Mr Mason were paid, through a Fairfax, Virginia, law firm, by the CIA.) I was given a gleaming black Lancia as big as an ocean liner: the sort of car that Bernard Mason, nouveau riche American businessman, would undoubtedly hire.

The cardiologist's office was located a short drive away, on the Corso del Rinascimento, a noisy, traffic-snarled main street just off the Piazza Navona. I parked in an underground lot a block and a half away and located the doctor's building, whose entrance bore a brass plaque that was engraved DOTT. ALDO PASQUALACCI.

I was early for my appointment, almost forty-five minutes, and I decided to walk over to the piazza. For a variety of reasons, I knew it was best to adhere to the schedule set for me. I was to meet the cardiologist at eight that evening – unusually late in the day, but deliberately so. The inconvenience, I suppose, was designed to further my legend: this was the only time that the reclusive American tycoon, Bernard Mason, could meet the physician. Thus inconvenienced, Dr Pasqualucci would presumably be more inclined to be cooperative and deferential. Pasqualucci was considered one of the finest cardiologists in Europe, which was surely why the former KGB chief had consulted him. So it was logical that Mr Mason, who resided several months of the year in Rome, would seek out his services. All Pasqualucci knew was that this

American had been referred by another physician, an internist whom Pasqualucci knew casually, and that a fair degree of discretion was called for, since Mason's extensive business empire would suffer incalculable financial harm if word got out that he were being treated for a cardiac problem. Pasqualucci did not know that the physician who had referred Mason was in fact on a CIA retainer.

At this time of the evening the baroque ocher edifices of the Piazza Navona were illuminated dramatically with klieg lights, a stunning sight. The square bustled with people, crowding into cafés, garrulous and excited and electric. Couples strolled, absorbed in each other, or eyeing others; in another time they would have promenaded. The piazza was built on the ancient ruins of the Stadium of the emperor Domitian. (I'll always remember that it was Domitian who once said, 'Emperors are necessarily wretched men since only their assassination can convince the public that the conspiracies against their lives are real.')

The evening lights glinted and sparkled off the spouting water of the two Bernini fountains to which people always seemed to gravitate: the Fountain of the Four Rivers in the square's center and the Fountain of the Moor at the south end. It was an odd place, the Piazza Navona. Centuries ago it was used for chariot races, and later the popes ordered the place flooded so that mock naval battles could be waged.

I walked through the crowd, feeling somewhat alienated from the others, their effervescent high spirits contrasting with my anxiety. I had spent quite a few nights like this, alone in foreign cities, and I'd always considered it oddly lulling to be surrounded by the babble of foreign voices. That night, of course, graced (or was it afflicted?) with this strange ability, I found myself increasingly confused, as thoughts blended with chatter and cries in one great indistinguishable rush.

I heard, aloud: '*Non ho mai avuto una settimana peggiore!*' and then, in that thought-voice: *Avessimo potuto salvarlo!*

And aloud: '*Lui e uscito con la sua ragazza.*'

And in that softer thought-voice: *Poverino!*

And then, another muzzy thought-voice, but this one distinctly American: *damn him left me all alone!*

I turned. She was obviously an American, in her early twenties, wearing a Stanford sweatshirt under an acid-washed denim jacket, walking by herself a few feet from me. Her round, plain face was set in a pout. She caught me staring at her and gave me an angry glance. I looked away, and just then I heard another phrase, in American-accented English, and my heart began to thud.

Benjamin Ellison.

But where was it coming from? It had to be close, had to be within six feet or so. Must have come from one of the dozens of people immediately surrounding me, but who? It took enormous restraint to keep from whipsawing my head around, from side to side, trying to catch a glimpse of someone who looked slightly out of place, an Agency type following me. I turned casually, heard –

can't let him notice

– and began to accelerate my pace, striding toward the church of St. Agnes, still unable to single out the follower from the crowds, and suddenly lunged left, knocking over a white plastic café-table, knocking an elderly man off balance, and plunged into the darkness of a narrow alley, which was fetid with urine. From behind I could hear shouts, a woman's voice and a man's, the sounds of a commotion. I ran down the alley, sensed footsteps following me, and ducked into a doorway, which appeared to be some sort of service entrance. I flattened myself against the tall wooden doors, feeling the crust of peeling paint sharp against my neck and head, and slowly bent my knees and sank toward the cold tile floor of the foyer. I could just see out through a broken glass pane in the middle of the exterior door. The darkness and shadows would, I thought, conceal me sufficiently.

Yes: a watcher.

A hulking, muscle-bound figure made its way down the alley, hands outstretched as if they were being used to keep balance. I had seen this man in the piazza, off to my right, but he had looked like every other Italian man; he had blended in too well for my unpracticed eye. Now he passed directly in front of me, moving slowly, and I saw his eyes peering directly into the tiny lobby where I knelt.

Did he see me?

I heard: *run to* . . .

His eyes stared straight ahead, not down at an angle.

I felt the cold steel of the pistol in my pants pocket, slowly withdrew it. Released the safety, and fingered the trigger tentatively.

He moved on, down the alley, peering into doorways on either side. I crept forward, watched as he reached the end of the alley, paused for a moment, and took a right.

I sat back, let out a long, slow breath. Closed my eyes for a minute, then leaned forward and glanced out again. He was gone. I had lost him for the time being.

Several endless minutes later I emerged and walked down the alley, in the direction the watcher had gone earlier, away from the piazza, and through a rabbit-warren of dimly lit back streets to the Corso.

At precisely eight o'clock, Dr Aldo Pasqualucci opened his office door and, with a slight bow of the head, shook my hand. He was surprisingly short, rotund but not fat, wearing a comfortably worn brown tweed suit with a camel sweater-vest. His face was kind. His brown eyes had a look of concern about them. His hair was black, peppered with gray, and looked recently combed. In his left hand he held a meerschaum; the air around him was vanilla-fragrant with pipe smoke.

'Please come in, Mr Mason,' he said. His accent wasn't Italian at all, but British, upper-class and crisp. He waved with his pipe toward the examination room.

'Thank you for seeing me at such an inconvenient time,' I said.

He dipped his head, neither assenting nor disagreeing, and said smilingly, 'My pleasure. I've heard much about you.'

'And I you. But I must ask first . . .'

I paused, concentrated . . . and found nothing audible.

'Yes? If you can please sit over here and remove your shirt.'

As I sat on the paper-covered examination table and took off my suit jacket and shirt, I said, 'I need to make sure I can count on your absolute discretion.'

He took a blood-pressure cuff from the table behind him, wrapped it around my arm, pressed the Velcro closures together, and said, 'All of my patients can count on complete confidentiality. I'd have it no other way.'

Then I said loudly, deliberately provocative: 'But can you *guarantee* it?'

And in the instant before Pasqualucci replied, pumping the bulb until the cuff squeezed my upper arm uncomfortably, I heard: . . . *pomposo* . . . *arrogante* . . .

He was standing so close to me that I could feel and smell his tobacco-scented breath hotly against me, sense a tension in him, and I knew I was reading his thoughts.

In Italian.

He was bilingual, I had been briefed: Italian-born but raised in Northumbria, Great Britain, and schooled at Harrow and then Oxford.

So what did that mean? What did it mean to be bilingual? Would he speak in English while thinking in Italian, was that how it worked?

He said, this time with considerably less warmth, 'Mr Mason, as you well know, I treat some very prominent and very reclusive individuals. I shall not reveal their names. If you feel uncomfortable about my discretion, please feel free to leave right now.'

He had left the cuff pumped up to its maximum rather too long, so that my arm throbbed. At least half deliberately, I suspected. But now, as if punctuating his declaration, he released the pressure valve, which gave off a loud hiss.

'As long as we understand each other,' I said.

'Fine. Now, Dr Corsini said that you have been suffering from occasional fainting spells, that once in a while your heart races seemingly without reason.'

'Correct.'

'I want to take a full history. Maybe a Holter monitor,

maybe a stress-thallium test, we'll see. But first I want you to tell me in your own words what brings you in here.'

I turned around to face him and said, 'Dr Pasqualucci, my sources tell me that you also treat a certain Vladimir Orlov, formerly of the Soviet Union, and that concerns me.'

He sputtered, 'I said – as I say – you are free to see another cardiologist. I can even recommend one to you –'

'I am merely saying, Doctor, that it worries me that Mr Orlov's files, or charts, or whatever they're called, are here in your office. If ever there's a break-in because of . . . shall we say, *interest* in him on the part of any intelligence agency, then aren't my files, too, vulnerable? I want to know what security precautions you take.'

Dr Pasqualucci looked at me hawkishly, angrily, his face reddening, and I began to receive his thoughts with an astonishing clarity.

An hour or so later I maneuvered the Lancia through the loud, crazed, snarling traffic toward the outskirts of Rome, to the via del Trullo, and then turned right down the via S. Guiliano, a modern and rather desolate section of the city. A few yards up on the right I located the bar and pulled over.

It was one of those all-purpose bars-cum-everything-else, a little white-painted stucco building with a striped yellow awning, white plastic outdoor furniture neatly stacked in front. A Lavazza coffee sign bore the inscription: ROSTICCERIA-PIZZERIA-PANINOTECA-SPAGHETTERIA.

It was twenty minutes before ten o'clock, and the place swarmed with teenagers in leather jackets, jostling with gray-haired laborers drinking at the bar. A jukebox blasted out an old American song I recognized: 'I Wanna Dance with Somebody.' Whitney Houston, I decided.

My CIA contact, Charles Van Aver – the man who had called me at the hotel earlier in the day – wasn't there. It was too early, and in any case he would probably be in his car in the parking lot out back. I settled on a plastic stool at the bar, ordered an Averna, and watched the crowd. One of the teenagers was playing a card game that seemed to involve a lot of slapping of cards against the deck. A large family gathered around a too-small table, toasting one another. No trace of Van Aver, and – with the sole exception of me – no one seemed to be there who didn't belong.

In the cardiologist's out-patient office, I was able to confirm what I had first observed with Dr Mehta, that a bilingual person thinks in two languages, a peculiar sort of melange. Dr Pasqualucci's thoughts were an odd twisting, blending of Italian and English.

My Italian was sufficiently workable to enable me to make out the sense of what he was thinking.

Concealed in the floor of his supply closet, a small room that evidently held cleaning substances, mops and brooms, photocopy paper, computer disks, typewriter ribbons, and the like, was a concrete-reinforced safe. It held samples of controlled substances, the files of an unpleasant malpractice case he had been involved in over ten years ago, and several patient files. These patients included several prominent Italian politicians of rival parties; the chief executive of one of Europe's largest automotive empires; and Vladimir Orlov.

As Dr Pasqualucci placed a cold stethoscope on my chest and listened for a long, long time. I agonized over how I could possibly get him to think the combination to the safe, how I could ever get to it, when all of a sudden I heard something, an almost-but-not-quite-distinct buzz, like a shortwave radio coming into and out of tune, the words:

Volte-Basse . . .

and *Castelbianco*

And again: *Volte-Basse* . . . *Castelbianco* . . . and *Orlov* . . .

And I knew then as much as I had to know.

Still Van Aver hadn't appeared. I had memorized his photograph: a large, flush-faced man, a hard-drinking southerner of sixty-eight. He wore his thick white hair so long that it curled over the collar at the back of his neck, at least in the most recent Agency file photo. His nose was large and webbed with the broken veins of an alcoholic. An alcoholic, Hal Sinclair used to say, is a person you don't like who drinks as much as you do.

At quarter after ten I paid the bill and slipped quietly out the restaurant-bar's front door. The parking lot was dark, but I could make out the usual assortment of Fiat Pandas, Fiat Ritmos, Ford Fiestas, Peugeots, and a black Porsche. After the din of the bar, I enjoyed the quiet of the dark lot, inhaling the cold air that somehow, in this part of Rome, seemed cleaner and crisper. A moped buzzed by, its flat, high-pitched whine piercing.

In the farthest row of cars was a gleaming olive Mercedes, license plate ROMA 17017. And there he was, asleep in the driver's seat, in an old man's slouch. I suppose I had expected that he'd have the motor running, impatient to set out for the three-hours-plus drive north to Tuscany, but the car was dark. Neither was the interior light on; Van Aver was, I figured, sleeping off the vast quantities of booze he regularly consumed, according to his personnel file. An alcoholic, yes, but a man who'd been around, who knew everyone, and so his peccadilloes were tolerated.

The windshield was partially fogged. As I approached, I considered whether I should insist that I drive, whether that would offend Van Aver's overendowed ego. I slipped into the car and found myself automatically straining to hear his thoughts, or at least those fragments I'd found I could perceive when someone is sleeping.

But there was nothing. A complete silence. I found it peculiar, illogical –

– and in a moment I was seized by a dizzy, vertiginous rush of adrenaline.

I could see Van Aver's long white hair curling at the back of his neck, against his navy blue turtleneck sweater, mouth open in what appeared to be a snore, and beneath it the old man's throat gaped grotesquely wide open. A terrible deep red stain crept down his jacket lapels, down his sweater, his pale, wrinkled neck a steaming, still-flowing lake of blood that my eyes at first refused to accept. I could see at once that Van Aver was dead, and I bolted from the car.

32

I ran out into the via del Trullo, my heart pounding, and found the rented car. I fumbled for a few moments with the key until I was finally able to unlock the door and sank into the front seat. Exhaling and inhaling slowly, measuredly, I managed to get a grip on myself.

You see, I had all of a sudden been plunged back into that nightmarish time in Paris. I found myself flashing back persistently, almost kaleidoscopically, on that hallway in the rue Jacob, on the sight of the two bodies, one of them my beloved Laura . . .

Whatever the mystique of clandestine intelligence work, it usually does not include murder and mayhem. That is by far the exception, not the rule, and although we were all trained to deal with the eventualities of bloodshed in the theater of the Cold War, rarely did such a thing actually intrude upon one's life.

Most clandestine operatives in fact see very little violence during their careers – a great deal of stress and anxiety, but very little outright violence. And when they encounter carnage, they customarily react the way anyone would: they are repelled and sickened; a fight-or-flight instinct takes over. Most operatives who are unlucky enough to face much bloodshed in their work will burn out early and retire.

But with me, something different happened. Exposure to blood and mayhem deadened me, tamped something down inside me. It switched something off: the essential human horror of violence. Instead, I became enraged, focused, tranquil. It was as if I'd been injected intravenously with a sedative.

As I struggled to make sense of what had just happened, I methodically ran down a list of possibilities. Who else had known that I was meeting with Van Aver? Who had Van Aver told? Who, that is, had he told – and would order him killed? And for what reason?

I would have liked to believe that Van Aver had been murdered by the same person or persons who had been following me since my arrival in Rome. Which begged the question of why I hadn't been eliminated. Obviously whoever had cut Van Aver's throat had preceded me by some time, so it was unlikely that he had been murdered by someone *following* me to this rendezvous (and in any case, I had taken elaborate precautions not to be followed leaving Pasqualucci's).

That indicated that it was someone, or some group, *within* the CIA who had had Van Aver killed. Someone who knew he was going to meet me, someone who had intercepted whatever communication had taken place between Toby Thompson in Washington and Van Aver in Rome.

And yet, the more I thought it through, the more I had to concede the possibility that the culprits weren't necessarily CIA at all – that they might have been ex-Stasi.

So that line of deduction didn't help one bit.

Then what about motive? It couldn't have been *me* they were after – Van Aver and I looked nothing alike; no one could have made that mistake. And presumably there had been other chances to get me, if that was the objective.

It wasn't as if Van Aver possessed some fund of information that someone wanted me not to gain access to. His mission, I had been briefed by Toby, was to escort me to Tuscany once I had learned Orlov's whereabouts, and to . . .

To get me in to see Orlov. I didn't know the protocol; I didn't know what would get me in to see the retired KGB chairman. Certainly I couldn't just knock on the man's door.

Could that be it? Could the motive for killing Van Aver have simply been to keep me from getting to Orlov? To 'discourage' me, frustrate me, make it as difficult as possible? To keep me from learning about the 'Wise Men'?

Suddenly I jolted upright.

My reasoning had been faulty. I had been late for my meeting with the CIA man. Deliberately, tactically so; but *late* all the same.

Like most field agents, Van Aver was probably impeccably precise in his timing. Whoever had surprised him there, knife in hand . . .

Had expected him to be meeting someone.

Me.

Whether they knew whom Van Aver was meeting . . . They knew he was meeting *someone*.

Had I been on time, might I now be slumped in the front seat beside Van Aver with a severed carotid?

I leaned back against the seat cushion and exhaled slowly.

Possible? Yes, of course.

Anything was possible.

By the time I had checked out of the Hassler and loaded my belongings in the trunk of the Lancia, it was well after midnight. The A-1 autostrada was fairly free of traffic, except for the occasional thundering delivery truck.

From the Hassler's concierge I had secured a very good map of Tuscany, a Touring Club Italiano map that appeared both comprehensive and accurate. It was a simple matter for me to commit it to memory. And then I had located a small town called Volte-Basse, not far outside of Siena, three hours to the north.

It took some time to acclimate to Italian drivers, who are not really reckless – compared to Boston drivers, the rest of the world is tame – but just elegantly aggressive. For a time concentrating on the amber-lit road calmed me, enabled me to think clearly.

So I watched the road and thought. I drove in the left lane at around 120 kilometers an hour. Twice I pulled off the road suddenly and waited with the engine and lights off, to make sure no one was following me. Elemental tradecraft, but it works. No one appeared to be following me, although I couldn't be sure.

A car approached from behind, drew closer, flashed its high beams, and my stomach tensed. Now it was almost upon me, and I floored the accelerator and swung the wheel to the right.

The other car was trying to pass, that was all.

My nerves were frayed. This is the way they pass in Italy, I told myself. You're losing it. Get a grip.

I found myself talking aloud to myself. 'Stay with it, Ben,' I said. And, 'You're there.' And, 'You'll make it.'

The thing was, by attaining this . . . talent . . . I had become a freak. I had no idea how much longer I would have it, but it had already changed my life forever, and had come close several times to getting me killed. And most disturbingly, the talent, and everything it brought with it, had transformed me into the very thing I never wanted to be again, the ruthless, fearless automaton created by my CIA work.

This form of ESP I had was, I now believed, a terrible thing. Not fantastic and wonderful, but in truth horrible. One should not be able to penetrate the protective walls that surround others.

So now I had been plunged into the middle of something that had taken my wife away from me and turned me back into the ice man and threatened to kill me as well.

Who were the bad guys? Some faction of CIA?

No doubt I would know soon. In the town of Volte-Basse, in Tuscany.

It was, I discovered, the tiniest of villages, a mere blip on the map. A cluster of ancient dun-colored stone buildings crowded together on either side of a narrow road, Number 71, which led directly into Siena. There was a bar, a small grocer/ butcher, and not much else.

And at three-thirty in the morning the town was utterly still, shrouded in silence and darkness. The map I'd memorized, comprehensive as it was, indicated nothing called 'Castelbianco,' and there was no one around to ask at this time of the morning, or, really, night.

I was exhausted, badly in need of a rest, but the road was far too exposed. My instincts told me to pull off somewhere concealed. I headed away from Siena on 71, through the modern town of Rosia, and up into the wooded hills beyond. Immediately past a stone-cutting yard I spotted a turnoff for a private estate, an immense tract of Tuscan forest with a castle planted quite a ways into it. The road was tiny and dark, its surface a treacherous paving of gravel and large stones. The Lancia bumped and scraped its way over the path. Soon I located a copse, and pulled the car into it so that I was invisible, at least as long as it remained dark.

I shut off the engine, retrieved from the trunk one of the blankets that I had guiltily stolen from the Hassler, and threw it over me. I reclined the front seat as far back as it would go and listened to the engine tick as it cooled, feeling very alone, until I was fast asleep.

33

Bruised and groggy, I awoke at sunrise and experienced a momentary sense of dislocation. Where was I? Not at home in my comfortable bed, snuggled up against Molly, I remembered with a sinking feeling, but in the front seat of a rented car somewhere in a forest in Tuscany.

Tilting the seat back upright, I started the car up, backed out of the copse, and drove a few miles into the town of Rosia. The air was chilly, and the sun, which was just edging over the horizon, cast golden beams against the terra-cotta buildings. Everything was still, utterly quiet until a broken-down delivery truck thundered by, through the town center, then groaning, whining as the driver downshifted to take it up the winding hill to the stone quarry I'd passed the night before.

Rosia seemed to consist of two main streets, the rows of buildings low-slung and red-roofed, evidently built in the middle of this century. Most of the buildings contained small shops – a bakery, a hardware store, a few fruit and vegetable places (FRUTTA & VERDURA), a newsstand. At this time of the morning they were all closed except for a Jolly Caffè Bar-Alimentari bar-cum-delicatessen down the quiet street, from which I could hear male voices. I walked up to it. Workers were having their coffee, reading sports papers, sparring verbally. They looked up as I entered, fell silent, looked me over curiously. I picked up scattered thoughts in Italian, of course, and not of any consequence.

Dressed as I was in a pair of somewhat rumpled pants and a heavy woolen sweater, they probably didn't know what to make of me. If I were one of the foreigners (most often British) who owned or rented the nearby Tuscan villas at exorbitant rates, why hadn't they seen me before? And what was this crazy foreigner doing awake at six o'clock in the morning?

I ordered an espresso and sat down at one of the small round plastic tables. The workers' conversations slowly resumed, and when my coffee arrived, a small Illy-Caffè cup filled with steaming dark espresso topped with a golden-tan layer of *crèma*, I took a long, appreciative sip and felt the caffeine do its work in my bloodstream.

Thus fortified, I got up and approached what appeared to be the most senior of the workers, a potbellied, round-faced, balding man whose face was covered with gray stubble. He was wearing a grimy white apron over a navy blue work uniform.

'*Buon giorno*,' I said.

'*Buon giorno*,' he replied, regarding me with suspicion. He spoke with the soft, gentle accents of Tuscany, in which a hard C becomes an H, a hard *ch* becomes a soft *sh*.

In my rudimentary Italian, I managed to say: '*Sto cercando Castelbianco, in Volte-Basse.*' I'm looking for Castelbianco.

He shrugged, turned to the others.

'*Che pensi, che questo sta cercando di vendere l'assicurazione al Tedesco, o cosa?*' he muttered: Think this guy's trying to sell the German guy insurance, or what?

The German: Is that what they thought Orlov was? Was that his cover legend here, a German émigré?

Laughter all round. The youngest of them, a dark-skinned, gangly man in his early twenties who looked like an Arab, said: '*Digli che vogliamo una parte della sua percentuale.*' Tell him we want part of his commission. There was more laughter.

Another one said, '*Pensi che questo sta cercando di entrare nella professione del muratore?*' You think this guy's trying to get into the rock business?

I laughed companionably along with them. '*Voi lavorate in una cava?*' I asked. You guys work in the quarry?

'*No, è il sindaco di Rosia,*' the youngest one said, slapping the oldest on the shoulder. '*Io sono il vice-sindaco.*' No, he's the mayor of Rosia, he was saying, and I'm the deputy mayor.

'*Allora, Sua Eccellenza,*' I said to the balding man, and asked whether they were doing stone work for the 'German.'

'*Che state lavorando le pietre per il . . . tedesco . . . a Castelbianco?*'

He waved his hand at me dismissively, and they all laughed again. The youngest one said, '*Se fosse vero, pensi che staremmo qua perdendo il nostro tempo? Il tedesco sta pagando i muratori tredici mille lire all'ora!*' If we were, you think we'd be wasting our time here? The German's paying stonemasons thirteen thousand lire an hour!

'You want veal, this is the guy to see,' another said of the older man, who got up, brushed his hands against his apron (which I now realized was spattered with animal blood), and walked toward the door. He was followed by the man who'd just spoken.

After the butcher and his assistant had left, I said to the swarthy young man: 'So where's Castelbianco anyway?'

'Volte-Basse,' he said. 'A few kilometers up the road toward Siena.'

'Is Castelbianco a town?'

'A town?' he said with an incredulous laugh. 'It's big enough to be a town, but no. It's a *tenuta* – an estate. Most of us kids used to play at Castelbianco years ago, before they sold it.'

'Sold?'

'Some rich German just moved in there. They say he's German, I don't know, maybe he's Swiss or something. Very secretive, very private.'

He described for me where Castelbianco was located, and I thanked him and left.

An hour later I found the estate on which Vladimir Orlov had gone into hiding.

If, indeed, the information I had 'gotten' from the cardiologist was right. At that point I didn't know for certain. But the talk at the bar about a reclusive 'German' seemed to confirm it. Did the townspeople think Orlov was some East German grandee who had gone into hiding when the Wall came down? The best covers follow the contours of reality.

Set on a hill overlooking Siena, Castelbianco was a magnificent ancient villa built in the Romanesque style. It was large and somewhat shambling; restoration was obviously being done on one wing. The villa was surrounded by gardens that were probably once beautiful but were now overgrown and in disarray. I found it at the end of a winding road in the hills above Volte-Basse.

Castelbianco had no doubt been a Tuscan family's ancestral home, and centuries before that had probably been a fortified bastion of one of the many Etruscan city-states. The forest that surrounded the disheveled gardens overflowed with silvery-green olive trees, fields of enormous sunflowers, and grapevines, great cypresses. I realized quickly why Orlov had chosen this particular villa. Its location, the way it was set high upon a hill, made it easy to secure. A high stone fence surrounded the estate, topped, I saw, with electrified wire. Not impenetrable – virtually *nothing* was impermeable to someone skilled in black-bag jobs – but it did a fairly good job at keeping out the unwanted. From a tiny stone booth, recently constructed, at the only entrance, an armed guard checked all visitors. The only visitors seemed to be, just as I'd learned that morning, workers from Rosia and the area, stonemasons and carpenters who arrived in dusty old trucks, were carefully looked over, and proceeded in to do their day's work.

Probably Orlov had brought this guard with him from Moscow. And if one got past this guard, there would certainly be others within. So crashing the gates seemed like an eminently bad idea.

After a few minutes of surveillance, from the car and on foot, I devised a plan.

A few minutes' drive away was the sprawling town of Sovicille, the capital of this area, this *comune* west of Siena, but as unassuming a capital city as I had ever seen. I parked in the center of town, in the Piazza G. Marconi, in front of a church, next to a San Pellegrino bottled-water truck. The square was peaceful, disturbed only by the lewd whistling of a bird in a cage in front of a Jolly Caffè, the chatter of a few middle-aged women. There I spotted the yellow rotary-dial sign of a public telephone, and as I walked toward it, the peace was broken by the loud ringing of the town bell.

I entered the café and ordered a coffee and a sandwich. For some reason, there is no coffee in the world like Italian coffee. They don't grow it, but they know how to brew it, and in any truck stop or cheap dive in Italy you can get better cappuccino than you can in the finest so-called 'Northern Italian' restaurant on Manhattan's Upper East Side.

I sipped, and I thought, which is something I had done quite a bit of since leaving Washington. Yet for all my cogitation, I still had no idea where things stood.

I was in possession of the most extraordinary talent, but what had I been able to do with it? I had tracked down a former head of Soviet intelligence – a neat bit of espionage that, frankly, the CIA would certainly have been able to accomplish, given more time and a little ingenuity.

And now what?

Now I would, if everything went as planned, find myself in proximity with the old KGB spymaster. Perhaps I'd learn why he had met with my late father-in-law. Perhaps not.

This much I knew, or thought I knew: Edmund Moore's fears had been borne out. Toby had confirmed it. Something was going on, something involving CIA, something substantial and frightening. Something, I suspected, of global consequence. And it was accelerating. First Sheila McAdams, then Molly's father. Then Senator Mark Sutton. And now Van Aver, in Rome.

But what was the pattern?

Toby had sent me to find out what I could from Vladimir Orlov. I had almost been killed in the process.

For what?

For learning something that Harrison Sinclair knew? Something he was killed for knowing?

Embezzlement, elemental greed, was not an adequate explanation. My instincts told me it was something more, something much greater, something of enormous and pressing concern to whoever the conspirators were.

And if I was fortunate, I would learn it from Orlov.

If I was fortunate. A secret that certain people of immense power wanted kept secret.

And as likely as not, I'd learn nothing. They would release Molly, I felt confident, in any case, but I would return home empty-handed. And then what?

I would never be safe, and neither would Molly. Not as long as I possessed this terrible gift; not as long as Rossi or any of his cronies knew where to find me.

Dispirited now, I left the café and found, on the winding main street, Via Roma, a small store called Boero, whose window displayed ammunition and hunting supplies for this hunting-obsessed region. The cases and boxes in the inelegant display bore such names as Rottweil, Browning, Caccia Extra. What I didn't find there I managed to turn up in a much fancier hunting-supply store in Siena, a place on the tiny Via Rinaldi called Maffei, which boasted pricy hunting jackets and accessories (for those wealthy Tuscans, I imagined, who wanted to look fashionable while they went out for a day's sport hunting, or who wanted to at least *look* like they hunted). Next, I arranged the transfer of a great deal of money from my old Washington account to an American Express office in London, and from there to Siena, where it was given to me in American dollars.

Finally there was enough breathing room – and I had sufficiently collected my thoughts – to place a telephone call. On Via dei Termini in Siena I located an SIP office (the Italian telephone company) where, from one of the booths, I dialed an international number.

After the customary clicks and hums and staticky interludes, the phone on the other end was answered on the third ring, as it was supposed to be.

A female voice said, 'Thirty-two hundred.'

I said, 'Extension nine eighty-seven, please.'

Another click, and the timbre of the connection was altered almost imperceptibly, as if the call were being routed through some special, insulated fiber-optic cable. Likely it was: from a communications outpost near Bethesda, to a switching station in Canada (Toronto, I believe) and back to Langley.

A familiar male voice came on the line. Toby Thompson.

'The *Cataglyphis* ant,' he said, 'goes out in the noonday sun.'

234

This was a coded exchange he had devised, a reference to the Saharan silver ant, which is able to withstand temperatures higher than any other animal in the world, as high as 140 degrees Fahrenheit.

I responded: 'And they sprint faster than any other animal, too.'

'Ben!' he said. 'What the hell are you – *where* the hell – ?'

Could I trust Toby? Perhaps yes, perhaps no, but it was best to take as few chances as possible. After all, what if Alex Truslow were right and the Agency was infiltrated? I knew that the security precautions of the telephone connection, the multiple switchbacks and so forth, would give me more than eighty seconds before my location could be traced, so I would have to speak quickly.

'Ben, what's going on?'

'You might want to fill *me* in, Toby. Charles Van Aver is dead, as I'm sure you know –'

'Van *Aver* – !'

As far as I could divine through the miracle of modern telecommunications, Toby sounded genuinely shocked. I glanced at my watch, and said, 'Look into it. Ask around.'

'But where are you? You haven't checked in. We agreed . . .'

'I just wanted you to know that I will not be checking in according to your schedule. It's not secure. But I'll be in touch. I'll call back tonight between ten and eleven my time, and I want to be connected immediately with Molly. You can do it; you guys are wizards. If the connection isn't made within twenty seconds, I'll disconnect.'

'Listen, Ben –'

'One more thing. I'm going to assume your . . . apparatus is leaky. I suggest you plug the leaks, or you'll lose contact with me entirely. And you don't want that.'

I hung up. Seventy-two seconds: untraceable.

I strolled through the crowds along Via dei Termini, preoccupied, and found a kiosk that had a good selection of foreign newspapers: the *Financial Times* and *The Independent*, *Le Monde*, the *International Herald-Tribune*,

Frankfurter Allgemeine Zeitung, Neue Zürcher Zeitung. I picked up a copy of the *Trib* and glanced at the front page as I continued walking. The lead story, of course, was the German election.

And a small headline below the fold on the left-hand side of the page read:

U.S. SENATE COMMITTEE TO INVESTIGATE CORRUPTION IN CIA

Wholly absorbed, I jostled a glamorous young Italian couple, both attired in olive green. The male, who was wearing Ray-Ban aviator sunglasses, shouted out some imprecation in Italian I didn't quite understand.

'*Scusi,*' I said as menacingly as I could.

Then I noticed the headline at the top left:

ALEXANDER TRUSLOW NAMED TO HEAD CIA.

White House sources say that Alexander Truslow, a longtime CIA official who was acting director of the CIA in 1973, will be named as the new director. Mr Truslow, who heads an international consulting firm based in Boston, vowed to launch a major cleanup of the CIA, which is being rocked by the allegations of corruption.

Things had begun to make sense. No wonder Toby had spoken of a 'grave urgency.' Truslow represented a threat to some very powerful people. And now, having just been named as Harrison Sinclair's replacement, he was in a position to do something about the 'cancer,' as he called it, which was overtaking the Agency.

Hal Sinclair had been killed, as had Edmund Moore, and Sheila McAdams, and Mark Sutton, and perhaps – probably – others.

The next target was obvious.

Alex Truslow.

Toby was right: there was no time to lose.

34

At a few minutes after three in the afternoon I drove up to the stone quarry near where I had spent the previous night.

One hour and fifteen minutes later I was seated in the front passenger seat of a beat-up Fiat truck, pulling up to the main gate of Castelbianco. I was wearing workclothes, heavy blue twill trousers and a light blue workshirt, well worn and covered in dust. Driving the truck was the gangly, dark-skinned young worker I'd met at the bar in Rosia early that morning.

His name was Ruggiero, and he turned out to be the son of an Italian man and a Moroccan émigré woman. Correctly sizing him up as cooperative, pliable, and very susceptible to a bribe, I had found him at the quarry and taken him aside to ask for information.

Or, rather, to pay for it. I explained that I was a Canadian businessman, a real-estate speculator, and I was willing to pay handsomely for information. Slipping Ruggiero five ten-thousand-lire notes (about forty dollars), I told him I needed to somehow get to the 'German' in order to talk business – specifically, to make a generous (if somewhat illegal) cash offer for the Castelbianco property. I had a potential buyer; the 'German' would turn a quick, easy profit.

'Hey, wait a second,' Ruggiero said. 'I don't want to lose my job.'

'There's nothing to worry about,' I replied. 'Not if we do it right.'

Ruggiero supplied me with all the information I needed about the renovation taking place at Castelbianco. He told me that a member of the housekeeping staff dealt directly with the quarry, placing orders for marble and granite tiles.

Apparently, the 'German' was overseeing a rather thorough-going renovation; the crumbling wing was being restored with deep green Florentine marble tiles for the floor and granite for the terrazzo. He had hired expert stonemasons, real old-world craftsmen, from Siena.

Ruggiero drove a hard bargain. It cost me seven hundred thousand lire – more than five hundred dollars – for a few hours of his time. He called his contact at Castelbianco and informed him that the last order of Florentine marble they had delivered, three days before, was short, as it turned out. An employee who'd since been fired had made a dreadful mistake. The remainder of the order would be delivered immediately.

It was unlikely that anyone at Castelbianco would argue over the quarry's willingness to supplement the earlier order, and indeed, no one did. In the worst case – if, somehow, Orlov's staff became suspicious, tallied up the marble already delivered, and learned that no mistake had actually been made – then Ruggiero would simply say that he'd been mis-informed. And nothing would happen to him.

Minutes later we were at the gate of Castelbianco. The guard emerged from his stone booth, holding a log sheet on a clipboard, and approached the truck, blinking in the sun.

'Sì?'

His intonation and accent were such that, had we been a few hundred miles to the north, I could quite easily imagine him saying 'Da?' with just the same brusqueness. With his close-cropped yellow hair, his healthy, ruddy complexion, he was unmistakably of Russian peasant stock, the sort of complaisant, beefy thug so often employed at the Lubyanka.

'Ciao,' Ruggiero said.

The guard nodded with recognition, made a check mark on the visitors' log, glanced at the load of marble slabs we were hauling, then saw me.

And nodded again.

I gave him the barest shrug of acknowledgment and scowled as if I could hardly wait for this shift to be over.

Ruggiero revved the engine and guided the truck slowly between the massive stone pillars. The dirt road wound past a few small stone houses with slanted roofs, which I assumed belonged to workers. Chickens and ducks roamed the tiny brown yards in front of the houses, chortling and honking angrily. A couple of workers were spreading white powder from a large sack of fertilizer over a sparse patch of lawn.

'His people live there.'

I grunted, not wanting to ask who 'his people' were, if indeed Ruggiero knew.

A small flock of sheep was scattered on a hillside on our left. They had slender pink faces, quite different in appearance from any sheep I had seen in America, and bleated suspiciously, in chorus, as we passed.

Up ahead, the house loomed. 'What's it like inside?' I asked.

'Never been inside. I've heard it's nice, but a little run-down. Needs work. The German got it cheap, I heard.'

'Good for him.'

We rounded a bend above a narrow ravine, passed another low stone building. This one had no windows.

'Rat house,' Ruggiero said.

'Hmm?'

'I'm joking. Half joking. It's where they used to keep the food garbage. It swarms with rats, so I stay away from it. Now they use it to store stuff.'

I shuddered at the image. 'How do you know so much about this place?'

'Castelbianco? My friends and I used to play around here when we were kids.' He shifted into neutral, coasted the truck up next to a terrace where several hunched, sun-bronzed middle-aged men were cutting and fitting limestone tiles in an ornate pattern of concentric circles. 'In those days, when Castelbianco belonged to the Peruzzi-Moncinis, they'd let kids from Rosia play here. They didn't care. Sometimes we helped out with chores.' He reached behind to the backseat, pulled out two pairs of coarse canvas gloves, and handed me a pair. As he pulled at a lever that mechanically lowered the load of marble to the ground, he said, 'If you get someone to buy it from the German, try to find someone who'll get rid of the barbed wire. This place used to belong to the whole *comune.'*

He jumped out of the cabin, and I followed him around to the back, where he began to lift marble slabs and set them gently down in a neat pile near the terrace.

'Che diavolo stai facendo, Ruggiero?' one of the masons shouted, turning toward us and waving a hand, asking what the hell he was doing.

'Calmati,' Ruggiero said, and kept working. Take it easy. *'Sto facendo il mio lavoro. È per l'interno, credo. Che ne so io?'* Just doing my job, he was saying. I joined him in unloading the marble. The thin slabs, rough on one side, smooth and finished on the other, weren't heavy, but were fragile, and we had to set them down carefully.

'No one told me anything about a delivery of marble,' the same mason, who appeared to be a foreman, continued in Italian, his hands gesticulating. 'The marble was last week. You guys fuck up or something?'

'I just do what they tell me,' Ruggiero said, and gestured to the house. 'The last delivery was short, so Aldo offered to make it up. Anyway, it's none of your fucking business.'

The mason picked up a trowel, smoothed a line of cement, and said resignedly, 'Fuck you.'

We worked in silence for a while, lifting, carrying, setting down, finding a rhythm. I said quietly, 'The guys know you, huh?'

'He does. My brother worked for him for a couple of years. Real asshole. You want us to finish unloading this stuff?'

'Almost,' I said.

'Almost?'

As we worked in silence, I surveyed the house and grounds. Up close, Castelbianco was no palazzo; it was large, and in its way magnificent, but at the same time shabby and in disrepair. Perhaps a million dollars of renovation would restore it to a grandeur it hadn't seen for centuries, but Orlov was barely spending a fraction of that. I wondered where he had gotten the money, but then, why should the former head of Soviet intelligence not have found clever ways to pocket some of the unlimited budget he once controlled, divert hard currency funds to Swiss accounts? And what was he paying his security guards, who might number half a dozen? Not much, I suspected, but then, he was providing these fellows asylum, protection from the arrest and imprisonment they'd face back home in Russia for having so faithfully served the now-discredited KGB. How quickly things had reversed course: the feared, mighty officers of state security, the sword and shield of the Party, were now hunted down like rabid dogs.

But it bothered me that I had been able to get into the grounds of Castelbianco so easily. What sort of security was this for a man in fear for his life, a man driven to strike a deal with the head of the CIA to give him protection, like some shopkeeper in Chicago buying protection from the minions of Al Capone?

The security was modest: there appeared to be no snipers, no closed-circuit cameras. Yet this made a certain sense. His *real* security system was his anonymity, which apparently was so successful that even my own employers didn't know where he was. Too *much* security would have been a . . . well, I could not help thinking 'red flag.' Too thorough a system would have attracted undue attention. An eccentric rich German might employ a few guards, but too sophisticated a system would have been risky. So I was inside, and according to the information I had received, Orlov was inside too. The problem was, how was I going to get into the house? And more to the point, once inside, how would I get out?

For what must have been the twentieth time, I mentally rehearsed my plan, and then signaled to my Italian accomplice to put down the marble slabs and follow me.

'*Aiutatemi!*' Help me! '*Per l'amor di Dio, ce qualcuno chi aiutare?*' Knocking wildly at the heavy wooden door that opened directly from the outside to the kitchen, Ruggiero was bellowing, 'For the love of God, can someone help me?' His right forearm was a frightful mess, a long gash bleeding profusely.

Squatting in the bushes nearby, behind a rusty set of metal

barrels that held food refuse, I watched. A noise inside signaled that someone had heard his desperate knocking. Slowly, with a squeak of the hinges, the door swung open to reveal a rotund old woman wearing a green canvas smock over a shapeless floral-print housedress. Her brown eyes, small circles in a large mass of wrinkles beneath a wild flyaway mane of gray hair, widened suddenly when she saw Ruggiero's wound.

'*Shto eto takoye?*' she said in a high, scared voice. '*Bozhe moi! Pridi, malodoi chelovek! Bystro!*' What's this? she was saying in Russian. My God, come in, young man!

Ruggiero replied in Italian: '*Il marmo . . . Il marmo é affilato . . .*' The marble is sharp.

She was, I presumed, the Russian housekeeper, perhaps a servant who had worked for Orlov in his days of power. And as I anticipated, she behaved with all the motherly concern of a Russian woman of her generation. She naturally wouldn't have guessed that Ruggiero's wound had not been caused by an accident with the sharp-edged marble tiles but had instead been created by me, using stage makeup from a shop in Siena.

Neither did the poor woman suspect that the instant she turned her back to direct this young Italian man into the kitchen for first aid, someone else would jump from the bushes to subdue her. Swiftly, I clamped a chloroform-soaked rag over her mouth and nose, smothering her scream, and supporting her large, awkward body when it went limp.

Ruggiero quietly closed the kitchen door. He glanced at me, alarmed, no doubt thinking: what kind of 'Canadian investor' is this? But his assistance had been bought and paid for, and he would not let me down.

From his childhood days playing at Castelbianco, Ruggiero had known where the entrance to the kitchen was. Already, as far as I was concerned, he had earned his money. When I pulled the coil of slender nylon rope from my overalls, he helped me tie the housekeeper up, taking care that the rope not chafe her, and placing a gag in her mouth, secured by rope, for when she came to. Then, silently, he helped me move the unconscious body from the onion-fragrant kitchen into the large pantry.

242

He shook my hand. I gave him the final payment, in American dollars, and with a quick nervous smile, he said, 'Ciao,' and was gone.

A small, dark set of stone steps led from the kitchen up to a dark corridor, off of which appeared to be unoccupied bedrooms. I crept noiselessly, making my way by feel as much as anything else. Somewhere in the house I heard a faint buzzing, but it seemed quite far off, as if from miles away. There were none of the normal noises a house makes, though, even an ancient castle such as this.

I came to an intersection of two corridors, a bare landing that held only two small, shabby wooden chairs. The insistent buzzing noise was closer, louder now. It came from some-where below. I followed it downstairs, turning left, going straight for a few feet, then left again.

Slipping my hand into the front pocket of my overalls, I touched the Sig-Sauer. I felt the reassuring cold of the pistol's steel.

Now I stood before high oak double-doors. The buzzing came, in irregular intervals, from within.

I grabbed the pistol and, crouching as low to the ground as possible, slowly pulled one of the doors open, not knowing what or whom I'd see inside.

It was a large, empty dining room with bare walls and bare floors and an immensely long oak table set for lunch for one person.

Lunch, evidently, had been eaten.

The single diner, who sat at one end of the table, buzzing furiously for a housekeeper who was not able to answer his calls, was a small, bald old man, an innocuous-looking man wearing thick, black-framed glasses. I had seen pictures of the man hundreds of times before, but I had no idea how small Vladimir Orlov actually was.

He was wearing a suit and tie, strangely: who would come to see him, hiding as he was in Tuscany? The suit wasn't smartly British, as so many modern Russians in positions of power seemed to favor; it was old-style, boxy, of Soviet or Eastern European manufacture, probably several decades old.

Vladimir Orlov: the last head of the KGB, whose likeness, stiff and unsmiling, I had seen countless times in Agency files, in newspaper photographs. Mikhail Gorbachev had brought him in to replace the traitorous KGB chief who had plotted to overthrow Gorbachev's government, during the last convulsions of Soviet power. We knew little about the man, except that he was deemed 'reliable' and 'friendly to Gorbachev' and other traits vaporous and unprovable.

Now he sat before me, furled and small. All the power seemed to have been drained out of him.

He looked up at me, scowled, and said in clipped Siberian-accented Russian, 'Who are you?'

Not for a few seconds was I able to reply, but when I did, it was with a smoothness that I hadn't expected. 'I'm Harrison Sinclair's son-in-law,' I said in Russian. 'I'm married to his daughter, Martha.'

The old man looked as if he'd seen a ghost. His heavy brow lowered, then shot up; his eyes grew narrow, then widened. He seemed to pale at once. '*Bozhe moi,*' he whispered. Oh, my God. '*Bozhe moi.*'

I simply stared, my heart hammering, not understanding what he meant, who he thought I was.

He got slowly to his feet, scowling and half pointing at me accusingly.

'How the hell did you get in here?'

I didn't reply.

'You are foolish to come here.' His words were a whisper, barely audible. 'Harrison Sinclair betrayed me. And now we will both be killed.'

35

I walked slowly into the cavernous dining room. My footsteps echoed against the bare walls, the high vaulted ceilings.

Beneath his glacial calm, his imperious demeanor, Vladimir Orlov's eyes flicked back and forth with great anxiety.

Several seconds of silence passed.

My thoughts raced. *Harrison Sinclair betrayed me. And now we will both be killed.*

Betrayed him? What did this mean?

Orlov spoke now, his voice clear and resonant and reverberating: 'How dare you appear before me.'

The old man reached a hand to the underside of the dining table and depressed a different button. From somewhere in the hallway I heard a long, continuous buzzing noise. Footsteps came from somewhere in the house's interior. The housekeeper, probably returned to consciousness by now but unable to move or be heard, was not answering his summons. But perhaps one of the guards had heard the noise, suspected that something might be wrong.

I withdrew the Sig from the overalls pocket, leveled it at the KGB chairman. I wondered whether Orlov had ever had a gun pointed at him in earnest before. In the circles of intelligence in which he had always worked, at least according to the career assessments I'd read, one's weapons were not guns or Uzis or poison darts, but fitness reports and memoranda.

'I want you to know,' I said, now holding the gun under the table, 'that I have no intention of harming you. We must have a brief chat, you and I, and then I will be gone. When the guard appears, I want you to assure him everything's all right now. Otherwise, you'll most certainly die.'

Before I could elaborate, the door to the dining room flew open, and a guard whom I hadn't seen before leveled an automatic at me, calling out: 'Freeze!'

I smiled casually, gave the old man the briefest glance, and, after the barest moment's hesitation, he told the guard, 'Go on. Thank you, Volodya, but I'm fine. It was a mistake.'

The guard lowered the gun, sized me up – dressed as a workingman as I was, he remained suspicious – untensed slowly, and said, 'Sorry.' He withdrew and closed the door quietly behind him.

I approached the table and took a seat next to Orlov. Sweat glistened on his forehead; his face, up close, looked ashen. Glacial and imperious, yes – but deeply frightened at the same time and trying desperately not to show it.

I was sitting a few feet from him, too close for his comfort, and he turned his head away as he spoke. A disgusted expression crossed his face.

'Why are you here?' he croaked out hoarsely.

'Because of an agreement you reached with my father-in-law,' I said. There was a long pause, during which I concentrated, trying to hear that distinct voice, but getting nothing.

'You have been no doubt followed. You endanger both of us.'

Not answering, I compressed my lips in deep concentration, and suddenly heard a noise, a nonsense phrase, something I didn't understand. A wisp of a thought, surely, but nothing that registered.

'You're not Russian, are you?' I said.

'Why are you here?' Orlov said, twisting in his chair. His elbow caught a serving plate and shoved it, clatteringly, against other dishes. His voice gradually gathered strength, grew louder. 'You fool!'

I heard another floating phrase as he spoke, something I didn't understand, something in a foreign language. What was it? It wasn't Russian, it couldn't be, it sounded unfamiliar. I grimaced, closed my eyes, listened, heard a stream of vowels, words I couldn't decode.

'What *is* it?' he asked. 'Why are you here? What are you doing?' He moved his high-backed carved oak chair back. It squealed loudly against the terra-cotta floor.

'You were born in Kiev,' I said. 'Is that right?'

'*Leave!*'

'You're not Russian-born, are you? You're Ukrainian.'

He got up and started backing out of the room slowly.

I got to my feet too and pulled the Sig out again, reluctant to threaten him again. 'Stay there, please.'

He froze.

'Your Russian has a slight Ukrainian accent. Your Gs give you away.'

'What are you here for?'

'Your native language is Ukrainian. You *think* in Ukrainian, don't you?'

'You know that,' he snapped. 'You didn't need to come here, to endanger me, to learn something that Harrison Sinclair must have told you.' He took a step toward me, as if to menace, a clumsy attempt to regain the psychological advantage. His old Stalinist suit hung on his frame like a scarecrow's. 'If you have something to say to me, or to give to me, it had better be of earth-shaking consequence.'

Another step. He resumed: 'I will assume it is, and I will give you five minutes to explain yourself, and then you had better be gone.'

'Sit, please,' I said, gesturing with the barrel of the gun to his chair. 'This will not take long. My name is Benjamin Ellison. As I said, I am married to Martha Sinclair, the daughter of Harrison Sinclair. Martha inherited the entirety of her father's estate. Your contacts – I am sure you have extensive contacts – can confirm I am who I say I am.'

He seemed to relax – and then he lunged, seeming to lose his footing as he vaulted toward me, hands outstretched. With a loud, almost subhuman, guttural sound – a choked, twisted *aaaghgh*! – he threw himself at me, grabbing my knees, trying to throw me off balance. I twisted, then grabbed his shoulder and forced him to the ground.

He sprawled on the floor at the base of the oak table,

gasping, his face crimson. 'No,' he gasped. His eyeglasses clattered to the ground a foot or so from his head.

Keeping the gun trained on him, I reached to retrieve his glasses, and with my free arm I somewhat awkwardly helped him up. 'Please,' I said, 'please don't try that again.'

Orlov sagged into the nearest dining chair like a marionette, exhausted yet wary. It has always fascinated me that world leaders, once out of power, are so palpably diminished in an almost physical sense. I remember once meeting Mikhail Gorbachev at the Kennedy School in Boston, shaking his hand after a lecture he gave a few years after he was so unceremoniously booted out of the Kremlin by Boris Yeltsin. And Gorbachev struck me as a small, very mortal, very ordinary person. I felt a pang of sympathy for the man.

A Russian phrase.

I heard it, heard his thoughts: a recognizable phrase, in Russian, amid a stream of Ukrainian, like a slug of uranium embedded in graphite.

Yes; he was born in Kiev. At the age of five his family moved to Moscow. Like the physician in Rome, he, too, was bilingual, though he thought mainly in Ukrainian, with the occasional bit of Russian interspersed.

The phrase he thought translated as *wise men*.

'You know very little,' I said, feigning great assurance, 'about the Wise Men.'

Orlov laughed. His teeth were bad, gapped and uneven and stained. 'I know everything, Mr . . . Ellison.'

I watched his face closely, concentrating, seeing what I could pick up. Again, most of it seemed to be in Ukrainian. Here and there I could pick up cognates, words that sounded similar to those in Russian, or English, or German. I heard *Tsyurikh*, which had to be Zurich. I heard *Sinclair*, and something that sounded like *bank*, although I couldn't be sure.

'We must talk,' I said. 'About Harrison Sinclair. About the deal you struck with him.'

Again I leaned close to him, as if thinking deeply. A stream of strange words came at me now, low and fuzzy and indistinct, but of them one word screamed out at me. It was, again, *Zurich*, or something that sounded like it.

'Deal!' he scoffed. The old spymaster gave a loud, dry laugh. 'He stole billions of dollars from me and from my country – *billions* of dollars! – and you dare to call this a deal!'

36

So it was true. Alex Truslow was right.

But . . . *billions of dollars?*

Was this all about money? Was that it? Money, throughout history, has motivated most of the great acts of evil, when you come right down to it. Was money why Sinclair and the others were killed, why the Agency was, as Edmund Moore warned me, being torn apart?

Billions of dollars.

He regarded me arrogantly, almost superciliously, and attempted to straighten his glasses.

'And now,' he said with a sigh, switching to English, 'it is only a matter of time before my own people find me. Of that I have no doubt. I'm not entirely surprised that you people tracked me down. There is no place on earth – no place on earth one would bear to live – where one can't eventually be found. But what I don't know is *why* – why you decided to endanger my life by coming here, whatever your reasons. That was enormously foolish.' His English was excellent, apparently fluent, and British-accented.

Inhaling sharply, I said: 'I was extremely cautious in getting here. You have little to worry about.' His expression did not waver. His nostrils flared slightly; his eyes, steady, betrayed nothing.

'I am here,' I continued, 'to put things right. To rectify the wrong my father-in-law did to you. I am prepared to offer you a great deal of money for your assistance in locating the money.'

He pursed his lips. 'At the risk of being vulgar, Mr Ellison, I would be extremely interested to know your definition of "a great deal." '

I nodded and got up. Replacing the gun in my pocket, and backing up just beyond his range, I reached down and raised the legs of my overalls, easing the canvas up to expose the banded wads of American dollars strapped to my calves. I released the Velcro restraints that I had purchased at a sporting goods store in Siena, and the money came off each leg in two segments.

Those I placed on the table.

It was a great deal of money – probably more than Orlov had ever seen, and certainly more than I had ever seen – and it had its persuasive effect.

He scanned the wads, rifled through them, apparently satisfying himself cursorily that it was real. He looked up and said, 'There is – what? – perhaps three-quarters of a million dollars here?'

'An even million,' I said.

'Ah,' he said, his eyes wide. And then he laughed, a harsh, derisive caw. Theatrically, he pushed the bundles toward me. 'Mr Ellison, I am in very difficult financial straits. But as much as this is – it is as nothing compared to what I was supposed to receive.'

'Yes,' I said. 'With your help, I can locate the money. But we must first talk.'

He smiled. 'I will accept your money as a good-faith payment. That proud I am not. And, yes, we will talk. And then we will come to an agreement.'

'Fine,' I said. 'In that case, let me put my first question to you: Who killed Harrison Sinclair?'

'I had hoped you would be able to tell *me* that, Mr Ellison.'

'But it was Stasi agents,' I said, 'who carried out the order.'

'Quite likely, yes. But whether it was Stasi or Securitate, it had nothing to do with me. Certainly it would not have been in my interest to eliminate Harrison Sinclair.'

I cocked a brow questioningly.

'When Harrison Sinclair was killed,' Orlov said, 'I and my country were cheated out of over ten billion dollars.'

I felt my face flush, hot and prickly. From everything I could tell, he was speaking the truth. My heart thudded slowly and evenly.

Certainly there was nothing modest about Orlov's Tuscan villa, but neither was he living in great wealth, as some of those high-level Nazis did in Brazil and Argentina in the years after the Second World War. A great sum of money would purchase not only a life of luxury but, far more important, protection for a lifetime.

But *ten billion dollars*!

Orlov continued: 'What was that memoir written by the CIA Director under Nixon, William Colby? *Honorable Men*, isn't that what it was called?'

I nodded warily. I didn't much like Orlov, though for reasons having nothing to do with ideology or the bitter rivalry people used to imagine existed between the KGB and the CIA. Hal Sinclair once confided to me that when he was station chief in various world capitals, some of his best buddies were his opposite numbers in KGB station. We are – I should say *were* – far more alike than different.

No, I found Orlov's smugness repellent. Moments ago he had been lunging at me like an old woman; now he sat there like a pasha – and thinking mostly in *Ukrainian*, for God's sake.

'Well,' Orlov continued, 'Bill Colby was, is, an honorable man. Perhaps too honorable for his profession. And until he betrayed me, I thought Harrison Sinclair was too.'

'I don't understand.'

'How much of this did he tell you?'

'Very little,' I admitted.

'Just before the collapse of the Soviet Union,' he said, 'I secretly contacted Harrison Sinclair, using back channels that had not been used in many years. There are – were, rather – ways. And I asked his help.'

'To do what?'

'To remove from my country most of its gold reserves,' he said.

I was astonished, even overwhelmed . . . but it made a certain sense. It gibed with what I knew, what I had read in the press as well as heard from spook friends of mine.

The Central Intelligence Agency had always calculated that

the Soviet Union had tens of billions of dollars in gold reserves, in their central vaults in and around Moscow. But then suddenly, immediately after the hard-line Communist coup d'état failed in August 1991, the Soviet government announced that it had a mere *three* billion dollars in gold.

This news had sent shock waves throughout the world financial community. Where on earth could all that gold have disappeared to? There were all manner of reports. One reliable one had it that the Soviet Communist Party had ordered 150 tons of silver, eight tons of platinum, and at least 60 tons of gold to be hidden abroad. It was alleged that Communist Party officials may have hidden as much as fifty *billion* dollars in Western banks, in Switzerland, Monaco, Luxembourg, Panama, Liechtenstein, and a whole array of offshore banks, such as the Cayman Islands.

The Soviet Communist Party, it was reported, laundered money furiously in its last years of existence. Heads of Soviet enterprises were creating fake joint ventures and shell companies to spirit money out of the country.

In fact, the Yeltsin government even went so far as to hire an American investigative firm, Kroll Associates – one of Alex Truslow's chief competitors, by the way – to track down the money, but nothing ever turned up. It was even reported that one massive transfer to Swiss banks was ordered by the Party's business manager, who committed suicide – or was murdered – a day or so after the coup collapsed.

Might it have been Orlov's former comrades, seeking to stop me from tracking down the gold, who killed the CIA man Charles Van Aver in Rome?

I listened in dull amazement.

'Russia,' he said, 'was falling apart.'

'You mean the *Soviet Union* was falling apart.'

'Both. I mean both. It was clear to me and to everyone else with a brain that the Soviet Union was about to be cast on the ash-heap of history, to use Marx's tired phrase. But Russia, my beloved Russia – it was about to collapse as well. Gorbachev had brought me in to run the KGB after Kryuchkov had

253

attempted a coup. But the power was slipping from Gorbachev's fingers. The hard-liners were pilfering the country's riches. They knew Yeltsin would take over, and they were lying in wait to destroy him.'

I had read and heard a great deal about the mysterious disappearance of Russia's assets, in the form of hard currency, precious metals, even artwork. This was not news to me.

'And so,' he went on, 'I came up with a plan to spirit out of the country as much of Russia's gold as I could. The hard-liners would try to regain power, but if I could keep their hands off the country's wealth, they would be powerless. I wanted to save Russia from disaster.'

'So did Hal Sinclair,' I said, as much to him as to myself.

'Yes, exactly. I knew he would be sympathetic. But what I was proposing frightened him. It was to be an off-the-books operation, in which the CIA helped the KGB steal Russia's gold. Move it out of the country. So that one day, when it was safe, it could be returned.'

'But why did you need the help of the CIA?'

'Gold is very difficult to move. Extraordinarily difficult to move. And given how carefully I was being watched, I could not have it moved out of the country. My people and I were under constant scrutiny, constant surveillance. And I certainly could not have it liquidated, sold – it would be traced back to me in a second.'

'And so you two met in Zurich.'

'Yes. It was a very complicated procedure. We met with a banker he knew and trusted. He set up an account system to receive the gold. He agreed to my condition, that I be allowed to "disappear." He had all pertinent location data on me deleted from the CIA's data banks.'

'But how did Sinclair – or the CIA – manage to get it out?'

'Oh,' he said wearily, 'there are ways, you know. The same channels that were used to smuggle defectors out of Russia in the old days.'

These channels, I knew, included the military courier system, which is protected by the Vienna Convention. This particular method was used to extract several famous defectors from behind the Iron Curtain. I remember hearing gossip about one legendary defector, Oleg Gordievsky, on the Agency rumor grapevine, to the effect that he'd been taken out in a furniture truck. It wasn't true, but at least it was plausible.

He continued: 'An entire military aircraft is treated as a diplomatic pouch, allowed to leave the country uninspected. And of course there are sealed trucks. Quite a few methods that the CIA has access to, which we did not, because we were being watched so closely. There were informants everywhere, even among my own personal secretaries.'

Something didn't entirely click, however. 'But how did Sinclair know he could trust you? How the hell could he be assured you weren't one of the bad guys?'

'Because,' Orlov said, 'of what I offered him.'

'Explain.'

'Well, he wanted to clean up CIA. He believed it was rotten through and through.

'And I gave him the evidence that it was.'

37

Orlov looked up at the door as if he expected one of his guards to appear. He sighed.

'In the early 1980s we finally began to develop the technology to intercept the most sophisticated communications between your CIA headquarters and other government agencies.' He sighed again, then gave a perfunctory smile. It was as if he'd told the exact story before.

'The satellite and microwave equipment on the roof of the Soviet embassy in Washington began to pick up a broad range of signals. They confirmed information we had already received from a penetration agent at Langley.'

'Which was?'

Another perfunctory smile. I began to wonder whether that was simply the way he smiled, a quick twitch of the mouth, the eyes unchanging, wary. 'What was the CIA's great mission from its founding until, oh, 1991?'

I smiled, one case-hardened cynic to another. 'To defeat world communism and generally make life hell for you guys.'

'Right. Was there ever a time when the Soviet Union was realistically a threat to the United States?'

'Where do I begin? Lithuania, Latvia, Estonia? Hungary? Berlin? Prague?'

'But to the *United States*.'

'You had the bomb, don't let's forget.'

'And we were as afraid to use it as you were. Only *you* used it; we did not. Did anyone at Langley seriously believe that Moscow had either the means or the will to take over the world? And what were we supposed to have *done* with the world once we took possession – run it into the ground the way, I'm sorry to say, our great esteemed Soviet leaders did the once-great Russian empire?'

'There was self-delusion on both sides,' I conceded.

'Ah. But this . . . *delusion* . . . certainly kept the CIA working overtime for years, did it not?'

'What's your point?'

'Simply this,' Orlov said. 'Your great mission now is to defeat corporate espionage, is that right?'

'So I'm told. It's a different world now.'

'Yes. International corporate espionage. The Japanese and the French and the Germans all want to steal valuable trade secrets from your poor, beleaguered American corporations. And only the Central Intelligence Agency can make America safe for capitalism.

'Well, by the mid-1980s, the KGB was the only intelligence service in the world equipped to fully monitor communications coming out of CIA headquarters. And what we learned simply confirmed the darkest suspicions of some of my most deeply-dyed Communist brethren. From intercepts obtained between Langley and its outposts in foreign capitals, Langley and the Federal Reserve, et cetera, we learned that CIA had for years been rather busily engaged in directing its formidable espionage abilities against the *economic* structures of ostensible allies like the Japanese and the French and the Germans. Against private corporations in these countries. All for the sake of protecting American national security.'

He paused, turned to look at me, and I said, 'So? Normal part of business.'

'So,' Orlov continued, settling comfortably back in his chair, and lifting both palms at once as if he'd made his point. 'We thought we'd picked up the contours of a normal money-laundering operation – you know, money flows out of Langley's accounts at the Federal Reserve in New York to the various CIA stations around the world. Wherever it's needed to fund covert operations for democracy, yes? New York to Brussels, New York to Zurich, to Panama City, to San Salvador. But no. Not at all.'

He looked at me and twitched another smile. 'The more our

financial geniuses dug –' He noticed my skepticism, and said, 'Yes, we did have a few geniuses among all the fools. The more they dug, the more they confirmed their suspicions that this wasn't standard money-laundering at all. Money wasn't just being channeled. Money was being *made*. Money was being *amassed*. Earned from corporate espionage. Intercept after intercept proved this.

'Was it the CIA as an institution? No. Our asset inside Langley confirmed that it was just a few people. Privateers. These operations were controlled by a small cell of individuals in CIA.'

'The "Wise Men." '

'An ironic name, I must assume. A tiny group of public servants inside CIA was becoming enormously rich. Using the intelligence they obtained from these espionage operations to enrich themselves. Rather handsomely too.'

The fact is, it's quite common for CIA operatives to skim from their budgets, their funds, which are fluid and poorly documented (for reasons of secrecy: no CIA director who's ordered a covert operation in some third-world country wants to leave a paper trail for some congressional oversight committee). Many operatives I have met make a habit of leeching – *tithing*, some of them call it – ten percent of the funds to which they have access, and squirreling it away in a Swiss numbered account. I never did it, but those who did, did it to provide themselves with a security blanket, protection in case anything went wrong. The green-eyeshade accounting types back in Langley routinely write off these sums, knowing full well where they've gone.

I said as much to Orlov, who shook his head slowly in response. 'We are talking about vast sums of money. Not tithing.'

'Who were – *are* they?'

'We had no names. They were too protected.'

'And how did they amass their fortunes?'

'It doesn't take a deep understanding of business or microeconomics, Mr Ellison. The Wise Men were privy to the most intimate conversations and strategy sessions in boardrooms and corporate offices and automobiles in Bonn and Frankfurt and Paris and London and Tokyo. And with the intelligence thereby gathered . . . Well, it was a simple matter to make strategic investments in the stock markets of the world, particularly New York, Tokyo, and London. After all, if you *knew* what Siemens or Philips or Mitsubishi was up to, you knew what stock to buy or sell, isn't that right?'

'So it wasn't embezzlement, really, at all?' I said.

'Not at all. Not *embezzlement*. But manipulation of stock markets, violations of hundreds of American and foreign laws. And the Wise Men did quite well, really. Their bank accounts in Luxembourg and Grand Cayman and Zurich flourished. They made quite a fortune. Hundreds of millions of dollars, if not more.'

He looked up again at the double doors, and went on, a small look of triumph on his pinched face. 'Think of what we could have done with the evidence – the transcripts, the intercepts . . . The mind reels. We couldn't have asked for anything better to use in propaganda. America is stealing from its allies! We couldn't have anything better. Once we leaked that, NATO would have been destroyed!'

'My God.'

'Oh, but then came 1987.'

'Meaning what?'

Orlov shook his head slowly. 'This is not known to you?'

'What happened in 1987?'

'Have you forgotten what happened to the American economy in 1987?'

'The economy?' I asked, puzzled. 'There was the great stock market crash in October 1987, but apart –'

'Exactly. "Crash" may be an overstatement, but certainly the American stock markets collapsed on, I believe, October 19, 1987.'

'But what does that have to do with –'

'A stock market "crash," to use your word, is not necessarily a disaster to one who is prepared for it. Very much the opposite; a group of savvy investors can make huge profits in a

259

stock market crash, by short-selling, futures and arbitrage, and other means, correct?'

'What are you saying?'

'I am saying, Mr Ellison, that once we knew what these Wise Men were doing, what their conduits were, we were able to follow their activities quite closely – unknown to them.'

'And they made money in the 1987 crash, is that it?'

'Using computerized program trading and fourteen hundred separate trading accounts, calibrating precisely with Tokyo's Nikkei and pulling the levers at exactly the right time, and with the right velocity, they not only made vast sums of money in the crash, Mr Ellison, they caused it.'

Dumbfounded, I could do no more than stare.

'So you see,' he continued, 'we had some very damaging evidence of what a group within the CIA had done to the world.'

'And did you use it?'

'Yes, Mr Ellison. There was a time when we did.'

'When?'

'When I say "we," I refer to my organization. You recall the events of 1991, the coup d'état against Gorbachev, instigated and organized by the KGB. Well, as you well know, your CIA had advance information that this coup was being planned. Why do you think you did nothing to forestall the plan?'

'There are theories,' I said.

'There are theories, and there are facts. The facts are that the KGB possessed detailed, explosive files on this group that called itself the Wise Men. These files, once released to the world, would have destroyed America's credibility, as I've told you.'

'And so the CIA was made inert,' I said. 'Blackmailed by the threat of disclosure.'

'Precisely. And who would give up such a weapon? Not a dedicated opponent of the United States. Not a loyal KGB man. What better proof could I offer.'

'Yes,' I said. 'Brilliant.'

'Who knows of the existence of these files?'

'Only a handful of people,' he said. 'My predecessor at the

KGB, Kryuchkov, who is alive but fears for his life too much to talk. His chief aide, who was executed – no, excuse me, I believe *The New York Times* published a story that said he had "committed suicide" just after the coup, am I right? And, of course, I.'

'And you gave him these amazing files.'

'No,' he said.

'Why not?'

A brief shrug, a twitch of a smile. 'Because the files had disappeared.'

'*What?*'

'Corruption was rampant in Moscow in those days,' Orlov explained. 'Even more rampant than it is now. The old order – the millions of people who worked in all the old bureaucracies, the ministries, the secretariats – the entirety of the Soviet government knew that their days were numbered. Factory managers were selling off their goods to the black markets. Clerks were selling off files in the Lubyanka offices of the KGB. Boris Yeltsin's people had taken many files from KGB headquarters, and some of *those* seized files were changing hands! And then I was told that the file on the Wise Men had disappeared.'

'Files like that don't simply disappear.'

'Of course not. I was told that a rather low-level file clerk in the KGB's First Chief Directorate had taken the file home with her and sold it.'

'To whom?'

'A consortium of German businessmen. I was told she sold it to them for something over two million deutsche marks.'

'About a million American dollars. But surely she could have gotten far more.'

'Of course! That file was worth a great deal of money. It contained the tools to blackmail some of the highest-ranking officials in the CIA! It was worth far, far more than this foolish woman sold it for. Greed can make one irrational.'

I suppressed the urge to smile. 'A German consortium,' I mused. 'Why would a group of Germans be interested in blackmailing the CIA?'

'I didn't know.'

'But you do now?'

'I have my theories.'

'Such as?'

'You are asking me for facts,' he said. 'We met in Zurich, Sinclair and I – in conditions of absolute secrecy, naturally. By this time I had left the country. I knew I would never return.

'Sinclair was furious to learn that I no longer had the incriminating files, and he threatened to cancel the deal, to fly back to Washington and put an end to this. We quarreled for many hours. I tried to make him believe the truth, that I was not deceiving him.'

'And did he?'

'At the time I thought he did. Now I do not.'

'Why?'

'Because I thought we had a deal, and as it turned out, we did not. I left Zurich for this house – which Sinclair, incidentally, had found for me – and awaited further word. Ten billion dollars was now in the West. Gold that belonged to Russia. It was an enormous gamble, but I had to trust in Sinclair's honesty. More than that, in his own self-interest. He wanted to keep Russia from becoming a right-wing, Russian-chauvinist dictatorship. He too wanted to spare the world that. But I think it was the files. The fact that I did not have the Wise Men files to give him. He must have felt that I was not playing fair. Why else would he have double-crossed me?'

'Double-crossed you?'

'The ten billion dollars went into a vault in Zurich. Sitting in a vault beneath Bahnhofstrasse with two access codes required to secure its release. But I could not gain access to it. And then Harrison Sinclair was killed. And now there is no hope of taking back the gold. So I hope you understand that I certainly had no interest in having him killed, now, did I?'

'No,' I agreed. 'You would not. But perhaps I can help you now.'

'If you have Sinclair's access codes –'

'No,' I said. 'There are no codes. None were left to me.'

'Then I am afraid there is nothing you can do.'

'Wrong. There *is* something I can do. I need the name of the banker you met with in Zurich.'

And at that moment the tall double-doors at the far end of the dining room flew open.

I jumped to my feet, not wanting to pull out my gun in the event that it was one of his guards again, in which case everything should look normal; I could not risk appearing to be threatening the master of the house.

I glimpsed a flash of deep blue cloth, and knew at once. Three uniformed Italian policemen entered, pistols directed at me.

'*Tieniti le mani al fianco!*' one of them commanded. Keep your hands at your sides.

They advanced into the room, in SWAT formation. My pistol was useless at this point; I was outnumbered. Orlov backed away from me until he was against a wall, as if avoiding the line of fire.

'*Sei in arresto,*' the other said. '*Non muoverti.*' Don't move – you're under arrest.

I stood there dumbly, confused. How could this have happened? Who had called them? I didn't understand.

And then I saw the small black call button set into the broad oak leg of the dining table, at the point at which it rested on the terra-cotta floor. It was the sort of button you could set off by tapping your foot, the way bank tellers can, unseen, summon the police. It would set off a noiseless alarm far away – in this case, I suspected, as far away as the municipal police headquarters in Siena, which explained why they took so long to arrive. Police, no doubt, in the pay of this mysterious 'German' émigré who required excellent security.

That lunge that Orlov had made at me, his only clumsy move. He knew I would push him to the ground, that he'd be able to roll over and set off the emergency button with his hand or knee or foot.

But something was wrong!

I looked at the ex–KGB chief and saw that he was terrified. Of what?

He was looking at me. 'Follow the gold!' he croaked. Meaning what exactly?

'The name!' I shouted out to him. 'Give me the name!'

'I can't say it!' he croaked, his hands flailing, indicating the policemen. 'They –'

Yes. Of course he could not say it aloud, not in front of these men. 'The *name*,' I repeated. '*Think the name!*'

Orlov looked at me, baffled and desperate. Then he turned to the policemen.

'Where are my people?' he said. 'What have you done with my –'

Suddenly, he appeared to jerk upward. There was a spitting sound, a sound I knew at once, and I turned and saw that one of the policemen was targeting Orlov with a submachine gun, its automatic fire cutting a grotesque swath into the old man's chest. His arms and legs danced around for a second as he expelled one last, horrifying scream. Blood flew everywhere, spattering the stone floors, the walls, the burnished dining table. Orlov, his neck half severed from his body, was crumpled into a nightmarish, bloodied heap.

I let out an involuntary shout of horror. I had pulled out my pistol, outmanned though I realized I was, but there was no point.

Suddenly there was silence. The submachine-gun fire had stopped. Numbly, I raised my hands and gave myself up.

38

The carabinieri led me, handcuffed, through the vaulted door of Castelbianco, and slowly over to a beat-up blue police van.

They looked and dressed like carabinieri, but of course they were not. They were murderers – but whose? Dazed from the horror, I could barely think straight. Orlov had summoned his own people, his protection, only to be surprised when *others* had arrived. *But who were they?*

And why hadn't they killed me as well?

One said something quickly and quietly in Italian. The other two, surrounding me closely, nodded and guided me into the back of the van.

It was not the proper time to move, to do anything sudden, so I went along with them bovinely. One of the policemen sat across from me in the back of the van, while another took the wheel and the third kept watch from the front seat.

None of them spoke.

I watched my police escort, a chubby and dour young man. He sat maybe two feet from me.

I concentrated.

I 'heard' nothing; just the loud muffled roar of the engine as the van negotiated the dirt road out of the estate. Or so I assumed, since there were no windows in the back of the van. The only illumination came from a dome light. My wrists, cuffed in front of me at my lap, chafed.

I tried, again, to empty my mind, to concentrate. In the last week or so this had become reflexive. I would free my mind as much as possible of distracting thoughts – let it become a blank slate, in a way; a receiver. And then I would hear the eddies and floes of thoughts in that slightly altered tonality that indicated I wasn't actually hearing anything spoken aloud.

I made my mind as blank, as receptive as possible, and in time . . . I 'heard' my name . . . and then something else that sounded familiar . . . in that faint, floating way that told me it was thoughts.

In English.

He was thinking in English.

He wasn't a policeman, and he wasn't Italian.

'Who are you?' I asked.

My escort looked up at me, betraying only for an instant his surprise, then shrugged mutely, hostilely, as if he didn't understand.

'Your Italian is excellent,' I said.

The van's engine quieted, then stalled. We had stopped somewhere. It couldn't be far outside the estate – we had been moving for only a few minutes – and I wondered where they had taken me.

Now the doors to the van slid open, and the other two climbed in. One covered me with a gun while the other gestured to me to lie down. When I had done so, he began to attach black nylon restraints to my ankles.

I made it as difficult for him as possible – kicking, wriggling. But with a crisp Velcro crunch he managed to fasten the wide black bands, binding my feet together. Then he discovered the second pistol, concealed in a holster at my left calf.

'One more, guys,' this one said triumphantly.

In English.

'Better not be any others,' said the one who seemed to be in charge. His voice was deep, raspy, cigarette-husky.

'That's it,' the other said, running his hands along my legs and arms.

'All right,' the one in charge said. 'Mr Ellison, we're colleagues of yours.'

'Prove it,' I said, lying prone. All I could see was the dome light immediately above me.

There was no response. 'You can choose to believe us or not,' the one in charge said. 'Makes no difference to us. We

266

just have to ask you a couple of questions. If you're completely honest with us, you have nothing to worry about.'

While he was speaking, I felt something cold and liquid spread over my bare arms, then my face, neck, then ears: a viscous liquid was being applied with a brush.

'Do you know what this is?' the fake policeman in charge asked.

I could taste the sweetness at the edge of my mouth.

'I can guess.'

'Good.'

The three of them hoisted me out of the dark van, into the blinding brightness of the day. There was no point to struggling now. I wasn't going anywhere. Looking around as I was carried out of the van, I saw trees, brush, a flash of barbed wire. We were still on the grounds of Castelbianco, not far from the entrance, in front of one of the small stone buildings I had noticed on the way in.

They set me down on the ground just before the building. I could smell the loamy earth, then the putrescent odor of rotting garbage, and I knew where I was.

Then the one in charge said: 'All you have to do is tell us where the gold is.'

Lying prone on the ground, the back of my head cold from the moist earth, I said, 'Orlov wouldn't cooperate. I barely had the chance to talk with him.'

'That's not true, Mr Ellison,' the middle one said. 'You're not being honest with us.' He lowered a small, shiny object, which I now saw was a razor-sharp scalpel, to my face, and I closed my eyes instinctively. God, no. Don't do it.

There was a swift stroke across my cheek. I felt the shock of cold metal, then a needlelike, sharp pain.

'We don't want to cut you too badly,' the senior one said. 'Please, just give us the information. Where is the gold?'

I felt something hot and sticky oozing down the right side of my face. 'I have no idea,' I said.

The scalpel was now resting on my other cheek, cold and oddly pleasant.

'I really dislike this, Mr Ellison, but we don't have any choice. Again, Frank.'

I gasped out, *'No!'*

'Where is it?'

'I told you, I have no –'

Another stroke. Cold, then stingingly hot, and I felt the blood on my face, running into the sticky bait-liquid they'd painted on me. Tears sprang to my eyes.

'You know why we're doing this, Mr Ellison,' the man in charge said.

I tried to wriggle over onto my stomach, but two of them were holding me firmly down. 'Goddamn you,' I said. 'Orlov didn't know. Is that so hard for you to understand. *He* didn't know – so *I* don't know!'

'Don't make us do it,' the elder said. 'You know we will.'

'If you let me go, I can help you find it,' I whispered.

He gestured with his pistol, and the junior two picked me up, one at my head, the other at my feet. I thrashed wildly, but my mobility was limited, and they had a firm grasp on me.

Now they thrust me into the cold, dark dankness of the tiny stone building, putrid with the high, ripe odor of rotting garbage. I heard rustling. There was another smell too, something acrid, like kerosene or gasoline.

'They removed the trash yesterday,' the elder said, 'so they're quite hungry.'

More rustling.

The crinkle of plastic; more rustling, this time more frantic-sounding. Yes; gasoline or kerosene.

They set me down, my feet bound. The only light in the tiny, awful chamber came in from the door, against which I could see silhouetted two of the false carabinieri.

'What the hell do you *want*?' I croaked.

'Just tell us where it is, and we will take you out.' It was the raspy, deep voice of the one in charge. 'It's that simple.'

'Oh, God,' I couldn't help saying aloud. Never let them see your fear, but it was uncontainable now. A scratching, more rustling. There had to be dozens of them.

'Your personnel file,' he went on, 'tells us you're

extremely phobic of rats. Please, help us out, and this will all be over.'

'I *told* you, he didn't know!'

'*Lock* it, Frank,' the one in charge barked out.

The door to the stone house was slammed shut and bolted. For an instant, all was pitch-black, and then, as my eyes acclimated to the dark, everything took on a doleful amber cast. From all around there was scurrying, rustling. Several large, dark shapes moved on either side of me. My skin prickled.

'When you're ready to talk,' I heard from outside the stone house, 'we'll be here.'

'*No!*' I yelled. 'I've told you everything I know!'

Something ran across my feet.

'*Jesus . . .*'

From outside I heard a hoarse voice addressing me: 'Did you know that rats are what you might call "legally blind"? They operate almost entirely by sense of smell. Your face, with its blood and its coating of sweet liquid, will be irresistible to them. They will gnaw at you out of desperation.'

'*I don't know anything more,*' I bellowed.

'Then I feel very sorry for you,' the hoarse voice came again.

I felt something large and warm and dry and leathery brush against my face, against my lips, several of them, then many of them, and I couldn't open my eyes, and I felt sharp incisions along my cheeks, sharp, unbearable jabs, a papery *whisk-whisk* sound, a tail whipping against my ear, moist feet against my neck.

Only the knowledge that my captors were standing outside, waiting for me to succumb, kept me from bellowing in terrible, indescribable fear.

269

39

Somehow – *somehow* – I was able to keep my mind focused.

I managed to wriggle upright, hurling off the rats as I did so, brushing them off my face and neck with my hands. In a few minutes I had the nylon restraints off, but little good that would do me, as the men waiting outside no doubt figured: the only way out of this massive stone structure was the door, which was securely bolted.

I felt around for a gun until I realized that of course they had taken both of them. I had a few rounds of ammunition strapped to my ankles, beneath my socks, but they were useless without something to fire them.

As my eyes grew used to the dark, I made out the source of the fuel odor. Several gallon cans of gasoline were stacked against one wall, beside an assortment of farm equipment. The 'rat house,' as my Italian friend had called it, may have been for storing garbage, but it also stored materials used in repairing Orlov's land – paper sacks of cement, plastic bags of fertilizer, rakes, fertilizer spreaders, mortar tools, scattered two-by-fours.

As the rats bustled about me – I kept my limbs in constant motion to discourage them from attempting to crawl on me – I surveyed the meager assortment of tools for a way out. A rake, I calculated, would hardly survive an assault on the steel-reinforced door, nor would any of the other farm tools. Gasoline seemed the most obvious means of assault – but assault on what? And what could I ignite it with? I had no matches. And what if I did spill out the gasoline and manage somehow to set it afire? Then what? I would burn alive. That would benefit no one but my captors. Utter foolishness. There had to be a way.

I felt the dry whisk of a rat's tail against my neck, and I shuddered.

From outside, a deep voice intoned: 'All we need is the information.'

The obvious thing to do was to make up information, pretend to break down and blurt it out.

But that would never wash. They would expect that; they would be too well briefed. I had to get out of there.

It was impossible; I was no Houdini; but I had to get out of there. The rats, fat brown little creatures with long, scaly tails, scurried around my feet, making little grunting noises. There were *dozens* of them. A few had climbed up the walls; two of them, crouched atop a fifty-pound bag of fertilizer, leapt toward me, scenting the blood that was congealing on my cheeks. Horrified, I flung out my hands to brush them away. One bit my neck. I thrashed wildly, managing to stomp a few to death.

I knew I would not survive here much longer.

It was the fertilizer bag that first caught my eye. In the dimness I was able to make out a label:

CONCIME CHIMICO
FERTILIZZANTE

A yellow, diamond-shaped label proclaimed it to be an 'oxidizer.' The stuff was used on grass, usually. Thirty-three percent total nitrogen content, the label stated. I moved closer, squinted. Derived of equal parts of ammonium nitrate and sodium nitrate.

Fertilizer.

Was it possible . . . ?

It was an idea. The likelihood of its working was not especially high, but it was worth it. There was simply no other way out.

I reached down and removed the Colt .45 magazine from the strap underneath my left sock. They had taken the gun but overlooked the slim magazine.

It was full: it contained seven rounds. Not much, but it might do. I extracted all seven rounds from the clip.

271

A voice from outside the rat house: 'Enjoy the rest of the day, Ellison. And the night too.'

Containing my horror, I made my way across the rat-crowded stone floor to one wall. One by one I jammed each cartridge into a narrow crack in the mortar. Now there was a row of them, their blunt gray tips sticking out.

With a rusty old pair of pliers I'd found, I whacked the nose of each bullet to loosen the tight friction fit between bullet and cartridge case. Carefully, I closed the jaw of the pliers over each bullet tip, pulling at it, wiggling back and forth, until the bullet came out of its casing. This part of the cartridge was the projectile, the business part, the part that was propelled into a target. But I had no need of it. I needed, instead, what remained in each cartridge: the propellant and the primer.

A trio of rats squirmed over my feet, one scampering over my knee, clawing at the fabric of my shirt, trying to make its unspeakable way up to my face. I gasped in terror, shuddered, slapped at the rats, knocked them to the stone floor.

Now, barely recovering, I removed each brass cartridge casing from the crack in the wall and slowly dumped the small amount of propellant from each one onto a scrap of paper I'd torn from one of the cement sacks. The six cartridges yielded a good little pile of propellant, a dark gray substance made of tiny irregular spheres of nitrocellulose and nitroglycerin.

By far the riskiest step was next: removing the primers. These are the small nickel cups, situated at the base of each cartridge, that contain a small quantity of the high-explosive tetracene. They are also extremely sensitive to percussive force. And, struggling as I was in the dark, surrounded by scurrying rats, my concentration was not at its height. Yet this had to be done with great caution.

So I searched the small stone house quickly for something like a drill bit, but there was nothing even approximating it. A thorough search of every dark corner of the small structure might have yielded me something usable, but I simply could not bring myself to plunge my naked hands into a dark, squirming niche. I am not proud of my terror of rats, but we all have our phobias, and this one was, as I'm sure you agree, not entirely irrational. I would have to make do with the ball-point pen in my pocket. It would do adequately. I removed its ink cartridge.

Very, *very* carefully, I inserted the tip of the ink cartridge into the flash hole at the base of the casing and nudged the first percussion cap out. The second one went much more easily, and in a matter of minutes I had extracted each of the primer cups from six of the cartridges, leaving one intact.

I felt something dry and scaly brush against the back of my neck, and I shivered. My stomach knotted instantly.

As dexterously as I could, I slipped each primer into the intact cartridge, stacking them up, one atop the other. Into the remaining space I poured the entire pile of propellant, then packed it down tight with a forefinger.

I had, now, a tiny bomb.

Next, I located a suitable length of two-by-four, a (rusty) length of pipe, a discarded soft-drink bottle, a cloth rag, a large rock, and an almost-straight long nail. This search took several minutes, an eternity it seemed, with the rats writhing across the ground, an ineffably horrifying moving carpet, it seemed to me. My stomach remained knotted, a tight, sore muscle of tension. I found myself shivering almost constantly.

With the rock I hammered the nail into the lumber until its point had just emerged from the other side. Now the fertilizer. Of the several fifty-pound bags, two had a nitrogen content that ranged from eighteen to twenty-nine. One had a total nitrogen content of thirty-three percent. That was the one I selected. I tore open the bag and scooped out a handful, sprinkling it onto another large scrap of cement-bag paper. A small claque of rats wriggled their way up to the pile, their whiskers twitching with curiosity and greed. With the soda bottle I knocked them away. Their bodies were far more solid and muscular than I had anticipated. If I had to speak, I could not have done so, I was so paralyzed with fright, but somehow my autonomic nervous system kept me working away robotically.

Rolling the soda bottle over the smooth, rounded prills of fertilizer yielded a fine powder. Repeating this process several times, I obtained a large pile of well-powdered fertilizer. In ideal conditions this step wouldn't have been necessary, but these were hardly ideal conditions. For one thing, the sensitizing agent should have been something like nitromethane, the blue fluid used by hot-rod enthusiasts to increase the octane in fuel. But there was nothing of the sort around. There was only gasoline, which would have to do, though it was far less effective. So powdering the nitrogenous fertilizer, thereby decreasing the diameter of the prills, increasing the surface area of the stuff and making it more reactive, was the least I could do.

I uncapped the can of gasoline and gently poured it over the fertilizer powder. There was a great rustling among the teeming rats; sensing danger, they scurried away, turned ghastly little pirouettes, backed up into the recesses of the chamber.

Gingerly, I packed the sensitized fertilizer into the rusty length of pipe, which I'd capped off by dropping in a stone just large enough to block off the end entirely. The pipe was about a half inch in diameter, which was about right. Into the nitrate I wedged the cartridge that I'd prepared.

I surveyed my handiwork and felt a sudden desperate, sinking feeling that the jerry-rigged bomb would not go off. The basic ingredients were there, but it was wildly unpredictable, especially given how hastily I had assembled the thing.

Now, with as much force as I could muster, I wedged the pipe into a crack in the ancient mortar between two stones of the wall.

The fit was extremely tight.

Yes. It might work.

If it did not work . . . If it *deflagrated* instead of *detonated*, it would fail miserably, filling this minuscule space with toxic fumes that would overwhelm me, probably kill me. There was a possibility, too, that a misfire of the pipe bomb would maim or blind me, or worse.

I placed the long two-by-four atop the protruding pipe bomb, the nail point just touching the base of the cartridge. Holding my breath, my heart thudding rapidly, I wrapped the filthy rag around my eyes, lifted the rock I'd used as a hammer a few moments before.

Held it in my right hand directly over the nail in the two-by-four.

And, pulling the rock back two feet or so, I hurled it with enormous force at the nailhead.

The explosion was immense, unbelievably loud, a thunder-clap, and suddenly everything around me was a nightmarish glaring orange visible even through the dirty rag tied tightly over my eyes, a vicious hailstorm of rocks and fire, a cataract of shrapnel, and my entire world was a ball of crimson fire, and this was the last thing I remembered.

Part Five

ZURICH

Le Monde

Germany Elects Moderate As Next Chancellor

Relief Sweeps World Capitals as Troubled Germany Turns Away from New Fascism to Select Centrist Wilhelm Vogel

BY JEAN-PIERRE REYNARD

IN BONN

Europe no longer has to fear the return of Nazism, as voters in the economically ravaged Germany voted overwhelmingly to . . .

40

White, the softest, palest linen-white: I became aware of the
color white, not the absence of color, but a full and rich and
creamy white that soothed me with its stillness and radiance.

And I became aware of soft murmurings from somewhere
far off.

I felt as if I were floating on a cloud, turning upside down,
then right-side up, but I didn't know which way was upside
down, and I didn't care.

More murmurings.

I had just opened my eyes, which seemed to have been
glued shut for an eternity.

I tried to focus on the murmuring shapes before me.

'He's with us,' I heard.

'His eyes are open.'

Slowly, slowly, my surroundings came into focus.

I was in a room that was all white; I was covered with white,
coarse white muslin sheets, white bandages on my arms,
which were the only part of my body I could see.

As my eyes focused, I saw that the room I was in was a
simple room with walls of whitewashed stone. Was I in a
farmhouse, or something like that? Where was I? An intra-
venous line fed into my left arm, but this didn't look like a
hospital.

I heard an accented male voice: 'Mr Ellison?'

I tried to grunt, but nothing seemed to come out.

'Mr Ellison?'

I attempted another grunt. Again nothing emerged, I
thought, but perhaps I was wrong. I must have made some sort
of noise, because the accented voice now said, 'Ah. Good.'

Now I could see the speaker, a small, narrow-faced man with a neatly trimmed beard and warm brown eyes. He was wearing a thick, coarsely knit gray sweater and gray woolen slacks, a pair of worn leather shoes. He was thick around the middle, in early middle age. He thrust a soft, plump hand toward me, and we shook hands.

'My name is Boldoni,' he said. 'Massimo Boldoni.'

With great effort I said: 'Where . . . ?'

'I'm a physician, Mr Ellison, although I know I don't look like one.' He spoke English with a mellifluous Italian accent. 'I don't have my doctor's costume on because I don't normally work on Sunday. In answer to your question, you are in my house. We have several vacant rooms, unfortunately.'

He must have seen the confusion in my face, for he continued: 'This is a *podere* – an old farmhouse. My wife runs this as a guesthouse, the Podere Capra.'

'I don't . . .' I tried to say. 'How did I . . . ?'

'You're doing very well, considering what you've been through.'

I looked down at my bandaged arms, and looked back at the physician.

'You were very fortunate,' he said. 'You may have sustained some hearing loss. You suffered burns only on your arms, and you should be recovering quickly. The burns are not serious; very little skin has been burned, as you'll see. You are a lucky man. Your clothes caught on fire, but they found you before the fire had a chance to do much damage to you.'

'The rats,' I said.

'No rabies or diseases or anything of the sort,' he reassured me. 'You've been thoroughly tested. Our Tuscan rats are healthy specimens. The superficial bites have been treated and will heal very quickly. There may be slight scarring, but that's all. I've put you on a morphine drip for pain relief, which is why you may feel as if you're flying at times, yes?'

I nodded. It really was quite pleasant; there was no sensation of pain. I wanted to know exactly who he was, and how I had gotten there, but I was finding it difficult to articulate words, and I seemed to be overcome with an inertia.

'Gradually I'll be reducing that. But now some friends of yours would like to pay a visit.'

He turned around and knocked lightly a few times on a small, rounded, wooden door. The door opened, and he excused himself.

I felt my throat begin to throb.

In a wheelchair, looking weary and diminished, was Toby Thompson. Standing beside him was Molly.

'Oh, God, Ben,' she said, and rushed toward me.

I had never seen her look so beautiful. She was wearing a brown tweed skirt, a white silk blouse, the strand of pearls I'd bought her at Shreve's, and the good-luck gold cameo locket her father had given her.

We kissed for a long time.

She looked me over, her eyes full of tears. 'I was – we were – so worried about you. My God, Ben.'

She took both of my hands.

'How did you two . . . get here?' I managed to say.

I heard the whir of Toby's wheelchair as he approached.

'I'm afraid we got here a little late,' Molly said, squeezing both of my hands. The pain made me wince, and she drew her hands back suddenly. 'I'm so sorry.'

'How are you feeling?' Toby asked. He was wearing a blue suit and a shiny pair of black orthopedic shoes. His white hair was combed neatly.

'We'll see when they take me off the painkillers. Where am I?'

'Greve, in Chianti.'

'The doctor –'

'Massimo is entirely trustworthy,' Toby said. 'We keep him on retainer – on occasion we need his medical services. Once in a great while we use Podere Capra as a safe house.'

Molly put a hand on my cheek, as if unable to believe I was really lying there before her. Now that I looked at her closely, I could see that she was exhausted, with deep circles under her bloodshot eyes she'd obviously taken pains to cover with makeup. But she looked beautiful despite it all. She was wearing Fracas, my favorite perfume; I found her, as always, irresistible.

281

'God, I've missed you,' she said.

'Me too, babe.'

'You've never called me "babe" before,' she marveled.

'Never too late,' I mumbled, 'to learn a new term of endearment.'

'You never cease to impress me,' Toby said gravely. 'I don't know how you did it.'

'Did what?'

'How you managed to blow a hole in the side of that stone house. If you hadn't done it, you'd probably be dead by now. Those guys were fully prepared to leave you there until you were eaten alive, or, more likely, died of fright. And certainly our people wouldn't have known where to look for you if it weren't for the explosion.'

'I don't understand,' I said. 'How did you know where I was?'

'Let's take this a step at a time,' Toby said. 'We were able to trace your call from Siena in eight seconds.'

'*Eight?* But I thought –'

'Our telecommunications technology has improved significantly since you left the business. You have the ability to ascertain that I'm telling you the truth, Ben. I'll move this damned chair closer if you like.'

For the time being, his assurance was enough; in any case, even if I'd wanted to, I was too woozy to focus my mind.

'As soon as we got a lock on where you were from the phone trace in Siena, we were able to get out here.'

'Thank God,' Molly said. She continued to hold my hands, as if I would slip away from her if she didn't.

'I immediately secured Molly's release, and she and I flew into Milan, accompanied by a few fellows from security. Just in time, I might say.' He smacked the arms of his wheelchair. 'Not too easy, in one of these. Italy doesn't have much in the way of handicapped ramps. In any case, we had a good warning system in place. Have I told you that if you place even a single tiny drop of water at the entrance to an ant nest –'

I groaned. 'Spare me the ants, Toby. I don't have the strength.'

But he continued, ignoring my interruption: '– the worker-ants will run through the nest, making alarm runs, warning of a possible imminent flood, even pointing out emergency exits. In less than half a minute a colony will begin to evacuate the nest.'

'Fascinating,' I said without much conviction.

'Forgive me, Ben. I do get carried away. In any event, your wife has been supervising Dr Boldoni rather closely, making sure you get the best treatment.'

I turned to Molly. 'I want the truth, Mol. How badly wounded am I?'

She smiled sadly, yet encouragingly. Tears still shone in her eyes. 'You'll be fine, Ben. Really, you will. I don't want you to worry.'

'Let's hear it.'

'You've got first- and second-degree burns on your arms,' she said. 'It's going to be painful, but not serious. No more than maybe fifteen percent of your body.'

'If it's not serious, why am I rigged up to all this stuff?' I noticed for the first time that some peculiar bandage, affixed to the end of my index finger, was glowing red, like the extraterrestrial in E.T. I held it up. 'What the hell is this?'

'That's a pulse oximeter. The red glow is a laser beam. It measures your oxygen saturation, which is maintaining at ninety-seven percent. Your heart rate is a little up, around one hundred, which is to be expected.

'Ben, you sustained a mild concussion during the explosion. Dr Boldoni suspected inhalation burns from the fire, which could have been trouble – your trachea can swell, and you can die, if you're not watched carefully. You were coughing up some stuff – he was afraid it was charred pieces of your own trachea. But I took a good look – it was only soot, thank God. We've ruled out inhalation burns, but there is some smoke inhalation.'

'So what's the treatment, Doc?'

'We've got you on IV fluids. D-5 one-half normal saline. With twenty of K at two hundred an hour.'

'English, please.'

'Sorry, that's potassium. I wanted to make sure to hydrate you well, give you plenty of fluids. You're going to have to have dressing changes every day. That white goop you can see under the bandages is Silvidene ointment.'

'You're lucky to have your own personal physician accompanying you,' Toby said.

'Plus, you'll need plenty of bed rest,' she concluded. 'So I've brought you some reading material.' She presented a handful of magazines. Atop the pile was a *Time* magazine cover which featured a close-up photograph of Alexander Truslow. He looked good, vigorous, although the photographer seemed to have made a point of emphasizing the pouches beneath his eyes. THE CIA IN CRISIS, the cover line read, and underneath that: A NEW ERA?

'Looks like Alex hasn't gotten a good night's sleep in ten years,' I observed.

'The next picture does him more justice,' Toby said. He was right; on the cover of *The New York Times Magazine*, Alex Truslow, his silver hair neatly combed, was beaming proudly. '*Can He Save the CIA?*' the headline asked.

Beaming proudly myself, I set down the thatch of magazines. 'When's his confirmation by the Senate?'

'He's confirmed already,' Toby replied. 'The day after the appointment – the Senate intelligence committee was persuaded by the President that we need a full-time director in there as soon as possible. A lengthy confirmation process would just cause turmoil. He was confirmed by all but, I think, two votes.'

'That's terrific,' I said. 'And I'll bet I know who his two opponents were.' I named the committee's most outspoken extreme-right-wing senators, both from the South.

'Right you are,' Toby said. 'But those clowns are going to be nothing compared to the real enemies.'

'Inside the Agency,' I said.

He nodded.

'So tell me this: Who were the thugs masquerading as Italian cops?'

'We don't know yet. Americans. Private mercenaries is my best guess.'

'Agency?'

'You mean, were they CIA personnel? No – there's no record of them anywhere. They're – they were killed. There was a . . . rather fierce shootout. We lost two good men. We're running prints, photos, and other essentials through the computers, see what, if anything, turns up.'

He looked at his watch. 'And just about now . . .'

A telephone on a nearby table rang.

'That should be for you,' he said.

41

It was Alex Truslow. The connection was a good one; his voice sounded so clear it had to have been electronically enhanced, indicating the line was very likely sterile.

'Thank God you're all right,' he said.

'God, and you guys,' I replied. 'You look a little ragged on the cover of *Time*, Alex.'

'Margaret says I look freshly embalmed. Maybe they chose such an unflattering shot because they ask if there's going to be a new era, and they conclude: No way, this chap isn't up to the task. You know – I'm such an old fossil. People always want new blood.'

'Well, they're wrong. Congratulations on the confirmation.'

'The President really twisted some arms on that one. But more important, Ben, I want you to come back.'

'Why?'

'After what you've been through –'

'I don't have the goods yet,' I confessed. 'You told me about a fortune – we're on secure, right?'

'We certainly are.'

'Okay. You talked about a fortune, a missing fortune, but I had no idea the magnitude of it. Or its origin.'

'Care to brief me?'

'Right now?' I looked questioningly at Toby.

He in turn glanced at Molly and said, 'Would you mind terribly leaving us to talk for just a few minutes?'

Molly's eyes were red and swollen, and tears started down her high cheekbones. She glared at him. 'Yes, I would mind terribly.'

Over the phone, Alex said: 'Ben?'

Toby went on apologetically: 'It's just that we need to get into some rather boring, technical things –'

'I'm sorry,' she said coldly. 'I'm not leaving. We're partners, Ben and I, and I won't be excluded.'

There was a long silence, and then Toby said pleasantly, 'So be it. But I have to count on your discretion –'

'Count on it.'

Over the telephone, and at the same time to Molly and Toby, I related the gist of what Orlov had told me. As I talked, both Toby's and Molly's faces registered their astonishment.

'Dear God in heaven,' Truslow breathed. 'Now it makes sense. And so damned wonderful to hear! Hal Sinclair wasn't engaging in criminal activity at all. The man was trying to save Russia. Of course. Now, please – I want you to come back.'

'Why?'

'For God's sake, Ben, these men who subjected you to that god-awful torture – they had to be employed by the faction.'

'The Wise Men.'

'Has to be. Nothing else makes sense. Hal must have confided in someone. Someone he depended upon to help him make the elaborate arrangements with the gold. Someone he confided in was a double. How else could they have learned about the gold?'

'Same deal in Boston?'

'Possibly. No, I'd say *probably*.'

'But that doesn't explain Rome,' I said.

'Van Aver,' he said. 'Yes. And you ask why I'm insisting you come back.'

'Who was behind that one?'

'On that I haven't a guess. There's no evidence to connect it to the Wise Men, though I can't rule it out. Certainly whoever did it knew the details of your planned meeting with him. Maybe through leakage of cable traffic between Rome and Washington. Or maybe it was local – who the hell knows?'

'Local?'

'Through monitoring of Van Aver's phone, maybe even the telephones of *everyone* at Rome station. You know, there's a good chance we're talking about some of Orlov's former comrades. We may never find out for sure. You know, it's odd.'

'How's that?'

'There was a time when I would have leapt at the opportunity to head CIA. I would have given anything for the directorship. But now – now that I have it – it feels like a deathtrap. The long knives are out for me. Far too many powerful people don't want me in there. It just feels like a deathtrap.'

'Were you able to read Orlov's thoughts?' Toby asked as soon as I had hung up.

I nodded. 'But there was a wrinkle,' I said. 'Orlov was born in the Ukraine.'

'He's a Russian-speaker!' Toby objected.

'Russian is his second language. When I realized that Orlov thought in Ukrainian, I was convinced I'd been defeated. A cruel twist. But then it came to me: That Agency fellow who tested me, Dr Mehta, had speculated that I was receiving not *thoughts* per se but extremely low frequency radio waves emitted by the speech-producing center of the brain. I could, in effect, listen in on words as the brain readied them to speak –or *not* to speak. So I switched our conversation back and forth between English and Russian, since I knew Orlov could speak both. And that enabled me to understand what he thought, since his mind was now putting English words to his Ukrainian thoughts.'

'Yes,' Toby said, nodding. 'Yes.'

'And I asked him several questions, knowing that whatever he chose to speak aloud, he would at least *think* the replies.'

'Very good,' Toby said.

'At times,' I said, 'he was trying so hard *not* to reply that he was thinking the English words he *didn't* want to say.'

The painkiller had begun to overwhelm me, and I was finding it hard to concentrate. I wanted nothing more now than to fall back asleep for a few days.

He shifted in his wheelchair, then moved it a few inches

closer by flicking a lever. It responded with a quiet whir. 'Ben, a few weeks ago a former colonel in the old Securitate' – the Romanian secret police under the late dictator Nicolae Ceauşescu – 'contacted a backstopper well known to us.' He was telling me that the Romanian had contacted a document forger who prepared bogus cover identity papers for freelance agents. 'Who in turn contacted us.'

I waited for him to continue, and after a minute or so, he did. 'We brought the Romanian in. Under intensive interrogation it developed that he knew of a plot to kill certain highly placed American intelligence officials.'

'Whose plot?'

'We don't know.'

'Who was targeted?'

'We don't know that either.'

'And you think it's connected to the diverted gold?'

'It's possible. Now, tell me this: Did Orlov tell you where that ten billion dollars was stashed?'

'No.'

'Do you think he knew and didn't want to say?'

'No,' I said.

'He didn't give you an access code or anything?'

He was visibly disappointed. 'Isn't it possible that Sinclair, in effect, pulled off a grand swindle? You know, told Orlov that he was going along with this scheme to remove ten billion dollars in gold, and then –'

'And then *what*?' Molly interjected. She gazed at him with a ferocious intensity. Two tiny red spots appeared on her cheeks, and I knew she had heard more than she could stand. She whispered, almost hissed: 'My father was a wonderful man and a *good* man. He was as honest and as straight as they come. For God's sake, the worst thing you could say about him was that he was *too* much of a straight arrow.'

'Molly –' Toby began.

'I was in the back of a cab with him in Washington once when he found a twenty-dollar bill wedged into the seat and gave it to the driver. He said maybe whoever lost it would realize it and contact the cab company or something. I said, Dad, the cabbie's just going to pocket it –'

'Molly,' Toby said, touching her on the hand. His eyes were sad. 'We must consider every possibility, no matter how unlikely.'

Molly fell silent. Her lower lip quivered. I found myself trying to tune in on her thoughts, but she was a little too far away, and I couldn't summon the mental energy. To be honest, I had no idea whether this strange gift was still with me. Maybe the experience in the burning rat house had knocked it out of me as suddenly as it had appeared. I think I wouldn't have minded very much if it was gone.

Whatever she was thinking, she was thinking with great passion. But in any case, I could imagine the turmoil she was going through, and I just wanted to leap out of bed and put my arms around her and comfort her. I hated seeing her like this. Instead, I lay there in the bed, arms bandaged, my head fuzzier by the minute.

'I don't think so, Toby,' I said musingly. 'Molly's right: it doesn't fit what we know of Hal's character.'

'But we're back to where we started from,' he said.

'No,' I replied. 'Orlov did supply me with one lead.'

'Oh?'

' "*Follow the gold*," he said. "*Follow the gold*." And he was thinking a city name.'

'Zurich? Geneva?'

'No. Brussels. There are ways, Toby. Since Belgium isn't known as a major gold center, it can't be all that difficult to figure out where in Brussels ten billion dollars worth of gold might be hidden.'

'I'll take care of your flight arrangements,' Toby said.

'*No!*' Molly exclaimed. 'He's not going anywhere. He needs at least a week of bed rest.'

I shook my head wearily. 'No, Mol. If we don't track it down, Alex Truslow is next. And then us. It's the easiest thing in the world to arrange "accidents." '

'If I let you leave this bed, I'm violating my Hippocratic oath –'

'Screw the Hippocratic oath,' I said. 'Our lives are in danger. An immense fortune is at stake, and if we don't find it . . . you won't be around to live up to that goddamned oath.'

Almost under his breath, I heard Toby say, 'I'm with you,' and with a high-pitched electric whine he began slowly to wheel away.

The room was quiet and peaceful. In the city, we become so habituated to the city's noises that we no longer hear them. But here, in a remote part of northern Italy, there was no noise outside. From the window I could see, in the pale Tuscan afternoon light, a field of tall, dead sunflowers, shriveled brown stalks bowing in pious rows.

Toby had left Molly and me alone to talk. She sat on my bed, absently stroking my feet through the blanket.

'I'm sorry,' I said.

'For what?'

'I don't know. I just wanted to say I'm sorry.'

'I accept your apology.'

'I hope it's not true about your father.'

'But in your heart –'

'In my heart I don't believe he did anything wrong. But we have to find out.'

Molly looked around the room, then gazed out the window at the spectacular view of Tuscan hills. 'You know, I could live here.'

'So could I.'

'Really? Could we, do you think?'

'You mean like, I open the Tuscany office of Putnam & Stearns? Come on.'

'But given your talent for making money . . .' She smiled wryly. 'We could just move here. You quit the law, we live happily ever after . . .'

A long silence, and then she continued: 'I want to go with you. To Brussels.'

'Molly, it's not safe.'

'I can be of help. You know that. Anyway, you shouldn't travel unless accompanied by a physician. Not in your condition.'

'Why aren't you objecting anymore to my traveling?' I said.

'Because I know it's not true about Dad. And I want you to prove it.'

'But can you deal with the possibility – even the likelihood – that if I find anything, it may not make your father look good?'

'My father's dead, Ben. The worst has already happened. Nothing you find's going to undo that.'

'All right,' I said. 'Okay.' My eyelids were beginning to close, and I couldn't gather the strength to fight it any longer. 'But now let me sleep.'

'I'll call ahead and find us a hotel in Brussels,' I heard her say from a million miles away. Fine, I thought; let her do that.

'Alex Truslow warned me of snakes in the garden,' I whispered. 'And . . . and I'm beginning to wonder . . . whether Toby is that snake.'

'Ben, I found something. Something that might help us.' She said something else, but I couldn't make it out, and then her voice seemed to fade away.

A little bit later – perhaps minutes, perhaps seconds – I thought I heard Molly slip quietly out of the room. I heard the bleat of lambs from somewhere far away, and very soon I was fast asleep.

42

Toby Thompson saw us off at the entrance to the Swissair terminal in Milan's international airport. Molly gave him a kiss, I shook his hand, and then we passed through the metal-detector gate. A few minutes later came the boarding call for Swissair's flight to Brussels. At the same moment, I knew, Toby was boarding a flight to Washington.

The painkiller that had kept me afloat for the last two days had begun to wear off (though I still felt too woolly-headed to 'read' Toby). I knew it was better to get off the stuff if I wished to remain alert. Now, my arms, particularly the insides of my forearms, felt as if they were on fire. They throbbed, each pulse sending knives of pain all the way to my shoulder. And on top of it all, since the painkiller had worn off, I'd had a terrible, unceasing headache.

Still, I was able to lift my two carry-on bags (neither of us checked any luggage) and make it to my seat without too much pain. Toby had purchased first-class tickets for us and provided us with fresh passports. We were now Carl and Margaret Osborne, owners of a small but prosperous gift shop in Kalamazoo, Michigan.

I had a window seat, as I'd requested, and I watched closely as the Swissair maintenance crew on the tarmac bustled here and there, completing their last-minute checks. My body was taut with tension. The front entrance to the plane from the Jetway had been closed and sealed a few minutes earlier. The first-class area afforded me an excellent vantage point from which to watch. Just as I saw the last crew member leave the cockpit area and descend the service steps toward the tarmac, I began to scream.

Thrusting my bandaged arms up in the air, I yelled: 'Let me out of here! My God! Oh, my God! Let me out!'

'What is it?' Molly shrieked at me.

Virtually all the passengers in the first-class cabin had turned toward us. They stared in horror. A flight attendant ran down the aisle toward me.

'Oh, Jesus,' I shouted. 'I've got to get off – *now!*'

'Sir, I'm sorry,' the flight attendant said. She was tall and blond, with a plain, mannish, no-nonsense face. 'We're not allowed to let passengers deplane at takeoff. Is there anything we can do for you –'

'What *is* it?' Molly asked me.

'Let me out!' I stood up. 'I have to get out of here. The pain is incredible!'

'Sir!' the Swiss woman protested.

'Get our bags!' I commanded Molly. My arms still thrust in the air, moaning and keening, I began to shove my way into the aisle. Molly quickly grabbed our bags from the overhead compartment, and somehow managed to wriggle the shoulder straps of two of the valises over each of her slight shoulders and, at the same time, grab the others with her hands. She followed me down the aisle, toward the front of the plane.

But the flight attendant blocked our way. 'Sir! Madam! I'm terribly sorry, but regulations stipulate –'

An elderly woman screamed out in terror: 'Let him out of here!'

'My God,' I shouted.

'Sir, the plane is about to take off!'

'*Move!* Out of our way!' It was Molly, ferocious in her anger. 'I'm his physician! If you don't let us off of this plane at once, you'll have a goddamn *huge* lawsuit on your hands. I mean you *personally*, lady – and you'll take the whole goddamned *airline* down with you, do you understand me?'

The Swiss woman's eyes widened as she backed down the aisle and then flattened herself against one row of seats to let us pass by. With Molly in tow, struggling mightily with our luggage, I ran down the service stairway, which was, thank God, still bolted to the side of the plane.

We ran across the tarmac and reentered the terminal. There, I grabbed all the bags from Molly – it was painful, but I was certainly able to do it – and pulled her toward me as I ran to the Swissair ticket counter.

'What the *hell* is going on?'

'Quiet . . . Just – quiet for a while!'

The Swissair ticket agents, fortunately, hadn't seen where we had come from. I pulled out a wad of cash (courtesy, too, of Toby) and bought two first-class tickets to Zurich. The flight was leaving in ten minutes.

We would just make it.

Although the Swissair flight from Milan to Zurich was pleasant and uneventful – I've always preferred Swissair to any other airline – I found myself in almost constant physical agony.

I nursed a Bloody Mary and tried to make my mind a blank. Molly was fast asleep. Before getting on the plane, even before the whole business with switching flights, she'd complained of feeling ill, queasy. She dismissed it as insignificant, though: some bug she'd picked up on the flight over to Italy in what she called a 'toothpaste tube' and a 'Petri dish' of a 747. She obviously didn't much like to fly.

I had decided that it would be folly to trust Toby at this point. Perhaps I was being overly suspicious. But we could no longer take chances, and if Toby were the serpent in the garden . . .

Hence my telling him that I was headed to Brussels. No, Orlov had not thought 'Brussels,' but only I knew that. In an hour or so, I was sure, CIA personnel in Brussels would realize that Mr and Mrs Carl Osborne had not arrived from Milan, and alarms would go off. So this was at best a temporary diversion; but it was better than nothing.

Follow the gold, Orlov had called out to me a few seconds before his gruesome murder. *Follow the gold*.

I knew now what he had meant. At least I thought I did. He and Sinclair had transacted their business in Zurich. He hadn't told me the name of the bank, but he had *thought*

295

something, thought a name. *Koerfer*: it had to be a name. Was it the name of a bank? Or an individual? I would have to locate the bank in Zurich where the two spymasters had met.

Follow the gold meant follow the paper trail, which was the only way to learn the nature of the beast that had killed Sinclair. And most likely, the only way for Molly and me to remain alive.

I tried to relax. One of the first questions he'd asked me, after we had finished the debriefing, was whether my . . . *ability*, as he delicately put it, had survived the fire intact. And the truth was, I didn't know what to answer then; I didn't yet have the strength, or the will, necessary to concentrate sufficiently.

Now, however, I gathered my resources, and as Molly slept, I tried. My head ached – worse now, it seemed, than any headache I'd ever had before. Was this related to the injuries I'd sustained in the fire?

Or, more ominously, did it have something to do with the power I'd acquired in the Oracle Project's laboratory? Was something beginning to degenerate, to go wrong? Who was it – Rossi? Toby? – who had mentioned, ever so casually, that the only person on whom the protocol had worked, the Dutchman, had gone crazy? The clamor in his head had driven him to suicide. I began to understand the impulse.

Yet at the same time I worried that this damned telepathic ability, which had gotten me into all this, after all, might no longer be with me.

So I furrowed my brow, squinted my eyes, frowned, tried to make my mind receptive, and found it difficult. I was surrounded by sound, which made it maddeningly difficult to separate out the ELF waves. There was the noise of the plane's engines, muffled and droning and lulling; the mostly in-distinct chatter of nearby passengers; a loud, whooping laugh from somewhere back in the smoking section; an infant wailing a few seats behind us; the clatter and clink of the serving carts moving down the aisle, loaded with miniature bottles and cans.

Asleep next to me was Molly, but I didn't particularly want

to violate my pledge to her. The nearest fellow passenger – this was first class, after all – was a good distance away.

Furtively, I bent my head toward Molly, focused, and heard her murmur something aloud. She shifted suddenly, as if she'd detected my proximity, and opened her eyes.

'What are you doing?' she asked.

'Checking on you,' I said quickly.

'Oh, yeah?'

'How do you feel?'

'Lousy. Queasy still.'

'Sorry.'

'Thanks. It'll pass.' She sat up slowly, massaged her neck. 'Ben, do you have a clear idea what you're going to be doing in Zurich?'

'Fairly,' I said. 'The rest I'll play by ear.'

She nodded, touched my right hand. 'How's the pain?'

'Subsiding,' I lied.

'Good. I mean, a nice try at playing the macho man, but I know how badly it hurts. Tonight, if you'd like, I'll give you something to help you sleep. The nights are the worst, when you can't stop yourself from rolling over on your arms.'

'Won't be necessary.'

'Just let me know.'

'I will.'

'Ben?' I looked at her. Her eyes were red-rimmed. 'Ben, I had a dream about Dad. But you probably know that.'

'I told you, Molly, I won't –'

'Never mind. This dream I had . . . You know all those places we lived when I was growing up – Afghanistan, the Philippines, Egypt? From as early as I can remember, I felt his absence. I guess that's pretty common among CIA brats – Dad's always gone, and you don't know where, or why, or what he does, and your friends are always asking why's your dad never there, you know? It always seemed like Dad wasn't around – it wasn't until much later that I understood *why* – but I remember thinking that if I were just nicer to Mom, he'd spend more time at home playing with me. When I got older, and he told me he worked for the CIA, I took it okay – I think

I'd pretty much figured it out, and a couple of my friends had already speculated as much to me. But it didn't make it easier.'

She slowly tipped her seat back until it was almost horizontal, then closed her eyes, as if she were in analysis. 'When he went overt, when he was publicly identified as a CIA officer, it wasn't any easier then either. He worked all the time, a real slave to his career. So what did I do? I became a slave to *my* career, went into medicine, which in some ways is even worse.'

I noticed she'd begun to cry, which I attributed to her being tired, or the trauma we'd both just been through.

She continued, heaving a soulful sigh. 'I guess I always thought that he and I would get to know each other better after he retired, and when I had a family. And now –' Her voice got small, choked, high-pitched. A little girl again. 'And now, I'll never . . .'

She couldn't continue, but I stroked her hair to let her know she didn't need to.

The last time I saw Molly's father was on a business trip to Washington. He had been Director of Central Intelligence for several months. I was in Washington on legal business. There was no good reason for me to call him from the Jefferson, where I was staying. Probably I wanted, on some level, to share in the excitement of Hal's new importance, of having my father-in-law in such a prominent office. Selfish? Naturally. I wanted to bask in the reflected glory. No doubt, too, I wanted to return to CIA headquarters in some triumphal manner, even if the triumph was someone else's.

On the phone Hal said he'd be delighted to get together for a quick lunch or a drink (he'd become a health fanatic, had given up all alcohol; he'd drink some nonalcoholic beer or his favorite pseudo-cocktail, cranberry juice, seltzer, and lime).

He sent a car and a driver for me to take me to McLean, which made me nervous: what if *The Washington Post* caught wind of Hal's abuse of office? Harrison Sinclair, that avatar of rectitude, had sent a government limo, at taxpayer expense, to pick up his son-in-law. Who could have gotten a cab. Would I see my picture on the front page of tomorrow's *Post*, getting into a big black government limo?

Unlike my last time at CIA, when I skulked out with a cardboard box under one arm, trudging alone through the cavernous lobby to the parking lot, this time was indeed triumphal. I was met in the lobby by Sheila McAdams, Hal's thirtyish, attractive executive assistant, who brought me up the elevator to Hal's office.

He radiated good health. He really did seem delighted to see me. Part of it, I think, was that he was excited to show off his new digs. We had lunch in his private dining room: Greek salads and grilled-eggplant sandwiches and tall, icy glasses of cranberry juice, seltzer, and lime.

We talked for a bit, perfunctorily, about the business that had brought me to Washington. We talked about how the Agency had changed since the demise of the Soviet Union, about what he planned to do in his tenure as director. We gossiped about people we knew. A little political talk. Altogether, a pleasant if unremarkable lunch.

But I will never forget something he said as I left. As I walked out, he put his arm around my shoulders and said: 'I know we haven't ever talked about what happened in Paris.'

I looked quizzical.

'What happened to you, I mean –'

'Yes –' I said.

'Someday I want us to talk,' he said. 'There's something I want to tell you.'

I felt instantly nauseated. 'Let's talk now,' I said.

I was relieved when he said, 'I can't.'

'Your schedule must be –'

'Not just that. I can't. We'll talk. Not now, but soon.'

We never did.

When Molly and I arrived at Kloten airport, we took a Mercedes taxi into the center of Zurich. We passed the mammoth, newly renovated Hauptbahnhof, swerved around the statue of Alfred Escher, the nineteenth-century politician who's credited with making Zurich a modern banking center.

299

I had booked us at the Savoy Baur en Ville, the oldest hotel in the city and a favorite among well-to-do American lawyers and businessmen. It had been nicely renovated, in 1975, and was right on the Paradeplatz, near everything – and, most important, next to the Bahnhofstrasse, where nearly every other building is a bank.

We signed in, and went up to our room, which was pleasant – a lot of brass and pearwood marquetry cabinets – and neither modern nor antique. We talked for a while until we were both too drowsy to continue. Once again she offered to get me a sedative; I refused. I watched Molly begin to drift off; I tried to join her. I desperately needed sleep, but it wouldn't come. The pain in my hands and arms was surging with a tingling heat, and my mind was spinning with the events, the revelations, of the last several days.

In one of the vaults under the Bahnhofstrasse, just a few yards from our hotel, lay the answer to what had happened to more than ten billion dollars in gold stolen from the former Soviet Union, the answer to the enigma of Sinclair's death. In a few hours, quite likely, we'd be much closer to solving the mystery. I wished it were morning already.

On the end table next to the base of the lamp was the *International Herald-Tribune* the hotel had left for us in the room. I picked it up and idly scanned the front page.

One of the articles, a one-column piece on the right-hand side of the page, was headed by a photograph of a face that was by now quite familiar. Although I was not surprised to see the notice there, its contents were ominous.

Last KGB Chief Is Found Slain in Northern Italy

BY CRAIG RIMER

WASHINGTON POST SERVICE

ROME – Vladimir A. Orlov, the last head of the Soviet intelligence agency the KGB, was discovered dead by local police at his residence 25 kilometers from Siena. He was 72.

Diplomatic sources here revealed that Mr Orlov had been in hiding in the Tuscany region of Italy for several months since his defection from Russia.

Italian authorities confirm that Mr Orlov was killed in an armed attack. His assailants have not been identified, but are believed to be either political enemies or members of the Sicilian Mafia. According to unconfirmed reports, Mr Orlov may have been engaged in illicit financial operations before his death.

The Russian government refused to comment on Mr Orlov's death, but in a statement released this morning from Washington, the newly appointed head of the CIA, Alexander Truslow, said: 'Vladimir Orlov presided over the dismantling of the greatest agency of Soviet oppression, for which we must all be grateful. We mourn his passing.'

I sat up in bed, my heart pounding along with my throbbing head, hands, and arms. The adjacent article concerned the new leader of Germany. '*Vogel*,' the headline read, '*Embraces American Ties.*'

It began: 'Chancellor-elect Wilhelm Vogel of Germany, whose recent landslide election occurred just days after the German stock market crash plunged the nation into widespread panic, has invited the newly confirmed head of the CIA, Alexander Truslow, to Germany for consultations on how best to ensure stable U.S.–German relations. The new intelligence chief accepted the invitation immediately as his first official state visit, and is believed to be flying to Bonn for a meeting with the chancellor-elect as well as Mr Truslow's German counterpart, the director of the *Bundesnachrichtendienst*, or the German Federal Intelligence Service, Hans Koenig . . .'

And I knew that Truslow was in danger.

It was the juxtaposition.

Vladimir Orlov had warned about hard-line Russians

301

seizing his country. What was it that my British correspondent friend Miles Preston had said about a weak Russia being necessary for a strong Germany? Orlov, who with Harrison Sinclair had tried to save Russia, was dead. A new German leader had been vaulted into power in the wake of a weakened, straitened Russia.

Conspiracy theorists, of whom (as I've said) I'm not one, like to write and talk about neo-Nazis, as if all of Germany wanted nothing more than a return to the Third Reich. It's nonsense, absolute foolishness – the Germans I came to know, eventually to like, during my brief sojourn in Leipzig, were nothing like that. They weren't Nazis, or brownshirts; they weren't swastika-wearers, or anything of the sort. They were good, decent, patriotic people, no different in essence from the average Russian, the average American, the average Swede, the average Cambodian.

But the point wasn't the *people*, was it?

Germany, man, Miles had said. *The wave of the future. We're about to see a new German dictatorship. And it won't happen accidentally, Ben. It's been in the planning for a good long time.*

In the planning . . .

And Toby had warned of an impending assassination plot.

And then a light went on, a flash of illumination in the murky darkness, a brief moment of insight.

It was the picture of the slain Vladimir Orlov that did it. He had talked about the American stock market crash of 1987.

A stock market 'crash,' to use your word, is not necessarily a disaster to one who is prepared for it. Very much the opposite; a group of savvy investors can make huge profits in a stock market crash. . . .

Did the Wise Men, I had asked, make money in the stock market collapse?

Certainly, he had replied. *Using computerized program trading and fourteen hundred separate trading accounts, cali- brating precisely with Tokyo's Nikkei and pulling the levers at exactly the right time, and with the right velocity, they not only made vast sums of money in the crash, Mr Ellison, they caused it.*

If the Wise Men had caused the significant – yet, at the same time, relatively benign stock market crisis of 1987 –

– had they done the same in Germany?

There was, Alex had warned darkly, a cancer of corruption in CIA. A corruption that included gathering and using top-secret economic intelligence from around the world to manipulate stock markets, and thus nations.

Could this be?

And could, therefore, there be a darker motive for Chancellor-elect Vogel's invitation to Alexander Truslow to visit Germany?

What if there were protests in Bonn against this American spy chief? After all, neo-Nazi demonstrations were in the news constantly. Who would be all that surprised if Alexander Truslow were slain by German 'extremists'? It was a perfect, logical plan.

Alex, who must certainly know too much about the Wise Men, about the German stock market crash . . .

It was nine o'clock in the evening in Washington by the time I reached Miles Preston.

'The German stock market crash?' he echoed gruffly as if I had taken leave of my senses. 'Ben, the German crash happened because the Germans finally formed a single, unified stock market, the Deutsche Börse. It couldn't have happened four years ago. Now tell me: What brings about this interest in the German economy all of a sudden?'

'I can't say, Miles –'

'But what are you doing? You're in Europe somewhere, am I right? Where?'

'Let's just say Europe, and leave it at that.'

'What are you looking into?'

'Sorry.'

'Ben Ellison – we're friends. Level with me.'

'If I could, I would. But I can't.'

'Look here – all right, fair enough. If you're going to stay with it, at least let me help you. I'll ask around, dig around for you, talk to some friends. Tell me where I can reach you.'

'Can't –'

'Then you call me –'

'I'll be in touch, Miles,' I said, and terminated the call.

Only then did I begin to have an inkling.

For a long while I sat there, on the edge of the bed, staring out the window at the elegant view of the Paradeplatz, the buildings glinting in the sunshine, and I was momentarily paralyzed with a great, dull terror.

43

I didn't sleep; I couldn't.

Instead, I placed a call to one of the several lawyers I knew in Zurich, and was fortunate enough to find him in town, and in his office. John Knapp was an attorney specializing in corporate law – the only practice duller than patent law, which pleased me. He had been living in Zurich, working for an outpost of a prestigious American law firm, for five years or so. He also knew more about the Swiss banking system than anyone I knew, having studied at the University of Zurich and supervised quite a few less-than-reputable secret transactions for some of his clients. Knapp and I had known each other since law school, where we were in the same year and section, and we occasionally played squash together. I suspected that deep down he disliked me as much as I disliked him, but our business dealings frequently brought us together, and so we both faked an easygoing, boisterous comradeship so integral to male friendships.

I left a note for the sleeping Molly, telling her I'd be back in an hour or two. Then, in front of the hotel I got into a taxi and asked the driver to take me to the Kronenhalle on Ramistrasse.

John Knapp was a short, slim man with a terminal case of short man's disease. Like a chihuahua trying to menace a Saint Bernard, he swaggered and affected imperious gestures that were faintly ridiculous, cartoonlike. He had small brown eyes and close-cropped brown hair speckled with gray, cut in bangs that made him look like a dissolute monk. After all this time in Zurich, he'd begun to take on the local coloration and dress like a Swiss banker; he wore an English-tailored blue suit and burgundy-striped shirt that probably came from Charvet in Paris; certainly his woven silk cuff links did. He'd arrived fifteen minutes late – almost certainly a deliberate power move. This was a guy who'd read all the books on power and success and how to do a power lunch and how to get a corner office.

The bar at the Kronenhalle was so crowded I could barely squeeze through to get a seat. But the patrons were clearly the right sort of people, the Zurich glitterati. Knapp, who liked high living, collected places like this. He regularly skied at St. Moritz and Gstaad.

'Jesus, what happened to your hands?' he asked as he shook my bandaged right hand a little too firmly and saw me wince.

'Bad manicure,' I said.

His look of horror transformed instantly into one of exaggerated hilarity. 'You sure it's not paper cuts from your exciting life of thumbing through patent applications?'

I smiled, tempted to unleash my arsenal of put-downs (corporate lawyers are especially vulnerable, I've learned), but said nothing. It's important to keep in mind, I think, that a bore is someone who talks when you want him to listen. And in any case, within a moment he'd forgotten all about the bandaged hands.

After we'd gotten through the preliminaries, he asked, 'So what the hell brings you to Z-town?'

I was drinking a Scotch; he made a point of ordering a *kirschwasser* in Schweizerdeutsch, the Swiss dialect of German.

'This time, I'm afraid, I'm going to have to be a little circumspect,' I said. 'Business.'

'Ah-*ha*,' he said significantly. No doubt he'd heard from one or another of our mutual friends that I'd done time in the Agency. Probably he thought that was the key to my legal success (and, of course, he wouldn't be so far off). In any case, I figured that with Knapp it was better to be mysterious than to give a bland cover tale.

I pretended to relent a bit. 'I've got a client who has assets here he's trying to locate.'

'Isn't that sort of outside your line of work?'

'Not entirely. It's related to a deal my firm is putting together. If you don't mind, I can't say a whole lot more than that.'

He pursed his lips and grinned, as if he knew more about what I was alluding to than even I did. 'Let's hear it.'

So high was the ambient noise level here that the thought of trying to read his mind was preposterous. I did try in a few instances, leaning toward him, focusing as hard as I could, but nothing. Still, there was nothing I wanted to know from him that he wouldn't say aloud. To say nothing of how banal, how mind-numbingly and teeth-achingly dull Knapp's thoughts surely were.

'How much do you know about gold?'

'How much do you want to know?'

'I'm trying to track down a deposit of gold made to one of the banks here.'

'Which one?'

'I don't know.'

He snorted derisively. 'There's four hundred banks registered here, big guy. Almost five thousand branch offices. And there's millions of ounces of new gold coming into Switzerland every year, from South Africa or wherever. Good luck.'

'Which ones are the biggest?'

'The biggest banks? The Big Three – the *Anstalt*, the *Verein*, and the *Gesellschaft*.'

'Hmm?'

'Sorry. The Anstalt's what we call Credit Suisse, or *Schweizerische Kreditanstalt*. The *Verein* is the Swiss Bank Corporation. The *Gesellschaft* is the Union Bank of Switzerland. So you're looking for gold deposited in one of the big three, only you don't know which one?'

'Right.'

'How much gold?'

'Tons.'

'*Tons?*' Another snort. 'I doubt it seriously. What are we talking about here, a *country*?'

I shook my head. 'A prosperous enterprise.'

He gave a low whistle. A blond woman in a pale green, tight-fitting, spaghetti-strap outfit glanced over at him, mistakenly thinking she was being admired, then quickly looked away. Presumably she had no interest in a dissolute monk in a blue suit. 'So what's the problem?' he asked, draining his *kirschwasser* and snapping his fingers at the waiter to signal for another. 'Someone misplaced the account number?'

'Stay with me for a second,' I said. I was beginning to sound like Knapp, and I didn't like it. 'If a significant amount of gold were shipped into Zurich and placed into a numbered account, where would it go, physically?'

'Vaults. It's an increasing problem for the banks here, actually. They've got all this money and gold to stash, and they're running out of space and the municipal laws won't permit them to put up taller buildings, so they have to burrow underground like gophers.'

'Under the Bahnhofstrasse.'

'Exactly.'

'But wouldn't it be more convenient to sell the gold here, put it into liquid assets? Deutsche marks, Swiss francs, whatever?'

'Not quite. The Swiss government is terrified of inflation, so they have limits on the amount of cash foreigners can keep. There even used to be a limit of a hundred thousand francs on foreign accounts.'

'Gold doesn't earn interest, right?'

'Of course not,' Knapp said. 'But come on, you don't bank in Switzerland to earn *interest*, for Christ's sake. Their interest rates are, like, one percent. Or zero. Sometimes you have to *pay* for the privilege of keeping your money here. I'm not kidding. Lots of the banks charge something like one and a half percent for all withdrawals.'

'All right. Now, you can tell by looking at gold where it's from, isn't that right?'

'Usually. Gold – the sort of gold that central banks use as their monetary reserves – is kept in the form of gold ingots, usually four hundred troy ounces per bar. Usually "three nines" gold, which means it's 99.9 percent pure. And usually it's earmarked, stamped with numbers and assay numbers, the ID and serial numbers.' The waiter came with his *kirschwasser*, and Knapp took it without acknowledging where it had materialized from. 'For every ten bars of gold that are poured, one is assayed, by drilling holes in six different locations on the bar, taking a few milligrams of shavings, and assaying it. Anyway, yeah, most gold bars you can tell where they're from.'

He chuckled, sipped his drink thoughtfully. 'You should try this stuff. You really get to like it. Anyway, the gold market is a funny, high-strung thing. I remember when the gold market went crazy not too long ago. The Soviets were trying to sell a shipment of gold bars here, and someone noticed that some of the bars had *czarist eagles* on them. The gnomes flipped out.'

'Why?'

'Come on, big guy. This was back in Christmas 1990. Gold bars with Romanoff eagles on it! The Gorby government was in the process of going down the tubes and was selling off the last of its gold! Scraping the bottom of the barrel! Why else would they be dipping into the czarist reserves? So the price of gold shot up fifty bucks an ounce.'

I froze in mid-sip, felt the blood rush to my head. 'Then what?' I asked.

'Then what? Then nothing. It turned out to be an elaborate hoax. A pretty sophisticated bit of financial disinformation on the part of the Sovs. Turned out they'd mixed a few old czarist bars in the pile deliberately. Watched the market go haywire, as they knew it would, then unloaded their gold at the higher price. Pretty clever, huh? The Sovs weren't total numbskulls.'

I thought in silence for a moment. What if it hadn't been disinformation? I wondered. What if . . . But I couldn't make any sense of this. Instead, I set my glass down and continued, as unflustered-seeming as possible: 'So can gold be *laundered*?'

He paused a moment. 'Yeah . . . sure. You just melt it down – re-refine it, re-assay it, get rid of the earmarks. If you're trying to be secretive about it, it's sort of a pain in the ass to move it around and get it done, but it's possible. And it's cheap. Gold's completely fungible. But Ben, I don't get this. You're looking for a huge load of gold that belongs to one of your clients, and you don't know where it *is?'*

'It's a little more complicated than that. I can't be too specific. Tell me this: When you talk about the secrecy of Swiss banking, what does that mean? How difficult is it to penetrate the secrecy?'

'Whoa,' Knapp said. 'Sounds a little cloak-and-dagger to me.'

I glared at him, and he replied, 'It ain't easy, Ben. Some of the most revered words in this town are "the principle of confidentiality" and "the freedom of currency exchange." Translation: the inalienable right to hide money. That's their reason for being. Money is their religion. I mean, when Huldrych Zwingli launched the Reformation of Zurich by chucking all the Catholic statues into the Limmat River, he made sure first to salvage the gold from the statues and give it to the town council. Thus giving birth to Swiss banking.

'But the Swiss – well, you gotta love 'em. They're mad about secrecy, unless it benefits them to break confidentiality. Mafiosi, drug kingpins, corrupt third-world dictators with briefcases full of embezzled funds – the Swiss protect their secrecy like a priest in a confessional. But don't forget, when the Nazis came during the war and started putting pressure on them, suddenly the Swiss got real accommodating. They gave the Nazis the names of the German Jews who had Swiss accounts. They like to spread this myth that they stood up to the Nazis, real steadfastlike, when they came to grab the Jews' money, but no way. Unh-unh. Okay, not all the banks, but a lot. The Basler Handelsbank laundered Nazi money, and that's a documented fact.' His eyes were roaming the crowd as if he were looking for someone. 'Look, Ben, you're looking for a needle in a haystack.'

I nodded, traced a pattern in the condensation on the side of the glass. 'Well,' I said, 'I have a name.'

'A name?'

'A banker's name, I think.' A name, I didn't say, that Orlov had thought in connection with the gold and Zurich. 'Koerfer.'

'Well, all *right*,' he said triumphantly. 'Why didn't you say so earlier? Dr Ernst Koerfer's the managing director of the Bank of Zurich. Or, at least, he was, until a month or so ago.'

'Retired?'

'Died. Heart attack or something. Although I wouldn't swear for the fact that he *had* a heart. A real son of a bitch. But he ran a tight ship.'

'Ah,' I said. 'Do you know anyone who's at the Bank of Zurich now?'

He looked at me as if I'd lost my mind. 'Come on, big guy. I know *everyone* in Swiss banking. That's my job, man. The new managing director there is a guy named Eisler. Dr Alfred Eisler. If you want, I can make a call, set up an introduction for you. You want that?'

'Yeah,' I said. 'That would be great.'

'No problem.'

'Thanks, big guy,' I said.

Procuring a gun in Switzerland proved to be more of a challenge than I'd anticipated. My contacts were limited, virtually nonexistent. I was afraid to contact Toby or anyone connected with the CIA; there was no one here I trusted. If absolutely necessary, I could reach Truslow, but that route was to be avoided: how could I be sure that the channels of communications hadn't been penetrated? Far better not to call him. Finally, after bribing a manager of a sporting goods and hunting supply store, I got the name of someone who might be able to 'help' me: the manager's brother-in-law, who ran, of all things, an antiquarian bookshop.

I found it a few blocks away. Gilt letters in the window, in old-style German *Fraktur* script, read:

BUCHHÄNDLER
ANTIQUITÄTEN UND MANUSKRIPTE

A bell mounted on the door jingled as I entered. It was small and dark and redolent of mildew and dankness and the vanilla smell of ancient, crumbling bookbindings.

High black metal shelves, overcrowded with haphazard

stacks of books and yellowed magazines, took up virtually every available square inch of floor-space. A narrow path between the shelves led back to a small, chaotic-looking oak desk piled high with papers and books, at which sat the proprietor. He called out, '*Guten Tag!*'

I nodded a greeting and, peering around as if searching for a particular volume, asked the shopkeeper in German: 'How late are you open?'

'Until seven,' he replied.

'I'll be back when I have more time.'

'But if you have just a few minutes,' he said, 'I have some new acquisitions in the back room.' He got up, locked the front door, and placed a Closed sign in the window. Then he led me back to a tiny, cluttered room piled high with crumbling leather-bound books. In several shoeboxes he had a pitifully small selection of guns, the best of them being a Ruger Mark II (a decent semiautomatic but only a .22), a Smith & Wesson, and a Glock 19. I chose the Glock. It is a gun that has had more than its share of problems, or so my Agency friends tell me, but I've always liked it. The price was exorbitant, but this was Switzerland, after all.

Throughout dinner at the Agnes Amberg on Hottingerstrasse, neither one of us brought up what was weighing so heavily on each other's minds. It was as if we both needed to take a tension break and be ordinary tourists for a little while. With my hands bandaged I found it difficult, and not a little painful, to cut into my fowl.

Follow the gold . . .

I had a name now, and a bank. I was several steps closer.

Once I had a direction, a path, I might come closer to learning why Sinclair was killed – that is, *what conspiracy* had to be covered up. Whether my midnight epiphany would be borne out.

We sat in glum silence. Then, before I could say anything, Molly said, 'You know, this is a place where women didn't get the right to vote until 1969.'

'What about it?'

'And I thought the medical profession in the U.S. didn't take women seriously. I'll never say that again after the doctor I saw today.'

'You saw a doctor?' I said, although I knew. 'About the stomach thing?'

'Yep.'

'And?'

'And,' she said, folding her white linen napkin neatly, 'I'm pregnant. But you knew that.'

'Yes,' I admitted. 'I knew that.'

44

We could barely make it back to the hotel, Molly and I. There
is something about the joy – and the terror – of discovering you
are creating a human being that can be quite arousing, and
that night we were both certainly feeling amorous. Although
Laura had been pregnant with our child, I hadn't known that
while she was alive. So this was a first for me. And as far as
Molly was concerned – well, for years she'd been sounding so
antiprocreation that I fully expected her to be morose and even
talk about getting rid of the child or something awful like that.

But no. She was thrilled, overjoyed. Did it have something
to do with the recent loss of her father? Probably, but who
really knows the workings of the unconscious mind?

She was tearing the clothes off me before we had the hotel
room door closed. She was running her hands across my chest,
under my belt to my buttocks, and then sliding them around to
the front, all the while kissing me wildly. I responded with no less
passion, tugging at her cream silk blouse, fumbling impatiently
with the buttons (a few of which popped off onto the carpet), and
reaching in to stroke her breasts, her nipples, which were already
erect. Then, remembering my burned and bandaged hands, I
instead used my tongue, licking in tighter and tighter concentric
circles toward her nipples. She shuddered. With my shoulders
and upper body – my throbbing arms averted like pegged lobster
claws – I pushed her backward onto the enormous sleigh bed and
fell on top of her. But she would not be dominated so easily. We
tussled, wrestled with an aggressiveness I'd never before seen in
our lovemaking but found I was enjoying immensely. Even
before I entered her, she was moaning and groaning with
pleasure, and anticipated pleasure.

And afterward, as they say, we lay there enjoying the sweatiness and stickiness and muskiness and the warm glow, stroking each other, talking quietly.

'When did it happen?' I asked. I remembered when we made love, shortly after I'd become telepathic, and we were both so aroused that she hadn't put in her diaphragm. But that was too recent.

'Last month,' she said. 'I didn't think anything would happen.'

'You forgot?'

'Partly.'

I smiled at her subterfuge, not at all resentful. 'You see,' I said, 'people our age try and try and try to conceive, buying ovulation kits and books and all that. And then you go and forget to put in your diaphragm once, and it happens by accident.'

She nodded and smiled enigmatically. 'Not entirely by accident.'

'I wondered.'

She shrugged. 'Should we have talked about it in advance?'

'Probably,' I said. 'But that's okay with me.'

Another pause, and then she said: 'How's the burn?'

'Fine,' I said. 'Natural endorphins are great painkillers.'

She hesitated, as if screwing up her courage to say something important. I could not help hearing a phrase – *horrible thing he used to be* – and then she spoke.

'You've changed, haven't you?'

'What's that supposed to mean?'

'You know. You've become what you swore you'd never be again.'

'It's the right thing, Mol. There really wasn't any choice.'

Her reply was slow and sad. 'No, I guess not. But you're already different – I can feel it. I can *sense* it. I don't need telepathy to see that – well, it's as if all those years in Boston have just been wiped away. And you're back in the thick of things. And I don't like it. It scares me.'

'It scares me too.'

'You were talking in the middle of the night.'

'In my sleep?'

'No, on the phone. Who were you talking to?'

'A reporter I know, Miles Preston. Met him in Germany in my early CIA days.'

'You asked him something about the German stock market crash.'

'And I thought you were fast asleep.'

'You think that has something to do with Dad's murder?'

'I don't know. It might.'

'I found something.'

'Yes,' I said. 'I remember your saying something when I was drifting off in Greve.'

'I think I now understand why Dad left me that letter of authorization.'

'What are you talking about?'

'Remember the document left to me in his will? There was the title to his house, and the stocks and bonds, and that bizarre financial "instrument," as the lawyers kept calling it, authorizing me to have all the rights of beneficiary, foreign and domestic?'

'Right. And?'

'Well, that would have been pointless for any *domestic* accounts, which automatically go to me anyway. As for *foreign* accounts, where banking laws vary so widely, a letter like that would come in handy.'

'Especially with a Swiss account.'

'Exactly.' She got up from the bed and walked over to the closet, opened a suitcase, and soon retrieved an envelope. 'The financial instrument,' she announced. She foraged a bit longer and then produced the book her father had for some reason bequeathed me, the first edition of Allen Dulles's memoirs, *The Craft of Intelligence*.

'What the hell did you bring this for?' I asked.

She didn't reply. Instead, she returned to the bed and set both items down carefully on the rumpled sheets.

Next, she opened the book. The predominantly gray jacket was immaculate, and the spine of the book cracked as she opened it to the middle. It had probably been opened a few times before. Maybe just once, when the legendary Mr Dulles had taken out his Waterman fountain pen and written on the title page in blue-black ink in his neat script: 'For Hal, With deepest admiration, Allen.'

'This was the only thing Dad left to you,' she said. 'And for a long time I wondered why.'

'As did I.'

'He loved you. And although he was always sort of frugal, he was never cheap. And I wondered why he'd leave you just this book. I knew his mind pretty well – he was a game-player. So when they let me pack up my things, I collected all the documents Dad left me, and I decided to take this along and look through it carefully for any kind of markings – that's the sort of thing he'd do for me when I was young, mark books up for me so I'd make sure not to miss the important passage. And I found it.'

'Hmm?'

I looked at the page she was indicating. On page 73, which dealt with codes and ciphers and cryptanalysis, the phrase 'Pink Code' was underlined in the text. Next to it, scrawled lightly in pencil, was 'L2576HJ.'

'That's his seven,' she explained. 'And definitely his two. And his J.'

I understood immediately. 'Pink Code' really meant the Onyx Code; Dulles had clearly wanted not to give away the actual name. The Onyx Code was a legendary World War I codebook that the Agency had inherited from the U.S. Diplomatic Service. It was still kicking around, though rarely used, since it had long ago been cracked. L2576HJ was a coded phrase.

Hal Sinclair had left Molly the legal means to access the account.

He had left me the account number. If only I could decrypt it.

'One more,' she said. 'The page before.'

She pointed. At the top of Page 72 was a series of numbers, 79648, which Dulles had cited as an example for the general reader of how codes work. It was underlined lightly in pencil, and next to it Sinclair had penciled 'R2.'

R2 referred to a codebook of much more recent vintage, which I'd never used. I assumed that 79648 was another code that would translate into a different series of numbers (or perhaps letters) when the R2 code was applied.

I needed code information from within the CIA, yet I couldn't risk disclosing my whereabouts. So I placed a call to an Agency friend from Paris days who had retired some years ago and was teaching political science in Erie, Pennsylvania. I had saved his ass twice – once on an all-night stakeout that had gone bad, and once bureaucratically, by clearing his name in the subsequent investigation.

He owed me big, and he agreed without hesitation to place a call to a trusted friend of his, still in the Agency, and ask him, as a favor to an old friend, to take a quick stroll over to the cryptography archives one floor below. Since any codebook three quarters of a century old was hardly a matter of national security, my friend's source read to him a series of codes. He then placed a call to the pay phone outside the hotel and read them to me.

And finally I had the account number in hand.

The second code, however, was a tougher nut to crack. The book wouldn't be stored in the crypto archives (the Crypt, as it was called), since it was still active.

'I'll do my best,' my friend in Erie said.

'I'll call back,' I replied.

We sat in silence. I glanced through Dulles's memoir. He had begun the section 'Codes and Ciphers' with that famous stern dictum from Henry Stimson, the secretary of state in 1929: 'Gentlemen do not read each other's mail.'

He was wrong, of course, and Dulles took pains to point that out. Everyone in the spy biz reads everyone else's mail, and anything else they can. Maybe, though, spies aren't gentlemen.

And I wondered what the hell Henry Stimson would have declared about whether gentlemen read each other's *minds*.

I called Erie back an hour later. He answered the phone on the first ring. His voice was different, strained.

'I couldn't get it,' he said.

'What do you mean?' Had someone gotten to him?

'It's deactivated.'

'Huh?'

'Deactivated. All copies withdrawn from circulation.'

'As of when?'

'Yesterday. Ben, what's this all about?'

'Sorry,' I said, my chest tightening. *The Wise Men*. 'I've got to run. Thanks.' And I hung up.

The next morning we walked along Bahnhofstrasse, a few blocks from the Paradeplatz, until we found the correct street number. Most of the banks were headquartered in the upper levels of the buildings, above the fashionable shops.

Despite its grandiloquent name, the Bank of Zurich was small, family-owned, and very discreet. Its entrance was concealed on a small side street off Bahnhofstrasse, next to a *Konditorei*. A small brass plaque said simply *B. Z. et Cie*. If you had to ask, you had no business knowing.

We entered the lobby, and as we did, I sensed a movement behind us. I turned quickly, tensing, and saw that it was only someone, probably a Zuricher, passing by. Tall, quite thin, in a dove-gray suit, he was no doubt a banker or shopkeeper going to work; I relaxed and, my arm around Molly, entered the lobby.

But something stuck in my mind, and I glanced back again, and the shopkeeper was gone.

It was the face. Pale, extremely pale, with large, elongated yellowish circles under the eyes, pale, thin lips, and thin blond hair combed straight back.

He looked strikingly familiar, there was no doubt about it.

And for an instant I remembered the rainy evening of the gunfire on Marlborough Street in Boston, the tall, gaunt passerby . . .

It was him. My reaction time had been dismayingly slow, but now I was quite sure. It was him. The same man in Boston was now here, in Zurich.

'What?' Molly asked.

I turned back, continued into the bank. 'Nothing,' I said. 'Come on. We've got work to do.'

45

'What *is* it, Ben?' she asked, frightened. 'Was someone there?'

But before she could say anything further, a male voice came over the intercom, asking us to state our business.

I gave my real name.

The receptionist responded, with the barest hint of deference, 'Come in, please, Mr Ellison. Herr Direktor Eisler is expecting you.'

I had to give John Knapp credit; he obviously had some clout around here.

'Please be sure you have no metal objects on your person,' the disembodied voice implored. 'Keys, penknives, any significant number of coins. You can place anything for safekeeping in this drawer.' A small drawer now jutted out of the wall. We both divested ourselves of coins, keys, and whatnot, and placed them in the drawer. An impressive and thorough operation, I thought.

There was a faint hum, and a set of doors in front of us were electronically unlocked. I glanced up at a twin set of miniature Japanese surveillance cameras mounted near the ceiling, and Molly and I passed into a small chamber to wait for the second set of doors to open electronically.

'You're not carrying, are you?' Molly whispered.

I shook my head. The second set of doors opened, and we were met by a young, plain blond woman, a little chunky, wearing oversize steel-rim glasses that would probably have been fashionable on anyone else. She introduced herself as Eisler's personal assistant, and led us down a gray-carpeted corridor. I made a quick stop in the rest room and then joined up with the two women.

320

Dr Alfred Eisler's office was small and simple, paneled in walnut. A few pastel watercolors in blond wooden frames adorned the wall, and not much else. None of the decorating touches I had expected – no Oriental rugs, grandfather clocks, mahogany furniture. The director's desk was a simple, uncluttered glass-and-chrome table. Facing the desk were two comfortable-looking white leather armchairs of Swedish modern design and a white-leather-upholstered couch.

Eisler was fairly tall, about my height, but somewhat portly, wearing a black wool suit. He was somewhere in his forties, with a round, jowly face, deep-set eyes, and large protruding ears. Deep lines were scored around his mouth, across his forehead, and in the furrow between his eyebrows. And he was completely bald, shiny-bald. Eisler cut an arresting if somewhat sinister figure.

'Ms Sinclair,' he said, taking Molly's hand. *He* knew who the proper center of his attention should be: not the husband, but the wife, the legal heir to her father's numbered account, according to the provisions of Swiss banking law. He gave a slight bow. 'And Mr Ellison.' Eisler's voice was a low, growly basso profundo; his accent was a mélange of Swiss-German and high-Oxbridge English.

We sat in the white leather chairs; he sat facing us on the couch. We made introductions, and he had his secretary bring in a tray of coffee for each of us. As he spoke, the lines that creased his brow deepened even more, and he gesticulated with his manicured hands in a manner so delicate, it seemed almost feminine.

He smiled tautly to signal that the meeting had begun; what was it, his expression asked, that we wanted?

I pulled out the authorization document signed by Molly's father and handed it to him.

He glanced at it and looked up. 'I trust you desire access to the numbered account.'

'That's correct,' Molly said, all business.

'There are a few formalities,' he said apologetically. 'We must confirm your identity, verify your signature, and such. I assume you have bank references in the United States?'

Molly nodded haughtily and produced a set of papers on which was all the information he needed. He took them, pressed a button to summon his secretary, and handed the papers to her.

Not five minutes of idle chat went by – about the Kunsthaus and other must-sees in Zurich – before his phone buzzed. He picked it up, said, '*Ja?*' listened for a few seconds, and replaced the receiver in its cradle. Another taut smile.

'The miracle of facsimile technology,' he said. 'This procedure used to take so much longer. 'If you would – ?'

He handed Molly a ball-point pen and a latex clipboard on which was a single sheet of Bank of Zurich letterhead, and asked her to write out the account number, in words – her numerical signature – on the thin gray line at the center of the page.

When she had finished writing the account number that her father had encoded so elaborately, he summoned his secretary again, handed her the paper, and chatted a bit longer while her handwriting was optically scanned, he explained chattily, compared with the signature card faxed from our bank in Boston.

The phone buzzed again; he picked it up, said '*Danke,*' and hung up. A moment later his secretary returned with a gray file folder marked 322069.

Clearly, we had passed the first hurdle. The account number was correct.

'Now,' Eisler said, 'what precisely can I do for you?'

I had deliberately chosen the seat closest to him. I leaned forward, focused.

Cleared my mind. Took advantage of the moment of silence. Focused.

It came. German, naturally, a tumble of phrases.

'Please?' he said, watching me sitting with head bent and brow furrowed.

Not enough to go on. I had learned German, had gone through intensive language training in it at the Farm, but he was thinking too quickly for me.

I couldn't do it.

I said, 'We'd like to know how much is in the account.'

I leaned toward him again, tried, *focused*, tried to isolate from the flow of German something, *anything* I could understand, grab on to.

'I am not permitted to discuss particulars,' Eisler said phlegmatically. 'In any case, I do not know.'

And then I heard a word. *Stahlkammer*.

Unquestionably, that was the word that leapt out at me. *Stahlkammer*.

Vault.

I said, 'There is a vault attached to this account, is that correct?'

'Yes, sir,' he admitted, 'there is. A rather sizable one, in fact.'

'I want access to it at once.'

'As you wish,' he said. 'Certainly. At once.' He rose from his couch. His bald head glinted in the pinpoint lights recessed in the ceiling. 'I assume you have the combination access code.'

Molly looked at me, signaling that she was out of her element.

'I believe it's the same as the account number,' I said.

Eisler laughed once and then sat down again. 'I really wouldn't know. Although for security reasons we would certainly discourage our clients from doing that. And in any case, it's not the same number of digits.'

'We may have it,' I said. 'I'm quite sure we do – somewhere. My wife's father left us quite a collection of papers and notes. Perhaps you can help us. How many digits are in the code?'

He glanced down at the file. 'I'm afraid I can't say.'

But I heard it, a few times, a number he thought but was defiantly *not* saying, articulating somewhere in the speech center of his brain . . . '*Vier*' . . .

Four digits, did that mean?

I said, 'Might it be a four-digit code?'

He laughed again, shrugged: this game is fun, his body language said, but now we are all through.

'There is a numbered account, which we administer and service,' he explained patiently as if to a slow child. 'You are permitted by law to withdraw or transfer those funds, as you wish. But there is also a vault – in effect, a safe deposit box, which we are charged with keeping safe. But we do not have access to it. We never do, except in the most extraordinary circumstances. As the late Mr Sinclair stipulated, in order to open the vault, an access code is required.'

'Then you can provide it to us,' Molly said, summoning all of her hauteur.

'I'm sorry, but I cannot.'

'As legal heir to his account, I request it.'

'If I could, I would gladly give it to you,' Eisler said. 'But under the terms of the arrangement set up here, I cannot.'

'But –'

'I'm sorry,' the banker said with finality. 'I'm afraid it is not possible.'

'I am the legal heir to *all* of my father's estate,' Molly said indignantly.

'I am deeply sorry,' Eisler said, unperturbed. 'I very much hope you did not come all the way here from – Boston, is it? – to learn this. A simple phone call would have saved you the time and expense.'

I sat in silence, barely listening to this exchange, absently unzipping my leather portfolio.

And then I heard it again: . . . 'Vier' . . . and then a string of other numbers. 'Acht' . . . 'Sieben' . . . I watched him studying the file, and then, in sequence and quite distinctly, it came:

'Vier . . . Acht . . . Sieben . . . Neun . . . Neun.'

'You see, Ms. Sinclair, this is,' the banker said aloud, 'a double-passkey system, designed –'

'Yes,' I interrupted. Shuffling through the notes in my portfolio, I feigned examining one sheet closely. 'It's here. We have it.'

Eisler paused, nodded, then examined me suspiciously. 'Excellent,' he said as I spoke the numbers. 'By the terms established by the owners of the account, now that you have accessed it, this account is altered from dormant to active status –'

'Owners?' I interrupted. 'There is more than one?'

'Yes, sir. It is a double-signature account. As legal beneficiary, your wife is one of the owners.'

'Who's the other one?' she asked.

'That I cannot disclose,' Eisler said, at once apologetic and
disdainful. 'Another signature is required. To be perfectly
truthful, I don't know the identity of the other owner. When
the second owner presents us with the access code, the
sequence of numbers is inputted into our computers. The co-
owner's signature is encoded in the data base, and when the
proper code is entered, the signature is printed out graphically.
This is our bank's security system to ensure that no bank
personnel can be implicated in the event of a claim against us.'

'So what does that mean?' Molly demanded.

'It means,' Eisler said, 'that you are legally permitted to
inspect the vault and to ascertain its contents. But without the
authorization of the second owner, you may neither transfer
nor withdraw the contents.'

Dr Alfred Eisler escorted us into a cramped elevator down
several flights. We were descending below Bahnhofstrasse, he
explained, and into the catacombs.

We emerged into a short gray-carpeted corridor, a cage
lined with steel bars. At the end of the corridor stood a beefy
security guard in an olive-green uniform. He nodded at the
bank's director, then unlocked the heavy steel door.

None of us spoke as we passed through the door, down
another steel-bar-lined corridor, until we reached a small
enclosed area marked *Sieben*. Steel bars comprised three walls
of the cage. The other wall was entirely metal, made of some
sort of brushed chrome or steel. At its center was an enormous
steel wheel with six spokes, evidently the mechanism by which
the metal wall could be caused to open.

Eisler pulled a key from the ring attached to his belt and
unlocked the cage.

'Please sit, if you would,' he said, indicating a small gray
metal table in the center of the cage at which were two chairs.

In the center of the table was a beige desk phone without any buttons, and a small black electronic keypad.

'The stipulation of the account,' the banker said, 'is that no officer of the bank is permitted to remain in this area while the combination is being accessed. Enter the digits of the access code slowly, checking the digital readout to be sure you have not made a mistake. If you have, you are permitted a second try. If that fails, the electronic locking mechanism will seize. Access will not be permitted for at least twenty-four hours.'

'I see,' I said. 'What happens after we enter the access code?'

'At that point,' Eisler explained, pointing toward the six-spoked wheel, 'the inner vault will electronically unlock, and you then turn the wheel. It's much easier than it looks, fear not. And the vault door will open.'

'And when we're done?' Molly asked.

'When you are finished examining the contents, or if there are any problems, please call me by simply lifting the handset.'

'Thank you,' Molly said as Dr Eisler left.

We waited a moment until we heard the second steel door shut.

'Ben,' Molly whispered. 'What the hell do we –'

'Patience.' Slowly and carefully – my gauze-wrapped fingers had little dexterity – I entered 48799, watching as each number appeared in red electronic digits on the small black panel. When I had entered the final 9, there was a mechanical whooshing sound, as if a seal had been broken.

'Bingo,' I said.

'I can barely breathe,' Molly said, her voice choked.

Together we walked over to the wheel and turned it. It moved easily in our hands, gliding clockwise, and a large section of the steel wall jutted open.

Weak fluorescent lights illuminated the interior of the vault, which I saw was remarkably small, disappointingly so. The uneven, brick-walled inner chamber was maybe five feet by five feet. It was entirely empty.

And at second glance I realized that our eyes had been deceived by an optical illusion.

What at first had appeared to be the vault's brick inner walls, roughly seamed and scored, could now be seen, as our eyes adjusted to the insufficient light, to be something else entirely.

They were not bricks. They were bars of gold, dull yellow, with a reddish tinge.

The cavernous vault was filled – almost entirely, floor to ceiling – with gold bullion.

46

'My God,' Molly whispered.

I could only gape. Tentatively, almost gingerly, we advanced into the vault toward the walls of solid gold. They did not glitter or glimmer, as one might have imagined. The overall coloration was a dull, mustardy yellow, but upon closer inspection I saw that some of the closely packed bars were a bright butter-yellow (new, and almost one hundred percent pure), and some were reddish-yellow, which indicated copper impurities: they had probably been cast from melted gold coins and jewelry. Each bar was stamped at its end with large serial numbers.

Were it not for the deep yellow hues and mellow patina, these gold bars might have been bricks, neatly stacked bricks, of the sort you could find at any construction site.

Many were scarred and dented; these had probably been in existence in Russia for a century or more. Some, I knew, had been stolen from Hitler's armies by Stalin's victorious troops; most had been mined in the Soviet Union. The edges of several of them were notched: assay marks. The newer bars were of a trapezoidal formation, but by far the majority were rectangular.

'Jesus, Ben,' Molly said, turning to me. Her face was flushed, her eyes wide. 'Did you have any idea?' For some reason, she was whispering.

I nodded.

She went to lift one of the bars up, but failed. It was too heavy. With two hands she managed to hoist it. After a few seconds she put it down on top of the others. It made a dull thud. Then she sank her thumbnail into it.

'It's the real thing, isn't it?' she said.

I nodded mutely. I was nervous, naturally, and excited, and scared, and my bloodstream coursed with adrenaline.

There's a famous remark made by Vladimir Lenin: 'When we are victorious on a world scale, I think we shall use gold for the purpose of building lavatories in the streets of some of the largest cities in the world.'

Wrong on several counts.

More apt was the gripe by the Roman poet Plautus, two hundred years before the birth of Christ: 'I hate gold; it has persuaded many men in many matters to do evil.'

Quite right.

I was disturbed from my reverie by the sight of Molly sinking to the concrete floor, her back against the wall of gold bullion. The vitality seemed to have drained from her body. She had not fainted, but she appeared woozy.

'Who's the other owner?' she asked quietly.

'I don't know,' I admitted.

'A guess?'

'Not even that. Not yet.'

She wrapped her arms around her knees and hugged them to her chest. 'How much?'

'Hmm?'

'Gold. How much gold is here?' Her eyes were closed.

I surveyed the chamber. The stack was about six feet tall. Each bar was nine inches long, three inches wide, and an inch thick.

It took me quite some time, but I counted 526 stacks, each six feet high. Which was 3,156 linear feet. Which was . . . 37,879 gold bars.

Was I calculating right?

I remembered reading an article once about the Federal Reserve Bank in New York. I called it to mind. The Fed's gold vault, which is half the length of a football field, holds something like 126 billion dollars worth of gold if you calculate it at the market price of $400 an ounce. I didn't know what gold was selling for when Orlov and Sinclair raided the Soviet national treasury, but $400 an ounce sounded about right, for the sake of calculation.

No. That wouldn't do it.

All right. The largest gold compartment in the Fed's vault contained a wall of gold ten feet wide by ten feet high by eighteen feet deep. Which was 107,000 bars. Worth seventeen billion dollars.

My head swam with fevered calculations. The volume here was about a third of that.

I returned to my original calculation of 37,879 gold bars. Gold was now selling at not $400 an ounce, but more like $330. Okay. At $330 per ounce, one gold bar, of four hundred troy ounces, was worth $132,000.

Which brought us to . . .

Five billion dollars.

'Five,' I said.

'Five *billion*?'

'Right.'

'I can't even conceive of that,' Molly said. 'It's sitting here, stacked up – I'm leaning against it – and I can't *conceive* of five billion dollars – and all mine –'

'No.'

'Half of it?'

'No. It belongs to Russia.'

She fixed me with a cold stare, then said: 'You're no fun.'

'You're right.'

'He said ten,' I interrupted.

'What?'

'There's maybe five billion here. Orlov told me ten billion dollars.'

'Then he was wrong. Or lying to you.'

'Or half of it is gone.'

'*Gone?* What are you getting at, Ben?'

'I thought we'd finally found the gold,' I mused aloud. 'And we found only part of it.'

'What's this?' she said, startled.

'What?'

Sandwiched in the crack between two vertical stacks of gold, at floor level, was a small square ecru envelope.

'What the hell – ?' she said, tugging at it.

It came out easily.

Her eyes wide, she turned the blank envelope over, saw that there was nothing on either side, and gingerly tore open the flap.

It was a blue-bordered card – a Tiffany's correspondence card, from the look of it – which bore the name Harrison Sinclair in capital letters at the top.

Something was written at the center of the card in her father's hand.

'It's –' Molly began, but I interrupted.

'Don't say it aloud. Show it to me.'

Two lines.

The first was: 'Box 322. Banque de Raspail.'

The second was: 'Boulevard Raspail, 128, Paris 7e.'

That was all. The name and address of a bank in Paris. A box number, presumably a safe deposit box. What for? What was this supposed to mean? Boxes, literally, within boxes: that was what this whole matter had come to.

'What – ?' she said.

'Come on,' I said impatiently, pocketing the card. 'Let's have another chat with Eisler.'

47

'A dead man,' according to Plutarch's *Lives*, 'cannot bite.' It was, I believe, John Dryden who centuries ago wrote: 'Dead men tell no tales.'

Wrong, both of them. Hal Sinclair continued to tell tales long after his funeral, tales that remained mystifying.

The brilliant old spymaster Harrison Sinclair had surprised hundreds of people in his six decades on this earth – friends and associates, superiors and subordinates, enemies around the world and at Langley. And even after his death, it seemed, the surprises, the twists and reversals, did not stop. Who would ever have expected as much on the trail of a dead man?

By the time Molly and I had had a rapid whispered conference, Eisler's personal assistant was waiting in the corridor outside the vault. We had summoned her and demanded immediately to see the director.

'Is there a problem?' she asked, her face radiating concern.

'Yes,' Molly said but did not elaborate.

'We will be glad to help in any way,' she said, escorting us into the elevator and up to Eisler's office. She was all business, but her Swiss reserve had melted somewhat: she chirped familiarly, as if we'd all become old friends in the last hour.

Molly conversed with her politely, while I kept silent. In my right front pocket I fingered the Glock.

Getting it into the bank, through the metal detectors, was no mean feat, and for that I must acknowledge my CIA training. A casual acquaintance of mine from my Agency days, Charles Stone (whose extraordinary saga is no doubt familiar to you), once described to me how he had smuggled a Glock pistol through an airline security gate at Charles de

Gaulle Airport in Paris. The Glock is predominantly, though not entirely, composed of plastic, and Stone (rather ingeniously, I think) disassembled the gun into its components, placed the small metal parts into a sticky shaving kit and the larger metal parts into the frame of a garment bag – both of which went through the luggage X-ray machine – and the plastic pieces on his person.

Unfortunately, Stone's technique wouldn't have worked here, because I didn't have the luxury of dealing with both a metal detector and a luggage X-ray. Everything had to be on my body, and the gun would unquestionably have set off the alarms.

So I'd devised my own method, taking advantage of an anomaly in all metal detectors. These machines are nowhere near as sensitive at their extremities as they are at the center of the field. And the Glock is made up of a relatively small amount of steel. What I did, therefore, was to attach the pistol to a long nylon cord affixed to my belt and running through a small hole I'd cut in my right-hand front trouser pocket. The gun dangled in my right pant leg, close to my shoe; I held it steady by keeping a hand in my pocket and gripping the cord as I passed through the metal detector gate. Essentially, I was kicking the gun through the detector at the perimeter of the magnetic field, where it is so attenuated that it can detect virtually nothing. Naturally, as I went through, I was almost catatonic with fear that the trick wouldn't work, that my attempt to spoof the metal detector would somehow go wrong. But I passed through without incident, and by stopping off in the rest room shortly thereafter I had been able to retrieve the small pistol and place it comfortably in my pants pocket.

Dr Eisler, who appeared even more perturbed than his assistant, offered us coffee. We politely declined. His brow wrinkled in concern as he sat down on the sofa opposite us.

'Now then,' he said in his gravelly yet refined voice. 'What seems to be the problem?'

'The contents of the vault,' I said, 'are incomplete.'

He glared at me a long, long time, then shrugged imperiously. 'We know nothing of the contents of a client's vault. We are obligated only to maintain all security precautions, all –'

'The bank is liable.'

He gave a dry laugh. 'I'm afraid not. And in any case, your wife is merely the co-owner.'

'A rather large quantity of gold,' I said, 'seems to be missing. Rather too much to misplace. I'd like to know where it might have gone.'

Eisler exhaled through his nostrils and nodded kindly. He seemed to be relieved. 'Mr Ellison – Ms. Sinclair – surely you both understand that I am not free to discuss any transactions –'

'Since it was made on my account,' Molly broke in, 'I have the right to know where it was moved *to*!'

Eisler hesitated, nodded again. 'Madam, sir. In the case of numbered accounts, our responsibility is to permit access to anyone who fulfills the requirements stipulated by the person or persons who have established the account. Beyond that, in order to protect all involved, we must maintain total confidentiality.'

'We are talking,' Molly said steely, 'about *my* account. I want to know *where* the gold went!'

'Ms. Sinclair, confidentiality in these matters is a tradition of our nation's banking system and one which the Bank of Zurich is compelled to observe. I am awfully sorry. If there is anything further we can do –'

In one smooth motion I pulled out the Glock and aimed it at his high, broad forehead.

'This pistol is loaded,' I said. 'I am fully prepared to use it. *Don't*' – I released the safety when I saw him begin to slide his foot to the right, ever so subtly, toward what I now saw was a silent alarm button at the base of his desk, a few inches away – '*don't* be so foolish as to hit the silent alarm.'

I moved closer, so that the barrel of the pistol was barely an inch or two from his forehead.

I hardly had to concentrate now, his thoughts were flowing so discernibly now. I could pick up on a great deal: rushes of thought, mostly in German, but with the occasional patch of

English as he readied to speak sentences, objections, declamations of outrage.

'We are, as you see, desperate,' I said. My expression let him know that desperate though I was, I retained full composure and was prepared to shoot at any moment.

'If you are so foolhardy as to shoot me,' Eisler said with astonishing equanimity, 'you will accomplish nothing. For one thing, you will not leave this room. Not only will the gunshot be audible to my secretary, but there are motion sensors in this room that –'

He was lying; that much I could pick up. And he was understandably scared: this had never happened to him before. He continued: 'Even assuming I were to give you the information you seek, which I will not, you will certainly not make it out of the bank.'

On that, I concluded, he seemed to be telling the truth; but it did not take extrasensory perception to realize the logic in what he was saying.

'I am prepared, however, to call an end to this idiocy,' he went on. 'If you put down this gun and leave at once, I shall not report this. I understand that you are desperate. But you gain nothing by threatening me.'

'We're not threatening. We want transaction information pertaining to the account which rightfully, by American and Swiss banking laws, belongs to my wife.'

A few beads of sweat began to run down his forehead, starting at the smooth bald crown of his head and coursing across the deeply grooved parallel lines inscribed there. I could see that his resolve was weakening.

I heard a rush of thoughts, some angry, some pleading. He was going through an agony of indecision.

'Has anyone removed gold from this vault?' I asked quietly.

Nein, I heard distinctly. *Nein.*

He closed his eyes, seeming to brace for the shot that would end his life. The sweat came down in rivulets now.

'I cannot say,' he said.

No one had removed any gold. But . . .

Suddenly, I had a thought. 'There *was* other gold, though, wasn't there? Gold that wasn't moved into the vault.'

I held the gun steady, and then moved it slowly closer until the end of the barrel touched his damp temple. I pressed it against the skin. It compressed with an easy elasticity, forming tiny stretch marks all around the barrel's end.

'Please,' he whispered. I could barely hear him.

His thoughts were coming fast and jumbled now, incoherent; I could not make them out.

'An answer,' I said, 'and we will leave you.'

He swallowed, closed his eyes, and then opened them again. 'A shipment,' he whispered. 'Ten billion dollars worth of gold bullion. We received it all here at the Bank of Zurich.'

'Where did it go?'

'Some of it was moved into the vault. That is the gold you saw.'

'And the rest?'

He swallowed again. 'Liquidated. We assisted in its sale through gold brokers we deal with on a confidential basis. It was melted down and then recast.'

'What was the value?'

'Perhaps five . . . perhaps six . . .'

'Billion.'

'Yes.'

'It was converted to liquid assets? Cash?'

'It was wire-transferred.'

'Where?'

He closed his eyes again. The muscles around them tightened as if he were praying.

'I can't say.'

'Where?'

'I *mustn't* say.'

'Was the money wired to Paris?'

'No . . . please, I cannot –'

'Where was the money wired?'

Deutschland . . . Deutschland . . . München . . .

'Was the money wired to Munich?'

'You will have to kill me,' he whispered, his eyes still closed. 'I am prepared to die.'

His resolve surprised me. What possessed him? What sustained him in this foolish resolve? Was he attempting to call my bluff? By now he had to know, surely, that I wasn't bluffing. Or if I was, with this gun at his temple, what sane man would take the *chance* that I was bluffing, that the gun wasn't loaded? He would rather be killed than violate Swiss banking confidentiality!

There was a faint liquid sound, and I saw that he had lost control of his bladder. A dark spot spread in a large irregular area across the crotch of his pants. His fright was genuine. His eyes were still closed, and he was frozen still, paralyzed with fear.

But I did not let up; I couldn't.

Compressing the barrel still harder against his temple, I said slowly: 'All we want is a name. Tell us where the money was wired. To whom. Give us a name.'

Now Eisler's entire body was racked by a visible tremor. His eyes were not just closed, the lids were squeezed tight, screwed up in little wrinkled knots of muscular tension. The sweat poured down his face, across his jawline, down his neck. Sweat darkened the lapels of his gray suit and spotted his tie.

'All we want,' I said, 'is a name.'

Molly watched me, her eyes brimming with tears, from time to time wincing. The scene was too much for her to stand. Stick with it, Mol, I wanted to say. Hang in there.

'You know what name I want.'

And within a minute I had a name.

He remained silent. His lips trembled as if he were about to weep, but he did not. He did not speak.

He thought.

He did not speak.

I was about to lower the gun, when another question occurred to me. 'When was the last time funds were transferred to him from this bank?'

This morning, Eisler thought.

He squeezed his eyes tighter. Droplets of perspiration rolled down his nose, onto his lips.

This morning.

337

And then I said, lowering the gun, 'Well. I can see you are a man of steel will.'

Slowly, he opened his eyes and looked directly at me. There was great fear in them, of course, but there was something more. A glint of triumph, it seemed; a flash of defiance.

Finally, he spoke. His voice cracked. 'If you will leave my office at once –'

'You haven't talked,' I said. 'I admire that.'

'If you will leave –'

'I do not plan to kill you,' I went on. 'You're a man of honor; you're doing your job. Instead, if we can agree that this never happened – if you agree not to report this, and agree to let both of us leave the bank undisturbed, we will call an end to this. We will leave.'

I knew, of course, that the moment we left the bank he would call the police – in his position, I'd have done the same thing – but this would buy us a few much-needed minutes.

'Yes,' he said. His voice cracked again. He cleared his throat. 'Leave here immediately. And if you have any sense at all, which I seriously doubt, you will leave Zurich at once.'

48

We strode quickly out of the bank and then accelerated to a
run down Bahnhofstrasse. Eisler seemed to have abided by his
agreement to let us out of the bank (for his own safety and that
of his employees), but by now, I calculated, he had certainly
called in both bank security and the municipal police. He had
our real names, though not our cover names, which was an
encouragement, but it was probably only a matter of hours – if
that long – before we were apprehended. And once the Wise
Men's forces knew that we were here, if they didn't already –
but I didn't want to think along those lines.

'Did you get it?' Molly asked as we ran.

'Yes. But we can't talk now.' I was hyper-alert, keeping a
close watch on all passersby, searching for that one face that I
recognized, the washed-out face of the blond would-be
assassin I'd first seen in Boston.

Not here.

But a moment later I sensed that we once again had
company.

There are dozens of different techniques employed to follow
a man, and the really good operatives are seldom caught. The
problem for the blond man was that I had 'made' him, in
surveillance argot: I'd recognized him. Except in the loosest
sort of tail, he couldn't hope to follow me unnoticed. And
indeed, I didn't see him anywhere near us.

But, as I was to learn soon, there were others, tails I *didn't*
recognize. In the crowded foot-traffic of Bahnhofstrasse, it
would be difficult if not impossible to spot a tail.

'Ben,' Molly began, but I gave her a fierce look that shut her
up at once.

'Not now,' I said under my breath.

When we came to Barengasse I turned right, and Molly followed. The plate-glass storefronts provided a good reflecting surface for me to study who was following us, but no one seemed conspicuous. They were professionals. It was likely that since the moment I'd spotted him as we entered the bank, the blond man was determined not to be seen. Others, confederates, were now in play.

I would have to flush them out.

Molly let out a long, quavering sigh. 'This is *crazy*, Ben. This is just fucking *dangerous*!' Her voice grew softer. 'Look, I really hated seeing you hold a gun to that guy's head. I hated seeing what it did to him. Those things are so vile.'

We walked along Barengasse. I was keenly aware of pedestrians on either side of us, but wasn't yet able to get a fix on anyone.

'Guns?' I said 'They've saved my life on more than one occasion.'

She heaved a heavy sigh. 'Dad always said that too. He taught me to shoot a gun.'

'A shotgun or something?'

'Handguns. A .38 and a .45. Actually, I was pretty good at it. An ace, if you must know. Once I was able to hit the bull's-eye on one of those police silhouette target things at a hundred feet, I put down my dad's gun and never fired it again. I also told him never to keep one in the house again.'

'But if you ever have to use a gun to protect yourself or me –'

'Of course I'd do it. But don't ever make me.'

'I won't. I promise.'

'Thanks. But was all that necessary with Eisler?'

'Yes, I'm afraid it was. I have a name now. A name and an account that will likely tell us where the gold disappeared to.'

'What about the Banque de Raspail in Paris?'

I shook my head. 'I don't know what that note's supposed to mean. Whoever was meant to see it.'

'But why would my father have left that note there?'

'Don't know.'

'But if there's a safe deposit box, there has to be a key, right?'

340

'Generally, yes.'

'So where is it?'

I shook my head again. 'We don't have it. But there must be a way of getting into the box. But first, Munich. If there's any way of intercepting Truslow before anything happens to him, I'll find it.'

Had we eluded them?

Doubtful.

'What about Toby?' Molly asked. 'Shouldn't you notify him?'

'We can't risk contacting him. Or anyone at CIA now.'

'But we could use his help.'

'I don't trust his help.'

'How about trying to reach Truslow now?'

'Yes,' I said. 'He may be on his way to Germany. But if I can stop him –'

'What?'

In mid-sentence I swiveled around toward a public telephone on the street. It was far, far too risky to place a call to Truslow's office in the CIA, of course. There were other ways, however. Even on short notice; even improvised on the spot. There were ways.

Standing on the street, Molly next to me, I kept a close watch on my surroundings. No one – yet.

With the assistance of an international operator I called a private communications facility in Brussels, whose number I, of course, was able to recite easily. Once connected, I entered a sequence of numbers, which shifted the call to a rather complicated telephone switch-back system, a dead-end loop. The next call I direct-dialed would appear, in a trace, to originate in Brussels.

Truslow's executive assistant took my call. I gave him a name that Truslow would immediately recognize as signaling me, and asked him to pass it on to the director.

'I'm sorry, sir,' the assistant said. 'At this moment the director is aboard a military aircraft somewhere over Europe.'

'But he's accessible by satellite link,' I insisted.

'Sir, I'm not permitted –'

'This is an *emergency!*' I half shouted at the assistant. Truslow had to be reached, to be warned against entering Germany.

'I'm sorry, sir –' he replied.

And I hung up. It was too late.

And then I heard my name.

I turned toward Molly, but she hadn't said anything.

At least I *thought* I heard my name.

Quite an odd sensation. Yes, definitely my name. I glanced around the street.

There it was again, *thought*, not spoken, unquestionably.

But there was no man anywhere near us who could possibly –

Yes. It wasn't a man at all, but a woman. My pursuers were equal-opportunity employers. Very politically correct.

It was the lone woman, standing at a newsstand a few feet away, seemingly absorbed in a copy of *Le Canard Enchainé*, a French satirical newspaper.

She appeared to be in her mid-thirties, with short reddish hair, wearing a no-nonsense olive business suit. Powerfully built, from what I could tell. No doubt she was very good at her job, which I suspected was to do more than simply follow.

But *if* she was a follower, that was about as much as I could deduce. A follower employed by *whom*? By those in the CIA Truslow had warned of, the so-called Wise Men? Or by people associated with Vladimir Orlov – who knew of the existence of the gold and knew that I was on its trail?

They – her employers – knew I'd gone into the Bank of Zurich. Knew I'd emerged empty-handed . . .

Empty-handed, yes, but with a solid morsel of knowledge now. The name of a German in Munich who had been the recipient of some five billion dollars.

Now it was my turn.

'Mol,' I said as quietly as I could. 'You have to get out of here.'

'What –'

'*Keep your voice down.* Act as if nothing's wrong.' I smiled, as if at some witticism. 'We have company. I want you to leave.'

342

'But *where*?' she asked, frightened.

'Go grab our bags from the left-luggage claim near the main train station,' I whispered, and thought for a second. 'Then go to the Baur-au-Lac, on Talstrasse. Every cabbie in Switzerland knows where it is. There's a restaurant there called the Grillroom. I'll meet you there.' I handed my leather portfolio to her. 'Take this with you.'

'But what if –'

'*Move!*'

Frantically, she whispered in reply: 'You're in no shape to handle anything dangerous, Ben. Your hands – your dexterity –'

'*Go!*'

She glared at me, then without warning turned and stormed down the street. It was a clever piece of play-acting; an observer would think we had had a tiff, so natural was Molly's reaction.

The redhead looked up sharply from her newspaper, her eyes following Molly, turning to me, then returning to the paper. Clearly she had decided to stay with me, her chief quarry.

Good.

Suddenly I spun around and vaulted down the street. In my peripheral vision I could see that the red-haired woman had dropped her newspaper and, abandoning all subtlety and pretense, was running after me.

Just up ahead was a narrow, alleylike service street, into which I abruptly turned. From Barengasse behind me I heard shouts, and the woman's footsteps. I flattened myself against a brick wall, saw the redheaded woman in the olive suit lunge into the alley after me, saw her draw a gun, and I released the safety on my Glock and fired off a round at the woman.

There was a groan, an exhalation. The woman grimaced, spun awkwardly forward, then regained her balance. I had shot her somewhere in the upper leg, the thigh perhaps, and now without a moment's pause I leapt forward, firing away at her, no, not directly *at* her, really, but *around* her, circumscribing her head and shoulders, and momentarily thrown off balance, she contorted her body, twisting left and right, then, regaining her center of gravity, she leveled her gun at me, aiming for just an instant too long, and –

– her hand snapped open as a round from my gun sank into her wrist, and her gun clattered to the floor, and then, in one headlong rush I was upon her, slamming her to the pavement, my elbow smashing into her throat, pinning her down with my left hand.

For a moment she was still.

She had been wounded, in her thigh and her wrist, and the blood had soaked darkly through the olive silk fabric in several places.

But she was immensely strong, for all that, and of wiry build, and she reared up with a sudden surge of strength, almost knocking me off balance, until my right elbow cracked once against the cartilage in her throat.

The woman was actually younger than she had earlier appeared, perhaps in her early twenties, and she was a woman of extraordinary strength.

With one swift, sure motion, I grabbed her gun – it was a small Walther – and stuck it in the breast pocket of my suit.

Thus disarmed, and obviously in great pain, the would-be assassin moaned, a low, guttural animal sound, and I turned my pistol toward her, aiming precisely between her eyes.

'This gun holds sixteen rounds,' I said very quietly to her. 'I fired off five. That leaves eleven.'

Her eyes widened, but in fiery defiance, not fear.

'I will not hesitate to kill you,' I said. 'I assume you believe me, but if you don't, it's of no serious concern. I will kill you because I have to, to protect myself and others. But for the moment I would rather not.'

Her eyes narrowed slightly, as if conceding.

I could hear sirens now, growing louder, almost here. Did she think the arrival of the Swiss police would provide her with the opportunity to escape?

But I remained poised to fire, knowing that this woman was a professional and was probably possessed of a homicidal courage, and was surely being paid an enormous amount of money for her valor besides.

She would do almost anything. But she would, I calculated, rather not die if she did not have to. It is a human instinct, and even this killer had human instincts.

I had to move her as far away from the street as possible, so that neither of us could be seen. 'Now,' I said, 'I want you to get slowly to your feet. Then I want you to turn around and walk slowly. I will direct you. If you make the mistake of doing anything I haven't instructed you to do, I will not hesitate to fire.'

I pulled back, lifted my elbow from her now-bruised throat, and, the Glock aimed steadily at the center of her forehead, watched as she very slowly, and in obvious pain, struggled to stand.

Then she spoke her first word to me. 'Don't,' she said in an accent of indeterminate European origin.

'Turn,' I replied.

She turned around slowly, and I did a quick body search with my free hand. I turned up nothing, no second gun or even a knife.

'Now, move,' I said, shoving the gun against the back of her head, prodding her to move faster.

When we had come to a dark, deserted alcove toward the end of the block, I shoved her suddenly into it, keeping the Glock trained on the back of her head. Then I said, 'Face me.'

She turned slowly. Her face was set in a look of dour recalcitrance. Up close, it was a square, even mannish face, but not unattractive. She took pains with her appearance, whether out of vanity or out of concern for her cover. She wore eye liner of deep blue and eye shadow of a very pale blue mixed with a barely detectable glitter. Her round, pouting lips had been carefully painted with crimson lipstick.

'Who are you?' I asked.

She said nothing. There was a slight twitch below her left eye, but apart from that, her face remained frozen.

'You're in no position to hold out,' I said.

Her left cheek twitched, but her eyes regarded me with boredom.

'Who hired you?' I said.

Nothing.

'Ah, a genuine professional,' I said. 'They're so scarce these days. You must have been paid a great deal.'

A twitch; silence.

'Who's the blond man?' I persisted. 'The pale one.'

More silence.

She glanced at me, as if about to speak, then off into the distance. She was quite good, really, at concealing her fear.

For a moment I considered threatening her again, and then I remembered that there were other ways to learn what I wanted to learn. Other resources; other talents. I had forgotten the very thing that had brought me here.

The gun pointed steadily between her eyes, I moved closer.

I was at once greeted by that flow of indistinct sound I'd grown to recognize, that jumble of syllables and noises, but it was, strangely, what I now know to be the 'audible' thoughts of someone who was not in fear. And in a language I did not recognize.

Her left cheek was twitching out of tension, but not out of fear, an emotion we experience quite differently. This woman had been shoved into a dark alcove with a semi-automatic weapon pointed directly at her, and yet she was not afraid.

There were various drugs the clandestine people administer their agents to keep them calm and collected, a veritable pharmacopoeia of beta blockers and anxiolytics and such that over the years had been found to keep field agents calm yet focused. Perhaps this woman was under the influence of something like that. Perhaps, on the other hand, she was preternaturally calm, one of those peculiar human specimens, sociopaths or whatever they are, who do not experience fear the way the rest of us do, and who are therefore eminently suitable for their strange line of work. She had capitulated to me not out of fear, but out of a very rational calculus. She planned, I would bet, to surprise me at a moment when my defenses were relaxed.

But no one is entirely without fear.

Without fear we are not human. We all experience some degree of fear. Fear keeps us alive.

'His name,' I whispered.

I squeezed my finger against the blue metal trigger ever so slightly, but obviously, and told myself that if it came to it, I would without a doubt have to kill this woman.

Max.

I heard, quite distinctly, in that crystalline timbre, one very clear syllable. *Max.* A name, I assumed. A name that was understandable in any language.

'Max,' I said aloud. 'Max what?'

Her eyes met mine, with insouciance, not fear or surprise.

'They told me you could do this,' she said, speaking at last. Her accent was European. Not French, but – Scandinavian? Finnish, or Norwegian . . . ? She shrugged. 'I know very little. That was why I was hired.'

I recognized her accent now. Dutch, or perhaps Flemish.

'You know very little,' I agreed, 'but you can't possibly know *nothing*. Otherwise you'd be of no use. You have been given instructions, code names, and so on. What is Max's last name?'

I heard, again, *Max.*

'Try me,' she said with a hint of impertinence.

'What is his last name?'

She replied, pursing her lips slightly, 'I don't know. I'm sure Max isn't his real name anyway.'

I nodded. 'I'm sure you're right. But who is he with?'

Another shrug.

'Who hired you?'

'You mean, what company name is on my weekly pay-check?' she came back with a smirk.

I leaned closer, until I could feel her breath hot against my face, the Glock still pointed at her, my left hand pressing her against the brick wall.

'What is your name?' I asked. 'That I assume you know.'

Her facial expression was unchanged.

Zanna Huygens, she thought.

'Where are you from, Zanna?'

Back off, motherfucker, I heard. English.

Back off.

347

She spoke English, German, Flemish. Probably one of the Flemish hired killers that the world's espionage agencies like to employ as free-lance talent. The CIA used the Dutch and the Flemish, not just because they were good, but because they had a natural facility in many languages, which made it easy for them to blend in anywhere in the world, to submerge their true identity.

Something else I didn't understand. A floating phrase, repeated several times: *the name the name the name the name the name motherfucker the name give me the name the name give me the name.*

'I don't know *anything*,' she spat out at me, tiny gobbets of saliva stinging my face.

'You've been told to get a name out of me, is that it?'

A twitch of her left cheek; a sere pucker of her perfect crimson lips. Then, having considered for a moment, she spoke.

'I know you're some kind of freak,' she said. Without warning her words began to gush forth, in a prim, singsong Flemish accent. 'I know you were trained by the CIA. I know that somehow you have this weird thing, this thing where sometimes you can hear the voices inside the heads of other people, inside the minds of people who are afraid, I don't know exactly how, or why, or where this thing came from, or whether you were born with it . . .'

She was yammering, jabbering away almost mindlessly, and suddenly I knew what she was doing.

She was talking nonstop, filling her brain's speech center with word after word that was probably rehearsed, because if you keep talking, your brain is too busy producing the thoughts that lead to vocalized speech, too busy to be intruded upon, to be read.

'. . . or why you're here,' she blathered on, 'but I know that you're supposed to be ruthless, bloodthirsty, and I know that you're not going to return to the U.S. alive, but I can probably be of some help to you, and please, *please* don't kill me, *please don't kill me*, I was doing a job, and I didn't fire directly at you, you'll notice, *please –*'

Was she really pleading? I momentarily wondered. Was that fear in her eyes? Had the anxiolytic worn off, or had the stress and terror finally sunk in, and as I inhaled, thought how to respond, she abruptly jammed her hands in my face, her sharp nails grasping at my eye sockets, screaming shrilly, deafeningly, and slammed her knee upward into my groin, all of this happening in one bewildering, frightening instant, and I reacted, a little late, but not entirely too late, by steadying the gun, my bandaged, clumsy finger poised on the trigger, and the would-be assassin jolted my hand, certainly trying to dislodge the gun, but it didn't dislodge the gun at all; instead, it caused me to pull back instinctively, thus giving the trigger the slightest squeeze, and the woman's head exploded, and with a liquid sound the air was expelled from her lungs and she sank to the ground.

Calmly, I reached down, frisked her, searching for but not finding any documentation, any papers or wallets of any kind except a small billfold that contained a small amount of Swiss currency, probably just enough to get her through her morning's assignment, and then I ran.

For a long, awful, excruciating moment, as I searched for Molly in the Grillroom at the Baur-au-Lac, I *knew* she was dead. I knew they had gotten to her. As had happened once before, I had survived their onslaught but the others had gotten my wife.

The Grillroom is a clubby, comfortable place with an American-style bar, a large stone fireplace, and businessmen sitting at tables lunching on their *émincé de turbot*. I was decidedly out of place there, bedraggled and blood-spattered as I was, and I drew a number of hostile, disapproving looks.

And as I turned to leave, a young woman in the uniform of a waitress hurried up to me, and asked, 'Are you Mr Osborne?'

It took me a moment to remember that that was my cover. 'Why do you ask?'

She nodded shyly, handed me a folded note. 'From Mrs Osborne, sir,' she said, and stood there expectantly as I opened it. I gave her a ten-franc note, and she hurried off.

The blue Ford Granada in front, the note said in Molly's handwriting.

49

Munich was dark by the time we arrived, a clear and crisp evening twinkling with city lights. We had retrieved our bags from the left-luggage depot in the Hauptbahnhof in Zurich, and got the 15:39 train, which arrived at 20:09 in Munich's Hauptbahnhof. There was a momentary fright aboard the train when we crossed the German border, and I braced myself for passport control. There had been plenty of time for our false passports to be faxed to the German authorities, particularly if the CIA put a priority on it, which I would bet it did.

But times have changed. The old days, when you would be startled awake in the middle of the night, your train compartment door violently slid open, a German voice barking: '*Deutsche Passkontrolle!*' – those days were ancient history now. Europe was unifying. Passport checks were seldom.

Exhausted yet tense, anxious, wired, I tried to sleep on the train, but could not.

We changed some money at the Deutsche Verkehrs-Bank office at the train station, and then I made hotel reservations for the night. The Metropol, with the unique advantage of its location directly across from the Hauptbahnhof, was booked solid. But I was able to book us a room at the Bayerischer Hof und Palais Montgelas, on Promenadeplatz, in the city center – inordinately expensive, but any port in a storm and all that.

From a pay phone I placed a call to Kent Atkins, Deputy Chief of Station, CIA, in Munich. Atkins, an old drinking buddy of mine from Paris days, was, as I've said, a friend of Edmund Moore's – and, more important, was the one who had given Ed Moore documents warning of something 'ominous' in the works.

It was about nine-thirty by the time I called Atkins at home. He answered on the first ring.

'Yes?'

'Kent?'

'Yes?' His voice was sharp, alert, but it sounded as if he had been asleep. One of the vital skills you acquire in the business is the ability to snap awake, be perfectly attentive in a split second.

'Boy, you're asleep early. It's barely nine at night.'

'Who's this?'

'It's Father John.'

'Who?'

'*Père* Jean.' An old, inside joke; a reference I hoped he would remember.

Long silence. 'Who is – oh, God. Where are you?'

'Can we meet for a drink or something?'

'Can it wait?'

'No. Hofbraühaus in half an hour?'

Atkins replied quickly and sarcastically: 'Why don't we just meet in the lobby of the American embassy?'

I got it, and smiled to myself. Molly looked at me with concern; I nodded reassurance.

'See you at Leopold,' he said, and hung up. He sounded distraught.

Leopold, I knew – and he knew that I knew – meant Leopoldstrasse, in Schwabing, the section to the north of the city. That meant the Englishcher Garten, a logical meeting place, and specifically, the Monopteros, the classical temple built in the early part of the nineteenth century, on a bluff in the park. A good place for a 'blind date,' as we spooks call it.

Instead of taking the U-bahn directly from the train station, which had certain risks, we exited the station and strolled a bit, circuitously, to Marienplatz, the always-crowded central square of the city, overpowered by the Gothic monstrosity of the New Town Hall, its gray gingerbread façade illuminated frighteningly at night, and on the southwest corner a rather barbarous modern department store building, which utterly destroyed the kitsch-Gothic unity of the square, awful though it was.

In some ways Germany hadn't changed since last I saw it. I was reassured to see a crowd waiting bovinely at a flashing red Don't Walk sign on Maxburgstrasse, where not a single automobile was in sight and the whole bunch could have crossed without anyone noticing, but laws were laws. One young man hopped up and down on alternating feet, desperate with impatience, like a horse champing at the bit, but even he wouldn't violate the social etiquette.

Yet in significant ways Germany had changed drastically. The crowds in Marienplatz were louder and more threatening than the usually polite evening throngs there. Neo-Nazi skinheads lurked in spiteful little gangs, hurling racial epithets at passersby. Graffiti covered quite a few of the otherwise-tidy Gothic buildings. '*Ausländer raus!*' and '*Kanacken raus!*' – 'Foreigners get out,' in varying degrees of derogation. '*Tod allen Juden und dem Ausländerpack!*' – 'Death to the Jews and the foreign hordes.' '*Deutschland ist stärker ohne Europa*' – 'Germany is stronger without Europe.' There were attacks on the former East Germans: '*Ossis – Parasiten!*' Inscribed in Day-Glo pink on the front of an otherwise elegant restaurant, an evocation of an earlier time: '*Deutschland für Deutsche,*' 'Germany for the Germans.' And one plaintive cry: '*Für mehr Menschlichkeit, gegen Gewalt!*' meaning 'For more humanity, against violence.'

Dozens of homeless people slept on cardboard flats above grates. Many storefronts were boarded up, plate-glass windows were smashed and unrepaired, and many businesses seemed to be dying. '*Wegen Geschäftsaufgabe alle Waren 30% billiger!*' one sign read: GOING OUT OF BUSINESS ALL GOODS 30% OFF.

Munich seemed a city out of control. I wondered whether the entire country, which was in its biggest economic crisis since the days before Hitler's rise to power, was like this.

Molly and I took the U-bahn from Marienplatz to Münchner Freiheit and made our way through the Englischer Garten's asphalt tracks, by the artificial lake, the Chinese Tower. We quickly located the Monopteros, which has always reminded me of a bulimic Jefferson Memorial, all gawky columns and scrolled capitals. We circled it in silence. In the sixties the Monopteros was a hangout for street people and protesters and the like. Now it seemed to be a rendezvous point for teenage boys and girls in American college sweatshirts and black leather jackets.

'Why do you think the money was wired to Munich?' Molly asked. 'Isn't Frankfurt the financial capital of Germany?'

'Yes. But Munich is the manufacturing center. The industrial capital as well as the capital of Bavaria. The real city of money. Sometimes Munich's called Germany's secret capital.'

We were early, or, rather, Atkins arrived late, in his antique Ford Fiesta, little more than sheaths of rust held together by duct tape. He had the radio blasting, or maybe it was a tape: Donna Summer doing the old postdisco classic 'She Works Hard for the Money.' In Paris, I remembered, he'd had an embarrassing affinity for discothéques. The music died only when he keyed off the ignition and the car sputtered to a stop fifty feet from where we stood.

'Nice car,' I called out as he approached. 'Very *gemütlich*.'

'Very crappy,' he returned unsmilingly. His face showed great strain, the same anxiety I had heard in his voice. Atkins was in his mid-forties, lithe, with a mane of prematurely white hair contrasting with heavy dark brows. He had a long, thin face and virtually no lips, but he was good-looking all the same. He was also gay, which for a long while made career advancement difficult for him (the upper echelons in Langley have become enlightened only very recently).

Atkins had aged quite a bit since I had last seen him in Paris. He had deep circles under his eyes, which told of nights of insomnia. He hadn't been a worrier when I knew him in Paris, but something was obsessing him now, and I knew what it was.

I began introducing him to Molly, but he would have no social pleasantries. He reached out a hand and gripped my shoulder.

'Ben,' he said, alarm in his eyes. 'Get the hell out of here. Get the hell out of Germany. I can't afford to be seen with you.

'Where are you staying?' he asked.

'Vier Jahreszeiten,' I lied.

'Too public, too vulnerable. I wouldn't even stay in the city if I were you.'

'Why?'

'You're PNG.' Persona non grata.

'Here?'

'Everywhere.'

'So what?'

'You're on the watch list.'

'Meaning?'

Atkins hesitated, glanced at Molly and then at me, as if asking for permission to proceed. I nodded.

'Cauterization.'

'*What?*' In Agency lingo, a compromised or identified agent is 'cauterized' for his own protection by being swiftly yanked out of a hostile situation and taken into safety. But more and more often the term is used with irony – meaning the apprehension of an agent by his own employers when he's deemed to be dangerous to the organization.

Atkins was telling me that orders had been disseminated throughout the world that I was to be brought in by any Agency official who chanced to encounter me.

'It's a D-Sid.' A DCID, or Director of Central Intelligence Directive. 'Orders cut by some muckety-muck at the Agency named Rossi. What are you doing here?' Atkins was moving quickly now, probably an unconscious fear reflex. We kept up with him; Molly was forced into a kind of half-walk, half-sprint. She only listened, allowing me to do all the talking.

'I need your help, Kent.'

'I said, what are you *doing* here? Are you out of your *mind*?'

'How much do you know?'

'They warned me you might surface here. Have you gone private or something?'

'I went private when I quit and went to law school.'

'But you're back in the game,' he prodded. 'Why?'

'I was forced into it.'

'So they all say. You can never quit.'

'Bullshit. For a while, I did.'

'You were put through some sort of superclassified experimental program, they say. Some sort of research program designed to enhance your usefulness. I don't know what that means. The rumors are vague.'

'The rumors are barium,' I said. He got my reference: 'barium' is a KGB-inspired term for false information that's given to suspected leaks in order to detect them, much the same way barium is used in gastroenterology.

'Maybe,' he said. 'But you've got to go to ground, Ben. Both of you. Disappear. Your lives are in jeopardy.'

When we had gotten to a deserted spot, a copse of trees by a dirt path, I stopped. 'You know Ed Moore's dead.'

He blinked. 'I know. I talked to him the night before he was killed.'

'He told me you were scared to death.'

'Moore exaggerated.'

'But you *are* scared, Kent. You've got to tell me what you know. You gave Moore documents –'

'What are you talking about?'

Molly, sensing his reticence, announced: 'I'm going to take a stroll. I badly need some fresh air.' Her hand grazed the back of my neck as she walked off.

'He *told* me, Kent,' I continued. 'It never went any further than me, I promise. We don't have the time for this. *What do you know?*'

He bit his thin lower lip, frowned. His mouth was a straight line, an arc tilted downward. He consulted his watch, a fake Rolex. 'The documents I gave Ed were far from conclusive.'

'But you know more now, don't you?'

'I have nothing in writing. No documents. Everything I've learned is ears-only stuff.'

'That's often the most valuable intelligence. Kent, Ed Moore was killed over this. I have some information that might be useful –'

'I don't *want* your goddamned information!'

'*Listen to me!*'

'No,' he said. 'You listen to *me*. I talked to Ed a few hours before the fuckers made him commit suicide. He warned me about an assassination conspiracy.'

'Yes,' I said, my stomach tensing. 'Against whom?'

'Ed had only bits and pieces. Speculation.'

'Who?'

'Against the only guy who can clean the Agency out.'

'Alex Truslow.'

'You got it.'

'I'm working for him.'

'I'm glad to hear it. For his sake and the sake of the Company.'

'I'm flattered. Now, I need some information. Recently, a large sum of money was wired to a corporate account in Munich. The Commerzbank.'

'Whose account?'

Could I trust him or not? I had to rely on Ed Moore's good judgment. I plunged ahead. 'Are you with me or not?'

Atkins took a deep breath. 'I'm with you, Ben.'

'The recipient's name was Gerhard Stoessel. The corporate account belongs to Krafft A.G. Tell me everything you know.'

He shook his head. 'You got that wrong. Boy, you got something all screwed up.'

'Why?'

'Do you know who Stoessel *is*?'

'No,' I admitted.

'Christ! Haven't you been reading the papers? Gerhard Stoessel is the chairman of Neue Welt, an enormous real estate concern. Believed to own and/or control most of the commercial real estate in unified Germany. More to the point, Stoessel is the economic adviser to Wilhelm Vogel, the chancellor-elect. Vogel's already named him finance minister in the Vogel government. Wants Stoessel to rebuild the shattered German economy. He's known as Vogel's Svengali, sort of a financial genius. But as I said, you got something really screwed up.'

'How?'

'Vogel's real estate company has no links whatsoever to Krafft A.G. Do you know much about Krafft?'

'That's part of the reason I'm here,' I said. 'I know it's a huge arms manufacturer.'

'Only the biggest arms manufacturer in Europe. Head-quartered in Stuttgart. Way bigger than the other German defense companies – Krupp, Dornier, Krauss-Maffei, Messerschmitt-Bölkow-Blohm, Siemens, and let's not forget the Bayerische Motorenwerke. Bigger than Ingenieurkontor Lübeck, the submarine makers; or Maschinenfabrik Augsburg-Nürnberg, AEG, MTU, Messerschmitt, Daimler-Benz, Rheinmetall . . .'

'How do you know Stoessel has no links with Krafft?'

'It's the law. There was a ruling some years back by the Federal Cartel Office, when Neue Welt tried to acquire Krafft. The cartel office decided the two companies can't have anything to do with one another, that a merger would create an uncontrollable giant. Did you know the word cartel comes from the German *Kartell*? It's a German concept.'

'My information is right,' I said.

All this time I had been straining, while talking and listening, to pick up what I could of Kent's thoughts. Here and there something would come through. Each time it confirmed for me what I already knew, that he was telling me the truth, at least as he knew it.

'If – *if* your information is right, and I won't ask where you got it, I don't *want* to know – that's damned convincing proof that Stoessel's company has somehow, secretly, acquired Krafft!'

I turned to make sure Molly was within view; she was: she was pacing back and forth.

What this all meant, I thought but didn't say, was that the Bank of Zurich had funneled billions of dollars to a German corporation, the largest real estate firm combined with the largest munitions manufacturer . . . which was behind Wilhelm Vogel, the next chancellor of Germany . . . the next leader, functionally, of Europe.

I shuddered, not wanting to consider the ramifications of this, but not able to stop myself. The consequences, I knew at once, were even worse than I had suspected.

50

'Could it have been a bribe?' I asked.

'Stoessel's known as a Mr Clean type,' Atkins replied.

'Those are the types who most often take bribes.'

'All right, I'm not saying he wouldn't take a bribe. But the fact is that all campaign financing in Germany is scrutinized incredibly closely these days. That's to keep these industrial giants from controlling the politics. There are any number of ways to secretly channel money, but there isn't a corporation that would dare. German intelligence keeps a close watch. So if you have proof – *documentary proof* – of this, that's political dynamite.'

What was I to say? I had no documents. All I had was the thoughts in Eisler's head that I'd received. But tell that to Atkins!

'All the more reason,' I said, 'why billions of dollars or deutsche marks surreptitiously channeled into the country would be enormously valuable to a candidate. But I don't get it. I thought Vogel was a moderate, sort of a populist.'

'Let's walk,' he said. Out of the corner of my eye I could see Molly. We began to walk, and, keeping her distance, she followed.

'All right,' Atkins said, bowing his head as he walked. 'The German economy is in a disarray it hasn't seen since the 1920s, right? Riots in Hamburg, Frankfurt, Berlin, Bonn – all the major cities, and in many of the smaller ones as well. Neo-Nazis are all over the place. There's a wave of violence sweeping the country. You with me?'

'Go ahead.'

'So now the Germans have this big election. But what

happens a few weeks before election day? A massive stock market crash. A complete and utter catastrophe. The German economy – well, you can see it; you've heard it – is in ruins. A wasteland. It's in a depression that's in some ways worse than the Great Depression in the U.S. in the thirties.

'So the Germans panic. The incumbent is thrown out, of course, and the new face is elected. A man of the people. A man of honor – a former schoolteacher, a family man – who's going to turn it all around. Save Germany. Make it great again.'

'Yes,' I said. 'The way Hitler came to power in 1933 in the midst of the Weimar disaster. Are you suggesting Vogel is secretly a Nazi?'

For the first time, Kent laughed, more a snort than a laugh. 'Nazis – or, really, neo-Nazis, to be precise about it – are repellent. But they're extremists. They don't represent anywhere close to a majority of the German electorate. I think the Germans get a bum rap for that. Yes, Hitler *did* happen. But that was years ago, and people change. The Germans want to be great again. They want to reclaim their status as a world power.'

'And Vogel – ?'

'Vogel is not who he says he is.'

'What does that mean?'

'This was what I was trying to dig up when I couriered those documents to Ed Moore. I knew he was a good man, someone I could trust. Outside the Agency. Outside whatever's going on. As well as a specialist in the politics of Europe.'

'What did you dig up?'

'I was transferred here a few months after the Berlin Wall came down. I was assigned to debrief KGB agents, Stasi, all those guys. There were rumors – only rumors, mind you – about Vladimir Orlov having moved huge amounts of money out of the country. Most of these low-level guys didn't know diddly-shit. But when I tried to call up information on Orlov, I found that his whereabouts were marked 'unknown' in all the data banks.'

'His location was protected by CIA,' I said.

360

'Right. Odd, but okay. It happens. But then I debriefed one KGB guy, a fairly highly placed officer in the First Chief Directorate who – I think the guy was desperate for money, frankly – began gassing on about some file he'd seen on corruption in the CIA. Right, sure. Is the CIA corrupt? Does the Pope shit in the woods? A group of officials, I forget the name. It's not important.

'But here's what got me thinking: This KGB guy told me about some *American* plan – some *CIA* plan, he claims – to manipulate the German stock market.'

I just nodded and felt my heart thud against my rib cage.

'In October 1992 the Frankfurt Stock Exchange agreed to create one centralized German stock exchange, the Deutsche Börse. Given the interconnectedness of Europe, the way all the European currencies are linked now through the European Monetary System, a failure in the Deutsche Börse would devastate all of Europe, the guy says. Especially in this day of program trading and portfolio insurance, computer trading gone berserk. There weren't any circuit breakers in the German market. Computers were programmed to sell automatically, triggering massive sell-offs. Plus, it was a time of great currency instability, ever since the Bundesbank, Germany's central bank, was forced to raise interest rates. So the rest of Europe had to follow suit. That hurt stock market valuations. Anyway, the details aren't all that important. Point is, this KGB guy says there's a plan under way to undermine and destroy the European economy. The guy was a financial whiz, so I listened to him. He said all the levers are already in place; all it would take is the swift and sudden infiltration of capital –'

'Where is this guy, this KGB guy?'

'Measles.' Kent smiled sadly and shrugged. That's a killing that's meant to look like a death from natural causes. 'One of his own, I assume.'

'Did you report this?'

'Of course I did. It's my job, man. But I was told to drop it. Drop all efforts to investigate this; it's disruptive to German-American relations. Don't waste any more time on it.'

Suddenly I noticed that we were standing in front of Atkins's old rustbucket Ford Fiesta. We had made a large loop, though I was concentrating so hard I hadn't noticed. Molly joined up with us.

'You boys done?' she said.

'Yep,' I said. 'For now.' To Atkins I said: 'Thanks, buddy.'

'Okay,' he said, opening the car door. He hadn't locked it; no one, no matter how needy, would take the trouble to steal such a vehicle. 'But now take some advice, Ben, please. You too, Molly. Get the hell out of the country. I wouldn't even spend the night here if I were you.'

I shook his hand. 'Would you mind giving us a lift to the city center?'

'Sorry,' he said. 'Last thing I need is to be seen with you. I agreed to meet with you because we're friends. You've helped me through some tough times. I owe you. But take the U-bahn. Do me a favor.'

He got into the driver's seat and put on the seat belt. 'Good luck,' he said. He slammed the door, rolled down the window, and added: 'And get out of here.'

'Can we meet again?' I asked.

'No.'

'Why not?'

'Stay away from me, Ben, or I'm a dead man.' He turned the key in the ignition, smiled, and added: 'Measles.'

Taking Molly's arm, we started down the path toward Tivolistrasse. Kent's engine failed to turn over the first two times he tried, but the third time took and the car roared to life.

'Ben,' Molly began, but something was bothering me, and I turned around to watch Kent back his car up.

The music, I remembered.

He'd shut the car off with the music blasting, that Donna Summer stuff. The radio, he said. But now the radio was off.

He hadn't turned it off.

'Kent!' I shouted, vaulting toward the car. 'Jump out!'

He looked up at me, surprised, smiling uncertainly, as if wondering whether I were attempting some sort of joke.

That half-smile disappeared suddenly in a flash of white

light, an absurd, hollow pop like a piñata shattering, but it was the windows of Kent's Ford Fiesta, then a tremendous, thundering explosion like a clap of thunder, a sulphurous blaze that went amber and blood-red, run through with great leaping tongues of ocher and indigo flames, then a column of ashen cumulonimbus thunderclouds out of which sprayed oddments of the car high into the air. Something struck me in the back of the head: the face of his fake Rolex watch.

Molly and I clutched at each other in mute terror for a second, and then we ran as fast as we could into the gloom of the Englische Garten.

51

At a few minutes after noon we reached Baden-Baden, the famous old spa resort nestled in woods of pine and birch in Germany's Black Forest. In our rented, gleaming smoke-silver Mercedes 500SL (outfitted with burgundy leather upholstery, it was just the sort of car an ambitous young diplomat with the Canadian embassy would drive), we had made very good time. It had taken just under four hours of frantic yet careful driving on the autobahn A8 west-northwest of Munich. I was dressed in a conservative yet stylish suit that I had picked up off the rack at Loden-Frey on Maffeistrasse, on my way out of the city.

We had spent an agonized, sleepless night at our hotel on Promenadeplatz. The terrible explosion in the Englishe Garten, the horrific death of my friend: the images and the terror had lodged themselves in our minds. We comforted one another and talked for hours, each trying to allay the other's fears, trying to make sense of what had happened.

We knew it was now imperative to find Gerhard Stoessel, the German industrialist and real estate baron who had received the wire transfer from Zurich. He was at the center of the conspiracy, I felt sure. Somehow I would have to place myself in proximity to Stoessel and receive the conspirator's thoughts. And I would have to reach Alex Truslow, in Bonn or wherever he was, and warn him. Either he should leave the country, or he'd have to take appropriate security measures.

Early in the morning, having given up the battle to get some badly needed sleep, I called a financial reporter for *Der Spiegel*, whom I had known slightly in Leipzig.

'Elisabeth,' I said, 'I need to track down Gerhard Stoessel.'

'The great Gerhard Stoessel himself? I'm sure he's in Munich. That's where the headquarters of Neue Welt are.'

But he wasn't in Munich, as I had learned after some preliminary calling. 'What about Bonn?' I asked.

'I won't ask why you want to reach Stoessel,' she said, sensing the urgency in my voice. 'But you should know that he is not easy to get to. Let me make some calls.'

She called back twenty minutes later. 'He's in Baden-Baden.'

'I won't ask your source, but I assume it's reliable.'

'Very much so.' Before I could ask, she added: 'And he invariably stays at Brenner's Park Hotel and Spa.'

In the nineteenth century Baden-Baden had swarmed with European nobility; it was there that, having lost everything at the Spielbank casino, Dostoyevski in despair wrote *The Gambler*. Now Germans and other Europeans went there to ski, play golf or tennis, watch the horse races at Iffezheim Track, and partake of the mineral-rich baths fed by artesian wells deep beneath the Florentiner Mountain.

The day had started out overcast and quite cold, and by the time we approached Brenner's Park Hotel and Spa, surrounded by a private park by the Oosbach River, a chill drizzle had begun to fall. Baden-Baden seemed a town accustomed to grandeur and festivity; the tree-lined Lichtentaler Allee, with its vibrant adornments of rhododendrons, azaleas, and roses, was its centerpiece, its great promenade. But now it looked forlorn and deserted, resentful and furtive.

Molly waited for me in the Mercedes while I entered the hotel's spacious and quiet lobby. I had traveled such a distance in these last few months, I reflected. So much had happened to me, to both of us, since that rainswept March day in upstate New York when we laid Harrison Sinclair's coffin in the ground, and here we were, in a deserted German spa in the Schwarzwald, and once again it was raining.

The uniformed desk clerk who appeared to be in charge of the registration desk was a tall young man in his mid-twenties, towheaded and officious. 'May I help you, sir?'

'*Ich habe eine dringende Nachricht für Herrn Stoessel,*' I said as importantly as possible, holding in one hand a business-size envelope. I have an urgent message for Mr Stoessel.

I introduced myself as Christian Bartlett, a second attaché with the Canadian consulate on Tal Strasse in Munich. 'Will you please give him this letter?' I said in my heavily accented but still serviceable German.

'Yes, of course, sir,' the clerk said, reaching for the envelope. 'But he is not here. He is gone for the afternoon.'

'Where is he?' I slipped the envelope in my breast pocket.

'The baths, I believe.'

'Which one?'

He shrugged. 'I don't know. I'm sorry.'

There are really only two leading spas in Baden-Baden, both on Romerplatz: the Old Baths, also called the Friedrichsbad, and the Caracalla-Therme. At the first one I came to, Caracalla-Therme, I went through my routine, and was met by blank stares. There was no Herr Stoessel here, I was told. One of the older attendants, however, had overheard the conversation and said, 'Mr. Stoessel doesn't come here. Try the Friedrichsbad.'

At the Friedrichsbad, the attendant – bulky, sallow-faced, and middle-aged – nodded. Yes, he said. Mr. Stoessel was here.

'*Ich bin Christian Bartlett,*' I told him, '*von der Kanadischen Botschaft. Es ist äusserst wichtig und dringend, dass ich Herrn Stoessel erreiche.*' It is urgent that I reach Stoessel.

The attendant shook his head slowly, with mulelike truculence. '*Er nimmt gerade ein Dampfbad.*' He is taking the steam. '*Man darf ihn auf gar keinen Fall stören.*' He has instructed us not to disturb him.

The attendant was, however, awed and impressed by my imperiousness, and perhaps by my foreignness, and agreed to escort me into the private thermal steam bath where the great Herr Stoessel was. If it really was a matter of urgency, he would see what he could do. We passed white-uniformed stewards carting silver trays of mineral water and other cold drinks, and others carrying stacks of thick white cotton towels, and finally reached a corridor that seemed to be off limits to the other employees.

Outside the steam room sat a wide, potato-faced man in a gray security officer's uniform, sweating profusely and visibly uncomfortable. He was obviously a bodyguard.

He looked up as we approached and snarled: '*Sie dürfen nicht dort hineingehen!*' You can't go in there!

I looked at him, surprised, and smiled. In one lightning-fast motion I pulled my gun from my front pocket and slammed the butt against the side of the bodyguard's head. He groaned and slumped to the ground. Whirling the gun back the other way, I caught the attendant on the back of his head, with the same result.

Moving quickly, I dragged both bodies into a nearby service alcove and out of sight, then closed the doors to close the area off. The attendant's white uniform slipped off easily. It hung on me, but it would have to do.

I grabbed an empty tray from the stainless steel counter and several bottles of mineral water from a small refrigerator, and ambled casually to the steam room door. I gave it a hard tug and it came open with a loud hiss.

The steam swirled about me, thick and opaque like absorbent cotton, an undulating scrim. The room was unbearably hot, stifling, the steam sulfurous and acrid. I could taste it. The vaulted walls were tiled in white ceramic.

'*Wer ist da? Was ist los?*' Who's there? What's going on?

Through the gauzy mist I could just make out a pair of corpulent, reddened, nude bodies. They rested on a long stone bench, on white towels like carcasses in a slaughterhouse.

The voice came from the body nearest me, hairy-chested and round. As I advanced through the dense clouds, holding the tray aloft, I could make out his prominent ears, his balding dome, his large nose. Gerhard Stoessel. I had studied his photograph in *Der Spiegel* that morning; there was no question it was him. I couldn't quite see who his companion was, except that it was another middle-aged man, hairless, with short legs.

'*Erfrischungen?*' Stossel barked out. Refreshments? '*Nein!*'

Wordlessly, I backed out of the chamber, closing the door behind me.

The bodyguard and the attendant were still unconscious. Swiftly and deliberately, I paced the corridors outside the steam bath until I found what I wanted: a windowless door located at what would have been the rear of the chamber. It was the maintenance crawl space that I knew had to be there, in which the spa's workers could do repair work on the steam pipes. It was not locked; there was no reason for it to be. I opened it and quickly, nervously, ducked into the low-ceilinged space. It was completely dark. The walls were slimy with moisture and mineral deposits. Momentarily losing my balance, I reached up to steady myself and accidentally grasped a scalding-hot pipe. Only with great effort was I able to restrain myself from bellowing in pain.

As I crept along on my knees, I spotted a pinhole of light and moved toward it. The caulk fitting around a steam vent, where it entered the bath area, had come loose in one place, letting in a dot of light – and muffled sound.

After a minute or so my ears became sufficiently accustomed to the poor sound quality, and I could recognize phrases, then whole sentences. The conversation between the two men was of course in German, but I was able to understand much of what I heard. Crouched in the darkness, my hands braced against the slimy concrete walls, I listened with horrified fascination, overcome with fear.

52

At first there were just isolated phrases: *Bundesnachrichten-dienst*, the German Federal Intelligence Service. The Swiss Intelligence Service. The *Direction de la Surveillance du Territoire*, the French counterespionage organization, the DST. Something was said about Stuttgart, and an airport.

Then the conversation grew more fluid, more expansive. A scornful voice – Stoessel's? the other man's?: 'And for all their assets, their sources, their *data bases*, they have not a clue as to who this secret witness is?'

I could not hear a reply.

And a wafted phrase: 'To ensure victory . . .'

And: 'The confederacy.'

And: 'If a united Europe is to be ours.' Then: 'Such an opportunity comes along once or twice in a century.'

'Full coordination with the Wise Men . . .'

The other man, who I now decided was Stoessel: ' – at history. It is sixty-one years since Adolf Hitler became chancellor and the Weimar Republic was no longer. One forgets that at the beginning no one thought he would last the year!'

The other replied angrily, 'Hitler was a madman! We are sane.'

'We are not burdened with ideology,' came Stoessel's voice, 'which is always the downfall . . .'

Something I could not hear, and then Stoessel replied: 'So we must be patient, Wilhelm. In a few weeks you will be the leader of Germany, and we will rule. But to consolidate our power will take time. Our American partners assure us of their restraint.'

You will be leader of Germany . . . The other man was, had to be, Wilhelm Vogel, the chancellor-elect!

My stomach turned over.

Vogel, I was sure it was Wilhelm Vogel, made a noise, some sort of muffled objection, to which Stoessel responded, loudly and quite clearly: '. . . that they will watch and do nothing. Since Maastricht, the conquest of Europe has been made enormously easier. The governments will fall one by one. The politicians are not leaders anyway. They will look to the corporate leaders, because industry and commerce are the only forces capable of governing a unified Europe. They have no vision! We are visionaries! We can see much farther, beyond tomorrow and the day after. Beyond the immediate concerns of the day.'

Another demurral from the chancellor-elect. Stoessel said: 'A global conquest that is quite simple, because it is based on the profit motive, pure and simple.'

'The defense minister,' Vogel said.

'Will be easily done,' Stoessel replied. 'He wants the same thing. Once the German army is restored to its proper glory . . .'

Another muffled remark, and then Stoessel went on. 'Easily! Easily! Russia is no longer a threat! Russia is nothing. France . . . you are old enough to remember the Second World War, Willi. The French will curse and complain, bluster about a Maginot line, but they will capitulate without a struggle.'

Vogel seemed to object again, for Stoessel replied querulously, 'Because it is in their best economic interests, why else? The rest of Europe will roll over, and Russia will have no choice but to roll over as well.'

Vogel said something about Washington and a 'secret witness.'

'He will be found,' Stoessel said. 'The leak will be found and plugged. He assures us it will be contained.'

Vogel said something about 'before then,' and Stoessel said, 'Yes, precisely. In three days it will happen . . . Yes. No, the man will be assassinated. It will not fail. It is orchestrated. He will die. It is not to worry.'

There was a noise, a thump, which I realized was the door to the steam bath being opened.

Then, very distinctly, Stoessel said: 'Ah, you are here.'

'Welcome,' Vogel said. 'I trust your flight into Stuttgart was uneventful.'

Another thump; the door was closed.

'. . . wanted to tell you,' Stoessel's voice came again, 'how grateful we are. All of us.'

'Thank you,' said Vogel.

'Our heartfelt congratulations to you,' Stoessel said.

The newcomer spoke to them in fluent German, but with a foreign accent, probably American. The voice was a resonant baritone, and somehow familiar. The voice of someone I'd heard on television? On the radio?

'The witness is scheduled to appear before the Senate committee on intelligence,' the newcomer said.

'Who is it?' Stoessel demanded.

'We do not yet have a name. Be patient. We have obtained access to the committee's computer banks. This is how we can be sure that this secret witness will be testifying on the subject of the Wise Men.'

'And on us?' Vogel said. 'Does he know about Germany?'

'Impossible to know,' the American said. 'Whether he – or she – does, or doesn't, our link to you is a simple one to make.'

'Then he must be eliminated,' Stoessel said.

'But without knowing the witness's identity,' the American said, 'it is impossible to know who to eliminate. Only when the individual appears –'

'Only at that moment – ?' Vogel interrupted.

'At that moment,' the American said, 'it will be done. This I can assure you.'

'But they will take measures to protect the witness,' Stoessel said.

'There are no protective measures adequate,' the American went on. 'Do not be concerned. I am not. But the pressing concern now is one of coordination. If the hemispheres are apportioned – if we have the Americas, and you have Europe –'

'Yes,' Stoessel interrupted impatiently, 'you are speaking of the coordination between the two world governing centers, but that is easily accomplished.'

It was time to move.

As quietly as possible I turned around, awkward in this cramped space, and crept back to the door. I listened for any footsteps, and when I was sure no one was passing by, I quickly opened it and returned to the hallway, which now seemed grotesquely bright. There were dark mud stains on the knees of my white cotton pants.

I ran around to the entrance to the steam room, found the tray of bottled water, and yanked open the door. A large cloud of opaque steam swirled before me as I stepped into the chamber. Stoessel seemed to have shifted somewhat; he had moved to the right. The man I now identified as Vogel had not moved from the spot on the bench he was in earlier. The last arrival sat farther down the bench from Vogel, to the chancellor-elect's right, out of my range of sight.

'Hey,' the American said, still in German. 'No one comes in here, you understand me?' The voice was increasingly, maddeningly familiar.

Stoessel excoriated me in German: 'Enough with the refreshments! Leave us alone! I gave instructions to be left alone!'

I stood there, not moving, letting my eyes adjust to the opaque steam. The American seemed to be a middle-aged man, I couldn't tell for sure, and he was in better physical condition than the two Germans. Then a gust of air from somewhere nearby wafted the sulfurous clouds, an eddy parting a clear patch in the steam. The face of the American, swirling before me, was instantly recognizable, and for a moment I could not move.

The new Director of CIA. My friend, Alex Truslow.

Part Six

LAC TREMBLANT

Los Angeles Times

Germany to Rearm, Acquire Nuclear Weapons

Move Supported by Washington, Western Leaders

BY CAROLYN HOWE

TIMES STAFF WRITER

Relieved that Germany has resolutely turned away from neo-Nazism, the United States and a majority of governments around the world have lent their support to new Germany Chancellor Wilhelm Vogel's bid to 'restore Germany's national pride'. . . .

53

'*Wer ist denn das?*' Vogel called out. Who is this? '*Wo ist der Leibwächter?*' Where is the bodyguard?

Truslow's silver hair, I now saw, was still neatly combed; his face was red from the scalding heat, or from anger, but probably from both.

I came nearer to him.

And to me, in a voice soft and caring and gentle, he said: 'Please, Ben, stop right there. For your own sake. Don't worry. I've just told them you are a friend, that you must not be harmed. Nothing will be done to you. You will not be hurt.'

He must be killed, I heard. *He must be killed at once.*

'We've been looking all over for you,' Truslow continued sweetly.

Ellison must be eliminated, he thought.

'I must say,' he went on soothingly, 'this is the last place in the world I expected to find you. But you're safe now, and –'

I hurled the tray at Truslow, scattering glass mineral water bottles everywhere. One hit Vogel in the stomach; the others shattered loudly on the tiled floor.

Truslow commanded in German: '*Halten Sie diesen Mann auf. Er darf hier nicht lebend herauskommen!*'

'Stop this man!' he had shouted. 'He must not be allowed to leave here alive!'

I leapt through the door and ran with all my might, with as much speed as I could muster, toward the nearest exit, into the Romerplatz, Truslow's words echoing in my head. And I knew that for the last time, Alexander Truslow had lied to me.

Molly had the Mercedes idling for me at the Friedrichsbad's

side entrance. She threw the car into gear, sped to the city's outskirts, and found the autobahn A8. Echterdingen International Airport was only sixty miles or so east, a few miles south of Stuttgart.

For a long time, I didn't speak.

Finally, I told her what I had seen. She reacted just as I had, with shock, horror, and then white-hot anger.

We both knew now why it was that Truslow had recruited me, why it was that Rossi had deceived me into becoming an Oracle Project subject, why they were so elated to discover that the experiment had worked on me.

A great deal now made sense.

Aloud, as we barreled down the autobahn in Molly's skilled hands, I pieced it together. 'Your father didn't commit any crime,' I told her. 'He wanted to do whatever he could to save Russia. So he agreed to help Vladimir Orlov empty out the Soviet treasury of its gold reserves, help move it abroad, hide it. He had it moved to Zurich, where some of it was put into storage in a vault, and some of it was converted into liquid assets.'

'But where did it go from there?'

'It fell under the control of the Wise Men.'

'Alex Truslow, you mean.'

'Right. By asking me to help track down this missing fortune – which he told me had been diverted by your father – he was actually using me, using my talent, to locate the half of the gold *he couldn't get access to*. Because your father had locked it away in the Bank of Zurich.'

'But who's the co-owner of the account?'

'I don't know,' I admitted. 'Truslow must have suspected that Orlov had stolen the gold. That's why he employed me to find Orlov, which the CIA hadn't been able to do.'

'And once you found him – ?'

'Once I found him, I could read his thoughts, presumably. And learn where he had put the gold.'

'But Dad was co-owner of the account. So no matter what, Truslow would need my signature!'

'For some reason, Truslow must have wanted us to get to

376

Zurich. What was it that the banker said – by accessing the account, its status was altered from dormant to active?'

'Meaning what?'

'I don't know.'

Molly hesitated, let an eighteen-wheeler pass us. 'And what if the Oracle Project hadn't been successful on you?'

'Then he might not have found the gold. Or he might have. But in any case, it would have taken much, much longer.'

'So you're telling me that Truslow used the five billion he *did* have access to as – as a fulcrum, to cause the German stock market crash?'

'It fits, Molly. I can't be certain, but it fits. If Orlov's information is right, and the Wise Men – read Truslow, and probably Toby, and probably others –'

'Who now run CIA –'

'– Yes. If the Wise Men really used Agency intelligence to gather inside information on foreign markets, and were able somehow to engineer the U.S. stock market crisis of 1987, it must have been these same people who pulled off the far bigger German one.'

'But *how*?'

'You channel a paltry few billion dollars – deutsche marks – secretly and suddenly into the German stock market. Used swiftly and suddenly, by experts with access to computer trading accounts, it can be used to acquire vast sums of money on credit in order to destabilize an already weak market. To seize control of much larger assets. To buy and sell on margin, buy and sell, using computerized program trading, at a speed possible only in this age of computers.'

'But for *what*?'

'For what?' I echoed. 'Look at what's happened. Vogel and Stoessel are about to control Germany. Truslow and the Wise Men now control CIA . . .'

'And?'

'And – I don't know.'

'But who's going to be killed?'

I didn't have the answer to that exactly, but I knew that there was a leak – someone who knew about this conspiracy between

377

Truslow's people and Stoessel's, between Germany and America. And this person, whoever it was, was about to testify before the Senate Select Subcommittee on Intelligence hearings on corruption in CIA. 'Corruption,' that is, masterminded by the new Director of Central Intelligence, Alexander Truslow.

A secret witness was about to blow the whole thing in two days. If he (or she) was not killed first.

At Echterdingen Airport I tracked down a private airline and a pilot who was about to go home for the evening. I offered him double what he normally got for flying to Paris, and he turned around, donned his flight jacket, and guided us to his small plane. He radioed ahead for clearance to land, received it, and then we took off.

At something after two in the morning we arrived at Charles de Gaulle, went through the briefest of customs formalities, and got a cab into Paris. We got off at the Duc de Saint-Simon, on the rue Saint-Simon in the seventh arrondissement, woke the night clerk who dozed at the concierge desk, and wheedled a spare room. She was not happy about being disturbed. Molly halfheartedly insisted upon accompanying me on my nocturnal mission, but she was feeling queasy from the pregnancy and was easily dissuaded.

Paris, to me, wasn't just one of the world's great cities; it was, or at least it had become, a stage set for my recurrent nightmares. Paris wasn't the Île and the Left Bank and the rue Royale. It was the rue Jacob, that dark, narrow, echoing street where Laura and my future child were murdered and James Tobias Thompson III was paralyzed for life in a sequence that repeated and repeated itself, became more and more ritualized and grotesque and artificial. Paris had become a synonym for tragedy.

Yet I had no choice but to return.

Now I found myself in a depressing second-floor-walk-up photographer's studio on a seedy strip along the rue de Sèze. Below were forbidding little black-painted storefronts marked with signs that read SEX SHOP and VIDEO and SEXODROME and LINGERIE LATEX CUIR and the flashing green crosses of the Grande Pharmacie de la Place.

What appeared to have been once a tiny one-bedroom flat had been converted haphazardly over the years into a dismal little combination pornographic photographer's studio and porno-video rental outfit. I sat on a grimy molded plastic chair, waiting for Jean to finish his work. Jean – I never knew his last name and didn't care to know it – did a healthy sideline business producing excellent false documents, passports, and licenses, largely for free-lance operatives and small-time crooks. I had had occasion to do business with him a few times before, during my Paris assignment, and found him to be reliable and a good craftsman.

Could I trust him? Well, nothing in this life is certain, I suppose. But Jean had all the motivation in the world to be trustworthy. His livelihood depended upon his reputation for discretion, which a single act of betrayal would tarnish forever.

I had spent forty-five minutes glancing dully through a dog-eared movie magazine, having grown bored with inspecting the empty video boxes on display on his counter. There were more fetishes and variations in the porno biz than I had ever imagined ('Spanking' and 'Hard' and 'Trisex' and some deviations I'd never heard of), and all of them were available on video now.

It was after midnight. The photographer had locked the front door and drawn the shade to guard against what little street traffic might come by at that time of night. From the inner room I heard the whir of a hot-air photographic dryer.

At last Jean appeared from the darkroom. He was a small, wizened man in premature middle age, bald and worried-looking, wearing small round wire-rim glasses. He smelled strongly of potassium permanganate solution, which he'd used to artificially age the documents.

'*Voilà,*' he said, placing the papers on the counter with a flourish. He smiled with some pride. The job had not been terribly difficult: he had been able to work with the entire set of CIA-prepared documents that Molly and I had been given, in effect recycling them, reusing our photographs, and altering numbers where necessary. He had provided one set of Canadian passports and two sets of American ones for us. Molly and I were now fully documented as either American or Canadian citizens.

I inspected all four sets carefully. He did meticulous work. He also charged outrageously. But I was in no position to negotiate.

I nodded, paid him his small ransom, and walked down to the street. There was the whine of mopeds, the acrid stench of diesel fumes. Even at this time of night people roamed the streets of Pigalle, searching for quick gratification. A scraggly gang walked by, who looked to be of college age, dressed in the latest French take on the sixties – leather jackets in black or brown or American-type varsity letter jackets (the effect marred by odd emblazoned slogans like 'American Football,' which only made them seem all the more counterfeit); long hair, rolled-up jeans, and orthopedic-looking oxford shoes of the sort you might see nuns wearing. Someone roared by on an enormous motorcycle, a Honda Africa Twin 750.

In the next few minutes I placed several phone calls to old contacts from my CIA days. None of them was connected in any official way to governmental intelligence services; each worked mainly on the wrong side of the law (a difficult distinction in the espionage trade): from a souvlaki shop owner who laundered money for others (at a fee, naturally) to an armorer who custom-altered weapons for assassins and hit men. I succeeded in waking each one of them up with the exception of one night owl who seemed to be out at some dance club with a bimbo and a cellular phone. Finally, through an old friend who had been useful as an expediter years before, I located what my French operative friends sometimes call an *ingénieur*, an 'engineer,' or a fellow skilled at clever circumventions of the international telephone systems. Within the hour I was at the *ingénieur*'s apartment, in a decrepit 1960s-vintage high-rise in the twentieth arrondissement, off the Avenue de la République. He eyed me through the peephole for a few seconds, and then opened the door. His apartment, scantily furnished with cheap furniture, smelled of stale beer and sweat. He was small and pudgy, wearing a pair of dirty, paint-spattered jeans and a stained white Hard Rock Cafe T-shirt under which bulged an enormous pot belly. Obviously he had been sleeping, like most of the rest of Paris; his hair was disheveled and his eyes were half shut. Without so much as a grunt of social pleasantry, he thrust his thumb toward a smudged white telephone on a coffee table topped with fake-wood-grain Formica that was chipped around the edges. Next to the coffee table was a hideous mustard-yellow sofa whose stuffing was coming out in several places. The phone was precariously balanced atop a set of Paris phone directories.

The *ingénieur* didn't know my name and naturally didn't ask. He had been told only that I was an *homme d'affaires*, but then, probably all his clients were *hommes d'affaires*. He was making a very quick five hundred francs for allowing me to use an untraceable phone.

Actually, the call I was about to place *was* traceable, but the trace would come to a grinding halt somewhere in Amsterdam. From there, though, the link was routed through a series of pass-throughs to Paris, but no electronic tracing equipment yet invented could track it that far.

The *ingénieur* took my money, grunted porcinely, and shuffled off to another room. Had I had more time, I would have preferred a more secure arrangement than this one, but it would have to do.

The receiver was smudged with greasy fingerprints, I noted disapprovingly, and it smelled like pipe smoke. I punched in the number, and a sequence of strange tones followed. Presumably, the signal was gavotting somewhere around Europe, under the Atlantic Ocean, and perhaps even back to Europe, before it made its by-now-feeble way to Washington, D.C., where the Agency fiber-optic telecommunications system would enrich the signal and put it through its own electronic paces.

I listened for the familiar clicks and hums, waited for the third ring.

On the third ring the female voice announced, 'Thirty-two hundred.' How could the same woman always answer the phone, no matter the time of day or night? Maybe it wasn't even a human voice at all, but a high-quality synthesized one.

I responded: 'Extension nine eighty-seven, please.'

Another click and then I heard Toby's voice.

'Ben? Thank God. I heard about Zurich. Are you –'

'I know, Toby.'

'You know –'

'About Truslow and the Wise Men. And the Germans, Vogel and Stoessel. And the surprise witness.'

'Jesus Christ, Ben, what the hell are you talking about? Where are you?'

'Give it up, Toby,' I bluffed. 'It's all about to come out anyway. I've pieced enough of it together. Truslow tried to have me killed, which was a serious mistake.'

There was a quiet whoosh of static faintly in the background.

'Ben,' he said at last. 'You're mistaken.'

I checked my watch and saw that the connection was ten seconds old by now, long enough to trace the call . . . to Amsterdam. They would pinpoint my location as Amsterdam, which would be useful misdirection.

'Naturally,' I replied sardonically.

'No, please, Ben. There are things going on that can't be understood . . . without a full perspective. These are dangerous times. We need the help of people like you, and now with your ability, it's all the more –'

And I slowly hung up the receiver.

Yes. Toby was involved.

I returned to our hotel and got quietly into bed next to Molly, who was sleeping soundly.

Troubled and sleepless, I got out of bed, fetched the copy of Allen Dulles's memoirs that Molly's father had left to me, and began to leaf through it aimlessly. It isn't even that great a book, but it was all I had in the hotel room, and I needed to run my eyes over something, needed to distract my whirling thoughts. I skimmed a passage about the Jedburghs, who were parachuted into France; and about Sir Francis Walsingham, who was Queen Elizabeth's spymaster in the sixteenth century.

I looked again over the codes that Hal Sinclair had left for us, for me, to find, and I thought about his cryptic note in the vault in Zurich that told of a safe deposit box in a bank on the Boulevard Raspail.

And I thought, for the millionth time, about Molly's father and the secrets he had bequeathed us, the secrets within secrets. I wondered . . .

It was a hunch more than anything else, certainly nothing well grounded, that inspired me to get out of bed a second time and retrieve a razor blade from my shaving kit.

Publishers in America used to print books of a higher quality in the old days, and by the old days I mean as recently as 1963. Underneath the gray, red, and yellow jacket of *The Craft of Intelligence*, the heavy pasteboard case was covered with a fine-wove cloth and embossed with the publisher's insignia. The binding was sewn, not glued, of black and white cloth. I examined the jacketless book, turning it over and over and inspecting it from all angles.

Could it be? How clever was the old spymaster anyway?

Carefully, I sliced open the binding with the razor blade. I lifted back the black cloth of the binding, peeled away the brown kraft paper liner, and there it was, glinting at me like a beacon, a signal from Harrison Sinclair's grave.

It was a small, oddly shaped brass key stamped with the number 322: the key to what I assumed was the explanation, the answer to the mystery, somewhere in a vault on the Boulevard Raspail in Paris.

54

We strode quickly along the rue de Grenelle the next morning
toward the Boulevard Raspail and the Banque de Raspail.

'An assassination is scheduled to occur in *two days*, Ben,'
Molly said. 'Two days! We don't know who the victim will be;
all we know is that unless the surprise witness testifies, we're all
as good as dead.'

Two days: I knew it; I thought of the ticking clock virtually
all the time. But I didn't reply.

A neatly dressed older man in a blue overcoat walked toward
us, his short white hair slicked back, brown almond eyes
behind rectangular glasses. He smiled politely. I glanced in
the window of a storefront marked IMPRIMERIE, which
featured a display of *cartes de visite* pinned on a corkboard,
samples of their handiwork. In the glass I caught the reflection
of a woman, admired her figure, and then realized it was
Molly; and then saw the reflection of a small red and white
Austin Mini Cooper moving along slowly behind us.

I froze.

I had seen that same car from our hotel window last night.
How many other little red Austins were there with white tops?

'Shit,' I exclaimed, slapping my hand against my forehead
in a large, theatrical motion.

'What?'

'I forgot something.' I pointed in back of me without
turning. 'We've got to go back to the hotel. Do you mind?'

'What'd you forget?'

I took her arm. 'Come on.'

Shaking my head, I pulled her around and walked back up
the street toward the hotel. The Austin, which I now saw in a

quick, furtive glance was being driven by a young bespectacled man in a dark suit, sped up and disappeared down the street.

'You forget the documents or something?' Molly asked as I turned the key in the room door. I put a finger to my lips.

She gave me a worried glance.

I closed and locked the door, immediately tossing my leather portfolio on the bed. I emptied it of the sets of documents, then held it up to the light, unzipping each compartment, running my fingers along each fold, scrutinizing it closely.

Molly mouthed one word: *What?*

I said aloud, 'We're being followed.'

She looked at me questioningly.

'It's okay, Molly. You can talk now.'

'Of *course* we're being followed,' she said, exasperated. 'We've been followed since –'

'Since *when?*'

She stopped, frowned. 'I don't know.'

'Think. Since when?'

'Jesus, Ben, you're –'

'– the expert. I know. All right. There was someone waiting for me when I arrived in Rome. I was tailed pretty much constantly in Rome. Lost them in Tuscany, I assume.'

'In Zurich –'

'Right. We were followed in Zurich, to the bank and afterward. Probably in Munich, though it's hard to tell. But I sure as hell wasn't followed last night.'

'How do you know?'

'Well, the truth is, I don't know for absolute certain. But I was pretty damned careful, and I walked around a bit after I met with the documents guy, and if there was any indication, *I* sure as hell didn't see it. And I'm trained to look for this sort of thing. That skill doesn't go away no matter *how* much patent law you practice.'

'So what are you saying?'

'That *you* were followed.'

'And that's supposed to be *my* fault? We left the airport

together, you had the taxi take a pretty circuitous route – you said you were sure we weren't being followed. And I didn't leave the hotel.'

'Let me see your purse.'

She handed it to me, and I dumped the contents onto the bed. She watched in dismay. I went through everything carefully, then inspected the purse and its lining. I examined, too, the heels of our shoes; unlikely, though, since they hadn't been out of our sight. No.

Nothing.

'I guess I'm like your black cat,' she said.

'More like the bell on a sheep,' I said distractedly. 'Ah.'

'What?'

I reached over and carefully lifted her locket and chain off her neck, pulling it up and over her head. I popped the round gold case open, and saw inside only the ivory cameo.

'For God's sake, Ben, what are you looking for? A bug or something?'

'I figured it was worth a look, right?' I handed it back to her, and then a thought occurred to me, and I took it back.

I popped the locket open again, then looked very closely at the inside of the lid. 'What's inscribed on the inside of this?' I asked.

She closed her eyes, trying to recall. 'Nothing. The inscription's on the back.'

'Right,' I said. 'Which made it pretty easy.'

'Easy for what?'

I had a small jeweler's tool attached to my key chain, which was on the bed, and I grabbed it and inserted the tiny beveled screwdriver into the lid. A gold disc, roughly the size of a quarter and about an eighth of an inch thick, popped out. Attached to it was a tiny coil of wire almost as thin as a human hair.

'Not a bug,' I said. 'A transmitter. A miniaturized homing device with a range of up to six or seven miles. Emits an RF signal.'

Molly gaped at me.

'When Truslow's people captured you in Boston, you were wearing this, weren't you?'

She took a long while to respond. 'Yes . . .'

'And then, when they sent you to Italy, they returned this to you with the rest of your things.'

'Yes . . .'

'Well, then. Of course. Of course they wanted you with me. For all our precautions, they've known our location every second. At least, every second you've had the locket with you.'

'Right now too?'

I answered slowly, wishing not to alarm her any more than necessary. 'Yeah,' I said. 'I'd say it's a pretty fair guess they know where we are right now.'

55

The small, elegant, jewellike Banque de Raspail at 128 Boulevard Raspail in Paris's seventh arrondissement was a small, private merchant bank that seemed to cater to an exclusive clientele of wealthy, discreet Parisians who desired excellent personal service they apparently believed they could not find in banks open to the unwashed masses.

Its interior was an advertisement for its exclusivity: there wasn't a customer in sight. And in fact it barely resembled a bank at all. Faded Aubusson carpets covered the floor; clustered here and there along the walls were Biedermeier chairs upholstered in Scalamandre silk, fragile-looking Italian busts and urn lamps perched atop Biedermeier side tables. Architectural engravings in gilt frames hung in precise quadrants on the walls, completing the effect of stately elegance and great solidity. I, of course, would not have placed my money in a bank that spent so much on overhead, but I'm not French.

Both Molly and I knew we were operating under enormous time pressure. Two days remained before the assassination, and we still didn't know who the target was.

And now they – *they* being Truslow's agents, perhaps in addition to agents working for Vogel and the German consortium behind him – had pinpointed our location. They knew we were in Paris. They might not know *why*; they might not know about Sinclair's cryptic note concerning the Banque de Raspail; but they knew we were here for some reason.

And though I hadn't permitted myself to talk about this to Molly, I knew the odds were great that we would be killed.

True, I was worth a great deal to American intelligence

because of my psychic ability, but now I represented, more than anything, a threat. I knew about what Truslow's people were doing in Germany, or at least I knew a piece of it. I had no documentary proof, no evidence, nothing solid; so even if I went public now – if I called, say, *The New York Times* – I simply wouldn't be believed. I would be dismissed as a raving lunatic. Molly and I had to be eliminated. That was the only logical course for Truslow's people.

But if only we could make it – forge on ahead to determine who was to be assassinated two days from now in Washington, foil the assassination, make it public, let the sunlight in – we would be safe. Or so I believed.

The clock was ticking.

But who could it be? Who could the surprise witness be? Might it be an assistant of Orlov's, a Russian, someone he had entrusted with the truth? Or perhaps it might be a friend of Hal Sinclair's, someone in whom *he* had confided.

I even briefly considered the most farfetched possibility of all. Toby? Who else, after all, knew so much? Was it Toby who would be appearing suddenly before the Senate two days from now, testifying against Truslow, blowing the whole conspiracy sky high?

Ridiculous. For what possible reason?

Frightened, strung out, and at our wit's end, Molly and I had quarreled at the Duc de Saint-Simon, until finally we came up with a workable plan. We had to leave the hotel as soon as possible, in a matter of moments. Yet we had to go to the Boulevard Raspail; we had to see what it was that Molly's father had left behind. We couldn't take the chance of overlooking any piece of the puzzle. Maybe we'd turn up nothing; maybe the box would be empty; maybe there would no longer be a safe deposit box in his name at the bank. But we had to know. *Follow the gold*, Orlov had urged. We had done so. And now the trail of the gold led inexorably to this small private bank in Paris.

So, realizing there were few courses of action left to us, we had quickly packed our bags and had the bellboy send them on to the Crillon, tipping him generously for his discretion.

Molly explained to him that we were doing advance work for a prominent foreign statesman, that it was vitally important that our whereabouts be kept a secret, that he disclose to no one where he had dispatched our luggage.

The cameo locket, however, was a different matter. I had little doubt that the RF transmitter contained within the locket would in a matter of minutes draw the watchers to the Saint-Simon. Destroying it was one solution, but not the best. Diversion was always better. I took the locket with me and strolled aimlessly out of the hotel toward the Boulevard Saint-Germain. Across from the Rue du Bac Métro station is a café that is almost always crowded. I entered, sidled up to the bar, and ordered a *demitasse*. Jammed up next to me was a very soigné middle-aged woman with copper-colored hair up in a chignon, clutching an enormous, capacious handbag of green leather and reading a crisp new copy of V*ogue*. Ever so casually I slipped the locket into the woman's handbag, finished my coffee, left a few francs, and returned to the hotel. Since these transmitters send the RF signal along the line of sight, our followers would be flummoxed, at least temporarily: as long as my V*ogue*-reading friend continued to circulate in crowds, they'd never be able to pinpoint the signal, never be able to determine where in the throngs it was coming from.

We had left the hotel separately and by different means of egress – I'll spare you the details, but suffice it to say that it was highly unlikely we were followed – and from a rendezvous point at the obelisk on the Place de la Concorde, we made our way back, in a taxi, across the Seine on the Pont de la Concorde, down the Boulevard Saint-Germain, until it branched off onto the Boulevard Raspail.

A few sultry, exquisitely dressed young women sat busily working at mahogany tables a good distance from the glass and mahogany doors through which Molly and I entered, and a couple of them looked up with pique, annoyed at this interruption. They radiated attitude, but with a particularly French patina. Then a young man rose from one of the tables and hastened toward us anxiously, as if we were there to rob the bank and take everyone hostage.

'*Oui?*'

He stood before us, blocking us with an awkward stance. The young banker wore a navy serge double-breasted suit of exaggerated cut, and perfectly round black-framed glasses of the sort the architect Le Corbusier used to wear (and, after him, generations of affected American architects).

I deferred to Molly, who was the one with the official business there. She was wearing one of her odd but somehow stylish outfits, some sort of a black linen shift that would be equally appropriate on the beach or at a White House dinner. As usual, no one could carry off eccentricity the way she could. She began explaining, in her very good French, her situation: that she was the legal heir to her father's estate, that as a matter of routine she sought access to his safe deposit box. I watched the two of them speak, as if from a great distance, and pondered the strangeness of the situation. *Her father's estate.* Here we were, tracking down her father's assets, which seemed to include a vast fortune that didn't belong to him.

The silent spouse, I followed the two of them around the foyer to the banker's table to conduct our business. Although this was only the second bank I had visited in the course of this drama that had overtaken Molly and me since I'd attained this freakish telepathic ability, it seemed as if I had done nothing but go into bank after bank in the last week or so. The ritual, the forms, everything was entirely, cloyingly familiar.

And as we sat there, I found myself dipping into that particular recess of my brain with which I'd also become so familiar, that strange place into which floated words and phrases. Thoughts. I had some French, as they say, which is to say that I was reasonably conversant in the language, and I waited for the banker's Gallic thoughts to voice themselves . . .

. . . And nothing came.

For a moment I was gripped by a familiar fear: had this peculiar talent, which had been visited upon me so suddenly, now vanished just as suddenly? Nothing was coming across. I thought of the afternoon walking around Boston, after leaving the Corporation, when I was overcome by the incredible profusion of the thoughts of others, the rush of phrases, the thoughts of others, giddy and angry and remorseful, those scraps that came at me without my really having to concentrate at all.

And I wondered at that moment whether it might all be fading away to nothing.

'Ben?' I suddenly heard Molly say.

'Yes?'

She looked at me curiously. 'He says we can get into the box now if we'd like. All I have to do is fill out a form.'

'Then let's do it now,' I said, knowing she was trying to divine my intentions. *If you had the power, Mol, you wouldn't have to ask*, I thought.

The banker took from a drawer a two-page form evidently designed for one purpose alone: intimidation. When she had filled out the form, he glanced it over, pursed his lips, then got up and consulted an older man, probably his superior. A few minutes later he returned, and with a nod he led us into an interior room lined with tarnished brass compartments that ranged from about four inches square to roughly three times that. He inserted his key in one of the smaller boxes.

He pulled the brass-fronted box from its slot and carried it to a nearby private conference room, where he placed it on a table, explaining to us that the French system required two keys to open a safe deposit box: one belonging to the client, and the other to the bank. With a curt smile and a perfunctory nod, he left us alone in the room.

'Well?' I said.

Molly shook her head, a little gesture that conveyed so much – apprehension, relief, wonderment, frustration – and inserted in the second lock the tiny key that her father had hidden in the binding of Allen Dulles's memoirs. Harrison Sinclair, rest in peace, never lacked a sense of irony.

The brass plate at the front of the box popped open with a tiny click. Molly reached her hand inside.

My breath caught for an instant. I watched her intently. I said, 'Empty?'

After a few seconds she shook her head.

I let out my breath.

She pulled out from the safe deposit box's dark recesses a long gray envelope measuring perhaps nine inches by four inches. Quizzically, she tore open the envelope and pulled out its contents: a typewritten note, a yellowed scrap of a business envelope, and a small black-and-white glossy photograph. A moment later I heard her sharp intake of air. 'Oh, dear God,' she said. 'Dear God.'

56

I stared at the photograph that had so taken her aback. It was the most ordinary-looking snapshot taken from a family album: three inches by four, 1950s scalloped edges, even a crusty brown spot of dried mucilage on the back. A lanky, athletic-looking, handsome man stood arm in arm with a dark-haired, dark-eyed young beauty; in front of them, grinning mischievously, was a tomboyish little girl of three or four, twinkling light eyes, her dark hair cut in perfect bangs and tied in loose braids on either side.

The three of them were standing on the worn wooden steps of a large wooden house or a lodge, from the looks of it; the sort of ramshackle, comfortable summer house you might find on Lake Michigan or Lake Superior or in the Poconos or the Adirondacks, or on the banks of any rustic lake in any part of the country.

The little girl – Molly; there was no question about it – was a blur of hyperactivity, her image just barely captured by the wink of an aperture, for one sixty-fourth of a second or whatever it was. Her parents looked both proud and comfortable: a heart-melting family tableau that was so all-American, it was almost kitsch.

'I remember that place,' Molly said.

'Hmm?'

'I mean, I don't actually remember much about it, but I remember hearing about it. It was my grandmother's place in Canada somewhere – my mother's mother. Her old house on some lake.' She fell silent, continued staring at the photo, probably culling the details: an Adirondack chair on the porch behind them, missing one slat; the large, uneven stones that made up the front of the rough-hewn house; her father's seersucker jacket and bow tie; her mother's prim floral summer dress; the India rubber ball and baseball glove lying on the steps beside them.

'How odd,' she said. 'Sort of a happy memory. Anyway, the place isn't ours anymore. Unfortunately. My parents sold it when I was still little, I think. We never went there again, except that one summer.'

I picked up the scrap of envelope, which bore an address or a portion of an address in a spidery European scrawl: 7, *rue du Cygne, 1er, 23*. Paris, clearly, but what was it? Why here, locked away in a vault?

And why the photograph? A signal, a message to Molly from her late father – from (you'll pardon the triteness) beyond the grave?

And I picked up the letter, which had been composed on some ancient manual typewriter and was rife with cross-outs and typos, and was for some reason addressed 'To My Beloved Snoops.'

I looked up at Molly, about to ask what the hell that salutation was all about, when she smiled sheepishly and explained: 'Snoops was his pet name for me.'

'*Snoops?*'

'For Snoopy. My favorite cartoon character when I was a kid.'

'Snoopy.'

'And . . . and also because I liked to open locked drawers when I was a little girl. Look into things that were deemed none of my business. Stuff that all little kids do, but if your father was CIA station chief in Cairo, or deputy director of Plans, or whatever he was, you get chided a little too much for your curiosity. Curiosity killed the cat, and all that. So he used to call me Snoopy, and then Snoops.'

'Snoops,' I said, trying it out impishly.

'Don't you dare, Ellison. You hear me? Don't you fucking *dare*.'

I turned back to the letter, so badly typed on creamy Crane's

ecru stock, under the Harrison Sinclair letterhead, and began
to read:

To my beloved Snoops:
If you're reading this – and of course you're reading this, else
these words will never be read – let me first express, for the
millionth time, my admiration. You are a wonderful doctor,
but you'd also have made a first-class spy if only you didn't
have such disdain for my chosen profession. But I don't mean
by that any hostility: in some ways you were right to take such a
dislike to the intelligence trade. There is much in it that's
objectionable. I just hope someday you come to appreciate
what's noble in it too – and not out of some sense of filial
obligation or loyalty or guilt. When your mother's cancer had
progressed to the point that it was clear she wouldn't be around
for more than a few weeks, she sat me down in her hospital
room – no one could hold court like your mother – and told
me, with a wag of her index finger, that I should never
interfere in the way you choose to live your life. She said you
would never follow the conventional patterns, but in the end,
wherever you wound up, no one would have a more level
head, a firmer grasp on reality, a better perspective, than 'dear
Martha.' So I trust you'll understand what I'm about to tell
you.

For reasons that will soon become apparent, there's no
record of this box among my papers, in my Last Will and
Testament, or any other place. In order to have found this
note, you'll have found the key I left (sometimes the simplest
and most old-fashioned ways are the best) and also have gotten
into the vault in Zurich.

Which means that you have found the gold, which I'm sure
you'll agree requires some explanation.

I've never much liked chases and hunts, so please believe
that my intention was not to make things difficult for you – but
to make things difficult for anyone *else*. Nothing in this game
is foolproof, but if you've gotten this far, you'll understand why
I've done this. Everything is for your protection.

I am writing this a few hours after a momentous meeting in

Zurich with Vladimir Orlov, whose name you may recognize as the last chairman of the KGB. I made an arrangement with him that I must explain to you, and I learned certain things from him as well, which I must tell you.

Because I am about to be killed. I'm sure of it. By the time you read this, I may or may not be dead, but I wanted you to know why.

As you know better than anyone, Snoops, money has never held an attraction for me, beyond what one needs for food and shelter. So I trust when you're told that I was corrupt, an embezzler, and whatever else they may say about me now that I'm gone, you'll know the truth. You know it's nonsense.

But what you may not know is that as I write this, I've received a number of threats against my life, some of them hollow, some quite serious. They began (no surprise) shortly after I was appointed Director of Central Intelligence, when I took it upon myself to clean house, launched my foolhardy crusade to clean up CIA. I loved the place; I *believed* in the place. Ben, I'm sure you understand that the way no outsider can.

Something terrible is happening deep within the bowels of CIA. There is a small group that over the years abused the intelligence they were privy to in order to amass huge sums of money. I set out, from my first day as director, to unmask them. I had my theories, but I needed proof.

The atmosphere around Langley at that time was like a tinderbox, ready to combust at the slightest spark from a congressional investigating committee, or an enterprising reporter from *The New York Times*. There was a lot of open talk in the hallways about getting rid of me. Some of the old boys hated me even more than they used to hate Bill Colby! I happen to know that several highly placed, extremely influential Washington power brokers went to see the President to urge that I be replaced.

You see, there were rumors floating around of corruption on a breathtaking scale. I had heard tales of a small, faceless group of past and present intelligence officials known as the Wise Men, who met in conditions of extreme secrecy. These

Wise Men were said to be involved in massive fraud. It was believed that they were using intelligence gathered by the Agency to make huge amounts of money. But no one knew who these people were. Apparently they were so influential, so well connected, they had been able to elude detection.

And then one day I was contacted directly by a European businessman – Finnish, actually – who claimed to represent, as he put it, a 'former world leader' who had 'information' that might be of interest to me.

Protracted negotiations were begun, long before I even learned that the person he represented was none other than the last head of the Soviet KGB, Vladimir Orlov, who was living in a small dacha outside Moscow and wanted to leave the former Soviet Union and go into exile.

Orlov, the intermediary let me know, had an interesting proposition for me.

He needed my help in saving Russia's gold reserves from the hard-liners who would any day, he believed, unseat the Yeltsin government. If I would help him remove a massive quantity of gold – ten billion dollars! – he would be prepared to give me a valuable file he had on certain corrupt elements in the CIA.

Orlov, the intermediary said, had in his possession a file documenting, in extraordinary detail, massive corruption within the CIA. Vast sums of money amassed over the years by a small group of CIA insiders, making phenomenal money using intelligence gathered from corporate espionage around the world. He had all names, locations, amounts, records. Full evidence.

I, of course, agreed. I would have agreed to help him anyway – you know how badly I wanted to keep Russia from returning to dictatorship – but the lure of this file made his offer irresistible.

As it turned out, Orlov appeared in Zurich without this file – it had been stolen out from under him, a fact that made me nervous indeed. Initially, I suspected a blackmail attempt, but I deduced he was genuinely a victim. And having gone this far, I had to complete the deal.

But I needed help in making such an enormous transaction – help that originated *outside* the Agency. Removed from any possible taint of corruption. It was imperative, given the huge sum of money we were dealing with. Also, all the financial arrangements had to be handled completely off the books.

So I turned to the one Agency man who was now an outsider, a man whose personal integrity was above reproach: Alexander Truslow. It was the biggest mistake I ever made.

I made Truslow the joint owner of the account at the Bank of Zurich to which I moved half the gold. That meant that neither one of us could move the gold without the other's consent. And the gold could be moved or sold only when the account was activated – a mechanism that was triggered by access by either party. If ever a problem arose, I figured, we were both protected from any blame. I could not be accused of grand larceny on a world scale.

The other half we arranged to be transshipped by container through Newfoundland, by the St. Lawrence Seaway, into Canada. Or, I should say, *Truslow* arranged this.

But now something frightens me deeply. I fear for my life. As you know, Ben, we have people at Langley who are really quite skilled at making a murder look like a natural death.

So I am not long for this world.

I have only very recently learned that Wilhelm Vogel, who is running for chancellor of Germany, is being controlled by an enormously powerful German cartel. They seek, secretly, to rearm and rebuild Germany. Their intention is to control not only Germany, but through it, a unified Europe.

Their partners are this group within the CIA. The arrangement, I am told, amounts to a peaceful division of spoils. The CIA element will, through fronts, control the CIA, and by extension the economy of the Western Hemisphere. The German cartel will get Europe. All will become enormously, even inconceivably rich. It is a new, corporate neo-Fascism – seizing control of the levers of government during this fragile and uncertain time.

The leader of the Americans is Alexander Truslow.

And I am powerless to do anything about it.

But I believe I will soon have a way to stop it. There are documents to reveal. They must come out.

If I am killed, you two must find them.

To that end, I leave each of you a gift.

I left very little in my estate to pass on to you, which hardly pleases me. But now I'd like to bequeath to each of you a small gift – both of them gifts of knowledge, which, after all, is the most valuable possession.

For you, Snoopy, it's a memento of a very happy time in your life, in mine, and in your mother's. The *real* riches, as you'll learn, are to be found in the family. This photograph, which I think you've never seen, always conjures up for me a very happy summer we three spent.

You were only four, so I'm sure you don't remember much if anything of it. But I, a confirmed workaholic in those early days as well, was compelled to take a month off after my emergency appendectomy. I think perhaps my body was telling me to spend a little more time with my family.

You loved it there – you caught frogs in the pond, learned to fish, to throw a softball. . . . You never stopped moving, and I've never seen you so happy. I've always believed that Tolstoy was dead wrong when he wrote at the beginning of *Anna Karenina* that all happy families are alike. Every family, whether happy or unhappy (and our family has been both) is as unique as a snowflake. I am allowed, my dear Snoops, to be sentimental and cornball once in my lifetime.

And for you, Ben, I give you an address of a couple who may or may not be alive by the time you read this. I fervently hope at least one of them is alive to tell you a very important tale. Bring this scrap with you; it will serve as your admission ticket, a passkey of sorts.

Because I believe what they have to tell you will relieve you of the terrible burden you've been carrying around with you for so long.

In no way, Ben, were you responsible for the death of your first wife, as this couple will confirm. How I wish I could have shared this with you when I was alive. But for various reasons, I could not.

You will soon understand. Someone – I think it was La Rochefoucauld or one of those seventeenth-century French aphorists – put it best: We can rarely bring ourselves to forgive those who have helped us.

And one last literary reference, a line from Eliot's 'Gerontion': After such knowledge, what forgiveness?

All my love,
Dad

57

Tears coursed down Molly's cheeks, and she bit her lower lip. She blinked rapidly and stared at the note, then finally looked up at me.

I didn't know where to begin, what to ask about. So I wrapped my arms around her, gave her a big, long hug, and said nothing for a long while. I felt her rib cage hiccup with quiet sobs. After a minute or two her breathing became more regular, and she pulled away from me. Her eyes shone, and for an instant they were the eyes of the four-year-old in the photograph.

'Why?' she said at last.

'Why . . . what?'

Her eyes searched my face, back and forth, back and forth, and yet she was silent, as if trying to decide for herself what she really meant. 'The photograph,' she said.

'A message. What else could it be?'

'You don't think it could be . . . a simple, straightforward gift from . . . the heart?'

'You tell me, Molly. Is that like him?'

She sniffled, shook her head. 'Dad was wonderful, but you'd never call him straightforward. I think he learned how to be cryptic from his friend James Jesus Angleton.'

'Okay. So where was your grandmother's house in Canada?'

Again she shook her head. 'God, Ben, I was *four*. We spent exactly one summer there. I have virtually no recollection of it.'

'Think,' I said.

'I *can't*! I mean, what is there to think about? I don't *know* where it was! Somewhere in French Canada, probably in Quebec. *Jesus!*'

I put my hands on either side of her face, held her head steady, stared directly into her eyes.

'What are you – cut it out, Ben!'

'*Try* it at least.'

'Try – hey, hold on there. We have an agreement. You assured me – you *promised* me – you wouldn't try to read my thoughts.'

trem . . . tremble . . . trembling? . . .

It was just a fragment, a word or a sound I suddenly heard.

'You're trembling,' I said.

She looked at me quizzically. 'No, I'm not. What are you –'

'Tremble. Trembling.'

'What are you – ?'

'*Concentrate!* Trembling. Tremble. Trem –'

'What are you talking about?'

'I don't know,' I said. 'No, I *do* know. I *do* know. I heard you – you *thought* it –'

She looked back into my eyes, by turns defiant and bewildered. Then, a moment later, she said, 'I really have no idea –'

'Try. *Think*. Trembling. Trembley? Canada. Your grandmother. Trembley or something? Was that your grandmother's name?'

She shook her head. 'She was Grandmother Hale. Ellen. Grandpa was Frederick. No one in the family was Trembley.'

I sighed in frustration. 'Okay. Trem. Canada. Trembling. Canada . . .'

. . . tromblon . . .

'There's something more,' I said. 'You're thinking – or maybe you're subvocalizing – something, some thought, some name, *something* your conscious mind isn't entirely aware of.'

'What do you – ?'

Impatient, I interrupted: 'What's "Tromblon"?'

'What? – oh, my God – Tremblant. Lac Tremblant!'

'Where – ?'

'The house was on a lake in Quebec. I remember now. Lac Tremblant. Beneath a big, beautiful mountain called Mont-

403

Tremblant. Her house was on Lac Tremblant. How did I know that?'

'You *remembered* it. Not enough to speak it, but it was there anyway, in your brain. Probably you heard the name mentioned dozens of times when you were little, and you stored it.'

'And you think that's important?'

'I think that's *crucial*. I think that's why your father left that photograph of a place no one would be able to recognize but you. A place that's probably to be found in no records anywhere. So that if anyone got into this box somehow, they'd come to a dead end. The most anyone else except you could do would be to identify you and your parents, but then they'd be stymied.'

'I was almost stymied myself.'

'I suppose he counted on you to summon it up, track it down, something. This was for you. I'm quite sure of it. Your father left that for you to find.'

'And –'

'And to go there.'

'You think that's where the . . . the documents are?'

'It wouldn't surprise me greatly.' I stood up, straightened my pants and jacket.

'What are you doing?'

'I don't want to waste another minute.'

'Where? Where are we going?'

'You're staying here,' I said. I looked around the conference room.

'You think I'm safe here?'

'I'll tell the bank manager we'll require the use of this room for the rest of the day. No one is to be admitted. If we have to pay a rental charge for the use of it, we'll pay. A locked conference room inside a bank vault – we're not going to get more secure than that, at least not on more than a moment's notice.' I turned to leave.

'Where are you going?' Molly called out.

By way of reply, I held up the scrap of envelope.

'Wait. I need a phone in here. A phone – and a fax machine.'

'For what?'

'Just get it, Ben.'

I glanced at her with surprise, nodded, and left the room.

Rue du Cygne – the street of the swan – was a small, quiet street just a few blocks from what was once the Marché des Innocents, the great central market of Paris, the place Emile Zola called *le ventre de Paris*, 'the belly of Paris.' After the old neighborhood was cleared in the late 1960s, a number of gargantuan and impressively ugly modernistic structures were put up, including Le Forum des Halles, galleries and restaurants, and the biggest subway station in the world.

Number 7 was a shabby late-nineteenth-century apartment building, squat and dark and musty inside. The door to apartment 23 was of thick, splintery paneled wood that had, long ago, been painted white and was now quite gray.

Long before I had reached the second floor, I could hear the low, menacing bark of a large dog from within the apartment. I approached and knocked.

After a long time, during which the dog's bark grew more shrill and insistent, I heard slow footsteps, the tread of an old man or woman, and then the rattle of a metal chain, which I assumed was the door being unbolted from the other side.

The door swung open.

For an instant, the barest fraction of a second, it was like being in a horror film – the footsteps, the rattle of a chain – and the face of the creature that now stood in the shadows of the opened door.

It was a woman; the clothes were those of an old woman of bent posture, and the hair atop the head was long, silver-gray, and pulled back in a loose chignon. But the old woman's face was almost unspeakably ugly, a mass of welts and growths and lumps surrounding a kindly pair of eyes and a small, deformed, twisted mouth.

I stood in shocked silence. Even if I had the wherewithal to speak, I had no name, nothing more than an address. I stepped forward and wordlessly showed her the yellowed scrap of envelope. In the background, from the depths of the dark apartment, the dog whined and strained.

Wordlessly, too, she squinted at it, then turned and was gone.

A few seconds later, a man came to the door who appeared to be around seventy. Once, you could tell, he had been strong, even stocky; his coarse gray hair had once been jet black. He was now frail, but he still walked with a pronounced limp, and the long, thin scar on one side of his face, at the jawline, once an ugly, inflamed red, had faded to a pale, etiolated white. Fifteen years had aged him dramatically.

The man whose face and figure I knew I would never forget, because I had seen it night after night after night.

The man I had last seen limping away from the rue Jacob fifteen years ago.

'So,' I said with more calmness than I would ever have believed I could summon. 'You're the man who killed my wife.'

58

I did not remember seeing his eyes, which were a watery gray-blue: vulnerable eyes that did not belong to a KGB 'wet-work' specialist, to the man who had dispatched my beautiful young wife, fired off a shot to her heart without a moment's thought.

I remember only the thin red scar at his jawline, the shock of black hair, the plaid hunter's shirt, the limp.

A would-be defector, a KGB filing clerk in the Paris station who identified himself as 'Victor,' has information to sell. Information he says he's discovered in the archives in Moscow. Something to do with a cryptonym, MAGPIE.

He wants to defect. In exchange, he wants protection, security, comfort, all the things we Americans are known to dispense to defecting spies like some sort of intelligence Santa Claus.

We speak. We meet on the Faubourg-St. Honoré. We meet again at a safe-house flat. He promises us earthshaking, really explosive stuff, from a file on MAGPIE. Toby's interest is piqued. He is quite interested in MAGPIE.

We arrange to meet at my apartment on the rue Jacob. It is safe, because Laura is gone, I think. I arrive late. A man in a plaid shirt, a thatch of black hair, is limping away. I can smell blood, sharp and metallic, warm and sour, a stomach-turning odor that screams at me, louder and louder as I mount the stairs.

Can that really be Laura? It's not possible, certainly it can't be, that contorted body, that white silk nightgown, the large bright red stain. It's not real, it cannot be. Laura's out of town; she's in Giverny; this isn't her; there is a resemblance, that's all, but it can't be . . .

I am losing my mind.

And Toby. That tangle of a human form on the floor of the hallway: Toby, barely alive, paralyzed for life.

I have done this.

I have done this to both of them. To my mentor and friend. To my adored wife.

'Victor' examined the scrap of envelope, and then looked up. His gray-blue eyes regarded me with an expression I couldn't quite place: fright? Or nonchalance? It could have been anything.

Then he said to me: 'Please come in.'

The two of them, 'Victor' and the deformed woman, sat side by side on a narrow couch. I stood, gun trained on them, flushed with anger. A large color television set was on, its volume muted, playing some old American situation comedy I didn't recognize.

The man spoke first, in Russian.

'I didn't kill your wife,' he said.

The woman – his wife? – sat with her trembling hands folded in her lap. I could not bring myself to look at her face.

'Your name,' I said, also in Russian.

'Vadim Berzin,' the man replied. 'This is Vera. Vera Ivanovna Berzina.' He inclined his head slightly toward her, sitting at his right.

'You are "Victor," ' I said.

'I was. For a few days that is what I called myself.'

'Who are you, really, then?'

'You know who I am.'

Did I, in fact? What did I actually know of the man?

'Did you expect me?' I asked.

Vera shut her eyes, or, rather, they seemed to disappear into the swells of flesh. I had seen a face like hers before, I now recalled, but only in photos and films. *The Elephant Man*, a powerful film based on the true story of the famous Elephant Man, the Englishman John Merrick. He had been terribly disfigured with neurofibromatosis, von Recklinghausen's disease, which can result in skin tumors and deformities. Was that what this woman had?

'I expected you,' the man said, nodding.

'But you're not afraid to let me into your apartment?'

'I didn't kill your wife.'

'You won't be surprised,' I said, 'that I don't believe you.'

'No,' he said, smiling wanly. 'I am not surprised.' He paused, then said: 'You can kill me, or both of us, very easily. You can kill us right now if you want to. But why would you want to? Why, before you listen to what I have to tell you?'

'We have been living here,' he said, 'since the death of the Soviet Union. We bought our way out, as did so many of our comrades in the KGB.'

'You paid off the Russian government?'

'No, we paid off your Central Intelligence Agency.'

'With what? Dollars stashed away somewhere?'

'Oh, come. Whatever few dollars we could scrape together over the years are nothing to the great and wealthy Central Intelligence Agency. They don't need our grimy dollar bills. No, we bought our way out with the same currency all KGB officers –'

'Of course,' I said. 'Information. Intelligence, stolen from KGB files. Like all the rest of them. I'm surprised you had any interested buyers, after what you did.'

'Ah, yes,' Berzin said sardonically. 'I tried to entrap a bright young CIA officer whom Moscow Center had a grudge against. So I arrange a false defection, right out of the textbook, yes?'

I said nothing, and he went on. 'I show up, but the young CIA officer is not there. And so – because vengeance is not selective – I kill the young CIA officer's wife and wound an older CIA man. Do I have this right?'

'Approximately.'

'Ah. Ah, yes. A good tale.'

I had lowered my gun while he spoke, but now I raised it again, slowly. I believe that few things evoke truth the way a

409

loaded gun does in the hands of someone who knows how to use it.

For the first time, his wife spoke. She cried out, actually, in a clear, strong contralto: 'Let him speak!'

I glanced quickly at the disfigured woman, then turned back to her husband. He did not look frightened; on the contrary, he seemed almost amused, entertained by the situation. But then his expression turned suddenly grave. 'The truth,' he said, 'is this: When I arrived at your apartment, I was met by the older man, Thompson. But I didn't know who he was.'

'Impossible –'

'No! I had never met him, and you hadn't told me who would be joining you. For reasons of compartmentalization, I'm sure. He said he was assigned to vet me, that he wanted to begin the interrogation right then. I agreed. I told him about the MAGPIE document.'

'Which is?'

'A source in American intelligence.'

'A Soviet mole?'

'Not quite. A source. One of ours.'

'Code-named MAGPIE?' I used the Russian word *soroka*, for the bird.

'Yes.'

'So it was a KGB code name.' There was a long line of KGB code names taken from the names of birds, far more colorful than anything *we* ever came up with.

'Yes, but, again, it wasn't a mole, strictly speaking. Not a penetration agent, exactly. More like an agent we had managed to turn, bend our way, just enough to be of use.'

'And MAGPIE was . . . ?'

'MAGPIE, as it turned out, was James Tobias Thompson. Certainly I had no idea I was addressing the source himself, since I didn't know the real name – KGB files are far too compartmentalized for that. And there I was, chirping away about a file I wanted to sell on a sensitive Soviet operation, and there was the agent right there in front of me, listening with great interest as I tried to sell him information that would blow his cover.'

'My God,' I said. 'Toby.'

'Suddenly he became violent, this Thompson. He lunged at me, pulled a gun on me, a gun with a silencer, and demanded that I give him the document. Well, I was not so foolish as to bring it with me, not before we had made a deal. He threatened me; I told him I did not have the document with me. And he was about to kill me, I believe, when all of a sudden we both turned and saw a woman come into the room. A beautiful woman in white, in a white nightgown.'

'Yes. Laura.'

'She had heard everything. Everything I said, everything Thompson said. She told us she had been asleep in the other room, ill, and that the noise had awakened her. And now, suddenly, all became confusing. I took advantage of the interruption to get to my feet, try to escape. As I ran, I pulled out my own service revolver to protect myself, but before I could cock the pistol, I felt my leg explode. I looked, and I saw that Thompson had shot me. He had shot me, but he had not killed me, his aim had slipped in his haste, but by then I had my revolver out, and he froze, and I fired at him, out of self-defense. And then I leapt into the hallway, down a landing, and managed to get away before he could kill me.'

All I wanted to do was to sink down onto the floor, cover my eyes, seek refuge in sleep, but I needed my entire reservoir of willpower now. Instead, I lowered myself to a large boxy armchair, clicked the safety back on, and continued to listen in silence.

'And as I ran down the stairs,' Berzin continued, 'I heard another silenced shot, and I knew he had either killed himself or had killed the woman.'

The disfigured old woman's eyes were closed, I noticed; they had been closed for much of his narration. A long, long silence ensued. I could hear the far-off buzz of mopeds, a roar of a truck, the laughter of children.

At last I was able to speak. 'A plausible story,' I said.

'Plausible,' Berzin said, 'and true.'

'But you have no proof.'

'No? How closely did you examine your wife's body?'

411

I didn't answer. I had not been able to bring myself to look at Laura's corpse.

'Exactly,' Berzin said gently. 'But if someone with expertise in ballistics had inspected the wounds, he would have discovered that the shot had been fired by a gun belonging to James Tobias Thompson.'

'Easy to say,' I said, 'when the body's been in the ground fifteen years.'

'There must have been records.'

'I'm sure there were.' I didn't add: But none that I had access to.

'Then I have something you will find useful, and if you will let me get it, I will have settled my debt to Harrison Sinclair. Your father-in-law, yes?'

'He's the one who got you out of Moscow?'

'Who else would have enough influence?'

'But why?'

'Probably so that someday I could tell you this story. It's on top of the television set.'

'What is?'

'The thing I want to show you. To give you. On the television set.'

I turned my head slightly to look at the television set, which was now playing a rerun of *M*A*S*H*. Atop its wooden console was an array of things: a bust of Lenin of the sort you used to be able to buy anywhere in Moscow; a lacquered dish that appeared to be in use as an ashtray; a small stack of Russian-language, Soviet-published collections of verse by Aleksandr Blok and Anna Akhmatova.

'It's in the Lenin,' he said with a smirk. 'Uncle Lenin.'

'Stay there,' I said, walked over to the television and lifted the small, hollow iron head. I turned it over. A tag on its base said BERIOZKA 4.31, meaning that it had been purchased from one of the old Soviet hard-currency stores for four rubles and thirty-one kopeks, once a fair amount of money.

'Inside,' he said.

I rattled the bust, and something inside it shifted. I removed a scrunched-up loose ball of what appeared to be scrap paper,

412

and then a small oblong came out. I took it in one hand and examined it.

A microcassette tape.

I looked at Berzin questioningly. From one of the other rooms the dog (which I assumed had been tied up or somehow restrained) began to whimper.

'Your proof,' he said, as if that explained everything.

When I didn't respond, he went on: 'I wore a wire.'

'To the rue Jacob?'

He nodded, pleased. 'A tape made in Paris fifteen years ago bought me my freedom.'

'Why the hell did you wear a wire?' An answer occurred to me, but it made no sense: 'You weren't actually defecting, were you? You were working for the KGB even then, right? Planting information?'

'*No*! It was for *protection*!'

'Protection? Against whom? Against the people you wanted to defect to? That's ludicrous!'

'No – listen! This was a microcassette recorder the Lubyanka had given me for 'provocations,' entrapments, all of that. But that time I wore it to protect myself. To record any promises, assurances, even threats. Otherwise, if ever there was a dispute about what was promised me, it would be *my* word against *yours*. And I knew that if I had a tape recording, it would be useful somehow. What else did I have?' He took his wife's hand, which I noticed was somewhat disfigured with small tumors, but nowhere near as badly as her face. 'This is for you. A tape recording of my meeting with James Tobias Thompson. It is the proof you want.'

Stunned, I approached the two old people, pulled a chair very close to them, and sat. It was far from easy, given how my mind was whirling, but I bent my head and concentrated, focused, until I seemed to be hearing something, a syllable here, a phrase there, and then I was quite *sure* I could hear something, I was certain I had tuned in on his desperate, anxious thoughts, which fairly *shouted* at me.

Very quietly, methodically, I said in Russian: 'It is very

413

important to me that you are telling the truth about this whole thing – about my wife, about Thompson, about everything.'

He spoke: 'Of course I am!'

I didn't respond; I *listened*, the quiet of the room broken only by the dog's loud whimpering, but then something flooded into my consciousness.

Of course I am telling you the truth!

But was he, in fact? Was he thinking this? Or was he instead about to *say* this – two very different things? What made me think that I possessed the ability to divine the truth?

Clutched by this uncertainty as I was, I was hardly prepared for the next thing I heard.

A woman's voice, pleasant and deep, a contralto, but not a spoken voice.

A *thought* voice, calm and assured.

You can hear me, can you not?

I looked up at the woman, and her eyes were once again closed, vanished into that frightful landscape of welts and tumors. Her small mouth appeared to be arched slightly upward into a crude semblance of a smile; a sad, knowing smile.

I thought: *Yes, I can.*

And, looking at her and smiling, I nodded.

A beat of silence went by, and then I heard: *You can hear me, but I cannot hear you. I do not have the ability you have. You must speak aloud to me.*

'The tape –' Berzin began to say, but his wife put a finger to her lips to shush him. Puzzled, he fell silent.

'Yes,' I said. 'Yes, I can. How do you know?'

She continued to smile, her eyes still closed.

I know of these things. I know of James Tobias Thompson's projects.

'How?' I said.

While my husband served as a clerk in Paris, I was kept behind in Moscow. They liked to do that – to keep the husband and wife separated so that they would have leverage over you. My job, in any case, was very important. Too important for me to give up. I was the chief secretary to three successive KGB

414

chairmen. I was, in effect, the gatekeeper. I handled all of their secret papers, their correspondence.

'And so it was *you* that found the MAGPIE file.'

Yes, and many other files.

Berzin said, bewildered: 'What is going on?'

His wife said soothingly, 'Vadim, please. Silent for a few moments. I will explain all.'

And she went on, her thoughts as clear and understandable as her spoken voice.

All of my life I have had this disease. Her left hand fluttered toward her face. *But when I reached my forties, it attacked my face, and soon I became . . . unsuitable . . . to occupy a position of such visibility. The chairmen and their aides could no longer bear to look at me. Just as you cannot bear to look at me. And so they removed me from my job. But before I left, I took with me a document that I believed would at least let Vadim leave for the West. And when he visited me in Moscow, I gave it to him.*

'But how,' I persisted, 'how did you know about – about me?'

I didn't know. I guessed. In my position, I learned of the program that Thompson was working to develop. No one at the First Chief Directorate headquarters at Yasenyevo believed such a thing was possible. But I believed it was possible. I didn't know if he would ever succeed. But I knew it was possible. It's a remarkable, remarkable thing you have.

'No,' I said. 'It's a terrible thing.'

Before I could tell her, explain to her, she thought: *Your wife's father got us out of Russia. It was a generous and good thing for him to do. But we had more to offer than this tape.*

I furrowed my brow, silently asking, *What?*

Her thoughts continued to flow, impassioned and clear.

This man, James Tobias Thompson. Your mentor. MAGPIE. He continued to report to Moscow. I know; I saw his reports. He tells of people inside and outside the CIA who plan to take power. They cooperate with the Germans. You must find him. Thompson will tell you. He regrets what he did. He will tell you –

Then suddenly the dog's whimper became a sharp, loud bark.

'Something is wrong with Hunter,' Berzin said. 'Let me go find out –'

'No,' I said. The sharp barking grew steadily louder, faster, more insistent.

'Something is *wrong* with him!' Berzin said.

Then the bark became a horrible, horrible, piercing yowl, a cry that was almost human, almost a shriek.

And then there was a terrible silence.

I thought I could hear something, a thought. My name, *thought* with great urgency, from somewhere very close by.

I knew the dog had just been brutally slaughtered.

And that we were next.

59

It is amazing, really, how fast you can think when your life is at
stake. Both Vera and Vadim started at the dog's ear-splitting,
agonized scream, and then Vera shrieked and jumped up from
the couch and began awkwardly to run in the direction of the
sound.

'*Stop!*' I called out to her. 'Don't move – it's not safe! Get
down!'

Confused and terrified, the old couple grabbed at each
other, arms flailing wildly. Now the old woman began to
moan loudly, and her husband sputtered in protest.

'*Quiet!*'

Startled, they fell silent, and immediately there was an
ominous, unearthly quiet in the apartment. An absolute
silence, in which I knew someone – or several people – were
moving stealthily. I didn't know the layout of the apartment,
but I could surmise: the apartment was on the second floor – *le
premier étage*, as the French designate it – and probably a fire
escape wound up the rear of the building, where I assumed the
kitchen was located, where the dog had been tied up – and into
which the invaders had come.

The invaders. Meaning?

My thoughts raced: Who knew I was here? There was no
transmitter to guide my pursuers; and I hadn't been followed,
to the best of my knowledge. Toby Thompson . . . Truslow
. . . were they working together? Or at cross-purposes, against
each other?

Had this old Russian émigré couple been on a watch list?
Was it possible that someone with excellent access to Agency
secrets – and that described either Truslow or Thompson –

knew of the deal Molly's father had struck with this couple? Yes, certainly it was possible. And I was known to be in Paris; and it would be natural to intensify a watch that might otherwise have remained dormant. . . .

In no more than a second or two, these thoughts flashed through my brain, but as I paused momentarily, I saw that both of the Berzins were rushing, or really lumbering, toward the tiny dark hallway, presumably toward the kitchen. Fools! What were they doing? What were they *thinking*?

'Get *back*,' I said, almost shouted, but they had already reached the doorway, frantic and crazed as frightened deer, unthinking and illogical and reflexive. I lunged toward them to pull them back, to get them out of the way so that I could move unencumbered by fears of their safety, and as I moved I saw a flickering shadow in the hallway, a silhouette of a man, it seemed.

'Down!' I shouted, but at that very instant there was that sibilant, dull *phut phut phut* of a silenced automatic, and both Vera and Vadim began to slump forward and then topple in a grotesque, balletic slow motion, like fallen trees, great ancient trees that have been sawn at their base, and the only sound was a lowing, a deep caterwauling that suddenly emanated from the old man as he crashed to the ground.

I froze, and without thinking fired a volley of shots into the dark hallway. There was a shout, a high-pitched scream of pain that seemed to indicate I had hit someone, and several rapid, male voices shouting at once. Now the shots were returned, splintering the doorjamb. One bullet grazed my shoulder; another hit the television screen, and the set exploded. I sprang forward, grabbed the door handle, and fell against it, slamming the door to the sitting room, turning the lock as I did so.

For what? So that I could be trapped in this room? *Think*, dammit!

The only way out was the hallway, where the gunman or gunmen were, and that made no sense, but now what?

I had no time to think; there was time only to react as swiftly as possible, but I had put myself into this treacherous corner, and as I desperately calculated, a round of bullets was fired against the door, *through* the heavy wooden door.

Where now?

Jesus, Ben, *move* it, for Christ's sake!

I whirled around, saw the wooden chair on which I had been sitting just a few seconds earlier, and flung it toward the window. The window shattered, the chair lodged in between slats of the aluminum venetian blinds. I raced toward the window, yanked out the chair, and used it to clear away the remaining jagged edges of glass.

Another volley of shots came behind me; the doorknob was rattled; and then more shots.

And just as the door somehow came open behind me, I leapt – without looking – out of the second-floor window and into the street.

I bent my legs, bracing for the impact, my arms spread to protect my head in case I pitched forward.

I moved, it seemed, in slow motion. Time, for a moment, had stood still. I could see myself fall, almost as if I were watching on a movie screen, see myself tuck my legs in, see the street as it zoomed up toward me, shrubbery and concrete sidewalk and pedestrians and . . .

And in an instant I felt myself slam against the sidewalk, a crushingly hard blow: I had landed on the bottoms of my feet and vaulted forward, almost sprung upright, my arms outstretched to restore my balance.

I was hurt; that seemed clear; and I was in great pain. But I was alive, thank God, and I could move, and as I heard the bullets whistle by from behind and above, I lurched to one side, trying to ignore the stabbing pain in my feet, ankles, and calves. I ran with a speed I didn't even know I was capable of, instinctively down the street toward Les Halles. All around me passersby screamed and shouted, some pointing, some cringing as I tore through the crowds, but it was the crowds that would save me, I knew; the crowds would serve as underbrush to hinder the progress of any pursuers. But *were* there, in fact, any pursuers? Had I eluded them entirely? Were they all

419

upstairs, in the apartment that had belonged to the Russians? Or were –

But they were not all upstairs. No. I glanced back and saw that several men in dark suits, and several more in nondescript dark street clothes, were running after me, their faces set in grimaces of determination. I zigzagged around a mound of bricks, and something about them –

Hurl the goddamn bricks at them, dammit!

– reminded me that I had something more effective than bricks; I had a good, reliable pistol, with probably ten or twelve more rounds left in it, and I whirled around and fired off one shot, aiming as precisely as I could so as not to wound anyone I didn't intend to, and I saw one of the men in the dark suits go down, and now there was one of them, and I kept running, turning down the rue Pierre-Lescot, past a *tabac* and a bar, a bakery, weaving through the rush-hour crowds. I was a moving, darting, weaving target; a poor target for my one – was it one? – pursuer. He would face the choice of either stopping to aim with some degree of accuracy or to run as swiftly as he could, and my strategy seemed to be working: he chose to run, to try to overtake me. I could hear him behind me. It was just him and me now, the world had shrunk down to just him and me, life or death, no crowds, no passersby, just the man in the dark suit and fedora and black glasses coming after me, gaining on me, and I ran as I'd never run before. I was ignoring the siren of pain, ignoring the warning signs, and my body was punishing me for it. And now, as I ran, my abdomen and sides were gripped with terrible knifelike cramps. It was all I could do to keep going; my body, out of shape after years of practicing law and not tradecraft, was commanding me to stop, to give myself up: *What could they really want from me now? Information? Give it to them! Was I not too valuable to hurt, someone with my ability?*

Just up ahead loomed the modernistic forum of Les Halles, and as I ran toward it – why? what was the goal? was I planning to simply run myself into exhaustion, was that it? – my body warred with my mind. My poor body, racked with pain throughout now, tangled and screamed at my steely mental resolve, importuning and pleading, then cajoling silkily, *Give yourself up, they won't harm you, they won't harm Molly, all they want is your assurance of silence, and yes they might not believe you, but you can stall for time, you can play along with them, give yourself up, save yourself. . . .*

The footsteps, accelerating now, thundered behind me, and I found myself now in some sort of ground-level parking garage, at one end of which was a door marked with a red sign: SORTIE DE SECOURS and PASSAGE INTERDIT, and I pulled it open and shut it behind me. It gave off a rusty metallic groan, and then I was in a small, dimly lit stairwell which stank of garbage. A tall, overflowing trash barrel stood near the door.

It was made of aluminum: too light to serve as a useful obstruction.

Something slammed against the door from the other side. A foot, perhaps, or a shoulder; but the door didn't give way. Desperately, I tipped the barrel over. Trash, trash, more trash . . . and a battered half of a pair of scissors. It might do; it was worth a try.

Another thud against the door, and this time it came partway open: a sliver of light winked in the twilit stairwell and then was gone. I reached down, grabbed the slender elbow-shaped steel piece, and slid it into an opening in the door hinge, as far in as it could go.

The door thundered again, but this time no sliver of light: no movement. As long as the scissor would hold, the door was secure.

I vaulted up the stairs, which led directly into a corridor, which soon gave onto a bustling arcade.

Where was it? A station – the Métro station, yes, that was it. Chatelet les Halles. The biggest underground station in the world. A maze. Many directions to go now; many directions to lose him now if – if only my body would stay with me, if only it would permit me to keep on going.

And then I knew what to do.

60

It is fifteen years earlier, and I am a young man, a younger man, freshly graduated from the CIA's Camp Peary, newly posted to Paris, 'wet behind my ears,' as my boss and friend James Tobias Thompson III liked to jibe me. Laura and I have arrived in Paris that morning, having flown TWA coach from Washington National, and I'm exhausted. Laura's asleep in our bare apartment on the rue Jacob; I'm half asleep, sitting here in Thompson's office in the U.S. Consulate on the rue St.-Florentin.

I like the guy; he seems to take to me. It's a good beginning to a career I have had more than my share of apprehensions about. Most of the young field officers take an instant dislike to their superiors, who treat them as the callow and unreliable young guys they are.

'I'm Toby,' he insists. 'Either we're both on a last-name basis, in which case you're Ellison and I have to act like some fucking marine drill sergeant, or we're colleagues.' Then, before I can thank him, he shoves a stack of books at me.

'Memorize them,' he says. 'Memorize them all.'

Some of them are guidebooks available to any tourist (Plan de Paris par Arrondissement: Nomenclature des rues avec la station du Métro la plus proche) and some are published by the Agency for internal use only (detailed, classified maps of the Paris Métro, top secret listings of diplomatic and military sites throughout the city, suggested escape routes by train and car).

'I hope you're joking,' I say.

'Do I look like it?'

'I don't know your sense of humor.'

'I don't have one.' Spoken with just enough of a set to his

422

mouth to indicate otherwise. 'You've got a photographic memory. You can retain a hell of a lot more than the farina I've got upstairs.'

We laugh: he's dark-haired, lanky, youthful in appearance.

He says: 'Someday, friend, this information might come in handy.'

Someday, Toby, I now thought, eyes casting about the enormous Métro station to get myself oriented. It had been years since I'd been here. *Never thought it would come in handy against you, did you?*

Physically, I was a train wreck. My arms, though they hurt much less, were still bandaged; my legs, feet, ankles, all gave off sparks and spirals of fierce jabbing, searing pain like some Fourth of July firecracker.

Chatelet les Halles. *At forty thousand square meters, it is the largest underground station in the world.* Thanks, Toby. Came in handy, all right. Ah, me and that old photographic memory.

I glanced behind me, saw nothing, but didn't allow myself to experience that sense of relief that might mean lassitude. He had doubtless followed me up the stairs, delayed only by a quarter-inch of rusty, distressed steel, which at any second would probably snap or buckle with the application of repeated force.

When you're pursued, the biggest mistake you can make is to give in to ancient, atavistic human survival instincts like the fight-or-flight response that saved the lives of our cavemen ancestors. Instinct makes you react predictably, and predictability is the enemy.

Instead, you put yourself into your opponent's mind, calculate as you think he would, even if it means crediting him with more intelligence than he possesses.

So what would he do?

Just about now, if the door did not yield, he'd search out the nearest alternate entrance. No doubt one would be nearby. He'd enter the station, put himself in *my* head, decide whether I would choose to leave the station for the street – no, too risky

423

– or whether I would attempt to lose myself in the maze of corridors (a good possibility), or whether I would try to put the greatest distance possible between myself and him, and find the nearest train (an even better possibility).

And then, calculating, he would double back, eliminate the best (and therefore most obvious) escape route . . . and search for me in the concourses. Anywhere but a train platform.

I scanned the crowds. A stringy-haired teenage girl nearby was singing in French-accented English, in a dreadful twittering imitation of Edith Piaf, 'On the Street Where You Live,' against a synthesized background of swelling strings and angelic obbligatos emanating from a Casio machine. People were tossing francs at the coat spread out on the floor before her, more out of pity, I guessed, than appreciation.

Everyone seemed to be moving purposively somewhere. Best I could tell, no one inside the station was coming after me.

So where was he?

The station was a bewildering array of orange *correspondances* signs and blue *sortie* signs, with trains headed toward dozens of different destinations: Pont de Neuilly, Créteil-Préfecture, Saint-Rémy-Les-Chevreuse, Porte d'Orléans, Château de Vincennes . . . And not just the regular Métro trains, but also the RER, the Réseau Express Régional rapid commuter trains to and from the Parisian suburbs. The place was huge, sprawling, bewildering, endless. And that was to my advantage.

For a few more seconds, at least.

I headed in the direction my pursuer would consider most obvious, and therefore – perhaps – least likely: the way the greatest flow of traffic seemed to be heading. *Direction* Château de Vincennes and Port de Neuilly.

To the right of the long row of turnstiles was an area marked PASSAGE INTERDIT that was cordoned off with a chain. I sprinted toward it, got a running start, and vaulted over it. A long line of people holding copies of *Pariscope* snaked around a booth selling half-price theater tickets (*Ticket Kiosque Theater: 'Les places du jour à moitié prix'*), beside an odd bronze statue of a man and a woman, both artistically misshapen, reaching forlornly toward each other. I flew past an exit to the Centre Georges Pompidou and the Forum des Halles, past a cluster of three policemen equipped with walkie-talkies, guns, and nightsticks, who looked up at me with suspicion.

Two of them snapped to attention and began to run after me, shouting.

I came to an abrupt halt at a row of tall pneumatic doors, which couldn't be surmounted.

But that's why God invented the *Sortie de Secours*, the security entrance for officials only, toward which I swerved, and then, to the audible alarm of a gaggle of Métro workers, bolted through.

The shouts crescendoed behind me. A shrill traffic whistle trilled.

A clattering of footsteps.

Past a Sock Shop, then a flower stand ('*Promotion – 10 tulipes 35F*').

Now I came to a very long corridor, through which a set of moving conveyor belts – 'people-movers,' I believe they're called – were carrying pedestrians up a gradual incline. The adjacent belt carried people back the other way, down in the direction from which I'd come. Between the two conveyor belts was a waist-high meter-wide band of metal that flowed uphill like an endless steel carpet runner.

I glanced around, and saw that the Métro security officers clambering after me were now joined by a solitary, dark-suited figure vastly outpacing them, approaching me with frightening speed, as I found myself wedged in a crowd of people who were not moving, letting the steel and rubber conveyors do all the work. Stuck.

The man in the dark suit: the exact one I wanted to lose.

And as he came closer, and I once again turned to gauge the distance that separated us, I realized that I had seen the face before.

His heavy, black-framed glasses only partially obscured the yellowish circles under his eyes. His fedora was gone, lost in the chase no doubt, revealing his thin, pale blond hair combed straight back. Gaunt, ghostly pale, thin pale lips.

On Marlborough Street in Boston.

Outside the bank in Zurich.

The same man, no question about it. A man who probably knew a great deal about me.

And a man – the thought was chilling – who took few if any pains to disguise himself.

He didn't care if I recognized him.

He *wanted* me to recognize him.

I wriggled past the bottleneck of people, elbowing them out of my way, and leapt up onto the metal runner between the conveyor belts.

Stumbling, I realized that the metal surface was broken every foot or so by jutting blades of steel, put there, I was sure, to make what I was trying to do – run atop it – difficult.

Difficult, but not impossible.

What had the woman in Zurich called him?

Max.

All right, old friend, I thought.

Come after me, 'Max.'

Whatever you want, come and get it.

Try.

61

Unthinkingly, I ran.

Along the metallic ledge, uphill. Around me, from either side, were gasps and screams and shouts – *Who's the madman? A criminal? What is he escaping?* The answer was supplied immediately to anyone who looked a short distance down the commuter beltway and saw the uniformed officers, trilling their whistles like a French version of the Keystone Kops, wriggling through the crowds.

And now, doubtless to the amazement of onlookers, not one but *two* men were loping along the metal ledge, the one desperately trying to elude the other.

Max. The killer.

Barely thinking about what I was doing, I vaulted across the opposing lane of descending commuters, gaining a tenuous foothold for a second or two before I leapt over the glass siding and down, a good ten feet, to the deep stairwell below, and bounded up the stairs. I couldn't risk looking back, couldn't risk breaking my stride for even a second, and so I simply ran as fast as my weakened ankles would take me, all sound around me drowned out by the incessant, rapid staccato of my heartbeat, the wheezing intake and expulsion of breath from my lungs. Way up ahead of me, at the top of the stairs, was a blue sign: DIRECTION PONT DE NEUILLY. A beacon. I was a greyhound chasing a rabbit; I was a prisoner making a jailbreak. I was, in my fevered brain, anything, anything inspirational, anything that would keep me going, through the pain, ignoring my body's screams to stop, trying to block out the silkily seductive siren calls – *Give up, Ben. They won't hurt you. You can't win anyway, can't outrun them, you're outnumbered, just make it easy on yourself and give it up.*

No.

He will not hesitate to 'hurt' me, I replied in my manic internal dialogue. He will do what it takes.

A narrow escalator loomed just up ahead, at the top of the stairs.

Where were the . . . pursuers?

I allowed myself a quick glance around, a snap of the head before I headed up the escalator.

The subway cops, all three – was it three? – of them, had given up the chase. Probably radioed ahead to others.

That left one.

My old friend, Max.

He hadn't given up, of course. Not old Max. He continued striding up the metal ledge, a solitary coiled figure approaching, accelerating . . .

At the top of the escalator was a small landing, and to the right, an escalator marked SORTIE RUE DE RIVOLI. Well? Which way? To the street, or to the train platform?

Stick with what you know.

For just a second I hesitated, then instead barreled ahead toward the train platform, where crowds of people were surging into and out of the train.

He was perhaps ten seconds behind me now, which meant that he too would pause at the landing, and if I was unlucky, he would spot me just up ahead, on the train platform, a big fat target in his crosshairs.

Keep going.

Electronic tones pealed, signaling that the train was about to depart, and I knew I wouldn't make it. I put on one last desperate burst of speed, aiming for the nearest open door, but they all slid closed with a brusque finality when I was still twenty yards away.

And as the train pulled away, and I could hear Max entering the platform, I leapt forward crazily – *toward* the moving train – and grabbed at its exterior and my right hand gripped onto something solid.

A handhold.

Thank God.

Then my left hand found another handhold as I was whooshed along the platform, leaving Chatelet and Max behind, pressing my body flat against the moving train, and of course luck was no longer with me, it was a terrible idea, I was about to be killed.

My eyes wild, I saw what loomed just ahead as the front section of the train plunged into the tunnel.

A huge round mirror jutting out, mounted on the wall at the entrance to the tunnel.

The train, I could see, cleared it by a few inches, but I wouldn't, a protruding lump of human flesh that would be sheared in two as neatly as a Sabatier knife through a wheel of cheese.

Some vestige of logic now rose to the forefront of my fevered brain: *What the hell do you think you're doing? What kind of lunacy is this? Gonna ride the train through its narrow tunnel, so you'll be squashed like a bug, let the stone walls of the tunnel do what Max couldn't, is that it?*

I heard a long, loud cry escape from my lungs involuntarily, and, just as the enormous round metal disc rushed up to decapitate me, I released my grip on the handholds and tumbled onto the cold, hard platform.

I barely heard the gunshots around me. I was in another world, an almost hallucinatory land of fear and adrenaline. I cracked into the floor, slamming my head and shoulders, and tears of pain stung my eyes, and the pain was indescribable, white and searingly hot and blindingly bright and all-encompassing.

PASSAGE INTERDIT AU PUBLIC – DANGER

A yellow sign just above me penetrated my haze.

I could stop, and that would be it. I could lie there, and surrender.

Or – if my body would permit it – I could plunge ahead, toward the gleaming yellow sign, *toward* the mouth of the tunnel, and what choice, really, was there?

Something in me, some great reserve of strength, opened up, and a flood of adrenaline pumped into my bloodstream, and I stumbled groggily forward to a small set of concrete steps. The yellow warning sign was hinged, and I shouldered it aside, almost tumbled down the few steps, into the cold darkness of the tunnel, into the tailwind of the just-departed train.

There was a footpath.

Of course there was. What was it?

The *passerelle de sécurité*. The gangway. Constructed for Métro repair crews to work while the trains are running if need be.

As I ran – no, *limped*, really – along the footpath, I could hear a sound behind me, a pneumatic sound of brakes, the slight squeal of metal, the noise of another train pulling into the platform I had just left behind.

Coming at me.

But it was safe, wasn't it? I was safe here, was I not?

No. The path was *too* narrow; my body would be *too* close to the upcoming train, I could see that even in my adrenaline-and-fear-crazed state. And surely my pursuer wouldn't be suicidal enough to follow me; he would know that I was as good as gone; he would know enough to just let me plunge on through the tunnels, to my inevitable death, and then I heard something, a thought, and I knew I wasn't alone.

I turned back for an instant. He was in the tunnel with me.

I'm impressed, Max.

That's two of us that are going to die.

And from what was now a good distance I could hear the electronic chimes ringing out, then the clattering of the closing doors, and I froze in the tunnel as the train began to move toward me.

I felt something akin to vertigo. An itch in the back of my head. All of my synapses were jumping with a chemical message of fear –

move move move move

– but I overpowered the instinct, flattened myself against the tunnel wall as the rush of wind heralded the coming of the train and I couldn't help closing my eyes as the steel skin of the

430

train, a terrifying blur, whooshed by, so close I was sure I could feel it brush against me.

It kept coming, and coming.

And I opened my eyes.

And with my peripheral vision I saw that Max – ten yards away, maybe – had done the same. He too had flattened himself against the tunnel wall.

He was illuminated stroboscopically with a dim, flickering, sickly greenish-yellow fluorescent light from a bulb directly above his head.

But there was a difference.

His eyes weren't closed. They stared straight ahead. And not with fear: with concentration.

And there was another difference.

He wasn't standing still.

He was sidling, ever so carefully, toward me.

Coming closer.

62

He approached, and the train kept coming. It seemed the longest train in the world.

I felt as if I were frozen in time, standing in the center of a tornado. As I sidled away from him, deeper into the tunnel, I caught sight of something just up ahead. A recess in the wall, illuminated by a fluorescent bulb. A niche. If I could . . .

And just a few feet ahead, there it was, a deep niche. Safety.

A little more effort, crabwalking along the footpath, along the horrifying rush of air, the glass and steel and protruding steel handgrips perhaps two inches from my nose.

And I was there. In the niche. Safe.

No other underground transport system in the world has this system of gangways and niches, I remembered. I could see the page, the diagrams. *There is a niche every ten meters . . . Between each station is an average of six hundred meters of track . . . Two hundred kilometers of track comprise the regular routes between stations of the Paris Métro . . . The third rail is extremely dangerous, charged as it is with 750 volts DC of electricity.*

The recess was three feet deep.

Positively roomy.

I was able, now, to pull out the gun, release the safety, cock it, extend my hand out of the recess, and fire.

Score.

I had hit him. He grimaced in pain, and teetered forward. . . .

And just as the very end of the train thundered past, he fell forward, onto the tracks. But he was not wounded seriously, that was clear at once by the way he braced himself, legs crouched, against falling again.

The train was gone. It was just the two of us in the tunnel. He stood on the ballast between the tracks; I huddled for protection in the narrow cave. I pulled back, out of his line of fire, but he leapt forward, gun extended, and fired.

I felt a jab of pain in my left leg: I had been hit.

Once again I pulled the trigger and heard only that small, flat innocuous click, that taunting, sickening sound that told me the cartridge was empty. Reloading wasn't even a consideration; I had no spare magazines.

And so I did the only thing I could: with a great, open-throated bellow I sprang forward, toward the killer. I could just make out his facial expression an instant before I pummeled him to the ground: a look of dull incuriosity, or was it disbelief? In that split-second interval he tried to take aim, but even before he could raise his pistol, we crashed to the ground, his back thudding against the steel of the tracks and the sharp gray ballast stones, and I heard his gun clatter somewhere out of his hand.

He reared up with immense strength, but I had the advantage both of surprise and of positioning – I had his arms and legs pinioned – and I was able to force him backward, one hand slamming into his throat.

He grunted, reared up again, and then spoke for the first time, a few words in a heavy – German? – accent.

'No – use,' he moaned, but I was not interested in what he had to say, I cared only about what was going through his goddamned *mind*, but I could hardly draw back and concentrate, there wasn't time for that, and so I throttled and slammed against his torso.

Back toward the train platform, a glint of light was visible thirty or forty meters or so away.

And I *heard* a few snatches of thought-language, phrases that seemed to come at me with a bizarre urgency, loud and yet not quite distinct. *You can kill me*, he thought in German, *you can kill me, but there is another. Another will take my place. Another –*

– and for just a second, stunned, I lost my grip on his throat. He reared up again, and this time he was able to break my

433

hold, and I fell over backward, my shoes sliding in the gravel as if in a puddle of grease. My right hand flew out as I tried to break my fall, but there was nothing to grab on to except the air, and then –

750 volts DC of electricity

– my fingertips brushed ever so close to the cold, hard steel of the third rail, but I managed to yank them away just in time, in time to see him flying through the air toward me.

I reached around for my weapon, but it was gone.

With a sudden lurch I propelled myself upward, cracking into him, sending him flying over my shoulder toward the electrified third rail as the approaching train was upon us, thundering, unbelievably loud, and I saw his legs shudder from the electricity just a split second before the train, its emergency horn bellowing, bore down on him and, oh Jesus Christ, I couldn't believe what I was seeing, the legs were still shuddering, but they ended at the hips, the lower half of his body shivered, a bleeding stump severed entirely at the waist, a quivering chunk of human flesh.

Up ahead came the thunder of another approaching train. Serenely, in a glacial calm, I climbed up to the footpath and the safety of the nearest recess. The train came, and I flattened myself against the wall of the niche. When it had passed, I made my way out of the tunnel without looking back.

63

The village of Mont-Tremblant was a tiny cluster of buildings – a couple of French country restaurants, a Bonichoix supermarket, and a hotel fronted by a green awning, oddly out of place, looking like a scale model of one of the grand hotels in Monte Carlo. Looming all around were Quebec's Laurentian mountains, green and lush.

Molly and I had flown separately to Montreal's two international airports from Paris on different commercial airlines, she into Mirabel via Frankfurt and Brussels; I into Dorval via Luxembourg and Copenhagen.

I had employed several standard tradecraft techniques to ensure that neither one of us could easily be followed. We'd each used the Canadian passports that my French contact in Pigalle had forged for us, which meant that both sets of American passports – in the names of Mr and Mrs Alan Crowell, and Mr and Mrs. John Brewer – were still virgin; they could be used at some time in the future if an emergency arose. We had departed from different airports, Molly from Charles de Gaulle, I from Orly. Most important, we had flown first-class and on European carriers – Aer Lingus, Lufthansa, Sabena, and Air France. The European airlines still treat first-class passengers as important personages, unlike the American ones, which give their first-class fliers a bigger seat and a free drink and that's it. As an important personage, your seat will be held until the very last moment; in fact, they usually page any first-class passenger who's checked in but not yet boarded. For every leg of our journey we boarded at the last possible second, which meant that our forged passports were given only the most cursory of glances as we were ushered aboard.

Although we had taken circuitous routes, miraculously we were able to land within two and a half hours of each other.

I'd rented a car from Avis, picked Molly up, and began our 130-kilometer journey up 15 North. The highway could have been anywhere in the world, the industrial and then suburban outskirts of Milan or Rome or Paris or, for that matter, Boston. But by the time 15 became 117 – the *Autoroute des Laurentides* – the broad, well-paved road cut a handsome swath through the magisterial Laurentian mountains, through Sainte-Agathe-des-Monts and then Saint-Jovite.

And we sat there, over our uneaten plates of *escargots Florentine* and pan-fried trout, like a couple of dazed prizefighters, barely talking. We hadn't talked on the way either.

Partly it was because we were both so exhausted, and jet-lagged on top of it. But partly we were silent, I think, because we had been through so much in the last days, together and separately, that there was far too *much* to talk about.

We'd gone through the looking-glass: everything was getting curiouser and curiouser. Molly's father was a victim, then a villain, and . . . now what? Toby had been a victim, then a savior, then a villain, and . . . now what?

And Alex Truslow, my friend and confidant, the crusading new director of the CIA – was in fact the leader of the faction that for years had profited illegally off the Agency.

An assassin code-named Max had tried to kill me in Boston and in Zurich and in Paris.

Who was he, really?

The answer had come in the last, amazing few moments of my telepathic ability, as the assassin and I struggled on the tracks of the Paris Métro. With one last burst of concentration I had tuned in; I had read his thoughts.

Who are you? I had demanded.

His real name was Johannes Hesse. 'Max' was only his code name.

Who hired you?

Alex Truslow.

Why?

436

A hit.

Who was the target?

His employers didn't know. All they knew was that the victim-to-be was the surprise witness before the Senate Select Committee on Intelligence.

Tomorrow.

Who was it? Who could it be?

Twenty-four hours or so remained.

Who was it?

So why were we here, in this isolated and remote place in Quebec? What had we expected to find? A hollow tree containing documents? A jack-o'-lantern with microfilm inside?

I had my theories now, theories that would explain everything, but the final piece of the puzzle still remained. And I was convinced that we were about to find it buried in an abandoned stone lodge on the shores of Lac Tremblant.

The registry of deeds for the village of Mont-Tremblant was located in the nearby larger town of St.-Jerome. But it turned out to be of little assistance. The stolid Frenchman who kept the records and issued licenses and did sundry other bureaucratic tasks, a man named Pierre La Fontaine, curtly informed us that all of Mont-Tremblant's records had been entirely destroyed in a fire in the early 1970s. All that remained were deeds registered since then, and he was unable to turn up any record of the sale or purchase of a house on the lake involving the names Sinclair or Hale. Molly and I spent a good three hours combing through the records with him, to no avail.

Then we took a drive around as much of Lac Tremblant as we could, past the Tremblant Club and the other new resorts, the MontTremblant Lodge, with its clay tennis courts and sandy lakefront beach, the Manoir Pinoteau, the Chalet des Chutes, and houses both elegant and rustic.

The idea, I suppose, was that either or both of us might recognize the lodge, whether (in Molly's case) from memory or from the photograph. But no luck there either. Most of the houses were not visible from the dirt road that abutted the lake. All we could see were names on signposts, some hand-lettered, some professionally drafted. Even if we'd had the time to drive off the road, down each path to every lakefront house – and that would have certainly taken days – it would have been in fact impossible, for a number of the driveways were rather persuasively blocked to incoming traffic. And then, quite a few houses were located on the lake's secluded northern part, which could be reached only by boat.

At the end of our little reconnaissance mission, discouraged, I pulled the car up in front of the Tremblant Club and parked.

'Now what?' Molly asked.

'We rent a boat,' I said.

'Where?'

'Here, I imagine.'

But it was not to be. There were no boat-rental places to be seen, and none of the hotels we stopped into rented boats. Evidently the town made it as difficult for tourists as possible.

Then the buzz of an outboard motor broke the silence of the beautiful, glassy lake from a distance, which gave me an idea. At LacTremblant-Nord (which was in fact not at the northernmost tip of the lake, but the end of the road, beyond which there was no access) we found several deserted gray-painted aluminum and wood boat-sheds. They were padlocked, of course. This seemed to be a docking area for residents of the lake who had no waterfront access.

Picking the padlocks was a matter of a few minutes. Inside was an array of small crafts, mostly fishing boats. I spotted a yellow Sunray with a seventy-horsepower outboard motor – a good, fast boat, but more important, its keys had been left in the ignition. The motor kicked right in, and a few minutes later, amid clouds of blue smoke, we were zipping along the lake.

The houses were various: modern ersatz Swiss chalets and rustic cabins, some right up on the water, some barely visible through the trees, some perched prominently on the mountainside. There was a false alarm, a stone and mortar house that at first looked right and then turned out to be a modern architect's pun on an old lodge.

And then it appeared without warning, the old stone-fronted lodge on a gently rising hill maybe a hundred meters from the shore. A veranda faced the lake, and on the veranda were two white Adirondack chairs. It was unmistakably the house in which Molly had spent a summer. In fact, it appeared not to have changed one whit since the picture had been taken decades before.

Molly stared at it, stricken and entranced. The color drained from her cheeks.

'That's it,' she said.

I killed the motor as close to the shore as I dared, and let it drift the rest of the way in, and then I tied it up to the rickety wooden pier.

'My God,' Molly whispered. 'This is it. This is the place.'

I helped her up to the dock, then clambered out myself.

'My God, Ben, I remember this place!' Her voice was a high-pitched, excited whisper. She pointed toward a white-painted wooden boat house. 'Dad taught me how to fish there.'

She began walking down the pier toward the boat house, lost in her nostalgic reverie, when I grabbed her.

'What – ?'

'Quiet!' I commanded.

The sound was barely audible at first, a rustling of grass from somewhere near the house.

A *thup thup thup*.

'What is it?' Molly whispered.

I froze.

The dark shape seemed almost to fly toward us over the overgrown lawn, down the hill, the *thup thup thup* mingling now with a whine.

A low growl.

The growl became a loud, terrifying, warning bark, as the creature – a Doberman pinscher, I realized – bounded toward us, teeth bared.

Moving so fast it was virtually a blur.

'*No!*' Molly shrieked, running toward the boat house.

My stomach turned inside out as the Doberman leapt into the air, bounding over a distance that seemed inconceivable, and just as I reached for my pistol, I heard a man's voice commanding: 'Halt!'

I heard a splash from the water behind us and whirled around.

'You could hurt yourself that way. He doesn't like surprises.'

A tall man in a boxy navy bathing suit emerged from the water. The water cascaded from his gray beard as he rose to his full height, a deeply tanned if aging Neptune come out of the underworld.

A sight that was so illogical it failed to register in my brain.

Molly and I both gaped, eyes wide, unable to speak.

Molly rushed to embrace her father.

Part Seven

WASHINGTON

64

So what do you say at such a moment?

For what seemed an eternity, no one spoke.

The lake was still, the water glassy and opaque. There was no buzz of motorboats, no shouts, not even the call of birds. Absolute silence. The world stood still.

Weeping, Molly squeezed her arms around her father's chest hard enough, it seemed, to crush him. She is tall, but he is taller still, and so he had to hunch forward to allow the two of them to hug.

I watched in dull shock.

Finally, I said: 'I barely recognized you with the beard.'

'Isn't that the point?' Harrison Sinclair said solemnly, his voice raspy. Then he cracked a wrinkled, lopsided smile. 'I assume you made sure you weren't followed here.'

'Best I could.'

'I knew I could count on you.'

Suddenly Molly broke her embrace, drew back, and slapped her father across the face. He winced.

'Damn you,' she said, her voice breaking.

The lodge was dark and still. It had the distinctive odor of a house that has long been closed up: of countless crackling fires over the years that have permeated the floors and walls; of camphor and mothballs; of mildew and paint and rancid cooking oil.

We sat together on a love seat whose muslin upholstery was discolored with years of dust, watching her father as he spoke. He sat in a canvas chair that was suspended from the high ceiling on a cable.

He had changed into a pair of baggy khaki shorts and a loose navy blue pullover sweater. With his legs sprawled in front of him, casually crossed at the ankles, he looked as relaxed as could be, the amiable host settling down for a martini with his weekend houseguests.

Sinclair's beard was full and untrimmed; it appeared to be the result of several months' growth, which made perfect sense. He had gotten a lot of sun, probably swimming and boating on the lake, and his face looked tough and leathery, the skin of an old mariner.

'I had a feeling you'd find me here,' he said. 'But not this quickly. Then Pierre La Fontaine called me a few hours ago and told me a couple had been asking questions in St.-Jerome about me and the house.'

Molly looked baffled, so he explained: 'Pierre's the keeper of the records, the mayor of Lac Tremblant, the chief of police, and the general chief factotum. He's also the caretaker for a number of summer residents. An old and trusted friend of mine. He's looked after this house for quite some time now – years, in fact. Back in the fifties he arranged the sale of this place – quite cleverly, I must say – so that it passed out of Grandma Hale's hands and basically disappeared, its ownership tangled and impossible to trace.

'Wasn't my idea, by the way. It was Jim Angleton's. Back when I began to get involved with covert stuff, Jim felt strongly I should always have a place to disappear to if things ever got too hot. Canada seemed to make as good sense as any place, since it's outside of U.S. borders. Anyway, Pierre rented it out during the summers occasionally, more often during ski season. And always on behalf of a fictional Canadian investor named Strombolian. The rental income more than paid for the upkeep and his fee. The rest Pierre kept in trust.' He gave his crinkled smile again. 'He's an honest guy.'

Without warning, Molly erupted in anger. She had been sitting next to me in silence, contemplatively I thought, no doubt in an advanced state of shock. But as it turned out, she had been smoldering, seething.

'How . . . could . . . you do this to me? How could you put me through this?'

'Snoops –' her father began

'Goddammit! Have you any *idea* –'

'Molly!' he shouted hoarsely. 'Hold on! I didn't have a choice, don't you see that?' He drew in his lanky legs until he was sitting upright, then hunched forward toward his daughter, his eyes beseeching, glistening.

'When they killed my dear Sheila, my love – yes, Molly, we were lovers, but I'm sure you knew that – I realized it was only a matter of hours before they got to me. I knew I had to hide.'

'From the Wise Men,' I said. 'From Truslow and Toby –'

'And half a dozen others. And their security forces, which aren't exactly small-time.'

I said: 'This all concerns what's happening in Germany, isn't that right?'

'It's complicated, Ben. I don't really have –'

'I knew you were alive,' Molly interrupted. 'I've known it since Paris.'

There was something steely in her tone, a quiet assurance, and I turned to look at her.

'It was his letter,' she continued, looking at me. 'He mentioned an emergency appendectomy that forced him to spend an entire summer with us here, at Lac Tremblant.'

'And?' I prompted her.

'And – it sounds trivial now, but I didn't remember seeing an appendix scar. The face was pretty much destroyed, but the body wasn't, and I guess I would have remembered, would have registered it on some subconscious level. I mean, it might have been there, but I *wasn't certain*. You understand? And you remember I tried to get the autopsy a while back, but it was sealed? Order of the Fairfax County district attorney. So I pulled some strings.'

'Which is why you wanted the fax machine in Paris,' I said. At the time, she had told me only that she had a thought about her father's murder, an idea, a way to prove something.

She nodded. 'Every pathologist – at least, every pathologist *I* know – keeps a copy of his work in his own locked drawers.

You do that in case you ever run into trouble later on, so you can turn to your notes and all that. So I'm not without resources. I called a friend at Mass. General, a pathologist, who called a colleague at Sibley in Washington, where the autopsy was done. Routine inquiry, right? Bureaucratic? It's incredibly easy to circumvent security channels in a hospital if you know where to pull the strings.'

'And?' I prompted her again.

'I had the autopsy report faxed to me. And sure enough, it listed the presence of an appendix. And at that point I knew that wherever Dad was, it wasn't beneath that gravestone in Columbia County in upstate New York.' She turned back to her father. 'So whose body was it?'

'No one who'll be missed,' he replied. 'I'm not without my *own* resources.' Then he added, quietly: 'It's a lousy business.'

'My God,' Molly said under her breath, her head bowed.

'Not quite as evil as you must be thinking,' he said. 'A fairly thorough sweep of John Does – unidentified cadavers in hospital morgues – netted us someone of approximately the right build, age, and – toughest of all – good health. Most homeless people are afflicted with a dozen different ailments.'

Molly nodded, smiled fiercely. Bitterly, she said: 'And what's one less vagrant?'

'The face wasn't important,' I said, 'since it was to be mostly destroyed in the crash anyway, right?'

'Right,' Sinclair replied. 'Actually, it was destroyed *before* the crash, if you must know. The restorative artists at the mortuary, who had no idea they weren't laboring away on the real Harrison Sinclair, were given my photograph to work from. Whether there's to be a public viewing or not, they generally like to make the body as presentable as possible.'

'The tattoo on the shoulder,' I said. 'The mole on the chin –'

'Easily done.'

Molly had been silently observing this matter-of-fact exchange between her father and her husband, and at this point she began to speak again, her voice tinged with bitterness. 'Ah, yes. The body was in terrible shape after the car crash. Plus which some decompositional bloating had set in.'

She nodded, flashed a broad smile that was not pleasant. Her eyes shone with ferocity. 'It *looked* like Dad, sure, but how closely did either of us look, really? How closely could we *bear* to look at such a time, under such circumstances?' She was staring at me, but at the same time she wasn't seeing me; she was looking *through* me. There was something awful in her tone now: a monotone with underpinnings of steel, anger, sarcasm. 'They bring you into the morgue, they slide open a drawer and unzip the body bag. You see a face, partially destroyed in an explosion, but you see enough of it to say, yeah, sure, that's my own father, that's his nose as far as I can tell, as far as I want to look, that's part of his *mouth*, for Christ's sake! You say to yourself, I'm seeing my own flesh and blood, the man who helped bring me into the world, the guy who gave me piggyback rides, and I never want to remember that I ever saw him this way, but they want me to look, so I'll give a perfunctory look, *there*, now take it away!'

Her father had put one hand up to his craggy face. His eyes were sad. He waited, didn't speak.

I watched my dear Molly, saw she couldn't go on. She was right, of course. It wasn't terribly difficult, I knew, using face masks and what is called the 'restorative art,' to make a cadaver resemble that of another.

'Brilliant,' I said, genuinely impressed, if still thoroughly befuddled.

'Don't credit me,' Sinclair said. 'The idea came from our old enemies in Moscow. You remember that bizarre case they lecture on during training at the Farm, Ben? About the time in the mid-sixties when the Russians had an open-coffin funeral in Moscow of a high-ranking Red Army intelligence officer?'

I nodded.

But he continued, addressing his daughter. 'We sent our spooks ostensibly to pay their respects, but actually to see who turned up at the funeral, take clandestine snapshots, and so on. Apparently this Red Army officer had been a significant American asset for a dozen years.

447

'And then, eight years later, it turned out that the guy was still alive. The whole thing had been an elaborate Soviet counter-intelligence operation, in effect, a sting. Complicated stuff. Evidently they'd made a life mask from the double agent – whom they'd turned into a *triple* in the meantime – and somehow put it on a corpse they happened to have handy. In those days, the good old Brezhnev years, the top brass thought nothing of having a guy shot if they needed to, so maybe they sent out an order for the body of a guy who looked like the mole, I don't know.'

'Wouldn't it have been simpler,' I asked, 'to just say you were so badly burned in the crash that nothing was left to identify?'

'Simpler,' Sinclair said, 'but in the end riskier. An un-identifiable body raises all manner of suspicions.'

'And the photograph?' Molly asked. 'Of you with – your throat slit?'

'These days,' Sinclair said wearily, 'even that's not impos-sible. A contact who was once affiliated with the Media Lab at MIT –'

'Sure,' I said. 'Digital retouching of photographs.'

He nodded; Molly looked puzzled.

I explained: 'You remember a couple of years ago when *National Geographic* ran a photograph on its cover, where they moved the Giza pyramid over a bit so it would fit?'

She shook her head.

'A big controversy in certain circles,' I said. 'Anyway, they're now able to retouch photographs in such a sophisti-cated way that it's pretty much undetectable.'

'That's right,' Sinclair said.

I continued: 'So that the focus would be not on *whether* you'd really been killed, but *how*.'

'Well,' Molly said to her father, 'you fooled me. I thought you'd been murdered, I thought your throat had been slit before the car crash, my own father had been murdered! And here you were all the time, sailing in a lake in Canada.' Her voice grew steadily louder, angrier. 'Was that the point? Was the point to make *me* think you'd been killed? Was the point to do that to your own goddamned daughter?'

448

'Molly –' her father tried to interject.

'To terrify and traumatize your own *daughter*? For *what*?'

'Molly!' he said almost desperately. '*Listen* to me! Please, hear me out. The point was to save my life.'

He took a deep breath, and then began.

65

The room in which we sat – all picture windows and spare, plain wooden furniture – was steadily darkening as dusk approached. Gradually our eyes became used to the darkness. Sinclair did not get up to switch on lights; neither did we. Instead, we sat, transfixed, watching his shadowed form, listening.

'One of the first things I did after moving into the director's office, Ben, was to order up from the archives the sealed transcript of your court-martial fifteen years ago. I'd always had my suspicions about it, and even if you wanted to put the whole thing behind you and never hear another word about it, I wanted to know the truth of what happened that day.

'Had this been the bad old days, the matter would have died there. But the Soviet Union had dissolved, and former Soviet agents were suddenly accessible to us. The trial transcript listed the true identity of the fellow who'd tried to defect – Berzin – and through a complicated channel I won't go into, I managed to contact him.

'Somehow, his own side had learned that he had tried to defect. I assume Toby had informed them. So Berzin was imprisoned – fortunately, they pretty much stopped shooting their own people when Khrushchev came to power – and later released, sent to live in some one-horse town about seventy-five miles north of Moscow.

'Well, the new, post-Soviet government had no interest in him. Therefore, I was able to strike a deal with the guy. I arranged safe passage for him and his wife. In exchange, he gave me the file he'd been trying to sell in Paris – proving that Toby was, or rather, had been, a Soviet asset code-named MAGPIE.'

Molly interrupted, 'But what does that mean, a Soviet "asset"?'

'MAGPIE was no ideological sympathizer of Communism,' Sinclair explained. 'That sort of thing went out in 1956, if not before. Apparently Toby had been caught by a sharp-eyed KGB type embezzling Agency funds. He was given an ultimatum: Either you cooperate with us, or we tell Langley what we know, and face the consequences. Toby chose to cooperate.

'Anyway, this Berzin fellow told me he had a tape of his meeting with you and Toby, and he played it for me. It confirmed everything. You'd been set up. I allowed Berzin to keep the original of the tape – I made a copy – if he would give it directly to you when the time came, when you asked for it.

'I checked, and learned that Toby was not in a sensitive position any longer. He was in charge of certain outside projects that seemed marginal to me – extrasensory perception and the like – and stood no chance of ever coming to fruition.'

'Why didn't you arrest him?' I asked.

'It would have been a mistake,' Sinclair said, 'to arrest him until I had the others. I couldn't risk alerting them.'

'But if Toby was one of the conspirators,' Molly asked me, 'why was he willing to be in such physical proximity to you in Tuscany?'

'Because he knew I was way too drugged to do anything,' I explained.

'What are you talking about?' Sinclair said.

Here Molly turned and gave me a significant glance. I turned away: what was the point of telling him, even if he did believe us?

I said: 'Your letter explained about the gold, about how you helped Orlov get it out. Apparently you wrote that letter right after you met with him in Zurich. What happened after that?'

'I knew the appearance of all that gold in Zurich would set off all kinds of alarms,' he said, 'but I had no idea what that

451

would mean. I sent Sheila over to meet with Orlov, to conduct a second round of negotiations, make final arrangements. Hours after she returned from Zurich, walking near her apartment in Georgetown, she was killed.

'I was heartbroken and terrified. I knew I had gotten in over my head. And I was sure I'd be next. I was witnessing a war over this gold, probably being waged by the Wise Men. I barely could think – I was in a state of shock, grieving for Sheila.

Although I could barely see Hal's face, I could see from his silhouette that his face was drawn, though whether from deep concentration or great tension, I couldn't tell. I focused my mind, trying to pick up any thoughts I could, but there was nothing; he wasn't close enough.

'And then they came after me. It was a matter of hours after Sheila's death – two men broke into my house. I was keeping a gun by my bed, naturally, and I killed one of the attackers. The other one – well, it was a standoff. But obviously he didn't want simply to knock me off; he had more elaborate plans. It had to look like an accident. So he was constrained somewhat.'

'You suborned him,' I said.

Molly said, 'What?'

'Correct,' Hal replied. 'I suborned him. I struck a deal with him. After all, the head of the CIA has his resources, does he not? In essence, I turned him, exactly as I had been taught to do in my tradecrafttraining days. I have my discretionary budgets. I could pay him handsomely – and more important, I could provide him with protection.

'I learned from him that Truslow had sent him to kill me, as he had had Sheila killed. And the gold would be out of my hands, out of American and Russian government hands – and into the hands of the Wise Men. Truslow had already begun his preparations to set me up, having false photos made that showed me in the Cayman Islands, dummied-up computer travel records, and whatnot. He was going to have me killed and then have me take the fall for the missing money.

'I knew then that Truslow was rotten. That he was one of the

Wise Men. That he wouldn't stop until he had gained full possession of the gold. And that I would have to disappear.

'So, I had a photograph created – one that showed me quite convincingly dead. It was all the evidence he needed to take to Truslow to collect his half-million dollars. And once I had "died" – once my look-alike had burned in the car crash – he was safe. For him it was a great deal. As it was for me.'

'Where is he?' Molly asked.

'Somewhere in South America, I believe. Probably Ecuador.'

And for the first time, I heard one of Hal's thoughts, clear as a bell: *I had him killed*.

By now the pieces had begun to fall into place, and I interrupted Sinclair's tale.

'What do you know,' I asked, 'about a German assassin code-named Max?'

'Describe him.'

I did.

'The Albino,' Sinclair replied immediately. 'That's what we used to call him. Real name is Johannes Hesse. Hesse was the Stasi's leading wet-work specialist until the day the Berlin Wall came down.'

'And then?'

'Then he disappeared. Somewhere in Catalonia, en route to Burma, where a number of his Stasi comrades had secured refuge. Went private, we figured.'

'Hired by Truslow,' I said. 'Another question: You expected the Wise Men to search out the gold?'

'Naturally. I wasn't disappointed.'

'How –'

He smiled. 'I hid the account number in several places, places I knew they'd look. The safes in my office and at home. My executive files. Encrypted, of course.'

'To make it plausible,' I said. 'But couldn't someone clever enough find a way to transfer the money out at a great remove? Undetectably?'

'Not the way the account was set up. Once I – or my legal

heirs – accessed the account, it became active, and Truslow could transfer the money. But Truslow would have to go to Zurich personally – and thereby leave his fingerprints.'

'Which is why Truslow needed us to go to Zurich!' I said. 'And why – once we'd activated the account – Truslow's people tried to have me killed. But you must have had a reliable contact in the Bank of Zurich.'

Sinclair nodded wearily. 'I need to get to bed. I need my sleep.'

But I continued: 'And so you had him. You had his "fingerprints," as you put it.'

'Why did you leave the photograph for me in Paris?' Molly asked.

'Simple,' her father replied. 'If I were tracked down and killed here, I wanted to make sure someone – preferably you – showed up here and found the documents I've concealed in the house.'

'So you have the proof?' I asked.

'I have Truslow's signature. It wasn't so bold of him – his people were watching Orlov, and as far as he knew, I was dead.'

'The old woman – Berzin's wife – told me to find Toby. She said he'd cooperate.'

Sinclair had begun to slow down, his eyelids drooping. His head began to nod. 'A possibility,' he said. 'But Toby Thompson tumbled down a steep flight of stairs at his home two days ago. The report is that his wheelchair caught on a corner of a rug. I seriously doubt it was an accident. But in any case, he's dead.'

Molly and I were speechless for a good twenty or thirty seconds. I didn't know what to feel: do you grieve for a man who killed your wife?

Sinclair broke the silence. 'I've got a meeting tomorrow morning with Pierre La Fontaine to make some rather pressing financial arrangements in Montreal.' He smiled. 'Incidentally, the Bank of Zurich has no idea how much gold is in the vault. Five billion dollars' worth was deposited. But a few gold bars are missing – thirty-eight, to be exact.'

'What happened to them?' Molly asked.

'I stole them. Had them removed and sold. At the going gold rate, I netted a little over five million dollars. Given how much gold is in that vault, no one's going to notice what's missing. And I think the Russian government owes it to me –to us – as a commission.'

'How could you?' Molly whispered, aghast.

'It's only a tiny fraction, Snoops. Five million bucks. You've always said you wanted to open a clinic for poor kids, right? So here's the money to do it. Anyway, what's a paltry five million compared with ten billion, right?'

We were all exhausted, and before long Molly and I had fallen asleep in one of the spare bedrooms. The linen closet held bedsheets that were clean and crisply ironed, if somewhat mildew-smelling.

I lay down beside her for a brief nap, after which I planned to draw up a plan of action for the next day. But instead, I slept for several hours, and I was awakened from a dream that had something vaguely to do with some sort of machinery that thumped rhythmically, like a perpetual-motion machine, and by the time I bolted upright in the moonlight that streamed in through the dusty windows, I knew that my dreams had been shaped by a noise from outside. A noise that began faintly grew steadily louder.

A regular thumping. A *whump-whump-whump* sound that was somehow familiar.

The sound of chopper blades.

A helicopter.

It sounded as if it had landed somewhere very near. Was there a helicopter pad on the property? I hadn't seen one. I turned to look out the window, but it faced out onto the lake, and the helicopter sounded as if it were off to one side of the lodge.

Racing out of the bedroom to a window in the hallway, I spied what was unmistakably a helicopter lifting up off a small bluff on the property. It was, I could just barely see, an asphalt-paved helicopter pad, which I hadn't noticed earlier in the day. Was someone arriving?

Had someone arrived?

Or – and the thought jolted me – had someone just left? Hal.

Flinging open the door to Hal's bedroom, I saw that the bed was empty. It was, in fact, made: either he had made it before he left (unlikely) or he hadn't slept at all (far more likely). Next to his closet was a small, neat pile of clothes, as if he had left in some haste.

He was gone. He had obviously arranged this surreptitious middle-of-the-night departure, deliberately without telling us.

But where had he gone?

I felt someone's presence in the room. I turned: Molly stood there, rubbing her eyes with one hand, pulling idly at her hair with another.

She said: 'Where is he, Ben? Where'd he go?'

'I have no idea.'

'But that was him in the helicopter?'

'I assume so.'

'He said he was going to meet with Pierre La Fontaine.'

'In the middle of the night?' I said, running to the telephone. In a few moments I had Pierre La Fontaine's telephone number. I dialed it; it rang for a long time before it was answered, by La Fontaine, in a sleepy voice. I handed the phone to Molly.

'I need to talk to my father,' she said.

A pause.

'He said he was meeting you in Montreal later this morning.'

Another pause.

'Oh, God,' she said, and hung up.

'What?' I asked.

'He says he's supposed to come here to see Hal in three days. They had no plan to meet in Montreal, today or any other day.'

'Why was he lying to us?' I asked.

'Ben!'

Molly held up an envelope addressed to her, which she'd found under the pile of clothes.

456

Inside was a hastily scrawled note:

Snoops – forgive me and understand please – I couldn't tell you two – knew you'd try with all your might to stop me, since you'd already lost me once – later you'll understand – I love you –

Dad

It was Molly who, knowing her father's idiosyncrasies so well – his scrupulous record-keeping – eventually found the thin brown accordion file in a drawer in the room Hal had been using as his study. Among miscellaneous personal documents he'd evidently needed in his seclusion – records of bank accounts, false identity papers, and so on – was a slender sheaf of papers that, taken together, told the entire story:

Apparently, Sinclair had rented a post office box in St.-Agathe under a false name, and in the past two weeks or so he had received a number of documents.

One of them was a photocopied schedule of a public, nationally televised hearing of the Senate Select Committee on Intelligence. The hearing was to take place tonight, in Room 216 of the Hart Office Building, the United States Senate, in Washington.

One item on the schedule was circled in red ink: an appearance at seven this evening – barely fifteen hours from now – by an unspecified 'Witness.'

I knew then.

'The surprise witness,' I murmured aloud.

66

Molly let out a cry.

'No!' she said. 'God, no! He's –'

'We've got to stop him,' I interrupted.

Everything fit together now; everything made terrible sense. Harrison Sinclair – the surprise witness – was the one scheduled to be assassinated. A terrible irony occurred to me: Sinclair, whom we thought we'd buried, was all of a sudden discovered to be alive, and now he would be killed in a matter of hours.

Molly (who must have been struck with this same thought) clasped her hands, held them to her mouth. She bit the knuckle of her index finger, as if to keep from screaming. She began pacing around the study in tight, frantic circles.

'My God,' she whispered. 'My God. What can we do?'

I found myself pacing as well. The last thing I wanted to do now was to further terrify Molly. We both needed to remain calm, think clearly.

'Who can we call?' she said.

I kept pacing.

'Washington,' she said. 'Someone on the Senate committee.'

I shook my head. 'Too dangerous. We don't know who we can trust.'

'Someone in the Agency –'

'That's preposterous!'

She resumed chewing on her knuckle. 'Someone else, then. A friend. Someone who can show up at the hearing –'

'And do what? Go up against a trained assassin? No; we have to catch up with him.'

'But *where*?'

I began to think aloud. 'There's no way he's taking the helicopter to Washington.'

'Why?'

'Too far. Much too far. The helicopter's way too slow.'

'Montreal.'

'Likely. Not definitely, but I'd calculate that there's a high probability the helicopter is taking him to Montreal, where he's either stopping for a while –'

'Or getting onto a plane for Washington. If we check all scheduled flights from Montreal to Washington –'

'Sure,' I said impatiently, '*if* he's taking a commercial flight. More likely, he's chartered a plane.'

'Why? Wouldn't a commercial flight be safer?'

'Yes, but a private plane is much more flexible and anonymous in its own way. I'd charter a plane. All right. Let's assume the chopper's taking him to Montreal.' I looked at my watch. 'Probably he's there by now.'

'But *where*? Which airport?'

'Montreal's got Dorval and Mirabel. That's two airstrips, not to mention any number of small unnamed airstrips between here and Montreal.'

'But there must be a limited number of airplane charter companies listed in Montreal,' Molly said. She pulled a telephone book from the floor, near the couch. 'If we call each one –'

'*No!*' I exclaimed too loudly. 'Most of them won't be answering the phone at this time of night. And who's to say your father made arrangements with a *Canadian* charter company? It might have been any of thousands of U.S. companies!'

Molly sank to the couch, her hands flat against her face. 'Oh, God, Ben. What can we do?'

I looked at my watch again. 'We don't have a choice,' I said. 'We have to get to Washington and stop him there.'

'But we don't know where he's going to *be* in Washington!'

'Sure we do. The Hart Senate Office Building, Room 216, at the Senate Foreign Relations Committee hearings.'

'But *before* that! We have no idea where he's going to be before that!'

She was right, of course. The most we could hope to do was to show up at the hearing room and –

And what?

How in the world could we stop her father, protect him?

The solution, I suddenly realized, was in my head. My heart began to pound with excitement and fear.

A few moments before he was so gruesomely killed, Johannes Hesse, alias 'Max,' had thought that another assassin would take his place.

I couldn't stop Harrison Sinclair, but I could stop his assassin.

If anyone could, I could.

'Get dressed,' I said. 'I've got it figured out.'

It was just after four-thirty in the morning.

67

Three hours later – at almost seven-thirty on the morning of the last day – our small plane touched down in a small airport in rural Massachusetts. Less than twelve hours remained, and although it was an unbroken stretch of time, I feared (with good reason) that it wouldn't be enough.

From Lac Tremblant, Molly had contacted a small private airplane charter company called Compagnie Aéronautique Lanier, based in Montreal, which had advertised the availability of twenty-four-hour emergency call service. Her call had been routed to the firm's on-call pilot and had awakened him. Molly explained that she was a physician who needed to be flown to Montreal's Dorval Airport on an emergency basis. She furnished the exact map coordinates of her father's helipad, and a little over an hour later we were picked up in a Bell 206 Jet Ranger.

At Dorval, we had made arrangements with another charter firm to fly us from Montreal to Hanscom Air Force Base in Bedford, Massachusetts. Given a choice of planes – a Seneca II, a Commander, a King Air prop jet, or a Citation 501 – we chose the Citation, which was by far the fastest, capable of flying at 350 miles per hour. At Dorval, we easily cleared customs: our false American passports (we used Mr and Mrs John Brewer, which still left one virgin set if ever we needed to become the Mr and Mrs Alan Crowells) were barely inspected, and in any case, once Molly explained that it was a medical emergency, we were rushed through.

At Hanscom we rented a car and I drove the thirty miles or so as quickly as I dared, at precisely the speed limit. Once I had fully explained my plan to Molly, we sat in grim silence. She

461

was terrified, but probably saw no logic in quarreling with me, since she was unable to devise any less risky plan to save her father's life. I needed to clear my mind as much as possible, to consider every possibility of failure. I knew that Molly would have appreciated some reassurance now, but I had none to offer, and besides, it was all I could do to think my plan through to its end.

I knew, too, that it would be a disaster to be stopped for speeding. I'd rented the car with a false New York State driver's license and counterfeit Visa credit card. We'd gotten by the car rental agency, but we would not survive the routine license check by a Massachusetts state trooper that inevitably accompanies a speeding ticket. There would be no record in their interstate computer data bank of my license, and the entire game would be over.

So I drove carefully through the morning rush-hour traffic to the town of Shrewsbury. At a little before eight-thirty we drove up to the small yellow ranch-style suburban house that belonged to a man named Donald Seeger.

Seeger was, to be honest, a calculated risk. He was a firearms dealer, the owner of two retail gun shops on the outskirts of Boston. He provided firearms for the state police and, as necessary, the Federal Bureau of Investigation (whenever the FBI needed to procure particular weapons quickly without going through cumbersome bureaucratic channels).

Seeger occupied a peculiar gray area of the legal firearms market, somewhere between the gun manufacturers and retail customers, who for one reason or another require such great discretion that they cannot deal directly either with distributors or the traditional retail outlets.

More important, though, I knew him just well enough to trust him. A law school classmate of mine had grown up in Shrewsbury and knew Seeger as a family friend. Seeger, who rarely dealt with lawyers, and (like virtually everybody, it seems) despised the lot of them, needed some quick (and free) legal advice on dealing with a disgruntled small-arms manufacturer, my law school friend told me. It certainly wasn't my area of expertise, but I had an associate dig up the answer for him. Seeger was duly grateful, and took me out to a thank-you dinner at a good steak house in Boston. 'If I can ever do anything for you,' he told me over filet mignon, hoisting his mug of Bass ale, 'you just give me a call.' At the time, I figured I'd never see the guy again. Now, however, it was time to collect.

His wife answered the door in a faded housedress decorated with tiny blue cornflowers.

'Don's at work,' she said, squinting at us suspiciously. 'He usually leaves between seven-thirty and eight.'

Seeger's office-cum-warehouse was a long, narrow, unmarked brick building on a busy main strip a few miles away, near a Ground Round. To all outside appearances, it might have been a public storage facility, perhaps a dry-cleaning plant, but the security system within was quite sophisticated.

He was naturally surprised to see me when I rang, but rushed toward the door with a broad smile. He was in his early fifties, physically quite fit, with a bull neck. He wore his blue blazer, which was about a size too tight on him, unbuttoned.

'The lawyer, right?' he said, ushering us past metal shelves stacked high with boxes of guns. 'Ellison. What the hell you doing in this neck of the woods?'

I told him what I wanted.

Seeger, who is basically unflappable, paused for an instant, shrewdly assessing me.

He shrugged. 'You got it,' he said.

'One more thing,' I added. 'Would you be able to obtain specifications for a Sirch-Gate III Model SMD200W walk-through metal detector?'

He looked at me for a long, long time.

'I might,' he said.

'It's important.'

'I figured as much. Yeah. I got a friend who's a security consultant. I can get him to fax them over in a couple of minutes.'

I paid in cash, of course. By the time we had finished our transaction, the medical supply house in Framingham, ten miles or so down the road, was open for business.

The shop, which specialized in equipment for invalids, had quite a few wheelchairs on display. Most of them I could rule out at once. Once I explained that I was purchasing one for my father, the salesman immediately recommended that I choose one of the lightweight chairs, which were easier to lift into and out of a car. I told him, however, that my father was particular and not a little eccentric, that he preferred a chair made of as much steel, and as little aluminum, as possible. He wanted something sturdy.

Eventually, I settled on a good, solid, old-fashioned wheelchair made by Invacare. It was extremely heavy; its frame was constructed of brazed, tubular carbon-steel, chrome-plated. But most important, the arm tubing was of sufficient diameter for my purposes.

I loaded it, enormously heavy in its cardboard carton, into the trunk, and dropped Molly at a nearby shopping mall to purchase a number of items: an expensive pin-stripe blue suit two sizes larger than I usually wore, a shirt, cuff links, and a few other things.

While she shopped, I proceeded to a small auto-body garage in nearby Worcester. The owner, a large, rotund ex-convict named Jack D'Onofrio, had been recommended to me by Seeger. He was temperamental, Seeger explained, but a master metal-worker. Seeger had called ahead and informed D'Onofrio that I was a good friend of his, that he should take care of me and I'd take care of him in return.

D'Onofrio, however, was not in good humor. He inspected the wheelchair irritably, distastefully, poking at the gray plastic armrests that were affixed to the steel arm tubing with Phillips-head screws.

'I don't know,' he said at last. 'It's not so easy trying to mill this kind of plastic. I could replace the armrests with teak. Make it a hell of a lot easier.'

I considered for a moment, then said, 'Go ahead.'

'The steel shouldn't be a problem. Cut and weld. But I'll have to change the diameter of the front tubing.'

'The join must not show, even at close inspection,' I said. 'What about using a surgical hacksaw to cut the tubing?'

'That's what I planned to do.'

'Good. But we need it in an hour or two.'

'An *hour*?' he gasped. 'You gotta be fucking kidding.' He waved his short, pudgy arms around the cluttered shop. 'Looka this. We're jammed. Totally raked. Up to our fucking eyeballs!'

An hour, even two hours, was pressing it, but not impossible. He was negotiating, of course. I had no time to waste, however. I pulled out an envelope of bills and flashed them.

'We're prepared to pay a premium,' I said.

'I'll see what I can do.'

The final meeting was the most difficult to arrange, and in some ways the riskiest. From time to time police forces, the FBI, and the CIA must call upon the services of specialists in undercover disguise techniques. Usually, they are trained in the theater, in makeup and prosthesis application, but undercover disguise is a highly specialized and rare art. The artist must be able to transform an undercover officer into someone else entirely unrecognizable, capable of withstanding the closest scrutiny. The techniques are therefore limited, and the artists few.

Perhaps the best, a man who had done occasional work for the CIA (as well as a long list of movie and television stars and several prominent religious and political leaders), had retired to Florida, I discovered. Finally, after several telephone calls to Boston costume and theatrical companies, I turned up the name of an old vet, a Hungarian named Ivo Balog, who had done some work for the FBI, so he was familiar with the requisite artistry. He had, I was informed, enabled the same FBI undercover officer to infiltrate a Providence-based Mafia family not once but twice. This was good enough for me. He worked out of an old office building in downtown Boston, as part owner of a theatrical makeup company. I reached him shortly before noon.

Since there was no time to drive into Boston and back, we arranged to have him meet me at a Holiday Inn in Worcester, where I had reserved a room for the day and night. In order to make time for me, he had to clear the remainder of his day; I let him know it would be more than worth his while.

'We have to split up,' I told Molly when we reached the Holiday Inn. 'You finalize the flight arrangements. Meet me back here when you're done.'

Ivo Balog was in his late sixties, with the coarse features and reddened complexion of a heavy drinker. It became apparent at once, however, that whatever Balog's personal failings, he was indeed a wizard.

Meticulous and acutely intelligent, he spent perhaps a quarter of an hour simply studying my face and form before even opening his makeup case.

'But who will you be *exactly*?' Balog demanded.

My answer, which I thought was perfectly reasoned out, did not satisfy him. 'What does the person you wish to become do for a *living*?' he asked. 'Where does he live? Is he wealthy or not? Does he smoke? Is he married?'

We conversed for several minutes, concocting this false biography. Several times he objected to my suggestions, saying over and over again, his mantra, in his thickly accented English: 'No. The essence of good design is *simplicity*.'

Balog bleached the color out of my dark brown hair and eyebrows and then combed gray dye through them. 'I can add ten, perhaps fifteen years to your age,' he cautioned. 'Anything more will be dangerous.'

He had no idea why I was doing this, but he unquestionably sensed the tension in both of us. I appreciated his thoroughness and caution.

He applied a chemical artificial-tanning lotion to my face, dabbing it on carefully to avoid any telltale lines. 'This will take at least two hours to develop,' he said. 'I assume we have that much time.'

'Yes,' I said.

'Good. Let me see the clothes you'll be wearing.'

He inspected the suit and highly polished black shoes, nodding with approval. Then he thought of something. 'But the armor –'

'Here,' I said, holding up the Safariland 'Cool Max' T-shirt, made of ultra-lightweight Spectra fiber, which Seeger had assured me is ten times stronger than steel.

'Nice,' Balog said admiringly. 'Quite slim.'

By the time the tanning creme had done its work, Balog had applied enamel paint to darken my teeth and had fitted me with a fully realistic-appearing, neatly trimmed salt-and-pepper-gray beard and a pair of horn-rimmed glasses.

When Molly returned to the room, she did a true double take, her hand to her mouth.

'My God,' she said. 'You fooled *me* for a second!'

'A second's not good enough,' I said, then turned to look at myself for the first time in the hotel room mirror. I too was astonished. The transformation was nothing short of extraordinary.

'The chair's in the trunk,' she said. 'You're going to have to give it a careful inspection. Listen . . .' She glanced at the makeup artist warily. I asked him to step into the hallway for a few moments so we could talk.

'What is it?' I asked.

'There was a problem with the hearing,' she said. 'Ordinarily, Senate hearings are open to the public, except for those designated specifically as closed. But this time for some reason – maybe because it's being televised live – they're admitting only members of the press and "invited guests." '

I replied calmly, unwilling to succumb to panic. 'You said *was*. "There *was* a problem." '

Her smile was wan; something was still troubling her. 'I placed a call to the office of the junior senator from the Commonwealth of Massachusetts,' she said. 'I told him I was the administrative assistant to a Dr Charles Lloyd of Weston, Massachusetts, who's in Washington for the day and wants to see a real-live Senate hearing in action. The senator's people are always delighted to do a favor for a constituent. A Senate pass is waiting for you at the hearing room.'

She leaned over and kissed me on the forehead.

'Thanks,' I said. 'But I don't have any ID in that name, and there's no time to –'

'They won't be requesting ID at the security check. I asked – I told them your wallet had been pickpocketed; they suggested you call the D.C. police about that. Anyway, they never request ID for admittance to open hearings – they rarely require passes, for that matter.'

'And what if they check and discover there's no such person?'

'They won't check, and even if they did, there *is* such a person. Charlie Lloyd is the chief of the surgical division at Mass. General Hospital. He always spends the entire month in the South of France. I double-checked. Right now Dr Lloyd and his wife are vacationing in the Îles d'Hyères, off the coast of Toulon, on the Côte d'Azur. Of course, his answering service is instructed only to tell callers he's out of town. No one likes to hear that their surgeon's boozing it up in Provence or whatever.'

'You're a genius.'

She bowed modestly. 'Thank you. Now, about the flight –'

I sensed immediately from her tone that all was not right. 'No, Molly. There isn't a hitch in the *flight*, is there?'

She replied with a sudden edge of hysteria. 'I called every single charter company within a hundred-mile radius. I could find only *one* that had a plane available at this late notice. Everyone else has been booked for at least a week.'

'So you booked that plane, I assume . . . ?'

She hesitated. 'Yes. I did. But it's not nearby. The company's at Logan Airport.'

'That's an hour away!' I thundered. I looked at my watch; it was after three o'clock in the afternoon. We had to be at the Senate before seven. That left us only four hours! 'Tell them to have the plane meet us at Hanscom. Pay whatever they ask. Just *do* it!'

'I *did* it!' Molly exploded in return. 'I *did* it, dammit! I offered to *double*, even *triple* their rates! But the only plane they had – a twin engine Cessna 303 – wasn't going to be available until noon or one, and then it had to be fueled and whatever else they –'

'*Shit*, Molly! We have to be in Washington by six o'clock at the latest! Your goddamned *father* –'

'I know!' She had raised her voice almost to a shriek; tears were coursing down her cheeks. 'You think I'm not aware of that every *second*, Ben? The plane'll be there at Hanscom in half an hour.'

'That barely gives us enough time! The flight takes something like two and a half hours!'

'There's a regular commercial shuttle leaving Boston every half hour, for God's sake! There should be no problem –'

'*No!* We can't take a commercial flight. That's insane. At *this* point? It's far too risky, if for no other reason than the guns.' Once again I looked at my watch and did a swift calculation. 'If we leave now, we should just barely make it to the Senate.'

I let Balog in, paid him, thanked him for his speedy assistance, and showed him out.

'Let's get the hell out of here,' I said.

It was ten minutes after three.

68

At a few minutes past three-thirty, we were airborne.

Molly had, as usual, come through in the clutch. The architectural plans of all public buildings in Washington, D.C., are a matter of public record, filed in the city records bureau. The problem, however, is obtaining them; but a number of private firms in Washington specialize in such searches for a fee. While I was becoming a dignified, wheelchair-bound older man, Molly had contacted one of these firms and – at an exorbitant cost for expediting the service – had had them fax her, at a local copy shop, photocopies of the blueprints of the Hart Senate Office Building.

While that was in the works, she had, posing as an editor of *The Worcester Telegram*, contacted the office of the senator from Ohio who served as vice-chairman of the Select Committee on Intelligence. The senator's press aide was more than happy to fax this editor the latest schedule for tonight's historic hearing.

Thank God, I told myself, for facsimile technology.

During the two-and-a-half-hour flight, we scrutinized the schedule and the plans until I felt sure my plan was workable.

It seemed to be foolproof.

At 6:45, the chair-car van I had hired at the airport pulled up to the entrance of the Hart Senate Office Building. A few minutes earlier, the driver had, as we requested, dropped Molly off several blocks away at a car-rental agency. She was angry about this aspect of my plan: if I was risking my life to save that of her father's, why should she be reduced to, in effect, driving the getaway car? She had done that in Baden-Baden, and didn't want to do it again.

'I don't want you there,' I told her on the way to the Capitol. 'Only one of us should be subjected to this danger.'

She sputtered in protest, but I went on: 'And even if you *were* in disguise, it's way too risky for both us to be there. People are going to be watching very closely – we can't afford to be seen together. Either one of us might be recognized; having two of us there at least doubles the chance that we'll be spotted. And this is a job that requires only one person.'

'But if you don't know the identity of the assassin, why is the disguise necessary?'

'There will be others – working for Truslow or the Germans – who will no doubt be briefed on my appearance. And who'll be instructed to find me – and to eliminate me,' I replied.

'All right. But I still don't understand why you can't just smuggle a gun through the press gallery and take out the assassin. I doubt there's a metal detector there.'

'Maybe there is a metal detector there tonight, though I doubt it. But in any case, it isn't just a matter of smuggling a gun in. The press gallery's on the second floor – too far away from the witness stand. And too far away from where the assassin will have to be stationed.'

'Too far?' Molly objected. 'You're a good enough shot. Christ, *I'm* a good enough shot!'

'That's not the point,' I said abruptly. 'I have to be there, in proximity to the assassin, in order to determine which one he is. The press gallery's too distant.'

I had overruled her, and she had reluctantly acquiesced. In matters of medicine she was the expert; in this *I* was – or, at least, I *had* to be.

The Capitol was lit up as I approached, its dome brilliant against the evening dusk. The traffic was snarled with weary commuters trying to get home from their government jobs.

Outside the Hart building a large crowd had gathered: spectators, onlookers, what appeared to be members of the press. A long line snaked out the door, presumably people waiting to be admitted to Room 216, dignitaries and the well connected who'd been issued special passes.

It was a glittery crowd, and no surprise: tonight's

extraordinary hearing was a hot ticket in Washington, gathering as it did some of the leading power brokers in the nation's capital.

Including the new Director of Central Intelligence, Alexander Truslow, who had just returned from a visit to Germany.

Why was he here?

Two of the four major American television networks were carrying the coverage live, preempting regularly scheduled programming.

How would the world react when they saw that the surprise witness was none other than the late Harrison Sinclair? The shock would be extraordinary.

But it would be as nothing compared with the assassination of Sinclair on live television.

When would he come out?

And from where?

How could I possibly stop him, *protect* him, if I didn't know when and how he would appear?

The driver secured my wheelchair to the platform at the back of the van and electrically lowered it to the ground. It gave off a high mechanical whine. Then he detached the wheelchair and helped me up the ramp. When he had wheeled me into the crowded entrance lobby, I paid him, and he left.

I felt exposed and vulnerable and deeply afraid.

For Truslow and his people, and the new Chancellor of Germany, the stakes were enormous. They could not risk exposure, that was certain. Two men – two insignificant men, really – stood between them and their own particular version of global conquest. Between them and dividing up the spoils of a new world; between them and an incalculable fortune. Not a measly five or ten billion, but hundreds of billions of dollars.

What, compared to that, were the lives of two spooks, Benjamin Ellison and Harrison Sinclair?

Was there any question now that they'd stop at nothing to have us, as they say in the spy business, neutralized?

No.

And there, in the room just beyond the crowd in which I sat, beyond the two sets of metal detectors, beyond the two rings of security guards, sat Alexander Truslow, beginning his opening remarks. No doubt his own security people were planted everywhere.

So where was the assassin?

And *who* was the assassin?

My mind raced. Would they recognize me despite the precautions I'd taken to disguise myself?

Would I be recognized?

It seemed unlikely. But fear is irrational sometimes, not subject to logic.

To all appearances, I was an amputee in a wheelchair. I had bound my legs underneath me, so that I was sitting on them. The wheelchair I had selected was wide enough to accommodate this. Balog, the makeup wizard, had hastily tailored the suit pants so that they looked like the sort of adaptation a real amputee would have made to an elegant suit. A lap blanket completed the effect. No one would be looking for a legless older man in a wheelchair.

My hair was quite convincingly gray, as was my beard, and the age wrinkles in my skin could withstand the closest scrutiny. My hands bore slight liver spots. My horn-rimmed glasses imparted a professorial dignity that, in combination with everything else, utterly altered my appearance. Balog had refused to do anything less subtle than that, and now I was glad of it. I appeared to be a diplomat or a business executive, a man in his late fifties or early sixties who had unfairly suffered the ravages of aging. In no way did I look like Benjamin Ellison.

Or so I was convinced.

Toby Thompson, of course, had been my inspiration for the disguise. A man I would never see again, never be able to confront directly. He had been killed, but he had given me an idea.

A man in a wheelchair both attracts attention and deflects it. This is one of the quirks of human nature. People turn to stare at you, but just as quickly – as anyone who's ever been wheelchair bound will tell you – they look away, as if embarrassed to be caught staring. As a result, the person in the wheelchair often attains a peculiar anonymity.

I had taken care, too, to arrive as late as possible, though, of course, not too late. An excess of time spent sitting in the hearing room, where I stood a chance, however small, of being recognized, would be dangerous.

I had taken another precaution as well, which was Molly's idea. Since one of the most powerful human senses is that of smell, which often works on us subliminally, she had suggested placing a small quantity of an acrid, medicinal-smelling chemical on the seat of the chair. This hospital odor would, subtly and unstatedly, complete my disguise. It was, I thought, brilliant.

Now I waited in the milling crowd, looking around with *gravitas* befitting my imagined station for a place to enter the line. A middle-aged couple kindly gestured to me to get in line ahead of them. I took them up on their offer, wheeled myself over, and thanked them.

There was a long table by the metal detectors, manned by young Capitol Hill staffers who were giving out pale blue passes to those on their lists of invited guests. When the line had reached the table, I took my card in the name of Dr Charles Lloyd of Massachusetts General Hospital, Boston.

One by one, people were being guided through the metal detector. As occasionally happens, there were several false alarms. A man ahead of me passed through the gate and set off the alarm. He was asked to remove all keys and change from his pockets. From the specs Seeger had provided for me, I knew that the metal detector was a Sirch-Gate III, that at its center it was sensitive enough to detect 3.7 ounces of stainless steel. I knew, too, that the security precautions would be extensive.

Hence, of course, the wheelchair. I knew that Toby had on more than one occasion carried a pistol through airport metal detectors simply by placing it beneath a sheet of lead foil under his chair's seat cushion. I didn't dare be quite that bold, though. A gun thus concealed would be too easily discovered in a perfunctory search.

The American Derringer Model 4, which is quite an unusual gun, had been built into an arm of the wheelchair. It would be indistinguishable from the surrounding steel.

So as I wheeled up to the search gate, I remained fairly confident that the gun would not be found.

But my heart pounded loudly and swiftly in my chest. It filled my ears with a rapid, thunderous beat that blocked out all other sounds.

I felt a rivulet of sweat run down my forehead, over my left eyebrow, and drop into my eye.

No, my heartbeat could not be heard. But my sudden perspiration was evident to all. Any security agent trained to look for signs of stress or nervousness would zero in on me. Why was this prosperous-looking gentleman in a wheelchair sweating so heavily? The lobby was neither stuffy nor particularly hot; in fact, a cool breeze ran through it.

I should have taken something to control my autonomic nervous responses, but I couldn't take the chance of dulling my reactions.

And as beads of sweat rolled down my face, one of the security guards, a young black man, beckoned me over to one side.

'Sir?' he said.

I glanced over at him, smiled pleasantly, and wheeled myself toward where he stood, on one side of the metal detector.

'Your pass, please?'

'Surely,' I said, and handed him the pale blue card. 'God, when does winter come? I simply can't bear this weather.'

He nodded distractedly, looked quickly at the pass, and handed it back. 'I love it just this temperature,' he replied. 'Wish it could stay like this all year. Winter gets here all *too* soon – I hate cold weather myself.'

'I love it,' I said. 'I used to love skiing.'

He smiled apologetically. 'Sir, are you . . .'

I guessed at what he was trying to say. 'I can't get out of this damned thing easily, if that's what you mean.' I smacked the gleaming teak armrests, in imitation of Toby. 'Hope I'm not disrupting anything.'

'No, sir, not at all. Obviously you can't go through the gate. I'm supposed to use one of those hand-held deals.'

He was referring to the Search Alert hand-held metal detection unit, which emitted an oscillating tone. When it came near metal, the frequency of the tone shot up.

'Go right ahead,' I said. 'Again, sorry about all the inconvenience.'

'No problem, man. No problem at all. *I'm* sorry to have to do this to you. It's just that they're stepping up security tonight for some reason.' From a table next to the gate he took the small hand-held device, a box attached to a long U-shaped metallic loop. 'You'd think it'd be enough they make you get these passes. But they're juicing up all the security. There's another gate up there' – he pointed at the security station at the entrance to the hearing room a few yards away – 'so you're gonna have to go through this all over again. Guess you're used to it, huh?'

'It's the least of my problems,' I said placidly.

The device whined as he brought it near me, and I tensed. He ran it up my legs, over my knees, and suddenly, when it got to my thighs – and the concealed pistol – the box whooped up to a high pitch.

'What've we got here?' he muttered more to himself than to me. 'Damn thing's too sensitive. The metal in the chair's setting it off.'

And as I sat there, dripping with sweat, the blood rushing in my ears, I suddenly heard the amplified voice of Alexander Truslow, coming from the loudspeaker system in the hall.

'. . . wish to thank the committee,' he was saying, 'for calling public attention to this grave problem besetting the agency I so love.'

The guard dialed down the sensitivity knob and ran it over me again.

Once again, as it neared the arm of the chair, where the gun was concealed, it emitted a shrill metallic wail.

I tensed again, and felt droplets of sweat falling off my brow, my ears, the end of my nose.

'Goddamned thing,' the guard said. 'Pardon my French, sir.'

Truslow's voice again, clear and melodious:

'. . . certainly make my own job easier. Whoever this witness is, and whatever the substance of his testimony, it can only benefit us.'

'If you don't mind,' I said, 'I'd love to get in there before Truslow's finished his testimony.'

He stepped back, switched the machine off in frustration, and said exasperatedly: 'I hate those things. Go on around this way.' He escorted me around the metal detector gate. I nodded, cocked my head gamely in a kind of salute, and wheeled ahead to the next security station. It seemed to be a bottleneck; a sizable crowd was gathered there. Some of them were craning their necks, trying to see into the hearing room. What was the problem? What was the delay?

Again Truslow's voice over the loudspeakers, calm and gracious: '. . . any testimony that can fling open the shutters and let in the light of day.'

Inwardly I cursed, my whole body screaming: Move it, damn it! Move! The assassin was already in place, and in a matter of *seconds* Molly's father would walk into the room.

And here I was, detained by a bunch of rent-a-cops!

Move, goddamn it!

Move!

Again I was waved around to the side of the metal detector gate. This time it was a woman, white, middle-aged, with brassy blond hair, a buxom figure within an ill-fitting blue uniform.

She inspected my pass sourly, glanced up at me, and summoned someone over.

Here I was, a matter of feet, mere *feet*, from the entrance to Room 216, and this goddamned woman was taking her goddamned *time*.

From the hearing room I heard a loud gaveling. A murmur in the crowd. The sudden dazzlingly bright flash of cameras.

What was it?

Had Hal arrived in the room?

What the hell was going on?

'Please,' I said as the woman returned with another middle-

477

aged woman, this one black and of thinner build, apparently her superior. 'I'd like to get inside as soon as possible.'

'Hold on a second,' the blond woman said. 'Sorry.'

She turned to her boss, who said, 'I'm sorry, Mister, but you're going to have to wait until the next recess.'

'I don't understand,' I said. *No!* It couldn't *be*!

From the hearing room, the stentorian tones of the committee counsel: 'Thank you, Mr Director. We all appreciate your coming here and lending your support to what can only be a painful time for the Central Intelligence Agency. At this point, with no further ado, we would like to bring in our final witness of these hearings. I would ask that there be no flash photography, and that everybody in the room please remain seated while –'

'But I have to get in there!' I objected.

'I'm sorry, sir,' the boss objected, 'but we have our instructions not to admit anyone further at this time, until there's a recess called or a break of some kind. I'm sorry.'

I sat, almost paralyzed with fear and anxiety, looking beseechingly at the two security guards.

In just seconds, now, Molly's father would be murdered.

I couldn't just sit here. I had come to far – *we* had come too far – to let this happen.

I had to do something.

69

Staring them down, eyes flashing with indignation, I said:
'Look, it's a medical emergency.'

'Of what sort, sir –'

'It's *medical*, dammit. It's *personal*. I don't have any *time*!' I
indicated my lap – my bladder, or my bowels, or whatever they
chose to conclude.

This was a desperate move. I knew from the blueprints that
there was no public rest room in the lobby. The only one
equipped for the handicapped was outside the hearing room.
But there was a public facility two flights up, which I could get
to without going through security. I knew that, but would
they? It was a calculated risk. And if they did?

The black woman shrugged, then grimaced.

'All right, sir –'

I felt my body flood with relief

' – go on through. There's a men's rest room off to the left
that has handicapped facilities. But, please, don't enter the
hearing room until . . .'

I didn't wait for her to finish. With a great spurt of energy I
wheeled off to the left, toward the entrance to the hearing
room.

Another guard manned the entrance. From where I sat, I
had an excellent vantage point. Room 216 of the Hart Senate
Office Building was a spacious, modern, two-floor chamber
built with television in mind. Standing floodlights illuminated
the entire room, for the sake of the television cameras. There
were panels inset in the walls for cameras to be trained down
on the hearing room; and, on the second floor, the press
gallery, behind plate glass and toward the rear of the room.

Where was he?

The press gallery? Had the assassin been infiltrated using false press credentials? Easily done, of course, but too far from the front of the room for an accurate shot.

He would almost certainly have to be using a small firearm, probably a handgun. Anything else would be too detectable within the space of the room. This was not a classic sniper situation with a rooftop and a rifle. He would have to use a pistol. Somehow he had to have smuggled a pistol into the room.

Which meant he would have to be within the killing field. He would have to be located somewhere at close range. In theory, a handgun is accurate at distances of three hundred feet or more, but the closer you can get, the more accurate, the more reliable, the shot.

Now I was out of the line of sight of the security guards who had admitted me through the second checkpoint.

Swallowing hard, I wheeled up the ramp and directly into the room.

Another uniformed guard stood by the entrance.

'Excuse me –'

But this time I plunged ahead, ignoring the guard. My calculation was accurate: he would not leave his post to chase down a man in a wheelchair.

Now I was in the main room. I scanned the crowded rows of seats. It was impossible to see everyone, but I knew he had to be here, *had* to be here somewhere!

Where – who – was the assassin?

Seated among the spectators?

I turned now toward the front of the room, where the senators sat at a raised mahogany semicircle. Some of them consulted notes; others held their hands over microphones planted in front of them as they chatted.

Behind them, against the wall, was a row of aides, well-dressed young men and women. In front of the high mahogany podium was a row of three stenographers, two women and one man, sitting at their keyboards, typing away silently with lightning speed.

And behind the row of senators, at the precise center, was a door, toward which the eyes of all spectators were trained. The room fairly crackled with tension. That was the door through which the senators entered. It had to be the door through which Sinclair would enter.

The assassin had to be within a hundred feet or so of that door.

So where the hell was he?

And *who* the hell was he?

I looked over toward the witness table, which faced the row of senators. It was empty, awaiting the surprise witness. Behind it was an empty row of chairs, cordoned off, probably for security reasons. A few rows behind the witness table I saw Truslow, dressed immaculately in a double-breasted suit. Despite having just returned from Germany, he didn't look a bit tired; his silver hair was combed and parted neatly. Was there a glint of triumph, of satisfaction, in his eyes? Beside him sat his wife, Margaret, and a couple I took to be his daughter and son-in-law.

I wheeled slowly down the side aisle, toward the front of the room. People glanced toward me, then quickly away, in that manner I'd become accustomed to.

It was time to begin.

Once again I scanned the layout of the entire room, affixing it pictorially in my memory. There was a limited number of positions from which a gunman could fire, hit his target – and plausibly attempt to escape.

I breathed deeply, tried to get my thoughts in some semblance of order. Rule out any positions beyond three hundred feet.

No – rule out any beyond *two* hundred feet. And within *one* hundred feet, the odds increased astronomically.

All right. Of those positions within one hundred feet, by far the most likely were those situated close to an exit. That meant, since the only exits were in the front or in the back, that the gunman would very likely be seated or standing front-center, front-right, or front-left.

Next . . . of those, rule out any without a direct line of fire

481

to the witness stand. Which meant I could safely rule out ninety-five percent of the seats in the room.

From where I was I could see mostly backs of heads. The assassin might be a man or a woman, which meant I couldn't rely on the standard search-image – the youngish, physically fit male. No; they were too clever. I couldn't discount the possibility that it was a woman.

Children were rule-outs . . . but an adult midget might pose as a child: bizarre, yes, but I could not afford to rule out the bizarre. Everyone within the area I had selected would have to be scrutinized. Systematically, I sighted each person in a strategic firing position, and was able to rule out only two: a young girl in a Peter Pan collar who really was a young girl; and a distinguished-looking old woman who my instincts told me really was an old woman.

If my calculations were right, then, that brought the pool of likely suspects down to perhaps twenty individuals, all near the front of the room.

Move.

I accelerated the wheelchair's pace until I neared the front. Then I slowed, and veered the chair to within a few inches of the people seated at the ends of the aisles.

Here and there I felt a jolt of recognition, but the audience, naturally, was filled with familiar faces. Not friends of mine, certainly, but dignitaries. Personalities. The sort of people who are written up in *The Washington Post* Style section, who appear on *Larry King Live*.

Where was he?

Focus. Dammit, I had to *focus*, to concentrate my powers of perception, to parse the ambient room noise from thought noise. And then separate the usual babble of human thought from the thoughts of a man or woman who was preparing to carry out a public, excruciatingly tense, methodically executed assassination. These would be the thoughts of someone concentrating with great intensity.

Focus.

Nearing a man in a three-piece suit – sandy-haired and early thirties, the build of a football player, seated at the end of the fourth row – I bowed my head and rolled by slowly as if I were finding it difficult to maneuver.

And heard: . . . *make partner or not and when? Because ah sweet Jesus if I don't know by* . . . An attorney; Washington crawled with them.

Keep on.

Next, a scruffy-looking late-teenage boy, acne-scarred face, dressed in an army-navy surplus pea coat. Too young? And it came: *won't call me because I'm not going to call her first* . . .

A woman who looked to be in her late fifties, primly dressed, sweet face, ruby red lipstick. *Poor man how does he get around the poor soul?* She was thinking about *me*, it had to be.

I rolled a little faster now, head still bowed.

fucking nest of spies hope they fucking do away with the goddamn thing totally. A tall man in his late forties in a workshirt, earring in his left ear, ponytail.

Was he possible? Not what I expected; not the intense, laser-beam concentration of a professional killer.

I stopped two feet from him, focused.

Focused.

get home I finish the piece tonight maybe revise tomorrow morning see what the Times *op-ed editor thinks.*

No. A writer, a political activist. Not a killer.

Now I had reached the front row and began slowly to wheel down the aisle, across the very front of the room, extremely conspicuous.

People were staring at me, wondering where I was going. *Guy's going to just wheel all the way across are they allowed to do that?*

And: *so close to all these senators how can I get closer –*

Stop!

get their autographs if they'll let me . . .

Move.

An ash blond woman in her fifties, anorexic-looking, with sunken cheeks, the too-tight facial skin that comes from excessive plastic surgery – a Washington socialite, from the look of her: . . . *chocolate mousse with raspberry sauce or maybe a nice big slab of apple flan with a mountain of vanilla ice cream and don't I deserve it I've been so good . . .*

I rolled faster, and faster, concentrating with all my might, glancing at the faces intermittently, head bowed, listening. The thoughts were coming in a torrent now, a confusing, kaleidoscopic, almost psychedelic rush of emotions and ideas and notions, glimmerings of the most private feelings, the most banal contemplations, anger, love, suspicion, excitement . . .

. . . promoted over me how can . . .

Faster.

. . . from the darned Department of Justice if . . .

Move!

Again and again my eyes swept the rows of spectators, then the row of well-dressed senatorial aides, then the stenographers seated before the mahogany podium at their silent keyboards, all of whom were bowed in ferocious concentration over their keyboards.

No.

didn't put anything in writing and there shouldn't be any records . . .

A murmur swept the room. I looked up toward the front of the room as I advanced across the front row of spectators, and saw the door at the front of the room open a crack.

Faster.

. . . Kay Graham's dinner party when the Vice President asked me . . .

I swiveled my head from side to side desperately. Where was the gunman? No sign of him yet, not a sign, and Hal was about to appear, and it would all be over!

. . . the legs on that babe if there's any way to get her phone number maybe I can ask Myrna to call personnel but then won't she . . .

And suddenly, with a jolt, I saw that I had completely overlooked the most obvious place of all! I whirled my head toward the podium, toward the steno pool, and when I noticed an odd discrepancy, I felt my stomach muscles tense.

Three stenographers. Two of them, the two women, were

typing away furiously, the continuous folded sheets of paper moving up out of their stenotype machines and around to the receptacle tray.

One of them, however, did not seem to be working. He, a dark-haired young man, was looking up at the door. Odd that he would have the leisure to look around when his colleagues did not; how easy it would be to insert a professional gunman into the stenographic pool. Why the hell hadn't I thought of it? I jerked my chair toward him wildly, studying him in quarter profile, and the stenographer glanced idly around at the audience, and . . .

. . . and I heard something.

Not from the stenographer, who was too far away for me to read his thoughts. But over my left shoulder, just ahead.

Zwölf.

Just a blip of a word, seemingly a nonsense word at first, but then it came clear: it was German. A number. Twelve.

Elf.

There it was again, from over my shoulder. Eleven. Someone was counting in German.

I whipped the chair back around, away from the row of senators, toward the audience. Someone seemed to be striding toward me; I could see a shape in my peripheral vision. And a voice, spoken: 'Sir? Sir?'

Zehn.

A security guard was moving toward me, gesturing to me to move out of the front of the room. A security guard, tall and crew cut, dressed in a gray suit, holding a walkie-talkie transmitter.

Where the hell? Where the hell? I ran my eyes up and down the front row, looking for a likely gunman, and glimpsed a pleasingly familiar face, probably someone I knew, some old friend, and kept searching –

And heard: *Acht Sekunden bis losschlagen*. Eight seconds to strike.

And saw that pleasingly familiar face again, and recognized it; Miles Preston. Just a few feet away.

My old drinking buddy, the foreign correspondent I had befriended in Leipzig, East Germany, years ago.

485

Miles Preston?

Why was he here? If he was covering the event, why wasn't he in the press gallery? Why would he be here?

No, of course.

The press gallery was located too far away.

The foreign correspondent I had befriended . . . No. He had befriended *me*.

He had come up to *me*, sitting alone at the bar. Introduced himself.

And then he was in Paris when I was there.

He had been *assigned* to me, a brand-new CIA boy. A classic black cultivation. His job had been to cultivate a friendship, subtly learn what he could –

Foreign correspondent: an ideal cover.

The security guard began to lope toward me, quickly and with great determination.

Miles Preston, who knew so much about Germany.

Miles Preston was not a British subject. He was – he had to be – a Stasi plant, a German agent, now gone freelance. *He was thinking in German*.

Zwölf Kugeln in der Pistole. Twelve bullets in the chamber.

And our eyes locked.

Sechs.

I recognized Miles, and he – I was sure – he recognized me. Beneath my disguise, my gray hair and beard and glasses, it was my eyes, the glint of recognition in my eyes, that identified me.

He gave me a cold, almost impassive stare, his eyes narrowing slightly. Then returned his fierce gaze to the precise center of the room. To the door that was now open a crack.

It *was* him!

Ich werde nicht mehr als zwei brauchen. I will need no more than two.

A man emerged from the door at the front of the room.

The room broke out in excited whispers. Spectators craned their necks, struggling to get a glimpse.

Sicherung gelöst. Safety off.

It was the chairman of the committee, a tall, gray-haired,

barrel-chested man in a dove-gray suit. I recognized him as the Democratic senator from New Mexico. He was engaged in conversation with someone entering behind him, a man in shadow.

Gespannt. Cocked.

But I recognized the silhouette.

Ausgang frei. Exit clear.

The man behind him was Hal Sinclair. The audience had yet to realize who it was, but in a second or two they would. And Miles Preston would –

No! I had to act *now*!

Hier kommt er. Los. Here he comes – now! *Bereit zu feuern*. Ready to fire.

And then Harrison Sinclair, tall and proud, dressed immaculately, his beard shaven, his hair neatly trimmed, strode slowly through the door, accompanied by a bodyguard.

There was an audible gasp throughout the crowd, and then the hearing room erupted.

70

The room was in an uproar, whispers becoming loud murmurings and excited exclamations, steadily louder and louder.

The unthinkable. The surprise witness was . . . a dead man. A man the nation had buried, had mourned, months ago.

The press gallery was in turmoil. Several people at the back of the room were running out, probably to place telephone calls.

Sinclair and the committee chairman, cognizant of the commotion Sinclair's appearance had caused, but oblivious of what was about to happen, continued walking across the hearing room floor to the witness box, where Hal was to be sworn in.

As the crew-cut guard rushed toward me, his hand at his holster, closing the gap between us, coming closer and closer . . .

Miles had gotten to his feet, unnoticed in all the pandemonium. Reached his hand inside the breast pocket of his suit jacket.

Now!

I depressed the button at the front of the right armrest, which caused the teak panel to flip upward, exposing the gun, grip up, barrel down, fitting snugly into the metal arm tubing.

Two shots only.

That was the drawback of the American Derringer, but it was a price I had to pay.

It was already cocked. I drew it out, slid the safety to the side with my thumb, and –

There was no clear line of fire between me and the assassin!
The guard, loping toward me, was blocking my path!

And suddenly, the chaos, the anarchy, was pierced by an earsplitting scream, a female cry from somewhere above us, and hundreds of heads were turned upward toward where the shrieking was coming from. It was coming from one of the square holes in the walls, one of the niches for television cameras, but there was no camera lens jutting out of this one; instead, it was a woman, shouting at the top of her lungs.

'Sinclair! Get down! Dad!

'He's got a gun!

'Get down!

'They're going to kill you!

'Get down!'

Molly!

How the hell did she get in here?

But there was no time even to think. The crew-cut guard froze, turned to his right, looked up in confusion, and now for an instant, for a split second, the target was clear.

– and at that instant, pointing the gun directly at the assassin, I fired.

It was not a bullet that I fired.

No, there was far too great a chance of missing with a bullet.

It was a specially configured .410 Magnum shotgun shell, containing one-half ounce of lead pellets. One hundred and twelve pellets.

A shotgun shell in a pistol.

The explosion filled the room, which was now a cacophony of terrified screaming. People were out of their seats, running for the exits, some of them throwing themselves to the floor, seeking cover.

In the two seconds before the guard leapt on top of me, slamming me into the wheelchair, I saw that I had hit the German whose cover was Miles Preston. He had thrown his head back, dazed, his left arm shielding his eyes but too late. Blood ran down his face as the highvelocity impact of dozens of lead pellets wounded him, maimed him, disabled him. It was like having a handful of hot broken glass thrown in your

489

face. He was thrown off balance, off his stride. In his right hand he was holding a small black automatic pistol. It dangled at his side, unfired.

Sinclair, I could see, had been tackled to the floor by someone, presumably his bodyguard, and most of the senators were crouching down, the whole chamber a Babel of screams and cries, deafeningly loud, and it seemed that everyone was rushing toward me all at once, everyone who wasn't running toward the exits, who hadn't flattened themselves on the floor.

I struggled with the guard, struggled to get the Derringer out of his powerful grasp. I barely managed to tumble out of the wheelchair, but my legs, which I had been sitting on for the better part of an hour, would not support me. The blood had left them; they were suffused with a dull tingling; they would not work. I could not get to my feet.

'Freeze!' he bellowed at me, wrestling over the gun.

One more shot! I had one more shot! One shot, and this one, the only one left in the chamber, was a .45 bullet, and if I could just get the goddamned gun free, and get the gun cocked, I could kill Miles, I could save Molly's father, but the guard had tackled me to the floor beside the wheelchair, and now others were upon me, and Miles, I knew for certain that Miles, that professional killer, wounded and maimed though he was, had his automatic pistol out, had it aimed at Harrison Sinclair, and had squeezed the trigger to silence him forever –'

– and then came the explosion.

I was overcome with a cold terror as I gave up struggling against the guard.

First one shot, and then two shots, one right after another, in all three enormous explosions, thundering in the room, followed by a split second of stunned silence and then an eruption of horrified screams and shouts.

Miles had fired three rounds.

He had killed Harrison Sinclair.

I had come close to immobilizing Miles. I had almost stopped him. Molly's diversion had almost stopped him. We had almost blocked the assassin from killing Molly's father.

But he had been too resourceful, too quick, too professional.

And, pinned against the floor by a half-dozen security guards now, the .45 round unfired in my gun, which the guard had wrested away from me, I felt myself go limp with exhaustion.

Tears – of frustration, of fatigue, of ineffable sadness – came into my eyes. I could no longer think.

Our plan, our brilliant plan, had failed. *I* had failed.

'All right,' I said, but it was a broken, hoarse whisper. I lay back, my back hard against the cold floor, while all around me chorused the shouts of horror.

As the crew-cut guard whipped out handcuffs, slipping them first over one wrist and then the other, I stared unbelievingly ahead, in the space between the guard's arm and his chest, at the front.

I did not believe what I was seeing.

The assassin, Miles Preston, was lying in a crumpled heap at the base of the witness stand, his forehead missing, along with most of the front of his face.

Dead.

Above him, watching in dazed incredulity, was the tall, lanky, somewhat disheveled figure of Harrison Sinclair.

Alive.

And the last thing I saw before they took me away, the last sight, extraordinary and wonderful, virtually a miracle, was Molly. Up in the camera niche, in that square hole in the wall, in which she had first begun screaming.

But she was holding in her extended right hand a matte black pistol, and she was looking at the gun with what seemed to be disbelief, and I am sure that I saw on her face the faintest glimmerings of a smile.

The Washington Post

CIA Revelations Stun Nation

Senate Hearing Room Explodes in Gunfire After Surprise Appearance by Ex-CIA Director Harrison Sinclair, Long Believed Dead

BY ERIC MOFFATT

WASHINGTON POST STAFF WRITER

The Hart Senate Office Building last evening was the setting for one of the most amazing scenes to take place in the nation's capital in recent memory.

During nationally televised hearings before the Senate Select Committee on Intelligence into alleged corruption in the Central Intelligence Agency, at approximately 7:30 last night, Harrison Sinclair, the former director of Central Intelligence who had been reported killed in a car accident last May, appeared without warning to give sworn testimony concerning what he said was a 'massive international conspiracy' involving the present director of Central Intelligence, Alexander Truslow, and the government of newly elected German Chancellor Wilhelm Vogel.

But as soon as Sinclair was brought into the hearing room by armed guards, gunfire erupted. One of the gunmen, who was killed, was identified only as a German national. The other assailant was reported to be Benjamin Ellison, 40, an attorney and former CIA operative. No other deaths were reported.

The New York Times

One Month After Incident at Senate Intelligence Committee Hearings, Questions Linger

BY KENNETH SEIDMAN

SPECIAL TO THE NEW YORK TIMES

WASHINGTON, Jan. 4 – In the aftermath of the remarkable events in the Senate last month, the nation remains gripped by the spectacle of a CIA director once thought dead suddenly making an appearance on live television, and the equally astonishing assassination attempt that followed immediately on its heels.

′ But for all the headlines the Sinclair-Truslow matter occasioned, and the weeks of news analysis, much of the affair remains a mystery.

As is by now well known, Harrison Sinclair, director of the CIA until May of last year, faked his own death in order to escape the threat of death posed by those he was seeking to expose. It is also known that, for several hours following the traumatic incidents in Washington, Mr Sinclair gave extensive testimony in closed session to the Senate Select Subcommittee on Intelligence, exposing the activities of Alexander Truslow and his colleagues.

But what has become of Mr. Sinclair since the bloodshed in the Hart Office Building last month? Intelligence sources speculate that he may have been killed, but refuse to comment on the record. Five days after the event, Mr. Sinclair's daughter, Molly, and her husband, Benjamin Ellison, were declared legally dead, after the small craft they were sailing off Cape Cod was discovered to have capsized. Intelligence sources would not confirm allegations that the couple, like Mr.

Sinclair, were murdered. The fate of the three remains a mystery.

A Capitol Hill security spokesman stated recently that Ms Sinclair was believed to have entered the hearing room through a loading dock beneath the building by posing as a food deliverywoman. The spokesman stated that Ms Sinclair had obtained blueprints of the Hart Office Building and was familiar with them.

GERMAN PLOT REVEALED

The would-be assailant, a former East German citizen identified as Josef Peters, was reported to be an ex-employee of the former East German secret intelligence service, the Stasi. According to intelligence sources, Peters was the true identity of a well-known journalist named Miles Preston, who claimed to be a resident of Great Britain. The place of birth listed on Miles Preston's passport is Bristol, England, but Bristol city officials have been unable to locate any birth record of a Miles Preston. Little is known about Josef Peters at the present time.

As for Alexander Truslow, Mr Sinclair's successor as Director of Central Intelligence, he remains in prison awaiting his treason trial in Washington Superior Court next month. The firm which he founded, Truslow Associates, Inc., has been charged with complicity in Mr Truslow's alleged treason, and has been shut down by government authorities pending further resolution of the matter.

The German government of Chancellor Wilhelm Vogel has resigned, and the heads of six German corporations, most prominent among them Gerhard Stoessel, the chairman of the Neue Welt real estate holding firm based in Munich, have been indicted and are facing trial.

Mr Sinclair had charged that, with the assistance of CIA Director Truslow, Chancellor Vogel and his backers engineered this fall's German stock market crash in order to gain election, after which they planned a corporate coup d'état of the German government and the establishment of hegemony over Europe. Whatever the truth of the Sinclair revelations, news of the Truslow-Vogel plot shook world governments and markets.

Yet it is still not known known whether we have learned the entire story of the CIA conspiracy.

A PACKET OF DOCUMENTS

Last week this reporter received by registered mail a packet of documents prepared and sent by a former CIA officer, James Tobias Thompson III, who died in an accident in his home several days before the events in Washington.

The documents appear to bolster Mr Sinclair's claims about Mr. Truslow's illegal dealings with the German consortium.

But the package, according to postal authorities, appears to have been tampered with. One document referred to in Mr Thompson's cover letter concerned a CIA covert program called the 'Oracle Project.'

That document, however, was missing from Mr Thompson's package. CIA spokesmen deny the existence of any such covert program.

Translated from *Tribuno de Siena*, p. 22

The Siena City Council welcomes with pleasure the establishment of the Crowell Clinic in the town of Costafabbri, in the Comune of Siena. The Crowell Clinic, a free medical clinic for children, is being run under the guidance of three new arrivals to the Siena area from the United States: Mr Alan Crowell; his wife, Dr Carol Crowell, who has an infant daughter, and Dr Crowell's father, Richard Hale.

Although the Oracle Project is fictional, this story is based on a number of intriguing, little-known historical facts. That a fortune in Soviet gold remains missing to this day is, according to reliable sources, a matter of record in international intelligence and finance circles. And the interest of the Central Intelligence Agency, the U.S. Department of Defense, and Soviet intelligence in psychic research has long been documented.